The Great Convergence

Joseph R. Lallo

DEDICATION

This book is dedicated...

To Gary, who inspired me to start writing the books.
To Sean, who encouraged me to keep writing the books.
To Cary, who convinced me to finish writing the books.
To Mom and Dad, who are the reason there is a me to begin with.

ACKNOWLEDGMENTS

I would like to acknowledge the hard work and contributions made by the following people, without whom this book would probably never have made it into your hands:

Nick Deligaris
For the magnificent artwork.

Anna Genoese
For the help in polishing my lackluster grammar.

My fans, bloggers, and friends:
For giving me the help, confidence, and exposure to come this far.

A story half told is a crime, and there is no crime greater. When this tale began it was the tale of a common woman in an uncommon circumstance. A woman unprepared, unskilled, and unready. When the last words were written, they spoke of a master many times over. She was a woman filled with resolve--fearless, steadfast, and, above all, determined. A woman firm in her belief and single in her focus, willing to charge into the jaws of doom for her cause. A job needed to be done, and she had the tools to do it. Imagine what the next pages will bring . . .

#

"I have lost my mind," Myranda muttered to herself. "Behind me is paradise. A warm bed waiting for me every night and hot meals waiting for me every day. The people there care for me, respect me, even admire me! I am turning my back on it in favor of a dark cave that will very shortly be filled with water, chasing a confirmed and shameless killer with hopes of convincing him to end a war and save the world."

The paradise was Entwell. It was a place of learning, populated by the wisest wizards and the mightiest warriors. All had come seeking a beast of legendary ferocity. A beast that each believed had taken the lives of all before them. A beast that had turned out to be the cave itself. For two short periods a year, the cave was dry and passable. The most recent such period was, in moments, going to come to an end.

The killer was a creature with seemingly no true name. Myranda first new him as Leo, then as Lain. The name most knew him by was the Red Shadow. He was an assassin, known and feared throughout the continent. He was also a malthrope, a hated and dying breed of creature that looked like a human and a fox combined. Most important, though, was what had days ago been revealed.

In a ceremony designed to both summon one divine warrior and identify another, he had been revealed as a Chosen One. A tool of the gods, fated to end the war that had been eating away the people of the Northern Alliance and Tressor for one and a half centuries. Rather than embracing his fate, he had turned his back on it. Now he was somewhere within this cave, heading for the war-torn world, with no intention of playing his role. And so she had followed.

"I *will* find him. I *will* convince him. I must," she insisted.

Myn merely shot her a quick look of acknowledgment before continuing on her task. The dragon, not yet a year old, hadn't spent a day away from Myranda, and she never intended to, no matter the difficulties the travel might bring. Her claws were better suited to the rough walls of a normal cave. The glassy walls of this one offered a challenge, but it was by no means the greatest challenge on the horizon. Already the pair was far enough along that the light from the entrance was dimming behind them. They were rapidly approaching the point of no return.

Myranda pulled the staff from her bag as the darkness deepened. The well-crafted tool was longer than her own had been, and stouter. No doubt perfectly suited to the height and grip of its former owner, her friend and former teacher, Deacon. She coaxed a light from within the crystal with ease. Being in the cave reminded her of just how recently she had come upon these new talents. When she was here last, she'd had to rely upon a torch. Now, thanks to Deacon's teachings, she could simply will light into being. She had dared not dream of such a thing months ago.

The pair had only been walking for a few minutes when the mountain let out a bone-shaking roar that each knew all too well. A blast of icy air was cast up from behind her as the way to safety was drowned in a flood of water. She quickened her pace while Myn practically jumped out of her skin, scrambling with renewed vigor along the glassy tube. When they had faced the flood last, it seemed to creep up at a few feet every minute. With any luck, she would be able to keep ahead of the rising water.

It was not long before it became clear that luck would most certainly not be with her. During their escape, they had thankfully been pulled from the basin of the waterfall before the falls had begun in earnest. Now she heard the roar of the mountain grow steadily. Before long, she could hear the restless rapids sloshing about behind her. They were not creeping along as she had hoped. They were surging. Myranda tried to quicken herself to a run, but the slick ground would not permit it. Finally, she stopped and strapped the bag of supplies to her waist. There would be no outrunning the water. Best, then, to brace herself for it. Myn, far from willing to meet her fate standing still, cast a pleading glance at her friend. When Myranda saw the terror in the beast's eyes, she knew the roaring water was upon them.

The wall of icy water met her with the force of a raging bull. She was swept along at a speed faster than she could run. Faster than a horse could run! A moment later, she collided with the familiar form of her dragon, and she held tight to the terrified creature with one arm as the other held firm to the staff. Amid the chaos of the water, she had precious little concentration to spend on light. What little she did have of her mind was devoted to a blur of spells aimed at keeping herself and her companion from being dashed apart against the walls. There was no telling how much of the cave was whisking by her, and her dim memory of the way she had come would be useless to her, even if she managed to survive the flood.

The unwilling trip she was taking ceased to be an upward one and doubled in speed as she found herself sliding down an increasingly steep incline. For a moment, Myranda wondered if this was a fortunate turn of events or an unfortunate one. As usual, fate made its answer to her prompt.

The ground sliding along below her suddenly dropped away, and in an instant she was plummeting. She released Myn and tried to set her mind to levitation, hoping to stop her fall--but there was a reason this mountain had been so trying to wizard and warrior alike. Crystal-strewn rock mangled and twisted all but the simplest of magic. This spell, it seemed, was just a bit too complex to slip past the cave's confounding effect, as she soon felt her hold on the mystic energies scatter.

She felt a sharp pain in her abdomen as she collided with a wall. Instinctively, she reached out with both hands, clutching madly at anything that offered a grip. Somehow she managed to cling to the rough surface of the wall. For a long moment, she held firm, and slowly reclaimed the wind that had been knocked from her by the impact. The roar of falling water surrounded her. She opened her eyes, though doing so was ultimately pointless, as the staff she had released would give off no more light until she willed it to do so. Indeed, before she could even think of illuminating the cave, she would have to *find* the staff. Having dropped it into the chasm below when she struck the wall, there was a stronger likelihood of the staff finding *her* than of she finding *it*.

As she sorted through the limited options open to her, Myranda felt a nudge at her shoulder. The unexpected feeling nearly jarred her from the wall.

"Myn! Myn, you are all right!" she cried.

Of course, the dragon was once again in her element. She could scamper up and down these uneven walls as easily as along the ground. The dragon flicked her hot tongue in and out, licking at Myranda's ears, thankful for getting her through that torrent.

"Yes, yes. You are welcome. Now it is time to pay me back. I can't cling to this wall forever. I need you to find a tunnel out of here--or, at least, a ledge to recover on," Myranda said.

Myn flapped from the wall and into the air. For a moment, Myranda wondered how the dragon would be able to see in the utter darkness. A moment later, the creature cast out a column of flame, bathing the gray walls and frothing white water in yellow light. In the flash, Myn's keen eyes took in the wall. In another moment, Myn was beside Myranda on the wall again. With a few helpful taps of the dragon's tail to guide her, Myranda managed to inch her way along the wall to a ledge and pull herself up.

"I don't suppose you might be able to find my staff. I let it go when I hit the wall," Myranda said to her friend, whom she imagined was sitting right before her.

When she held out her hand to give the creature a few rewarding scratches, she found that she was alone on the ledge. Myn was certainly eager to please. There were two or three more blasts of flame before she was joined again by a very pleased dragon clutching a staff in her teeth.

"Good, Myn. Very, very good," she said, feeling her way blindly to the dragon's brow and scratching it madly.

Myn squirmed with delight at the attention and dropped heavily into Myranda's lap, disturbing the large bag Deacon had provided her with. There was a metal clink, stirring thoughts of what Deacon imagined was a necessity. Myn deserved and required significantly more petting and rewarding before she allowed Myranda to indulge her curiosity.

She propped up the staff and brought about the light again as she looked through the bag. The first thing she withdrew was a page from a spell book. Myranda marveled at the torn edge. Deacon took better care of the books than he did himself, and yet when he learned that Myranda planned to find Lain, he'd torn this page free without a thought.

It was an old one, she could tell. Whatever it was that they used for paper in Entwell aged to an odd mahogany color. The black letters were difficult to read against the reddish paper. She carefully stored it away.

The metal clink was revealed to be a stout dagger he had provided. That would no doubt be quite useful. There was a small kit with bandages and potions. Thoughtful of him to include it. Finally, she found a stylus. There was no doubt. It was the very one that he carried with him at all times. She ran her fingers along the side of the pen, carefully feeling the point before stowing it with equal care.

Quickly she checked her tunic. Lain's tooth was mercifully still clinging to the inside of her waterlogged pocket. In a fit of anger during a training session with the warrior, she had managed to knock it from his mouth. He had presented it to her as a reminder of her anger. She removed the tooth from her pocket and fashioned a pouch for it from a bandage. Using a bit of thread, she hung it about her neck. With that done, she secured the bag again.

The time had come to find some way out of here.

Standing as best as she could on the somewhat precarious ledge, Myranda surveyed her position. There were numerous openings dotting the wall. Most were far too small to offer much in the way of an exit, and all were a fair distance up. Already the sound of the thundering water was that of a torrent falling upon a pool rather than hard ground. The water was gathering at the bottom of the crevice, and--though the level was still beyond the reach of her light--if the trip she had just taken was any indication, it would not remain so for long. She had to make the right choice the first time, lest she face a dead end with nothing but a wall of water behind her.

"Myn, I think this is another job for you. I need you to see if you can find Lain's scent. He had a head start, but I would wager that rush of water closed the gap for us," she said.

Before Myranda was through speaking, Myn had scrambled off, along the wall. She sniffed and flicked her tongue intently, traveling from hole to hole and sampling each. Shortly she returned and sniffed at the pouch about Myranda's neck.

"I'd feared as much. We are probably far from the safest or quickest route, so I would imagine there would be half of a mountain between us and Lain. Best to find a new plan," she said, patting the dragon for the effort.

Myranda set her mind to the task. Not having the benefit of Myn's sense of smell, she was not certain what sort of things would be reasonable to ask her to find. Finally she made up her mind.

"I need you to find fresh air, or failing that, some sort of animal that can be found outside of a cave occasionally. If they need to find a way out, then we can find their way," Myranda said.

Instantly the dragon scampered off again. It just so happened that the creature had found just such a scent in her search for that of Lain. She maneuvered swiftly to a wide, low opening more or less directly above Myranda's head and slipped inside. Her head then reappeared, looking down expectantly, as though she was surprised Myranda had failed to join her already.

The wall had countless narrow, smooth-edged cracks. It was ideal for climbing. However, the abrupt trip and its sudden and severe end had left Myranda a less than ideal climber. More than an hour of slow, tentative ascending had passed before she pulled herself onto the ledge. What she found there did little to improve her mood. The roof of the tunnel ahead was so low she would practically have to crawl. With a heavy sigh, she set herself to the task.

Myn led the way, thrilled to finally be so useful. Fortunately, the tunnel branched several times, eventually opening enough for a more comfortable posture. Also fortunate was the fact that Myn had chosen a tunnel that led steadily upward. At least if the water found its way to the tunnel, it would take longer to reach them.

Time passed slowly in the darkness of the cave. After enough travel to sap all but the last of the strength from her legs, Myranda began to notice the odor that had been pungent enough for Myn to follow all of this way. It meant that they were headed to a familiar chamber, albeit not the most pleasant one. Sure enough, another few minutes and the pair emerged into a chamber filled with quiet chattering and the worst of smells. This cavern was the home to a massive colony of bats.

Much to Myranda's dismay, her stomach growled at the terrible stench. She had been, after all, on the brink of starvation when last she had entered this place. At the time, she'd been accompanied by Lain, and they had made a rather unpleasant meal of some of the winged creatures. Alas, without the forethought to bring food, Myranda hesitated to think what state she would be in after another day of travel. Despite this, she decided that the next meal she ate would be eaten with the sky overhead. Myn was not so choosy, and was in the air in a flash to snatch up a few mouthfuls, sending Myranda running for cover to escape a blizzard of bats.

Now that they had found their way to a point Myranda knew, she could find her own way. They walked until the girl could no longer manage it, finally resting propped against the wall. With the morning came two sensations, constant companions of a traveler of the north, that she had all but forgotten during her time in Entwell: Stinging cold and gnawing hunger.

She had picked up the habit of eating breakfast, something that no doubt had contributed to her decision not to eat the one thing she could manage. Were one of those bats to fly by now, she would snatch it out of the air with her teeth, so hungry was she. At least her mind had not been idle while she rested. The many bruises and tender spots from the first half of the trip were healed up, the product of her white magic training working its wonders while she slept--though, upon standing, she found that she was still quite sore from the exertion. She continued regardless. If she remembered correctly, there was no less than another day of travel ahead of her.

There were two significant additions to their trip, now that she had made it this far. First, the stream that had smoothed the floor enough to guide them during their entry had begun to flow, providing, at least, water to drink. Second, Myn's attitude began to lift, as she undoubtedly began to pick up the scent of Lain. The little beast was nearly as fond of the warrior she was tracking as she was of Myranda, motivating her all the more to find him quickly.

The cold of the cave increased steadily as they neared its mouth. Myranda cursed herself for not grabbing something warmer to wear before she left. There would be many long, cold days ahead of her if she couldn't find something more suitable for the northern weather. Worse, the tunic she wore was bright blue. The residents of the north almost exclusively wore thick gray cloaks. Her current outfit would stand out like a sore thumb. That was the last thing she wanted right now.

Hour after long, weary hour passed. The growling of Myranda's stomach fairly echoed off of the walls. Myn seemed to take a more concerned attitude now. There was something in the air that she did not like. Myranda marveled at how well she could understand the thoughts and feelings of her friend, even without words. Indeed, without sound at all. Solomon, a small dragon in Entwell, was the only other dragon she had really known, and he spoke both her language and one of his own, along with no doubt countless others. Myn rarely made a sound.

Myranda frowned at the thought that, perhaps, growing up beside a human was robbing Myn of something, some language native to her kind.

The worrying thought was still on her mind when, off in the distance, the faintest glow of daylight could be seen. Myranda's heart leapt, and she would have run if she'd had the strength. Instead, she crept along at the same pace, though wary of Myn's deepening concern. All of a sudden, Myn stopped and absolutely would not proceed.

"What is it, Myn?" she asked.

The little dragon's body went rigid, tail straightening and teeth bared. There was an enemy. Judging from how protective Myn had been in the past, it might have simply been anyone, but on this side of the mountain, anyone was as good as her worst enemy. She doused the light and moved near to the wall, attempting to remain unseen.

Myn stalked, slowly and silently. When the mouth of the cave was near enough, Myranda saw what Myn had smelled. Not one but *two* of the Elites were standing dutifully at the cave's mouth. Elites, after all of this time!? A contingent of the small but legendary force of veteran soldiers had followed her here, but that was months ago. Surely they should have given up by now. Myranda's eyes darted about in near panic. They landed on Myn, who seemed ready to attack.

"Myn, no," Myranda whispered insistently into her friend's ear. "We can't. If we kill them, then when they do not report in, their superiors will know something has happened. Why else would Lain have left them alive? We have to get by them somehow."

Myranda quietly wished she had just an ounce of the stealth that Lain had. He had surely slipped by them with no trouble at all. Her mind turned to the spells that she had at her disposal. No disguise would do, and she doubted that she would be able to create one that was convincing, regardless. Invisibility would work, but Deacon had yet to perfect it, and Myranda had been less than successful at casting what little of it he had mastered. She had learned sleep, but simply dropping them into unconsciousness suddenly would be a clear indication that someone had passed. If she was to do this, she would have to do it with care.

Slowly, almost not at all, she passed her influence toward them. She made their eyes just a little heavy. With the utmost of care and restraint, she increased the spell. Slowly, slowly, ever so slowly. She noticed one of them waver, catching himself, and the other yawn. Slowly. One of the men moved to the wall to lean against it. A few minutes later, he slid to the ground to sit more comfortably. The other did likewise. In a few minutes more, the pair was asleep on opposite walls of the cave. As far as they knew, it had been their idea.

After reminding Myn to leave them be, Myranda walked past the unaware soldiers. Thankfully, there were no other soldiers in sight. There was, however, a two-man tent, a pair of horses, and a separate supply tent. Myranda peeked her head into the supply tent to find it mounded with all sorts of rations and equipment. The men had been stationed here for nearly half of a year, and they were equipped for months more.

She selected a coarse brown blanket from a stack of them near the back, and one each of the rations available, not bothering to see what, precisely, she was taking. She was far more concerned with her selections escaping notice. With the blanket wrapped around her and the supplies stowed in her bag, Myranda stalked off into the forest, directly away from the mouth of the cave.

Looking upon the landscape was a grim reminder of the life she had left behind when she entered the cave. The world was overwhelmingly white. Any color from evergreen leaves, lichens, or sky was muted to a sterile gray by frost. The air had a biting cold to it, one that the damp tunic and rough blanket did little to turn away. She forced the unpleasant sensations from her mind and quickened her pace. When she felt she had moved far enough to avoid discovery, she cleared a patch of ground, threw together a pile of frozen wood, and conjured a smokeless fire. She sat cross-legged and allowed Myn to crawl onto her lap before wrapping the blanket around the two of them.

When their combined body heat had made them at least somewhat comfortable, Myranda pulled the spell sheet from the bag. She held it in one hand while petting Myn with the other. The dragon's skin and scales felt more leathery than usual, and she had noticed that the little creature had a dingier color, but she could not spend any thoughts on that now. She had to focus on the spell.

The black letters on mahogany paper were barely visible in the light of the fire, but her eyes adjusted as the sun's light crept from the sky. Deacon had, alas, not cast a translation spell on this page, so she was left to her own knowledge to decipher it. While she had at least a loose understanding of the spoken languages of Entwell, the written ones had never been explained. This page, mercifully, must have been one of the few written by someone besides Deacon, because it was all in one language. Deacon had a mismatched patchwork language he tended to use when writing that took an expert to follow. Myranda wondered if perhaps that was the language he spoke when she was not around. Regardless, the spell seemed to be in the same alphabet as Northern. That at least would allow her to speak the words. Perhaps then she could understand them. She spent a fair part of the night sifting through the procedures described in the page until a particularly loud growl in her stomach actually woke Myn.

"I suppose I ought to eat and continue in the morning," she spoke quietly to her companion.

Myn seemed to want to get out from the blanket and retrieve a meal for her friend personally, but when she ventured a claw out into the bitter cold, she changed her mind and retreated back to beneath the covers.

The rations in Myranda's bag were many and varied. A rock-hard biscuit of some kind. Some salted meat. Dried fruit!? Myranda had heard that the best food was set aside for the troops, but aside from the apple that she had grown herself, the closest thing to fruit that she had seen in years was the awful wine that taverns served. That, she decided, would be for a special occasion. She chose some of the biscuit, ate it quickly, and propped herself against a tree to drop off to sleep.

In the morning, she woke and returned immediately to her task. Myn slipped from her blanket, stretched, and trotted off to get her own breakfast while Myranda gnawed on more of the biscuit. Myn returned with a rabbit and dropped it in front of Myranda. She prepared it as best she could. When she was through eating, Myn snapped up the rest.

Myranda deciphered more of the spell. It seemed that when she cast it, the item used to track the person in question would be drawn toward them. The strength of the attraction would indicate their distance. The duration would change depending on the will of the target. Myranda stood and removed the tooth from her neck. She held it by the strings in one hand and held her staff in the other. The spell was small but complex. She tried several times to cast it, with her final attempt prompting a tiny tug to the southwest. It wasn't much, but it was a start. Myranda wrapped the blanket about her shoulders, stowed the spell, donned the tooth, and moved to the southwest.

As days of walking passed and Myranda's stolen rations began to run low, she began to wonder what she was thinking. She couldn't enter a town with Myn, and the dragon simply would not leave her side. She could make do with the meals Myn brought her when the food ran out--but sooner or later, she would need warmer clothes at the very least. Even if she could convince Myn to wait while she entered a town to do business, she had no money, and no way to get any.

She remembered Lain's words. He had spoken of her as a creature of cities and roads, while he was of forests, mountains, and plains. Well, now she too was out of place in the world of humans. All the better, though. If this was where Lain was to be found, then it was where she must be.

Nearly a week of southward travel had led her to be comfortable with the sounds of the woods while she slept, though when a snowfall came, she missed her hood. Each morning she checked Lain's location with the spell. She knew that he would be traveling by night while she traveled during the day. This way, at least, he would not be moving when she cast the spell. It was becoming easier. He was getting closer. She had been heading almost entirely due south for the last few days. Lain had likely been keeping to the edge of the woods to remain unseen. Now, though, she checked to find that he was due west of her, traveling across the open plains.

Looking out across the plain, Myranda saw a thin, sparsely wooded area off in the distance. It was a bit less than half of the way between herself and the edge of Ravenwood, the massive western forest that was still visible at the base of the mountains on the horizon. The dangling tooth pointed her to the trees; they rustled with a stiff and constant breeze in the distance. Thus, she proceeded in that direction, carefully scanning for anyone who might spot her. For once, she was glad that the plains of the north were almost deserted. She hurried across the field as quickly as she could. As she did, she wondered why no roads led through this plain. There were at least five small towns nearby, yet the nearest road ran far to the west and circled completely around the plain to reach the furthest of the towns. A second road through this place would cut the travel time in half.

Myn seemed distracted. The slowly strengthening wind carried either the scent of Lain or something else, and it was making her anxious. When they reached the trees, Myranda noticed a handful of small brown creatures scurrying across the ground. Suddenly Myn froze. Myranda began to ask what might be the matter, but her voice caught in her throat when she realized the source of her friend's concern.

There was not merely a handful of the little creatures. Behind them there were dozens, perhaps a hundred. Each had the small size and long body of a weasel, but their eyes seemed absent, with slight indentations where they ought to be. They had six legs, each tipped with a trio of short, stout, cruel-looking claws. There were clusters of them, sniffing madly at the ground around her footprints.

The pair was surrounded by the things, and more were popping out of scattered burrows by the moment. As they each sniffed the air, row after row of needle-sharp teeth were bared in anger. They did not like the scent of the intruder. The creatures approached one at a time. Myn tried to frighten them off, but as she pounced at them, they scattered, keeping just out of her reach. In moments, the two of them were completely surrounded.

A chill of fear ran up and down Myranda's spine as she held her staff ready. She decided a spell of fire would hold them at bay, but she would need a minute or two to produce enough of it to protect her, while the fear burning at her mind increased that time greatly.

"Myn, fire!" she cried.

Myn tried to obey, but somehow the things with no eyes were able to avoid the flames, only a few getting even remotely singed. The creatures were swarming about Myranda's legs. With no spells swift or safe enough to ward them off now, she swatted at them with the staff, knocking a few away. Just as the first of them sunk its teeth into the girl's leg, there came a piercing whistle. The small creatures scattered. An instant later, blanket about the young woman's shoulders was torn from her back.

Turning quickly to discover the culprit, she found Lain, dressed in the black tunic of Entwell, holding his white cloak in one hand and her brown blanket in the other.

"You!" she cried furiously.

Myn scampered to him, leaping about joyfully.

"Pick her up," he ordered.

Before Myranda could object, Myn obligingly leapt into Myranda's arms. Lain threw his cloak about her shoulders and hurled her blanket into the mass of creatures who were already beginning to venture closer. The very moment that the blanket landed, the creatures converged on it, tearing it to ribbons.

"Quickly, this way. And do not speak until I tell you," he said.

The pair moved quickly to a more thickly wooded bit of the field. Every few moments, Lain would cast a glance at the chaotic frenzy behind them. When a handful of the furry creatures stood on their hindmost legs and sampled the air, only to turn away and return from whence they came, Lain broke the silence.

"You should have stayed in Entwell. You were there for your protection," he said.

"For safekeeping, you mean. So that you could go about your murder without fear of anyone else claiming my ransom," she said.

"Yes," he said.

Myranda was given pause by the frankness of his answer.

"So, what noble plans have you got that are more important than ending the war?" she asked.

"I must resupply and meet with my partner. The Elites will have been busy. It will take time to rebuild," he said.

"I cannot say that I am sorry to hear it. You deserve every hardship and misfortune that this world has to give until you turn yourself to your proper task," she said.

Lain weathered the assault in stoic silence. Somehow, Myranda could not bring herself to continue to give him the berating she felt he deserved.

"Thank you, by the way," she said, her voice still stern.

Lain grunted in reply.

"What were those things?" she asked.

"Oloes. They will attack, kill, and consume any creature with an unfamiliar scent or sound," he said.

"Then why didn't a single olo pay any attention to you?" she asked.

"My scent is familiar," he said.

They continued until they reached a tall, sturdy pine. Lain looked over the roots. In several places, they looped up above ground. After close inspection of one root in particular, he grasped it, put one foot against the tree, and pulled with all of his might. Slowly, not just the root but a square section of ground began to tip up. He pulled and strained until the square, now clearly a thick, wooden trapdoor with a few inches of soil disguising it, stood on end. He then crouched low to the ground and carefully reached his hand inside, feeling at the walls. Myranda peered inside. The pale light that made it through the thick clouds did not penetrate far into the darkness. When Lain found what he had been probing for, a soft click could be heard from within the hole that prompted him to quickly pull his arm free. A blade swiped across the shaft, and the swishing sound and puff of air from the door hinted at many more that had gone unseen.

"Put her down. This is the place," he said.

"After those blades nearly robbed you of your arm, you are going inside?" she said.

"Yes. And once the oloes get a whiff of the blood trickling down your leg, it is going to take more than a loud whistle to scare them off," he said.

Myranda had forgotten about the creature that had managed to bite her. She did not relish the thought of facing those things again. Reluctantly, she looked into the hole. Myn hopped to the ground and peered in curiously as well. Myranda searched for a ladder of some sort built into the walls, but found none. She lowered her bag down an arm's length and dropped it. From the sound, there was not much of a drop. She lowered her legs and slid into the opening, dangling for a moment by her fingertips before dropping a foot or two to a solid surface in the darkness below. Her eyes had only just begun to adjust when a light flashed in front of her. She scrambled back to the bag at the base of the opening and pulled out her staff, turning back in time for a second spark. This one lingered, as a lamp flickered to life, casting light on the room.

It was a small room. The walls were made of stone blocks, while the low ceiling was made of wood, with thick planks running across its length. Placed regularly through the room were sturdy support beams. There were heavy doors on three walls. The lamp was in the hands of a man standing in the open doorway opposite the entrance shaft. Its flickering yellow light fell upon a face with a look of confused recognition, a look that Myranda no doubt shared, as this was not precisely a stranger. After a moment of searching through crowded memories, each spoke the name of the other simultaneously.

"Desmeres?" she said.

"Myranda?" spoke the man.

Indeed, it was the odd fellow she had briefly met in a tavern when this great journey had only just begun. His youthful face, wild white hair, and expensive attire were unmistakable.

"I can't say I expected to see you here," he said.

Myn, hearing the voices within, darted down into the room and planted herself between Myranda and the potential threat. Desmeres took a step back.

"Well, now! That is yours, I trust!" he said, eying the intruding creature with amusement.

"Yes, yes. This is Myn," Myranda answered, eager to get it out of the way and have her own questions answered. "What are you doing here?"

"Well, for the time being, this is my home. A more appropriate question would be what are *you* doing here?" he countered.

Before she could answer, Lain dropped down. Desmeres glanced up, this time with recognition unmarred by confusion.

"L-L-L-L-Leo, right? Good lord, it has been ages! How has Sasha been treating you?" he said as though speaking with an old friend.

"Taken," he said.

"No! By who?" Desmeres said, dismayed.

"The Elites," he answered.

"Oh. I thought I'd never see the day," he said. "I trust she served well? A masterpiece, that one. She was silent when you needed her to be, but when she wanted to, she could *sing*. Shame on you for losing her. You'd better figure out how to get her back before they squeeze any secrets out of her, because if I--"

"Wait! What is going on here?" Myranda asked.

"I am catching up with my friend Leo," Desmeres said.

"You know him?" she said.

"Of course! I collect and craft weapons and he uses them. So, how has the business been? Any projects you feel like discussing?" he began.

"Never mind that. She knows," Lain said.

"Does she? How much?" Desmeres asked, surprised, but still with a sense of amusement.

"Enough," he said.

"Well . . . that's new," Desmeres replied.

"I suppose that it was no coincidence that you and I met in the tavern that day," Myranda said.

"No, no. Of course it wasn't. You can safely assume that each and every time I do anything, it has been meticulously planned out to benefit me in some way," Desmeres said, in a tone that made it difficult to tell if he was joking.

Lain pulled open one of the other doors and entered. Desmeres attempted to walk past Myranda, but Myn prevented it.

"Well, all right, fine. Myranda, would you do me a favor? There is a rope over there by the trapdoor. Give it a good strong pull. We've got to close the door and reset the blades," he said.

Myranda turned to do so. As she did, Desmeres continued to chat with her as though they were the best of friends.

"So, I recognize the old Entwell garb. Is that where you ended up?" he asked.

"Yes. How did you know about Entwell?" she asked.

"Born and raised there. Is my father still knocking about? He makes the master-level weapons," he asked.

"I don't know. I didn't meet any weapon makers except for . . . Wait, what is going on here?" she demanded. Desmeres had a way of making things seem so casual, she had nearly forgotten the ordeal that she had been through to get here.

"You just pull on the cord there and--" he began.

"Not that! Where am I? Why are you working with Lain? What do you really do?" she cried.

"Are we calling him Lain now? Eh, regardless. Just get the door closed, we'll join Lain inside, and all will be revealed. Well, *some* will be revealed. I don't want to make any promises I can't keep," he said.

Myranda sighed heavily and pulled hard on the rope. The heavy door began to drop shut, the weight of it apparently driving the machinery that reset the blades.

"Well done. This way, please. This is a bit of a reunion, so I've finally got a reason to open some of the vintage. That alone is reason enough to celebrate," he said.

They walked through the doorway to a larger room with various dried and smoked foods hanging along one wall. Along another was rack after rack of fine wine. Most of the rest of the room was littered and stacked with chests of various sizes. In the center was a table with two chairs. Desmeres lit a set of candles on the table and several lamps that lined the walls.

"As you see, we aren't equipped for guests. There is usually only the two of us here, if anyone at all. Pull up a chest or something to sit on. I dare say I've emptied quite a few waiting for this fellow to show up," he remarked, as he looked over the stock of wine.

Myranda did so. It was already quite clear that she would have no answers until Desmeres was ready to give them. The white-haired fellow opened a bottle and set it on the table, then set about finding enough glasses for all in attendance. After leaving the room, he returned with two heavy clay cups and one metal one.

"The honored guest gets the special glass," he said, setting it before her.

It was not until she watched him pour a splash of the wine that she realized that the chalice was of solid gold.

"Where did you get this?" she asked, admiring the work of art.

"I don't recall. Some people cannot afford payment in coins alone. I am willing to accept anything, so long as it is gold," he said, pouring the rest of the glasses.

Lain returned to his seat after fetching some manner of dried meat. Desmeres set out some cheese on a plate.

"To old friends and new ones," Desmeres said, raising his glass. Myranda joined in the toast, while Lain simply tore into his meal.

After sampling the wine, which was as subtle and delicious as any that she had ever tasted, Myranda set the glass down.

"May I *please* have some answers?" she begged.

"But of course. Just a moment, though. Lain, are we keeping any secrets for ourselves?" he asked.

"Use your best judgment," he answered.

"Oh, are we using our best judgment now? Because based upon your last few decisions, I thought the new policy was to try our very best to get ourselves killed and lose everything we have worked for. My mistake. Now that good judgment is the choice of the day again, perhaps things will get done. Questions please," he said. His words had been riddled with sarcasm, but still carried the necessary sting. Lain weathered them as though they were anything but rare.

"Who are you really? What exactly do you do?" she asked.

"I am this fellow's business associate," he answered.

"But he is an assassin. What could you possibly do for him?" she asked.

"Oh, not much. I make all of his weapons. I build, manage, and maintain networks of contacts and informants. I locate and contact prospective clients, manage cover businesses, handle finances, keep records, collect and negotiate payments. Basically everything but get my hands dirty," he said. "And in exchange, I get half of his fee."

Myranda frowned.

"So you are as much a murder as he is," she said.

"Heavens, no! If there is blood to be had, it is entirely upon his hands. I merely point him in the most profitable directions," he said.

"And arm him," she said.

"Bah. We've had this discussion. A weapon is merely a tool, and I merely make it. He is the one who decides what to do with it," he said.

"But--" Myranda began.

"But, but, but. I have had decades to hone my rationalizations. They are quite solid. I suggest you ask another question rather than lecturing me," he said, not a drop of anger in the voice. There was a sense of his having done all of this before. There was that sense to everything he did and said, as though this absurd life he lived was mundane.

"Well, what is this place?" she asked.

"A store room. One of many. A repository for surplus funds, a library for old records. I keep most of my better weapons here. Of course, in times of need, this place also serves as a safe house, and ever since that fellow there decided not to hand you over to the Undermine, the times have most certainly been of need. Clients tend not to react well when the person they hired to capture someone decides to release the target. When the client has an army at their disposal, it generally turns out poorly," he said.

"What is the damage?" Lain asked.

"The tavern and the inn have been seized. I still have access to a pair of the armories, but the rest have been closed as well. Our little enterprise has all but disappeared from the map," he said, almost grinning. "It will have to be rebuilt from the ground up."

"What are you talking about?" Myranda asked.

"We have a handful of legitimate businesses that we use for meeting places and to attract clients. Trigorah and her Elites have been taking them down one by one ever since her pet target vanished. She can be a real pain sometimes," he said.

Lain stood and headed for the door.

"Where are you off to?" Desmeres asked.

Lain continued silently.

"Well, enjoy. I had more to say, but it can wait," Desmeres said, obviously knowing Lain too well to expect a response.

"Get back here! I'm not through with you! I followed you here for a reason! You have a job to do and so do I!" Myranda cried.

Lain slipped out the door, shutting it behind him. Myranda rushed after him, but by the time she reached the door to the entry room, the heavy trapdoor was clicking back into place.

"Oh, never mind him. He will be back. There is no place else in this world that will have him right now. He is probably just out to hunt. Between you and me, he hates prepared food. At any rate, you must have more questions, and if you don't, I've got a few," he said, leading her back inside.

Myranda was helpless to follow Lain even if she had wanted to. She remembered the blades and knew neither how to deactivate them nor what triggered them. She entered the dining room and sat in Lain's chair.

"Any more questions?" Desmeres asked.

The young woman wondered for a moment why she had ever thought she could convince Lain of anything now that he had a whole world to hide in. In following him, she had left paradise for the sake of a hole in the ground, and perhaps nothing more.

"What does it matter? You will only lie to me," she said bitterly.

"Oh, not at all. As a matter of fact, I have a feeling you will very soon find me to be the most infuriatingly honest person you have ever met. So if you have any questions, feel free to ask," he said.

Myranda sat numbly and shook her head.

"Then I have a few for you. You say he has a job to do. I assume you are not speaking of his still pending task of turning you over to the Alliance Army. What then?" he asked.

"He is one of the Chosen," she said.

"The what? Oh, that's right. I remember them giving that speech at least a dozen times in Entwell," he said.

"But it is true. It is proven!" she said.

"How so?" he asked.

Myranda explained about the ceremony that had taken place in Entwell before she had left. She told of the summoning of an elemental, a Chosen One, and the fact that Lain was still standing when the creature was formed. The mystic being had even approached him. According to the peerless minds of Entwell, this was only possible if Lain was Chosen. Desmeres nodded thoughtfully through the entirety of the tale, sipping at the wine as it was told.

"Hmm. I always hated Hollow," he said when the recollection was through, speaking of the prophet who had predicted the ceremony and its meaning. "Frankly, I've never trusted the whole concept of prophecy. The fact that things occurred precisely as he'd predicted they would certainly punctures my theory that he has been speaking pure nonsense for all of these years. And you say that this other Chosen One, the one you conjured up, it just flew away?"

"Yes," she answered.

"That is a bit odd. You would think that after being brought into existence, one would be eager to get to the task for which one was summoned. I haven't heard anything about an elemental showing up and bringing widespread peace, though," he said.

"I believe that the Chosen will not turn to their task until all five have appeared and joined forces," she said.

"Ah, yes. The fabled 'Great Convergence.' I imagine that the meeting of the Chosen will be a rather difficult thing to arrange with Lain dedicating himself to other tasks, the mysterious elemental flying about waiting for something, and the others sight unseen," he asked.

"I've seen one. In the field. He was dead," she said.

"One would imagine that would only further complicate matters," Desmeres said. "Tell me. If he was dead, how did you discover that he was Chosen?"

"He had the mark. This mark," Myranda said, showing her scar.

"Say. That looks familiar," he said.

"There is one just like it on Lain's chest, one on the forehead of the elemental creature, and it was all over the dead swordsman's weapons and armor. It is the mark of the Chosen," she said.

"Am I to assume, then, that you are Chosen?" he asked.

"No, no. A Chosen One must be divine of birth and born with the mark. I am only human, and mine is a scar," she said.

"And yet you feel compelled to hunt the others down. You do realize that if the prophecy has come true thus far, it is likely to finish itself off without your help," he said.

"That is just it. I believe I am part of the prophecy. Hollow may have mentioned me," she said.

"I see. You don't suppose you are suffering from delusions of grandeur, do you? Well, I suppose you wouldn't be very well-suited to answer that. At any rate, this is all very interesting, but I hope you don't mind if I change the subject. I tend to enjoy talking about things that have already happened rather than things that are about to. Less chance of spoiling surprises that way," he said. "I take that you set your mind to magic back at Entwell. How far did you get?"

"Full master," she answered.

Desmeres tilted his head.

"No . . . in half a year?" he remarked in disbelief.

"A bit less than that," she said.

"And yet an olo got a hold of you. Not very fast with the spells yet?" he said, indicating the trickle on her leg.

"I manage," she answered, directing a bit of thought to the wound to close it.

"Hmm . . . I may need to renegotiate," he said.

"Renegotiate what?" she asked.

"Your price. It is already the highest that we've ever been offered, but now that you are a full wizard, I may just be able to squeeze a bit more out of them," he said.

"You are still thinking of turning me in?" she growled.

"Myranda, it is practically all I think about," he said, quite unapologetically.

"But now? After you know me? After you know what I must do? How could you?" she asked, appalled.

"Did Lain ever tell you what you were worth?" he asked.

"No! What does it matter?" she asked.

"Oh, with a number this large? It matters," he said, standing and hurrying out the door.

She stood to follow.

"No, no. Stay there. You were impressed with the gold goblet, right?" he said, amid door creaks and chest slams. Finally, he reentered and walked to the table. He slammed something down on it.

It an enormous brick, as thick as her arm and nearly as long. Gold.

"One gold ingot. Think of it as four hundred gold coins melted together. We currently have just under thirty of these, plus enough other gold coins and knickknacks to equal perhaps one hundred more. The Alliance Army, for a reason that we are not entirely certain of, is willing--nay, eager--to pay us one hundred and twenty-five of these for your corpse and the sword you carried," he said.

Myranda's eyes locked on the block of gold and widened.

"However! That is merely the base price. If you are still breathing when we hand you over, the price is increased tenfold. One thousand two hundred and fifty of these bits of auric masonry. That is equal to five hundred *thousand* gold coins. Five *million* silver coins. Two *hundred* and fifty *million* coppers. I would say that you are worth your weight in gold, but that is a massive understatement. You are worth something on the order of *three hundred times* your weight in gold. You are the single most valuable thing I have ever seen," he said.

"But . . . why?" she asked, dumbfounded.

"As I said, their motivation is a mystery to me. Most interesting is the fact that they did not even want specifically you. At least, not at first. Their orders were to retrieve that sword of yours--which we have, by the way--and anyone who touches it directly and lives. We were also told not to touch it ourselves, if we value our lives. I do and I have not," he said.

Myranda's mind began to stir.

"That sword . . . that sword belonged to the swordsman. That sword is what gave me the mark. It has something to do with the Chosen. And they want me, alive . . . " she thought aloud.

Deep in Myranda's mind, thoughts and instincts clashed together. Thoughts that had been forming since Lain had first told her the truth about why he captured her. Longings and hopes merged as she tried to find some explanation for such actions. Almost hammered into her mind at birth was the belief that the Alliance Army had the best interests of the people and the world at heart. That thought planted the seed of an idea. They wanted the person who touched the sword--alive, if possible. The seed grew until finally it found its way to her voice.

"They know! They know about the prophecy! They came to the same conclusion I did, that the person who is scarred with the mark by the sword is the one who will join the Chosen together. They must want my help!" she said, more certain of it with every moment.

"Possible. I have seen greater stretches of the imagination come true," he said, nodding thoughtfully, then frowning. "Not the least bit likely. In fact, now that I th--"

"Desmeres, I must meet with the Alliance Army at once!" she said.

"Not so quickly, I am afraid," he said, dropping the interrupted thought and embarking on a new one. "You see, when Lain decided to free you and keep them at arm's length from you, it made them believe that we were no longer willing to turn you over. That has put the two of us on a very exclusive list of insurgents who are to be killed on sight by the Elites. It is clear that those very same Elites are the ones who seek to claim you as well. Until we can establish that Lain's little idiosyncrasies are harmless and that we are indeed still willing and able to relinquish yourself and the sword, we are going to have to wait."

"I will just go to them myself," she said.

"That would not be wise. Lest you forget, the attempts to capture you have been less than pleasant in the past. The rest of the agents out after you are not so well-disciplined as the Elites, and I would wager to say that they have not been offered the same compensation as we. If you meet them first, which you most certainly will, they might be just as willing to turn over a corpse as a captive," he said.

"I will take my chances. I can take care of myself," she said.

"That freshly healed wound on your leg and the close calls of the past would seem to indicate the contrary," he said. "Besides, if you go off and turn yourself in, we will not get paid, and that would just be a tragedy."

"Hmm. And Lain is Chosen. I would have to find him again after all," she said.

"Precisely. So what do you say? You stay on as our guest until I can smooth out relations just enough to allow an exchange. That is, of course, unless you don't want to, in which case you will need to stay on as our prisoner. I would suggest choosing the former. It has better accommodations and the conversations are a tad less one-sided. That will give you time to convince Lain of his place in the cosmic way of things, and it will allow us to protect our investment. Then you and he can go off and find elementals and all manner of other eldritch companions and create a tale we can all tell our children about," he said, lifting the ingot to return it to its storage.

Myranda frowned at his mocking tone toward the end of the speech. When he reached for the gold, it made Myranda realize something.

"Wait. The war is good for you. Why would you allow me to help bring peace?" she asked.

"Do you honestly believe that you will be able to convince Lain to join forces with the Alliance Army and put his life on the line to somehow put this war to an end? They have hunted him for decades, and when they caught him, they tortured him for a month, if my sources can be believed. He will never work with them without what he considers to be a very good reason, and I doubt such a reason exists," he said frankly.

"He will see the light," Myranda said confidently.

"Yes, well, I sincerely doubt it. People like Lain have lived in the dark so long, when they see light, they tend to close their eyes. Say . . . why do you assume the war is good for us?" he said.

"Lain told me how the hatred it stirs up is what gets you your business," she said.

"Mmm. It would generally be true to say that war is good for the business. Of course, a war would generally only last a few years and be far less widespread. During a normal war, there are mad scrambles for power, people stabbing each other in the back to grab a hold of the largest slice of power and land. This war has been going on too long. Everything has stabilized. Anyone who wants power and has the means to get it has done so, often with our help. The rest are too weak to hope for anything better or too poor to manage it.

"Now, if this war were to come to a sudden end, chaos would ensue. The bottom would be pulled out from under society. The old guard would panic and throw money at anyone who could help them hold onto any power at all, and newcomers would jump at the dozens of holes in the hierarchy. We would barely be able to keep up with the clients," he said.

Myranda shook her head.

"You would end the war because it would be profitable to you? You would do the right thing for the wrong reasons," she said.

"I never said I would stop the war. And besides, who cares about the reason, so long as the right thing gets done?" he reasoned. "But enough philosophy. Would you care to have a look around? There isn't much to see, but I am quite proud of it all."

Myranda grudgingly agreed, and she and the dragon left the room, following Desmeres through the opposite doorway. There, Myranda found a chamber of equal size with three large bookcases, mostly filled, along the far wall. The rest of the room was filled with various valuables scattered in a haphazard manner. There were half-full chests of coins, some silver, most gold. There were statues, goblets, ornate daggers, swords, and helmets. Here and there, a satchel could be found filled with papers. Desmeres explained it all.

"The fortune is self-explanatory. These papers are deeds. We own a number of very large tracts of land as part of Lain's pet project. On the back wall is the catalog of our business to date. The first two shelves are the somewhat disorganized records--contracts. They hold the specifics of the deals that we have made, as well as anything worth noting about the way the task was performed. That last shelf has to do with Lain's little project, as well. He's been doing it since before I began working with him," he said.

Myn approached the third bookshelf and sniffed at it with much curiosity. Whatever those books held, they had enough of a scent to pique the interest of the dragon. Myranda approached the bookshelf and looked over the spines. They were unlabeled. Some of the books seemed old and well-used. Others were fresh. Myranda reached for one of the books.

"I wouldn't. You'll have to face Lain's wrath if you do," he said.

"I have reached an agreement with Lain that any question I have of him must be answered," she said.

"How did you manage that in less than a year when I haven't made so much progress in seventy? I have tried practically everything to gain his absolute trust," he said.

"I knocked one of his teeth out with a training sword," she said, pulling one of the books from the middle of the case.

Desmeres nodded thoughtfully.

"I hadn't tried that," he quipped.

"He made a wager that I would never be willing to draw blood, and if I did, I deserved to have my questions answered," she explained.

"Ah," he replied.

Myranda opened the book. There were no words, only brownish red stains, dozens of them, on every page. She flipped through, only to find more of the same. Replacing the book, she opened one of the older ones. More stains. She replaced it and chose a newer one. This had an addition. Below each small stain was a name, each scrawled in a different hand.

"What is this?" she asked.

"You'll have to ask Lain. This is a secret of his, not mine. Besides, I have more to show you. We've still got my favorite room left," Desmeres said.

Myranda shook her head, replaced the book, and followed. They entered the room that Desmeres had been standing in the doorway of when they had arrived. As soon as the light of his lamp entered, it glinted off of a dozen polished surfaces. He moved along the walls, lighting wall-mounted lamps as he went. Each new light revealed more of the room. The walls were hung with weapons of every type--swords with carved blades, bows, arrows, axes, and countless other weapons in racks, on stands, and even hanging from the ceiling. Other stands contained bottles, vials, tools, and books.

"Behold, my gallery. Nearly half of the weapons I have made since I began working with Lain are here. I tried to make one of every type, and Lain can use them all, but lately he has been using only daggers and the occasional light sword. I guarantee he will be asking me for a new one soon, what with Sasha's disappearance. No matter, I've got two in the works. I think I can finish one off in a week or so," he said, filled with pride.

"Look at all of them. You have spent so much time on making tools for killing," she said, slightly disgusted.

"Tools, yes. Killing--only sometimes. Besides, I have got widgets and gadgets for all sorts of purposes. Potions for healing, potions for sleep--frankly, I've got potions for everything. I never could get the hang of spell-casting, so I make potions instead. It isn't my greatest talent, but I get by. This one here is my favorite," he said, lifting a small, innocent-looking vial filled with clear liquid. "It is a poison that will kill anything but Lain."

Myranda shook her head.

"Why?" Myranda asked.

"Why the poison? Well, surely you see the usefulness of . . ." he began.

"No, why any of this?" she asked. "I can understand why you would spend your time on such things in Entwell, but why here? You seem like such a decent person. Why do you occupy all of your time with death?"

"Oh, so now it is just death? I liked 'tools for killing' better. Regardless of your terminology, I simply need something to do," he said.

"That is it? You need something to do?" she said.

"I see that you are confused. First of all, how old do you suppose I am?" he asked.

Myranda considered his appearance. His white hair was a bit less carefully kept than the last time she had seen him. His clothes were of the finest variety. Overall, he looked as though he might be her age, though the way he phrased the question made her believe he was older than he seemed.

"Thirty," she said.

"I was thirty when I left Entwell. I am now just about to celebrate my one hundred-third birthday," he said.

"What? No," she said.

"Father was, and is, an elf. I get the longevity from him. I get the appearance from Mother. It helps me blend with the human population. Never mind that, though. You were looking for an answer for why I squander my life so. Think of every old man or old woman you've met. I'd wager half of them are angry all of the time for no reason at all, or simply numb and apathetic. Why? They are world-weary. They have done and seen everything that they care to see or do. There is nothing left for them.

"Humans have the mixed blessing of a short lifespan. By the time you run out of ambitions and motivations, the end is usually near. Elves are not quite so lucky. We live on and on. As a result, if you are immortal, you need to find something to occupy your vast time. Something endless to fill your days. A passion. I have two.

"First, and foremost, I am a weapon crafter. I strive for perfection. I will never reach it--at least, I hope not--but I get closer with each new weapon. My second passion is more difficult to explain. I like making money," he said.

"How noble," she said with a smirk.

"I do not mean it in a greedy way. I lived the first thirty years without the need for money at all. I simply love the negotiation, the planning. I love reading people. It is as much an art as weapon craft, and just as rewarding. I don't care about the money once I have it. I would give it away, but that would rob me of the joy of haggling prices for the things I buy," he said.

"If you love money so much, why don't you just sell your weapons? At least then you wouldn't have to work with an assassin directly," she said.

"No. Never mix the passions. Weapons are weapons, money is money. I have only sold fifteen pieces in my lifetime, and I have spent the years since trying to hunt them down and buy them back. There are still three out there, and it burns my mind to think of it," he said.

"Why?" she asked.

"They are in the hands of inept fools! I can't stand to see one of my weapons misused. It soils the workmanship. My weapons can make an amateur into a master, but they can make a master invincible. That is why I work with Lain. He is one of only a handful of warriors I deem worthy of holding my handiwork, and his business offers limitless potential for my other skills. As long as he continues to satisfy my needs, I will work with him. If he ever ceases to, I will find someone who will. Simple," he said.

"That is so self-serving," Myranda said.

"That is another trait of immortals. Since we are going to outlive most of the people we know anyway, we tend to focus on ourselves. It is also the nature of things you are passionate about. You have a way of making very poor decisions to indulge them. Like, say, deciding that the people who have been hunting you for nearly a year are actually trying to help you," he said, not a hint of apology in his voice.

Myranda gazed at the weapons and armor. Were she able to bring herself to forget their purpose, she might have been struck by their beauty. Instead, all she saw was death. Her dark thoughts were interrupted by an odd scratching sound. She turned to Myn, the source of the interruption, to see her clawing madly at her neck. The dingy scales and skin were starting to give way.

"Well, well. Is our friend shedding? I'll get a blanket," he said, hurrying off to the supply room.

When he returned he placed the blanket on the ground. Myn seemed to know it was for her, as she rolled on top of it and began clawing at her belly. For the better part of an hour, Myranda and Desmeres discussed the specifics of her adventure that he had not learned on his own as Myn shed the old scales to reveal immaculate, gleaming ones underneath. When her focus returned to her neck, Myranda untied the charm and removed it.

"Say, you didn't mention that little thing. Let me see that," he said.

Myranda handed it to him. He turned it all about in his hands, held it up to the light, and tapped on the metal.

"I remember this. This was on Trigorah's helmet," he said.

"You remember seeing it there?" she said.

"I remember putting it there," he said, rubbing it on his shirt to restore its luster.

"You made her helmet?" Myranda said, shocked.

"No, just the charm. One of my better pieces. It lets healing and such through, but blocks most other spells. It was something of an anniversary gift," he said.

Myranda's jaw dropped.

"We weren't married. Not officially. But we were . . . involved for some time," he said, returning the charm to her. She was too stunned to reach for it, so he took it back.

"How . . ." she managed.

"How long? Six years. I gave this to her on our fifth," he said, trying to answer the half-asked question.

Myranda shook her head, still struggling to find the words.

"How long ago, perhaps? I'd say I first spoke to her perhaps thirty years ago. No, that still isn't it, eh? How . . . How involved? Well, I have a son she never told me about," he said, grinning at his last statement.

Myranda stopped searching for words and simply stared, dumbstruck.

"She's got him squirreled away somewhere up north. He's twenty-five now, with some military job. Croyden is his name, if I recall correctly. I wonder if she's given the boy my name or hers. Must check on that," he said.

Myranda finally found her voice again, and finished the question he had failed to guess.

"How could you?" she asked.

"Well, she has been after Lain since before I started working with him. She is no fool, so in following his trail, she found herself led to me time and time again. I have always felt that one should keep his enemies close, and she felt the same way. That is how it began. The entire time we were together was like a sort of dance, each of us trying our best to learn the intentions of the other. She is very attractive, and we share membership of a fairly unrepresented race. As we played each other for information, we found that we had a great many things in common. What can I say?" he said.

"But she wants to kill you!" she said.

"That is only a recent development. Back then she only wanted to kill Lain," he said.

"Even still, he is your partner!" she said.

"It began as a means to protect him. I feel no shame," he said with a shrug. "It is just the two of us in this partnership. We do what we must."

"Just the two of you . . . wait . . . didn't you mention a woman?" she asked.

"A woman. I don't believe I did," he said, attempting to recall.

"Yes, you did. Sasha," Myranda said.

"Oh . . . *Oh.* A misunderstanding. Sasha is a what, not a who. Sashat Mance. Bag of tricks. It is the sword Lain had been using," he clarified.

"What? No. You said that she never said a word, but she sang, and that they would try to coax secrets out of her," she objected.

Desmeres chuckled and pulled a sword from its mount on the wall.

"Listen," he said, swiftly drawing it from its sheath.

There wasn't a whisper of sound. He then ran his finger along the flat of the blade. The immaculate metal resonated with a crystal-clear tone.

"There are more than a few blacksmiths that would give their right hand to learn how I make these. Those are the secrets I'm worried about. A fellow by the name of Flinn has gotten wealthy off of one of my daggers . . ." he said, immediately changing the subject. "Say, you know what I haven't made in a dog's age? A staff. Lain doesn't use magic. Not a word of it. Frankly, it doesn't make any sense to me, because he swears by that 'warrior's sleep' they taught him back in the belly of the beast, and that is deeper and harder to manage than any trance. I've made normal staffs, but a casting staff would be a fine diversion. You say you are a full master? I suppose that I would be justified in giving you a piece of my handiwork, but . . . I just can't be sure. I would have to see you in action before I made something from scratch. I might not mind working on the one you've already got, though."

Myranda shook her head in disbelief again. He spoke of betraying his friend and having a relationship with his enemy as though it was nothing, but the very moment that the subject of weaponry was introduced, he latched onto it with boundless interest. Before she could object, Desmeres had fetched her staff.

"Good heavens. Have they still got Coda making these? I could improve this immeasurably. There are at least a dozen runes that could make this doubly resistant to hostile spells. A few potion infusions. Yes. This could be a fine weapon . . . Gracious, this is heavy. Did they give this to you?" he asked.

". . . No, Deacon gave it to me," she said. She knew by now that attempting to bring closure to anything that Desmeres wasn't interested in discussing anymore was useless.

"Well, Deacon must not be a weapon specialist, because this is the wrong size, weight, and shape for someone like you. The crystal could use work as well, but I haven't got the equipment for that. Not here, anyway," he said.

That was the last she heard from him for most of the day. He retired to a corner of the weapon room and set himself to work, flipping through books, selecting tools, and carving at the staff. Myranda watched for a time. He worked with a speed, grace, and enthusiasm that she admired. *He must truly love the work,* she thought. Before long, though, her mind became fixed on other things. She moved back to the dining room and retired to a chair.

Myn had finished shedding and looked to Myranda for attention. The girl moved to the ground to better dote upon her friend. She patted the little creature, whose scales were now as smooth and shiny as the day she was born. As she did, she thought.

She thought back to her encounter with Trigorah. It pained her to think of it. She had been desperate to escape. In her desperation, she'd nearly killed the commander. Now it was possible that all of this time they had been dedicated to the same goal. If she had only turned herself over, all of this could have been avoided. But, then, if she had turned herself in, she would not have helped to conjure the other Chosen in Entwell, and she would not know nearly as much magic. She would not have even been sure of Lain's place in the Chosen. Was it all part of the prophecy? All part of the plan for the world that she would not know the truth until she had earned it? So much hardship had come since then . . .

Her reverie was interrupted when Desmeres entered the room.

"Ah, excellent, the dragon has shed her skin," he said, gathering up the blanket and dumping the remnants of the act into a bag. "This is a very useful and very rare resource. I can think of a dozen or more things to do with this."

"Then when you put down the blanket, you didn't want to make Myn more comfortable, you wanted to make it easier to collect up the shedding?" Myranda said, annoyed that yet another seeming act of kindness was false.

"Yes. Would you stand up, please?" he asked.

"Why?" she asked.

"I need your exact height," he said, offering a hand to help her up.

Myranda reluctantly accepted the help. He looked her up and down, eventually asking to see her hands as well. Once he seemed satisfied with sizing her up, he told her so.

"Before you sit down, though, I imagine you might like something nicer than the floor to sleep on. We haven't got any beds, but there are a few bedrolls. One for each of us and a spare. If that dragon of yours--" he began.

"Her name is Myn," Myranda interjected.

"If Myn can hold onto her flame, I would not mind offering her the spare," he said.

"Myn likes to sleep on top of me," Myranda said.

"Do you like for her to sleep atop you?" he asked.

"I don't mind it," she replied.

"Then, by all means, let it continue. Sleep wherever you find room enough on the floor to do so, though I would not recommend directly below the entrance. It would lead to a rather rude awakening," he said.

Myranda accepted the bedroll and set it up, but she was not ready for sleep yet. She sat up longer and thought. It was perhaps a few hours more, in the dead of the night, when the door quietly creaked open and Lain deactivated the traps and slipped back inside. Desmeres was too busy at his task to notice the entry. Lain sat at the table in front of Myranda. He had nothing new with him. The dragon leapt from her lap to his, eager for the novelty of her other favorite creature in the world.

"Desmeres has shown me around," Myranda said.

Lain shifted his gaze to her without acknowledging her words.

"I have seen the books. The first two shelves are all about your business. Desmeres would not tell me what the third shelf's books were for," she said.

"Desmeres knows his place," he said.

"All I have to do is ask, you know. You have made a promise to me," she said.

"So I have," he answered.

"Then tell me. What is the purpose? Most of the pages do not even have names," she said.

"I am not interested in names. I am interested in people," he said.

"Tell me what I want to know," she demanded.

"Those are drops of blood. I collect one from each person who owes me a favor so that I can identify them by scent," he said.

"Owe you favors?" she asked.

"I have helped them in some way," he said.

"Oh? I suppose that you murdered someone for them and they have yet to pay you," Myranda said harshly.

"Now, now. That is an oversimplification of the services that we offer," Desmeres said, drawn by the voices. "We don't merely kill people. We also dabble in espionage. To wit, I have here every dispatch that we have managed to seize from the military through our various channels since you went missing.

"Allow me to condense. Up until about six weeks ago, dispatches were flying in every direction with inadequate and, frankly, rather skewed descriptions of Myranda here. Separately, there have been significant efforts put into reminding the populace of the evils of malthropes. Then the messages began to taper off. By the end, the rather thin selection of messages available all seemed to agree that the primary targets of late are dead or of no more concern.

"That is, of course, except for one that we managed to sneak a peek at en route from Trigorah herself to General Bagu, urging that the search not be ended until a body is found. I have reason to believe that Bagu agrees. He may even have sent one of the other generals to give Trigorah a hand, although other dispatches seem to indicate a second general has been involved for some time," he said.

"What does all of this mean for us?" Myranda asked.

"For *us* it means that we will be facing the Elites as a smaller, more focused, and much more powerful group. Fortunately, thanks to Lain's less than subtle actions prior to retreating to the Belly of the Beast, the Elite proper has been reduced to a handful of men, and with the way the combat on the front lines has been heating up, I cannot foresee many new members anytime soon. The rest are just mercenaries in uniforms, comparatively no threat at all. It also means that if we disguise you a bit, we may be able to transport you from one place to another without rousing too much suspicion. So long as you don't run into Trigorah herself, who knows your face," he said.

"But Trigorah is the one person I want to meet. She is the one who can deliver me to the Alliance Army safely so that I can begin finding the other Chosen," Myranda said.

Lain's gaze shifted sternly to Myranda.

"Yes. She has leapt to a rather lofty conclusion about the Alliance Army seeking to help her join the Chosen together," Desmeres explained.

"You agreed," Myranda said.

"I agreed it was possible. I also remarked that it was not at all likely. I would guessed that their intentions for you are not quite hospitable, but there is no sense guessing about one's intentions when we can read them in their own words. From Bagu to Trigorah a few months ago: 'I cannot stress the importance of this capture enough. As long as this target remains out of our reach, the possibility of failure exists. We must have her, if possible alive. She could be an invaluable resource.' Capture, target, resource, if possible alive? These do not sound like the words of a helpful and concerned party," he said.

"I don't care," she said.

"If you knew more about the people who want you, you might. You need to learn just who is really after you. The five generals are the ones most interested. Regardless of what you may have seen or heard, the generals are not the sort of people that you want looking for you. I know that you think that they have the best of intentions for you and the world, but keep in mind that if not for them, this war would have come to an end, possibly peacefully, decades ago."

"What do you mean?" she asked.

"There are standing orders from the generals to kill anyone sent to broker a peace. There is every indication that those have been the orders since the war began," he explained.

"So I have heard . . . wait. This war has been fought off and on for the past hundred and fifty years. How could the same five generals be at fault?" she asked.

"They aren't human. At least, four of them aren't for certain. Trigorah is an elf, as you know, but she was the last to be made a general, well after the war began. As for the others . . . I believe that they are D'karon," he said.

"D'karon? The inhuman creatures? The ones that created those wretched Cloaks and . . . and the dragon thing that killed the swordsman?" she cried. "I don't believe it."

"I don't expect you to. I only ask that you keep your eyes open, and listen for these names. They are bad people. There is a reason that few living men and women have ever seen them, and that is because those who see them seldom live long. The first is Trigorah. You know her well enough and she is, to a degree, the least of your worries. She is the decent and honorable sort and will only do what she is ordered to do. In the same vein, she will *always* do what she is ordered to do, and since she takes her orders from the other generals, she is capable of anything.

"Next is Teht. You won't likely run into her, but you may be brought before her if you get caught. She is fairly inactive, spending nearly all of her time in research, experimentation, and training others. A powerful wizard, and surrounded by many of the same.

"Now, Demont. He is one you had best keep away from. He doesn't seem terribly dangerous. A rather slight and weak-looking man, but he surrounds himself with the most vicious and twisted of D'karon creatures, and they take his will as law. Beasts snap to attention more readily and obediently than soldiers around him. He likes to spend his time researching as well, but research of a different sort. Many is the story I have heard of a patrol of soldiers torn to shreds by a swarm of creatures none had ever seen before while a man matching Demont's description watches. He tests these creatures.

"More disturbing is the man he often brings as a partner. Epidime. Nearly all of the information I have about this fellow is contradictory. This much I am certain of: He is an intelligence officer and a very good one, specializing in interrogation. His skills in that area are the stuff of legend. Those who come before him are never the same afterward. I have spoken with one or two of his victims. They ended up telling him things they didn't even know they knew.

"However, all of them report to one man, Bagu. Don't be fooled by the name. He is a masterful leader and, if what is said is true, every bit the wizard and warrior to keep the others in line by fear or force," he said.

"I can't imagine them being as evil as you make them sound," she said.

"It depends on your perspective. Frankly, most of our countrymen should be worshiping them. I guarantee you that without them, the north would have fallen to the south fifty years ago. It is on the strength of the five generals that the Alliance Army has withstood so many years against a far larger and healthier force. From your point of view, though, they are most definitely evil. These are the men and woman who want your freedom," he said.

"They want to help me, and the world," she said.

"If you choose to believe that," he said with a shrug. "Just remember, these are the most important and powerful people in the north. If you meet them, consider every breath from there after a gift. People don't tend to outlive their usefulness around them."

"Point taken," she said.

"I sincerely doubt that. Regardless, back to the business at hand. We need to do something soon. I believe these to be the last dispatches that we will receive until we can establish some new informants. We need manpower," Desmeres said.

"How much gold do I have?" Lain asked.

"Most of what we have left is yours. I'd say perhaps ninety bars worth," he said.

"That will be enough," Lain said.

"For what?" Desmeres said, in a tone of humoring a child.

"There is a mining company in the mountains to the northeast . . ." Lain began.

"No. No! Absolutely not. You know I cannot go out there. If you like, I'll show you the order by the Alliance Army demanding my head! I didn't even need an informant for it. *It was nailed to a tree.* You expect me to go out and negotiate a purchase *now?"* Desmeres objected fiercely.

"It will give us countless new opportunities," he countered, calmly.

"I don't care what it will give us, it is a terrible idea. I simply will not do it. And don't think that you'll be able to do it either. Unless those interrogators were kind enough to return that cloak that hides your face, you won't last three words into the first round of negotiations before either your throat is slit or you are forced to slit someone else's, and it will take me *months* to replace that little gadget. Not that anyone would conduct a negotiation with a man he couldn't look in the eye," he said.

"We'll send Myranda," he said.

"No! Absolutely not! I don't want anything to do with this awful business of yours!" Myranda objected.

"You want to send *her!?* We have only just gotten her back into the fold after you released her the last time! Now you propose that she be sent out, alone, with all of our money? I thought that you had mentioned *best* judgment as the standing order," he said.

"We do not have very many options," Lain said.

"That doesn't mean that we must choose the worst one! I've got a business or two left. We only need to get to one," he said.

"If it was so simple, you would have done it," Lain said.

"Perhaps I was waiting for you," Desmeres offered.

Lain looked calmly at his partner.

"How many?" Desmeres asked, defeated.

"Two hundred," Lain answered.

"It's Grossmer's? Grossmer's, the suppliers of half of the iron and copper in all of the Low Lands, is what you've got your eye on?" Desmeres said in disbelief.

Lain nodded.

"When did they even mention the possibility of putting that place up for sale? It isn't a gold mine, but it may as well be! They've got military contracts! Guaranteed business until the end of the war! Of course, long-standing military contracts mean that some of the older administrators could have fairly firm connections on the inside. That would be useful. We might have to bargain hard to take them for only ninety and have any left for your little practice in futility," he said thoughtfully. Finally he threw his hands up. "There is simply too much that needs to be done. I shall have to come along. We will need a carriage, an impressive one. With equally impressive horses and a driver. Impressive, but not extravagant. We need to convince them we are oozing with money, but we use it wisely. It will set the tone of the day and turn the deal in our direction before we even start. We will need a disguise for Myranda in keeping with her supposed social rank. The carriage will need a hiding place for me."

"Weren't you listening? I simply won't go!" Myranda objected again.

"You will change your mind. As for you, Lain. Since this was your idea, I will be expecting you to gather the necessary equipment. I will finish working on Myranda's staff and draw up the paperwork. And I'll mix up some of the smoke flares to keep the oloes away from the horses while we load up the carriage," Desmeres said.

"Meet me on the road east of here in seven days," Lain said.

With that, he rose and headed for the door.

"No, not again! Come back here! I haven't agreed!" Myranda called after him.

It was no use, she threw open the door that he had shut behind him, only to see him whisper a word or two to Myn, who sat obediently and watched as he whisked up to the hatch and slipped out.

"I'm not through with you!" Myranda called uselessly.

"You are beginning to repeat yourself. A word of advice from a veteran in dealing with that fellow: He and no one else decides when you are through with him. I have yet to finish a conversation with him that did not interest him," Desmeres said.

"Both of you are so selfish," she said.

"That is a fair opinion. One I happen to agree with, in fact," he said.

"How can you be so cocky? You take it for granted that I will help you," she said.

"You will. You are both intelligent and helpful. It is in your nature to do what others need of you. You are already becoming aware of how businesslike I am, and it is only a matter of time before you realize how useful it will be to have performed a valuable service for us," he said, walking back to his workshop.

"What do you mean?" she asked, following him.

"Your life, or death, depends entirely upon the value of each to us. You are alive because you are worth more to us in that state. Were I you, and I was after Lain's aid in this Chosen nonsense as you are, I would be spending most of my time and effort proving that I am more valuable as an ally than as a captive," he said, taking a seat at the bench and picking up the wood chisel.

"How could I possibly do that?" she asked.

"I don't have all of the answers, but I would say that helping us with this purchase would be a fine start. You might think about sabotaging our relationship with the Alliance Army while you are at it. That way, we would have a harder time turning you over for the reward to anyone but Trigorah. We would have to hold onto you longer, and you would have more time to convince Lain to end the war," he said.

"Why are you telling me this?" she asked.

"It will both plant the seeds of an idea, making it more likely for you to make the decision that benefits me most, and confuse your desire to do the opposite of what I say," he said.

". . . I wish you were not quite so forthcoming with your explanations," she said, less than pleased with this glimpse into the disturbingly well-crafted manipulations of her host.

"I'd warned that my honesty would become bothersome . . ." he said, looking up distractedly. "Lain . . . he didn't bring a weapon, did he?"

"I didn't notice. I suppose not. Why? Are you concerned for him?" she asked.

"No, for any who may face him," he said.

"I don't understand," she said.

"When . . . when he holds a weapon, particularly one of mine, he is a graceful, silent, clean killer. When he is unarmed, he is something else altogether. Vicious, forceful. He reverts to something primal. I dare say he is even more deadly that way, but in a way that is unmistakably animal," Desmeres said with a shudder.

"What do you care?" she asked.

"If a man must die, so be it, but there is no reason to be cruel. I must finish his weapon. But first I must finish yours, and the paperwork. So much to do, and only seven days to do it," he said, turning back to his task.

Myranda found her way back to the room with the table, where she had set up her bedroll, and retired. Try as she might, though, she could not bring herself to sleep. She was more at home on the freezing ground outside than in this place. Knowing that all that surrounded her was paid for by blood turned her stomach. She wondered how the peace of the world could be left to the whims of such twisted minds.

The best she could manage was a light doze, interrupted periodically by an odd sound or smell emanating from Desmeres's workshop. Myn, lying atop her as always, slept peacefully until what must have been morning. When the dragon roused, Myranda decided she may as well end this fruitless pursuit of sleep. She wandered into Desmeres's workshop.

The half-elf, visibly weary, was admiring what he had done to the staff. He noticed her walk in and held it up proudly. Myranda took it from his hands. It felt much lighter. He had carved a good deal of the exterior down and shaped it carefully. Her fingers fit easily and comfortably around it. The color was different, streaked with darker colors that made the formerly white surface resemble the gray bark of a tree, and covering the surface were dozens of small, intricately carved symbols. She had noticed the same symbols decorating the blades and handles of nearly every other weapon in the room. Lowering its tip to the floor, she found it stood at a more appropriate height than before. His improvements were apparent, though she wondered about the reasoning for some.

"Why the darker color?" she asked.

"A side effect of the solutions I soaked it in to strengthen it. Natural wood at the thickness that is appropriate for your hand size would not be strong enough for my tastes. I could restore the color, if you like," he said.

"I don't much care. What of the symbols?" she asked.

"Runes. Lain has put them to fine use over the years, and I see no reason why you couldn't do the same. He doesn't know a word of magic, as I've said, so he needed something that could turn the defensive skills he does have into something effective against magic. Those runes will allow you to defend against spells tossed in your direction as though they were conventional attacks. You can deflect a fireball as easily as a thrown stone, or shatter a conjured shield spell as though it were glass, all without wasting an ounce of your own mystic strength. Of course, a stronger spell is more difficult to deflect, just as a larger stone is. Also, though I stand by my work, I cannot guarantee that the enhancements will work against all magics. It is an ever-changing area, after all," he said.

Myranda tested the strength of the now-much thinner tool. Touching it for the first time in a day, she was struck by the clarity of mind it brought. Certainly the effect had not been so noticeable before. Seeming to notice her expression, Desmeres offered an explanation.

"Among other things, I treated the wood so that it will aid focus in absence of a crystal. With a crystal, the effect is doubled. Useful, yes?" he said.

The girl admired the work for a few more moments before a suspicion crept into her mind.

"You only did this to raise the price on my head again, didn't you?" she said.

"Heavens no. Not *only* that. I also needed some practice in the manufacture of mystical weapons. I almost never get the opportunity. I'm glad you thought to accuse me, though. It shows that you are developing a healthier outlook on the people around you," he said with a grin, as he searched around for some sheets of paper, some ink, and a quill.

"*Healthy?* I thought the worst of you!" she said.

"And you weren't completely wrong. You'll find that you seldom are when you think the worst of people," he said, finding some high quality parchment and ink.

"That is a terrible thing to say!" she objected.

"Prove me wrong," he said, dipping a quill and beginning to scribe in impressive calligraphy.

"What are you writing?" she asked.

"Paperwork. There is a fair amount of it involved in transferring land," he said.

"Aren't you going to sleep?" she asked.

"I prefer to wait until my affairs are in order," he said.

"And Lain? Does he ever sleep?" she asked.

"Not in the traditional sense. They call it 'the warrior's sleep,' but the two couldn't be more dissimilar," he said.

"You spoke of the warrior's sleep before. What is that?" she asked.

"It is . . . well . . . let us put it in mystical terms. It is like meditation, only far, far deeper, and not merely of the mind. It focuses the thoughts, and it brings the body near to death. They have been teaching it at Entwell since the beginning. I could never get the hang of it, but they say a few minutes like that will do the work of a few hours of real sleep. Back before he had someone to cook up healing potions, that is how Lain dealt with serious injury. It is not nearly as fast as a potion or a spell, but it is measurably better than simply waiting," he explained.

"He never sleeps normally?" she asked.

"If you ever find him lying down, especially in a bed, you can be certain it was not his idea," Desmeres answered.

As she watched him sculpt the official language of the paper with great care, she decided he had best be left alone. She found herself drawn to the room that contained the gold and the records. Myn's tapping claws followed her, and once inside, the little dragon leapt up onto one of the chests that was mostly coins, instinctively drawn to the gleaming treasure. She curled up and watched Myranda as she approached the second shelf.

The books that filled the shelf were in groups of four. All told, there were a few more than seventy such sets. She reasoned that, since Desmeres had been partnered with him for roughly seventy years, the groups must be by season and year, though if there was a written indication of exactly what year each represented, it was not in a form she recognized. It was just as well. The standard method for labeling the years these days was to measure from the day that the war had begun. By that measure, the year was 156. The thought depressed her.

In the days to come, days that seemed painfully long with nothing to fill them, she spent much time leafing through the books. The names of the people and places, as well as the prices, were the only things not written in some bizarre language that they had certainly learned at Entwell. As a result, she found herself scanning the pages for any places or names she knew. It seldom took long. A lifetime of journeying from town to town had taken her to most of the places in the north. Apparently Lain's business had done the same. People of much renown were frequently named in the pages as well. Wealthy landowners, merchants, and people of all walks of life had either hired his blade or fallen to it. Without understanding the language, it was impossible to tell which. Much of what she saw she had heard in the form of rumors over the years. The Red Shadow. The fact that he was real, the fact that she knew him, filled her with an icy, gnawing anxiety.

Soon it was the seventh day. Desmeres had long since finished his preparations, the last of which was the completion of some manner of sword for Lain. He refused to unveil it to her, claiming that Lain ought to be the first. He slipped out the entrance hatch, warning her that he would arrive back at the end of the day and they would have to move quickly when the time came. Until then, there was nothing to do but leaf through more books. She had worked her way backward through fifteen or so of the years, and came upon a name she had known about already. Rinthorne, the unfortunate man who had been in charge of Kenvard when the massacre occurred.

Dark memories filled her head at the glimpse of the name. She'd lost her home, her family, everything that day. Then something odd caught her eye. A line in the book was struck out. It was clearly written in a different hand than the rest. With a bit of effort, the words could still be read, not that it did any good. She still hadn't worked out what they meant. Something else was odd. There was no indication for whom or to whom the job was done. There was only one word that she did recognize.

Kenvard.

Her mind began to stir. How? He had told her of the job he had done for Rinthorne. It happened at the same time as the massacre. How could a job have been done in Kenvard afterward? Afterward there *was* no Kenvard. Kenvard the nation had been absorbed, and its capital of the same name had been razed. Was that why it was crossed out? And why no names? And no price? Rather, not one that could be counted in gold bars. The word that always preceded the number was present, but what followed was only another word. Myranda cursed herself for not spending more time in the warrior's section of Entwell. Had she, she might have learned this language, and this would have been clear.

A nagging feeling burned at her. This was important. She couldn't explain why, but she had to know what it meant. As she further pondered, her thoughts were interrupted by the creaking of the trapdoor and the whir of blades through the air.

"Myranda! Quickly! I am not sure how long we can keep the oloes at bay!" called Desmeres, struggling to yell over a powerful wind that whistled in the opening.

Myranda slipped the book into her bag and hurried to the entryway. The gold needed for the purchase had been transferred into twenty or so small crates. Though each held only four or five of the ingots, they were heavier than lead. A rope was lowered for Myranda to secure to one chest at a time, and the combined strength of Desmeres and Lain, topside, hauled each up. Myn, interested in the activity on the surface, scrambled up to them, and soon the chests were moving much faster. The little dragon had quickly determined the purpose of this little game and joined in, clamping the end of the rope in her jaws and lending her disproportionate strength to the effort. Soon, the chests were all loaded, and Myranda clutched the rope herself and was hauled out.

On the surface, it was night. She found the ground around them covered with a thin haze that smelled strongly of burning wood. The horrid brown creatures that guarded the place were completely surrounding them, staying at the exact distance where the mist faded to nothing. Waiting for them was a four-horse carriage. It was just as he had asked: elegant, but sturdy. Not a gaudy showpiece, a well-crafted vehicle. There was a very large cargo compartment in the back that was filled fairly to bursting with their precious load. In the front was a comfortable place for the passengers to sit, and just in front of that was a sheltered place for the driver. There was no one there.

Desmeres approached her, he was dressed as he'd been when he left, utterly cocooned in winter clothing in an attempt to stay warm and hide his identity. Lain was not disguised at all, wearing a lighter gray cloak with a white lining and a plain tunic underneath. Hanging from his belt was the new sword, concealed in a sheath.

"Do I take from your presence up here that you have chosen to aid us?" Desmeres asked, opening the door of the carriage for her.

"Certainly I do not want to spend the rest of my life in that hole. We shall see if I aid you or not. I want to know more about it first," she said, stepping inside and dropping her bag and staff on the floor.

"Fine, fine. I wouldn't expect you to do it without considerable instruction anyway," he said, starting to close the door.

"Aren't you coming inside?" she asked.

"Dawn will be here soon, and our driver is still a few hours away. Lain is the best there is, but even he couldn't drive a carriage in broad daylight without being seen. I will drive it until we meet the coachman," he said.

"What about Myn?" she asked.

"One of the lines in every description of you mentions that you will be in the company of the dragon. She will have to tag along with Lain," Desmeres said.

Myranda's heart sank as Myn turned to Lain in the distance, cast a goodbye glance, and trotted off to him.

"As for you, there is an outfit in the carriage; I suggest you change into it while you are alone," Desmeres said, closing the door.

A moment later, the carriage lurched into motion. Myranda looked around her. In all of her life, this was the first time she had been in a covered carriage, save the rather unpleasant trip in the back of the black carriage after the cloaks attacked her.

The seats were cushioned with deep red velvet. Doors that were better crafted than those on her childhood home kept even the slightest draft from breaking through. Over each of the glass windows, of which there was one on each door, there was a gauze curtain to keep prying eyes out but allow light in, and a heavy drape of the same red velvet to eliminate the light. She lowered the gauze curtains and looked over the outfit. It was exquisite. Fine lace, linen, and . . . silk! She had seen women pay a fortune for any one of these pieces of clothing. When she had put on the dress and petticoats, she found them to be just precisely her size, as though they had been hand-altered to suit her. She wondered for a moment how Lain had managed such a feat, but her thoughts were interrupted by the gleaming white fur coat that would protect her against the freezing cold.

Fur was not at all an uncommon thing to see someone wear in the north. If one had forsaken the ubiquitous gray cloak, a rough one of fur was generally in its place. In those cases, though, it was merely a skin, perhaps not even cleaned, draped about the shoulders and tied about the waist. This was, again, tailored to suit her. She slipped it on and found it to be more than warm enough.

If they wanted her to go unrecognized, they had certainly chosen a fine wardrobe. Dressed in this way, Myranda didn't even feel like herself. The crumpled pile of overused clothes on the floor of the carriage more closely resembled her true self than who she might have seen in a mirror. After stuffing her former self into the bag and attempting to gather her hair into something more becoming of her wardrobe, she drew the curtain on one side of the carriage and gazed outside.

After a few minutes, a fellow traveler passed in the opposite direction. He was an older man in a sleigh that was nearly falling apart. He wore a cloak so tattered that the hood was useless, replaced with a fur hat. He tipped it as he passed. Myranda smiled at him. It was the first time that anyone had acknowledged her as she traveled. She leaned into the soft seat and pondered why people were so willing to ignore their own, and so eager to acknowledge those who were better off. Her thoughts were interrupted when the carriage pulled to a halt just as the traveler disappeared from view. Desmeres appeared outside the window and pulled the door open.

"Has this curtain been open all along?" he asked.

"Yes," she said.

"Close it. You should know better," he said.

She obeyed and they were on their way again. It was nice to finally be able to travel in luxury, but without Myn to keep her company, she was beginning to feel loneliness creep back upon her. It was a feeling she'd not had to deal with since she'd found the little dragon, and she did not relish it. She pulled the bag from the floor and found the stylus inside. Rolling it slowly in her palm, she remembered the man who had given it to her. Fetching the torn spell page from the bag, she cursed it for not being written in his hand. She scratched the stylus along the page. A thin black line faded in swiftly behind it. It was enchanted to write without ink. In Entwell, it was nothing. Out here, it was miraculous. Smiling, she went back to admiring the simple tool. As she admired, her mind wandered to those happier times.

#

Meanwhile, a forest and a mountain away, Deacon sat at his table. He had found it increasingly difficult to keep his mind on his task, and self-imposed deadlines were quickly piling up. All of his life, he had kept to the schedules he made for himself. Faced with the daunting task of recording every piece of gray magic his former mentor had neglected to write down, if he hadn't forced himself to keep to a schedule, it would have consumed his life. Thanks to his diligence, he reasoned that in five short years he would have finished recording the teachings of Gilliam and would be free to begin his own contributions in earnest.

That was before. Now he was a full volume behind.

Even so, rather than writing, he was staring at the empty chair across from him. A motion drew his eye to the pen that sat in the pot of ink at the corner of his book. The pen rose shakily and touched to the paper. A slow, lazy line was drawn along one corner. With a curling flourish, the pen lifted from the paper and returned to the ink. Anxiously, Deacon watched the pen for any further movement. When it remained still, he pulled the page from the book and greedily took in the curve with his eyes. She had drawn it.

When he gave the stylus to her, he had meant it to be useful to her, a tool that would make her path easier. It was not until later that he supposed that the spell might persist regardless of distance. The moment that the thought came to him he had rushed to the paper to see if any of the words were not his own. From that day forward, he had awoken each morning with the hope of something new. Something from her. Slowly it occurred to him the madness of it. This was a simple line. It was no different than any meaningless scribble he might have made himself. Why should this one mean so much? He tried to convince himself that it was because of her task, that he couldn't keep his mind off of her because she had a part in the prophecy.

It was a lie. The prophecy was the last thing he thought of when he thought of her. He didn't think of anything. When she was in his mind, there was nothing else. He tried his best to shake the thoughts away, placing the paper in a drawer. There was nothing to be done about it. It would be months before the way was open for her to return. Until then, he would simply have to keep his mind on magic. If he could not scribe, at least he could study. Standing and approaching one of his many shelves, he plucked a volume he had written years ago. He flipped to a page in the center, where there was described a spell he'd never had much use for. Distance seeing. Perhaps . . . he may just find a use soon.

#

Back in the carriage, hours later, Desmeres pulled to the side of the road and stopped, joining her inside. Sitting on the seat across from her, he peeled off several of the outer layers of his winter covering until he was left with an outfit that was every bit as finely tailored as the one she had been given. Standing, he lifted the seat he had chosen to reveal a large compartment beneath it, obviously the hiding place he had requested. From inside, he pulled a pile of papers.

"Now, to complete your disguise," he said.

"What is on those papers? Spells?" she asked.

"Heavens no. I am no wizard. Any disguise spell I could manage would only attract *more* attention to you. No, these papers contain your new personality, by far the most important part of the disguise. That and your instructions, but those can wait. The driver will be showing up soon, and he will be your first test. We need to lay the groundwork before then," he said.

"I don't understand," she said.

"No need to worry. You will. You see, the most commonly used phrase in the dispatches that describe you is 'poor, nomadic girl.' Even if you manage to completely change your appearance, you would still fit that little phrase. And right now you are dressed as a noblewoman. If you do not act as one, you will draw attention even if you don't even remotely resemble a person to watch for. You need to act appropriately. As such, we will start from the bottom. Your name is Alexia Adriana Tesselor," he began.

Myranda tilted her head as she tried to recall where she'd heard the last name before.

"Of the West Kinsey Tesselors. It is a fact that you are endlessly proud of. Given the chance, you will mention it no later than the second sentence of any conversation, and as often afterward as possible," he said.

Myranda nodded. The Tesselors were an exceedingly wealthy family on the west coast of the continent, so much so that they practically owned the city that they hailed from. Though they were not nobles, there was not a single leader in all of the Northern Alliance who didn't have either a marital or financial connection to the clan. Rumor had it that the king himself owed a rather sizable debt to the patriarch of the Tesselors for the cost of his coronation.

Desmeres handed her a piece of paper and a small bag of jewelry.

"This is a family tree and a short description of the most prevalent members. Memorize it. Lord knows that they have. Rings and necklaces, gold, all bearing the family crest. Put them on. Now you know who you are. All that is left is to teach you how to *be* who you are. Listen up. I am about to give you the single most important piece of advice that you will ever receive. There are only two things that you will ever need to succeed, regardless of what you do: Confidence and experience. Of the two, confidence is paramount. No one, *no one,* is more confident and secure in their superiority than the extremely wealthy. You need to exude obnoxious amounts of confidence in all situations," Desmeres said.

"Like you," Myranda said mockingly.

"Precisely," Desmeres replied, ruining her joke. "I owe everything I have to--often unjustified--confidence. Now, rather than trying to fill in things you already know, we will do this as a test of sorts. First, what is your name?" he asked.

"Alexia Tesselor," Myranda replied.

"Alexia *Adriana* Tesselor. Adriana Tesselor is your grandmother and one of the more powerful members of your clan. You will never pass up an opportunity to flaunt your common name. Now, what is the name again?" he asked.

"Alexia Adriana Tesselor," she said.

"Right. Now, let us imagine that someone tries to exert some authority over you. Also, suppose that what you are doing is wrong, and they are justified in reprimanding you. What do you do?" he quizzed.

"I don't suppose I follow their orders," Myranda said, rolling her eyes at what was obviously a wrong answer.

"You are a Tesselor. What do you do?" he repeated.

"I . . . bribe them," she said.

"Better, but no. Criminals bribe. Besides, bribing acknowledges that you are at a disadvantage," he said.

Myranda thought hard, but couldn't find the answer.

"Threaten. Always threaten. The mere sound of your name should be enough, particularly if you repeat it, which you will. If it isn't enough, mention any name in the family line. On the off chance you have particularly duty-minded individual, the implied wrath of the patriarch of the family, Vander Tesselor, will stave off almost any authority figure," Desmeres instructed.

For an hour or so, Myranda was taught how to behave in a way opposite to what her heart and upbringing told her. Conversations with underlings are short and direct, always in the form of orders. She must assume that everything, in all situations, has been done for her benefit.

At first, she found it impossible to decide what to say or do to appear to be this new person, but her thoughts shifted to the one person in her life who she realized she was sounding more and more like. Ayna, the wind master in Entwell. When she began answering questions as Ayna would have, everything fell into place. Her first test came when the driver tapped on the window. Desmeres slipped quietly into concealment. Myranda pulled back the curtain.

"What is it?" she snapped irritatedly.

"Where does madam--" he began.

"Mistress Alexia Adriana Tesselor, not madam. You will refer to me as Mistress Tesselor. I want to be at Grossmer's mines in three days," she declared haughtily.

The driver, somewhat bewildered by the flurry of orders, hesitated.

"Well? Off with you!" she said curtly, dropping the curtain into place.

"Fine work," Desmeres said quietly, once the carriage had jerked into motion. He slipped from beneath the seat.

"Was it convincing?" she asked, somewhat proud.

"Exceptionally so. Voice down please. You are alone in here, remember. There is much for you to learn before we get there. Three days may not be enough," he said.

The rest of the day passed in much the same manner as the time she had spent in Entwell. Desmeres explained to her everything she might need to know about securing the ownership of the mines as quickly, easily, and cheaply as possible. She was told the prices of their ore, the success in recent years, and the likely success in the future. By sundown, her head was swimming. The carriage began to turn, signaling the approach of a town.

"Here is money. Give it to the driver when he opens the door. Rich people never pay for anything themselves. That case on the floor has five changes of clothes. He will carry it without being asked. Stay in the best room of the best inn in town. You won't need to figure out which is which, the driver will. I will stay in the carriage--slipping out for the necessities, of course," he said, climbing into the hiding place.

"Wait, what about the gold? Are we simply leaving it in the carriage? It will be stolen," she said.

"Lain is out there, somewhere. If anyone so much as lays a finger on a chest, they will have to pick it up off of the ground if they want it back," he answered, slipping out of sight.

A moment later, the door opened.

Without a word, Myranda thrust the bag of money into the hands of the driver and put out her hand to be helped from the carriage. He did so and they entered as nice an inn as was likely to be found in the area. It was not a tavern with rooms to let, as was typically the type of place Myranda would have selected. The difference was obvious from the moment that the driver opened the door for her. Inside were attentive porters and a remarkably comfortable room, with the first real bed she'd slept in since Entwell. Properly prepared food was a pleasant luxury as well.

Of course, for the duration of the stay, she belittled the quality of each and every little thing. It would have been suspicious if she hadn't. Spending the night alone was worse than she remembered. Worse yet was the fact she had left her satchel from Entwell in the carriage, and had nothing to do but stare at the painted walls of the room until her departure. Once she had checked out of the inn, she was led back to the carriage and they were on their way. Desmeres slipped out of his hiding place with a stern look on his face. He was holding the book that Myranda had brought along.

"What is this doing here?" he whispered harshly.

"I found something inside that I wanted to ask you about. Why were you going through my bag?" she asked, somewhat annoyed.

"I spent the night in a carriage. I needed something to do, but never mind that. This book contains very sensitive information. It was never to leave the storehouse," he said.

"Well, I didn't know that," Myranda said.

"You should have asked. What question have you got, anyway? It had best be an excellent one to warrant this sort of breach," he said.

Myranda took the book and flipped to the offending page. She indicated the crossed-out line and handed the book to Desmeres. He had only just glimpsed at the line when he shut his eyes tight and slammed the book closed.

"What? You didn't even read it," she said, taking the book away and trying to find it again.

"I didn't write that. If I didn't, then Lain did. If he wrote it, it was because he didn't want me to know about it. If he didn't want me to know about it, I don't want to know about it," he said, pushing the book closed again.

"If he didn't want you to know, then why would he write it down?" she asked.

"It doesn't matter. He knows that I respect his privacy. I would not have read it," he said.

"Well, tell me what it says," she said.

"If I could think of a way to do so without reading it myself, gladly. Why do you want to know so badly?" he asked.

"It is the entry directly following the . . . massacre at Kenvard. Yet, it mentions Kenvard. How can that be? There were no survivors aside from myself and my uncle," she said.

"I haven't a clue. All I can say is that, whatever that line says, it details a job that touched a nerve with Lain. If you want an answer, ask him, because the last thing I need is to give him a reason to distrust me," he said.

With the mystery of Lain's note still unsolved, Desmeres managed to bury it under two more days of instruction. By the time they had reached the crushed stone road that led to Grossmer's mines, Myranda felt she knew more about them than the old man himself did. What she understood less were the complexities of the art of haggling. She had always been able to get a decent price when she had to, but things were different on a scale as grand as this. Even as Desmeres laid out every move that she should make and every move he was likely to make in turn, Myranda became more lost.

Finally, Desmeres reluctantly endorsed a very different method.

"Perhaps three days is not long enough to teach you the intricacies of the land purchase, but I assure you, in three minutes I can teach you a surefire way to get this land for a decent price, whether he wants to sell or not. I wouldn't recommend it, though, because it will *only* work if you have the full amount you intend to pay with on hand. Such is never the case in situations such as this, which is precisely why this method works. Here we are.

"Rule one, always speak directly to the owner. If the underlings try to resist, mention that it is a matter of great importance regarding the price of their land. You won't have to wait long. Rule two, refuse any hospitality. Don't even enter their office. Do all of the negotiating outside. It will take them out of their environment and make it harder to think. Make up an excuse for why, but make it clear that you always do business this way. They may be reluctant to comply, but that brings us to rule three. Keep the money, the full purchase price, close at hand. When he gives you trouble, direct him to a chest and open it. He will cave. At the sight of that much money, anyone would.

"Rule four, set a maximum price--in this case, seventy thousand gold pieces--and if he tries to raise, open the rest of the chests. No one pays all at once. The thought of having all of that money in his hands will push the logic right out of his head. Finally, rule five. Get him out. Get him off of his land as quickly as possible, ideally by the end of the day. A swift cut will not only leave the land totally and completely yours in the shortest amount of time, but the chaos it creates will leave all who remain searching for someone to restore order, thus firmly installing you as the one in charge," he said.

Almost immediately, the carriage came to a stop and Desmeres slipped into the hiding place. A few moments later, the door was opened and the driver announced her.

"Mistress Tesselor," he proclaimed.

At the end of a crushed stone road was a mansion that would not have been out of place in the highest class sections of the north's wealthiest of towns. It *was,* however, quite out of place on one of only two level portions of an otherwise craggy mountainside. A stout man wearing an assortment of furs that matched one another only insomuch as they were not native to this forest hurried out to meet Myranda as she was helped down from her carriage.

"Mistress Tesselor, what brings you to my humble establishment?" asked Luther Grossmer, owner of the mines and, for that matter, the mountain.

It was clear from his beet-red face that he was unaccustomed to being anything less than the most important person on the mountain, and thus unaccustomed to hurrying.

"What brings me here, Luther, is the fervent hope that I can put this humble establishment under less humble management. My own," she stated, Deacon had made it clear to address him by his first name. The unbalancing effect it had on him was immediately obvious.

"You mean to make an offer for the mines?" Grossmer said, with an eyebrow raised.

"I mean to purchase the mines," Myranda corrected.

"I am certainly willing to discuss the matter, if you would like to join me inside, I've some excellent wine . . ." the owner offered.

"No need for that. We shall discuss it here or not at all," Myranda insisted.

"Surely you would be more comfortable inside. I could--" Grossmer attempted again.

"I am never comfortable beneath a roof I do not own, Luther. Besides, negotiations will be short," Myranda said, getting well into her character and, to her shame, rather enjoying it.

"I would never think of denying you the hospitality of--" the hardy owner persisted.

"Your dogged insistence to bring me indoors is beginning to lead me to believe that there is something about your place of business you do not want me to see. There *are* other mines, my good sir," Myranda said testily.

"No, no. Of course. This will be fine. In full view of the splendor of my mines. Hatchett, a table and two chairs, and the papers," Grossmer hastily ordered.

A rather slight, snakelike man who had been standing obediently beside his master quickly marched toward the estate. As he approached the door, a second man was trudging down the side path toward what looked to be a large shed of tools. Hatchett motioned for him to come inside immediately, and the two disappeared inside the enormous estate.

"I hadn't expected any offers. In truth, I'd only mentioned a desire to retire in passing. Do you mind telling me how you came to the decision to consider purchasing--" Grossmer attempted to ask.

"It is none of your concern," Myranda snapped quickly. "Suffice to say that little is said in the Northern Alliance that does not reach the ears of a Tesselor."

The two servants were already on their way back. Hatchett was carrying a few sheets of parchment, a pot of ink, and a quill. The other, through a complicated configuration, had managed to hoist a heavy oak table onto his back. Each hand held an ornamented chair, awkwardly positioned to prevent the table from sliding off. He set the chairs down and, with a bit of effort, managed to place the table right side up. It was all that Myranda could do to keep herself from lending a hand.

The laborer turned to go, but the as-yet completely silent assistant to Grossmer merely motioned that he should stay. The stoic worker nodded and stood to the side. He was stooped, and thus seemed a bit shorter than Hatchett. There was the air about him that, if he were to unfold himself, he would be a head and shoulders taller. His clothes looked vaguely as though they had once been used to hold potatoes. There was the hint that they might have been blue at some time in the distant past, but now they were the same color as their wearer--who, in turn, was the same color as the stone he was standing on. There was little doubt that this was a man pleased to be pressed into service in this case simply because it gave him a rare view of the sky, rather than a mine shaft.

Grossmer's chair was maneuvered into place and groaned under his weight as he sat. Hatchett hurriedly did Myranda the same courtesy. She sat in a carefully measured way, so as to make it clear to those around her that she was trying to place as little of her body in contact with the chair as possible, and was quite displeased at the prospect of touching it at all. Pages were laid out carefully on the table before Myranda, small bits of iron ore skillfully pinning them down against the constant mountain wind.

"Now, in the past few years we've seen a fairly stable profit of--" Grossmer began in a practiced way.

"Fifty thousand," Myranda stated.

"I'm sorry?" Grossmer said, searching the pages in front of her for some hint of the figure.

"Fifty thousand is the price," she elaborated.

"With all due respect, mistress, fifty thousand silver is only slightly more than we make in a single year. I could not dream of letting the place go for--" Grossmer objected.

"My good sir, the Tesselors do not deal in *silver,*" Myranda scoffed, doing her best to make it seem as though the mere sound of the word put a terrible taste in her mouth.

"Fifty thousand . . . gold?" Grossmer said, the word gleaming in his eye.

"Of course," Myranda said dismissively.

"That . . . that is a fair offer. But . . ." the proprietor struggled to say.

"You, the strong one, fetch a chest from the back of my carriage. Any one of them will do," Myranda ordered.

The worker glanced at Hatchett, who in turn glanced at Grossmer. A chain of nods sent him on his way. He trudged to the carriage, opened the storage area, and lifted one of the larger chests. His muscles bulged, giving him the look of a thing composed of little more than sinew and bone. His face remained stoic as ever.

"But, you see, the Grossmers have been the owners of this mountainside since the first mine was dug. My blood runs through these veins," he said, chuckling nervously. "A little joke, you see."

"Very little. On the table, please," Myranda instructed.

"Miss?" the worker said doubtfully, the words hissing from overworked lungs.

"On. The. Table," Myranda repeated standing and stepping aside.

The worker carefully placed the chest on the table as lightly as he could manage. The legs of the table creaked, then swiftly gave way, dumping the chest and its contents, a number of gold bars, across the gravel. The papers that were not buried beneath the gold fluttered into the air, but no one save Myranda noticed. All eyes were on the gold.

". . . a very generous offer, yes," Grossmer said, his voice lagging a few syllables behind his mouth. "But . . . I, ah . . . my sons. The . . . the legacy."

Myranda sighed with irritation. "Fine. Sixty thousand. I trust with ten thousand gold pieces, even the set-in-their-ways Grossmers can find a new legacy for themselves."

"Sold," Grossmer said automatically. "I presume that this represents the first payment."

"It does. The carriage contains the rest," Myranda said with a yawn. "Pack your things. I want you off of my property today."

"You brought all of . . . today!?" Grossmer sputtered, his mind at a loss for what to object to first. "I have generations of heirlooms, I have--"

"You have a day to remove them. However, I am a reasonable woman. Whatever you cannot take with you, I shall purchase. Another ten thousand should do, I would say. That makes seventy thousand for your land, your workers, your estate. The servants you may take with you or release. Some of my own will be by shortly. Oh, and send someone to tell the workers that they may have the rest of the day off," Myranda said, grinning as she finally reached the full price.

Grossmer objected no longer. He dismissed the worker and vanished inside. By sunset, everything he was particularly attached to was inside a caravan of carriages normally used for transporting ore. A hasty description of the day to day workings of the mine was delivered, and he was on his way. For the sake of ease, the surplus gold was removed from the chariot Myranda had arrived in and, after Desmeres had surreptitiously moved himself and his cargo into the mansion, it was taken by the Luther Grossmer and his equally corpulent wife.

Myranda watched through the window of the still-remarkably furnished estate as the last of the caravan disappeared from view. When they were gone, she heaved a heavy sigh and collapsed into a stuffed chair.

"Not the best price we've gotten, but overall a remarkable first performance," Desmeres said, startling Myranda with his sudden appearance.

"I sold it for the price you told me to. Besides, there is still twenty thousand gold pieces worth of ingots and such in chests in the bedroom. That should be enough for whatever you've got in mind," Myranda sneered.

"Easy now. I'd hate for all of this role playing to spoil your normally pleasant attitude," Desmeres said, his voice not betraying a hint of sarcasm. "The kitchen is rather well-stocked. Would you care for anything?"

"I'll get it myself . . . later," Myranda said, exhausted.

"See that you do. Big day tomorrow," Desmeres said before disappearing.

Myranda sat for a time in the emptiness of the mansion. She was surrounded by room after room of overly ornamental furnishings. If she had been in higher spirits, she might have realized she was, despite the situation, realizing a dream she'd had as a child. And yet, as she sat in a massive estate, dressed in clothes that no doubt cost a fortune, all she could think of was how empty it felt. As she ate food she could scarcely have imagined as a girl, her mind turned first to Myn, then to Deacon. Her thoughts lingered on him as she drifted off to sleep.

When the morning came, Desmeres awakened her.

"Enjoying the good life?" he asked.

Myranda sighed.

"What next? I'd like to get this whole unpleasantness behind me." She groaned.

"Well, you will be pleased to know that I will be playing the role of lackey today, at least until we can find one of the slaves that we can trust," Desmeres said.

"Slaves?" Myranda asked. "No. They are workers. They are paid a wage."

"Mm. Yes. In case you hadn't noticed, we are on a mountain and the only horses belong to the owner of the mines. Any money that they make is paid back in exchange for . . . well, room and board. Rather a clever system," Desmeres explained.

"How can you say that?" Myranda hissed.

"I said clever, not ethical or moral." Desmeres shrugged.

Myranda shuddered before asking, "Why can you show your face now?"

"Because the slaves are the only ones left. I assure you, no royal proclamations mandating my death will have reached them," Desmeres explained.

The pair bundled up and made their way to the workers' quarters. It was a small city of identical huts. Desmeres recruited a pair of the first workers he encountered to man a cart that handed out the rations for the day, and they set about handing them out.

"What precisely is the purpose of all of this?" Myranda whispered.

"We need to find someone to deliver 'the offer,'" Desmeres replied. "The whole reason for this purchase. We offer their freedom in exchange for a favor."

". . . truly? You are telling me that we cannot simply offer it ourselves?" Myranda asked.

"We can certainly try it," Desmeres said. "In fact, come with me."

The door to one of the huts was opened. The inside was little more than a room with a simple bed against one wall. The man and woman inside jumped to their feet when the well-dressed strangers entered. The two workers gave a sullen nod of acknowledgment as Desmeres ladled a share of stew into the pot over the meager fire and placed a coarse loaf of bread beside it. A single copper coin was handed over in exchange.

"Attention, slaves. If you desire your freedom, it will be provided in exchange for a favor and a single drop of blood," Desmeres announced.

Confusion came to the faces of the slaves.

"That . . . that won't be necessary. The ration is plenty. Paying us for these two days without work is generosity enough," said the man.

"He . . . he's offered you your freedom," Myranda said, momentarily breaking out of character.

"Yes, and a kind offer it is. But the ration is more than enough," the woman replied nervously.

"And if I force you do accept your freedom?" Myranda asked.

"No, please! You are the new owner, are you not? Miss, er, Mistress Tesselor, yes? Please, we will work. We will work gladly. We do not even require the ration for the day!" the woman blurted.

"Yes," agreed the man. "Yes, we did not work for it, we do not deserve it."

Myranda tried twice more to coax them into taking their freedom, but all she succeeded in doing was prompting more vigorous assertions of loyalty. The next three huts resulted in much the same reaction, to varying degrees.

"I . . . I don't understand. They live in squalor. They have no freedom. They barely have enough to survive. Why wouldn't they leap at the chance for freedom--at any price?" Myranda asked quietly.

"Because of where the freedom is coming from. The owners, old or new, would never offer it. To the slaves, this is a test. You are baiting them, trying to goad them into saying something that will let you make an example of them. They wouldn't have trusted their former master. They certainly won't trust a strange new one," Desmeres explained.

"Then how will we find one that will help us?" Myranda asked.

"We don't. We find one who doesn't care. We will know him when we find him," Desmeres replied.

Hut after hut of downtrodden workers attempted to quickly and enthusiastically assure their new master of their happiness and dedication. Finally, they came to a door that did not open immediately. Desmeres raised an eyebrow. This, it appeared, was a good sign.

"Open your door at once!" he barked.

There was a tap of footsteps, and finally the door opened. There was the flash of recognition in the stooping figure's eyes.

"Oh. It is you," he muttered, trudging back to his bed.

"You are the one who carried the chest of gold for me," Myranda recalled.

"And you are the one who made me smash a table with it. Come to dock my wages? Help yourself. Fat lot of difference it makes," the bitter man quipped.

Desmeres smiled. When the food and bread were ladled out, Desmeres had the other workers leave the hut, closing the door behind them.

"And what is *this* about? Punishment? If you are looking for someone to whip me, Hallern, the fellow two doors down, will be darn willing to lend a hand. Certainly hope you don't intend to use this fop. Let him do the whipping and I'm liable to forget he's even doing it," the man grumbled.

"What is your name, slave?" Desmeres asked.

"Slave, is it? Are we using the proper term now? I suppose you'll be wanting the coppers back then," he replied.

"Name!" he ordered.

"Udo," he said.

"Udo, are you happy here?" Desmeres asked.

"Happy as I *can* be," he remarked, in a tone that made it abundantly clear how he truly felt.

"Would you like to get out?" Desmeres asked.

"Why? You offering?" he asked, assuming a mock enthusiasm. "Golly, yes, master. I truly would love to escape. Thank you so much for asking."

"Right. Have a look around, Udo. How many guards to do you see? How many other owners? How many folks besides slaves like yourself?" Desmeres asked.

"None," Udo said.

"And what does that mean to you?" Desmeres prodded.

"It means either you are stupid or you are poor," Udo said.

"If you know there are no guards to stop you, why don't you just run away?"

"Getting hunted down by whatever bloodthirsty bounty hunters you're bound to hire for running out on that little pit of debt the fellow before you put us in doesn't strike me as an improvement."

"My employer here owns the debts now."

"Well she'd be the one doing the hiring then. Look, as much as I enjoy the conversation, I assume you'll be wanting me to work tomorrow, and if it is the same to you, I'd like some rest."

"Right, then. He's the one. Udo is it?" Desmeres decided.

Carefully leafing through a stack of pages he'd been carrying in a bag, he selected one.

"Udo, can you read?" he asked.

"Not as such," he said.

"Can you recognize your name?" Desmeres continued.

"Yeah," he replied.

"There, on that page, is your name. It says you owe seven silver coins," Desmeres explained.

"Lovely. I'll have it for you in a few years, assuming I don't need to eat or sleep till then," he sneered.

Desmeres tore the page up.

"What . . . what's that about?" Udo asked.

"You no longer have a debt. You have nothing to tie you here," he said.

"There's . . . there's other papers like that, yeah? This is a trick, yeah?" Udo said, emotion showing for the first time in his voice.

"Not that you'd believe me, but no, that is the only record of your debt," Desmeres explained. "Listen, my employer here is, well, not the generous sort, but the sort who has more unique tastes in labor. A lifetime of servitude is all well and good, but a single, legitimate favor at just the right time, that's something else. Never far from a friend, understand?"

"Oh, I understand, she's off her head," Udo said, glancing at her. "No offense. A nice sort of off her head."

"As though I honestly cared what you think," Myranda quipped quickly, not certain that she was supposed to leave character yet.

"The wealthy use the word eccentric," Desmeres corrected. "Regardless. What it boils down to is this. We will be leaving within the week. At the end of that time we expect to hear from every last one of you. There will be no work until then. Your options are simple. Come to us and agree to do my employer here a single favor, with a drop of blood in lieu of a signature on a contract, and you shall have your choice of either a share of this mine to continue your life here, or enough gold to start your life elsewhere."

With that, Desmeres opened the door and led Myranda out.

"You can do the rest of the rationing alone, workers. The mistress has grown weary of the tour," Desmeres instructed.

Myranda and Desmeres marched off toward the manor. When the others had returned to the task, she turned to him.

"Now what?" she asked.

"Now we wait. It doesn't usually take more than three days," Desmeres said.

"Just like that? He'll convince the rest?" she asked.

"Just like that," he replied.

The next few days were the very definition of tedium. Aside from a delivery of supplies and a supply caravan that had to be turned away due to the lack of recent work, the time was utterly filled with Desmeres tracing out two hundred names on the pages of a book. On the fourth day, there was a knock on the door. Desmeres answered it.

"I think . . . I think we've all decided," Udo said uncertainly.

Outside there were barely a dozen other slaves, likely the only others that shared Udo's apathy about life in general. Desmeres found their names, pricked their fingers, and rattled off a well-practiced speech.

"There will come a time when you will hear a voice, but not see a face. The voice will remind you of this day, the day when you were given your freedom in exchange for a favor. On that day, whether it comes today or in a generation, you will repay the debt if it is within your power. You will make your sons and daughters aware of the debt, and instruct them to do the same, for when you pass on, the debt passes to them. Understood?" Desmeres said.

This would invariably result in a wide-eyed nod. Those who wished to stay were given a slip of paper entitling them to a portion of the mine. Those wishing to leave were given a handful of coins. Gold coins. Then each was given the paper signifying their debt. In roughly the time it took for a pair of tired people to sprint to the huts, a second small group came to collect. The groups grew and compounded in size and enthusiasm as the promise of freedom and the spark of greed overcame their better judgment.

Strangely, a handful of the freed slaves lingered just outside the door, faces white as ghosts, dutifully putting to rest anything that seemed to be the beginnings of a riot. Before the sun had set on that fourth day, all of the slaves were accounted for. As night descended, the distant sounds of celebration took the place of the silence and howling of winds that had marked each night before.

"Why were those slaves keeping the peace of their own accord?" Myranda asked, still mystified by how smoothly the mad enterprise had gone.

"Lain called for the debt to be repaid immediately," Desmeres explained.

"But . . . how? I didn't see him," Myranda asked.

"He's an assassin. If he doesn't want to be seen, he won't be. And when you hear a ghost whisper an order in your ear and inform you that your life debt needs to be repaid, you tend to find yourself more eager to please than to find out what the penalty for failure is," he said.

A few days passed and, now working for themselves, a fair amount of the workers returned to the mines. Desmeres traced out a few official-looking documents that would ward off the authorities who might doubt the highly dubious story the freed men and women would tell. Myranda was left mainly with boredom and the soul-searing images of suffering she'd seen in her brief time among the enslaved to pass the time. She tried to imagine Lain in a similar situation, with the added stigma of being hated by his fellow slaves. A large part of who he was fell into place.

It was not until a full week had passed that the monotony was broken.

"We need to move--*now!*" Desmeres said, bursting into the dining room.

"What? Why?" Myranda asked, but Desmeres only rushed out the door.

The sun was just dropping below the horizon as Myranda rushed to the wagon her friend had run to. Desmeres had unhooked two of the horses, and one of them was saddled and ready.

"We have problems. An old friend of mine is about to pay us a visit," he said.

"Who?" she asked.

"Arden. He calls himself a bounty hunter, but headhunter is more appropriate. That tends to be the only part he brings back. He is one of those 'other agents' I told you about, the ones who want you as badly as we do and are not so picky about the state you are in when they receive you. What is worse, he has an escort. Soldiers. That means he is sanctioned by the military and will have all of the authority he needs to search this whole place. We cannot let him see you. More importantly, we cannot let them see *me,* because even if I wasn't on the 'kill on sight' list, he would put a knife in my back," he said, trying to fit a saddle onto the second.

"Why?" she asked.

"I have a contact at his place of business that feeds me the higher profile jobs he gets. If they are worth it, I put Lain on the trail and claim the reward out from under him. He knows I'm behind it. I cannot allow him to get his revenge on the verge of my greatest success," he said.

"Why would he come here?" she asked.

"How should I know? The man is a fool. He can barely form a sentence. He gets all of his information by finding someone he suspects knows something and clubbing them until they tell him. Probably the blasted supply wagons we turned away. I knew I should have delayed this whole madness until directly following a filled order," he answered, struggling with an uncooperative buckle. "The escort has got me worried. They think they are going to find someone important here. But who? Not that it matters--the fact is, if we don't get out of here now, they are going to find quite a few very important . . ."

Desmeres's eyes were locked on a faint gray dust cloud being kicked up by what must have been a half-dozen horses as they approached along the road. The *only* road.

"No. Damn it! We are in the mountains, no cover for miles! If we run now, they will certainly follow, and there is no way we will outrun chargers on draft horses. We have no options. Myranda, I hope you have learned your role well, because when they come here, you are going to have to be *very* convincing," he said, rushing to the house.

"But . . ." she said.

"No buts! Confidence and arrogance. I will be in the basement . . . no, they will look there first . . . the pantry. Do *not* let them look in the pantry. Good luck, for both of our sakes. If you fail, Lain will have quite a job ahead of him," Desmeres called before slipping inside.

Myranda readied herself and entered the house. She had managed to fool everyone thus far. Besides, this Arden fellow was a fool. There was no cause for concern. She simply had to prepare for any questions that they might have. There were no house servants. That would need to be explained. The slaves were at rest. That would surely draw curiosity. So long as she had the answers, this would be simple.

At least, that is what Myranda repeated in her head until the very moment that a harsh knock at the door came. She rushed to the door, but stopped. No. Alexia would never open the door herself. She hurried instead to the chair at the head of the table in the dining room. A second knock came, more insistent than the last. She ignored it. A third came, shaking the door on its hinges.

"I am *not* to be disturbed!" she shouted in a scolding tone.

"Official Alliance Army business," barked a voice.

"I am not taking visitors today," she dismissed.

"You! Open this door!" came an order.

"I most certainly will--" Myranda began to object.

It would appear that the order was not directed at her, as a massive blow forced the door open. A huge, heavily-armored man stepped aside to reveal the man who had issued the command. He was not familiar, but his armor was. He was Elite, and thus one of the few people who might know her on sight. She wondered for a moment whether this was a good thing or a bad.

He could take her to Trigorah and help her to begin her task in earnest, or he could identify her for Arden to behead. For now, she would play the character--at least until she was sure she would be safe.

As he stepped inside, Myranda pushed any fear she had aside and sprang to her feet.

"How *dare* you? With whom do you suppose you are dealing?" Myranda raged.

The Elite drew his sword and directed it at her. Myranda stopped short of the blade and conjured what she hoped was convincing look of anger and disbelief.

"You! You draw your weapon before *me?* Alexia Adrianna Tesselor?" she fumed.

The Elite's expression changed from one of anger to one of regret as he quickly sheathed his weapon.

"A thousand pardons, Madam--" he began.

"Mistress!" she corrected.

"Mistress Tesselor. I--" he began again.

"There is no use trying to explain yourself. There can be no excuse for what you have done. And an Elite, no less. If you are the best that our army can offer, then I weep for the future. Your sorry hide cheapens my uncle's superbly crafted armor. Leave this place," Myranda commanded.

"I can't, mistress. I am under orders from General Teloran herself. I am to--" he stated hurriedly, unsuccessfully attempting to avoid interruption.

"Trigorah? My dear boy, I know Trigorah, and she knows better than to do something as foolish as this," Myranda said, suddenly getting a thought. "Is she about?"

"No, mistress, she--" he half answered.

"Then do not speak to me of her orders. Do you actually expect me to take your word for truth? Show me a writ! Show me a signed and sealed order for you to force yourself upon my recently purchased dwelling and physically accost me!" she screamed with mounting anger.

The Elite scurried off like a struck hound, grumbling an order to the brute who had forced the door to close it. Myranda took a deep breath. Her heart was racing. She briefly marveled at the fact that a simple name was all that was needed to give her the power to intimidate an Elite, a man who was treated as a god normally.

She turned back to the door when a commotion was heard outside. The Elite was having a very spirited discussion with a man who was somehow even larger and stronger-looking than the one standing at attention just outside the doorway. He carried a thin-handled black halberd with a large bluish crystal set in the blade. The weapon didn't suit him. It was elegant, while everything else about him seemed to bring new meaning to the word barbaric. The armor he wore was, to say the least, excessive. There was an incomplete and rather ill-fitting suit of plate mail layered atop a rancid-looking leather under-fitting. As he moved, a chain mail shirt against his skin revealed that he was at least as foolish as he was war-minded. He turned to the house and began to storm toward her. This had to be Arden. Myranda prepared herself to deliver another tirade. The powerful man pushed inside.

"I've already told your idiot partner that I will not allow so much as a question without a writ," Myranda said.

The man reached into his bag and pulled out a scroll of high quality paper sealed with the official crest of the king pressed into wax. Myranda reluctantly took the paper and broke the seal. Unrolling it revealed line after line of very official language detailing all that the holder of the document was permitted to do. Disturbingly high on the list of permissions was the right to kill any person or persons who prevented the execution of duty. She placed the scroll back into the ham-sized hand extended before her. It was crumpled and stuffed unceremoniously back into the bag.

She made the mistake of looking him in the face. It would not have been out of place on a bear. Facial hair had grown wild into a matted beard with a fair accumulation of his last meal in it. His eyebrows were dense, bushy things, connected in the middle. Peering out from beneath them were a pair of undersized, enraged eyes.

"Very well. I suppose I can spare a moment or two," Myranda said, in as unconcerned a manner as she could muster.

"So, you're one o' those Tesselors. What're you doin' here?" he asked in a gruff voice.

Somehow he seemed to radiate hatred with his gaze. It was a heroic fight to keep from trembling.

"I am the new owner of this establishment," she said.

"What do you want with a bunch a mines for?" he asked.

"I 'want with a bunch a mines' because my uncle, the fellow who puts that armor on those soldiers' backs, grew weary of paying hand over fist for ore he could just as easily have for free," she said mockingly.

"No one out there is working. Slaves're supposed ta work," he said.

"As should be clear from the deplorable state of this house, the previous owner was terrible at managing this place. I am currently attempting to decide whether or not I will need to replace all of the workers. Until I decide they are capable, I do not want to risk one of those idiots collapsing a shaft or some such," she said.

His weak-minded manner of speech made her feel a bit safer. If his brain was as muddled as his mouth would make it seem, there was little chance he would see through her disguise. Any comfort she had taken, though, was lost when he started poking at her shoulder. He used only two fingers, but the offending digits combined were thicker than her wrist.

"You use big words. All o' you rich people use real big words. You tryin' ta make me feel dumb?" he accused.

Myranda swallowed hard. She couldn't help but feel she was digging her own grave, but with nothing left but the shovel she used, she had no recourse to continue digging.

"How dare you touch me? I am a Tesselor!" she declared. She hoped that she was the only one to notice the tremor in her voice.

She wasn't. Slowly, a look of clarity came to his eyes. It seemed even more out of place than the elegant weapon.

"You are familiar. In the fear--I can see it. But who?" he said. There was an unusual smoothness and an unmistakable intellect behind his words.

"I have told you, I am Alexia A--" she began, forcing the fear aside.

"Yes, yes, so I've heard. You play the part well, but it is most assuredly not so. Blast, if I could only remember. I was looking in the wrong place. Need to check again. It was something with an 'M'," he said, almost dismissively, as though he was lost in thought. He tapped the end of the halberd on the ground.

A different kind of fear coursed through her now. The fear of discovery. This man, as far as he knew, was advancing very threateningly on a completely innocent person. If he realized that she was wanted, there would be no escaping him. Myranda's heart fluttered in her throat as she pushed forward with the act.

"What are you doing here!? I feel I have answered my share of questions and it is high time you answered some of mine," she said.

The clarity and intellect dropped away.

"What am I doin' here? I was sent here by Gen'ral Teloran. She said I was ta see what was goin' on here. Said that when places like this get sold quick, some fella named Desmee-res or somethin' is behind it. Said he would be tough ta beat, might have a tough bodyguard," he said.

He walked to the door. For a moment, Myranda thought he might be leaving. Instead, he closed the damaged door and propped a chair against it to keep it shut. The burning in the pit of her stomach flared unbearably. Whatever he had in mind, he didn't want the other soldiers to see.

"Well, as you can plainly see, there is no person by that name here, nor is there a bodyguard," she said.

"Oh, I see that. No bodyguard. And here you are, just like all o' the other rich people. Lookin' down yer nose. Usin' yer big words. And no one ta fight yer fight for you," he said, approaching her menacingly.

"I don't know what you are thinking, but you can just stop now. I am a Tesselor. Do you have any idea what I can do to you? What I can have *done* to you?" she threatened in as convincing a way as possible, backing away until she reached the wall.

"They won't do nothin' 'til you say, and you won't be sayin' nothin'," he said, pressing the pole of the halberd to her throat. "You won't be sayin' nothin'."

Myranda managed a gasp before her air was cut off. She struggled and squirmed. Her mind raced as she fought helplessly against the weapon. Behind her, just on the other side of the wall, was Desmeres. She didn't know him very well, but what she did know of him suggested that he would probably stay hidden rather than offer aid. This was up to her. She tried to pull the tattered and panicked remains of her mind together. She'd learned magic, hadn't she? It hadn't been just a dream, was it? Her staff was on the table. In the state her mind was in, there wouldn't be much she could do without it.

Just as the gulp of air was almost spent, Myranda managed to cast a spell of fire on the handle of the halberd where the monstrous man gripped it. Her mind was in a frenzy as she tried to channel her desperation into the spell. There was a hideous sizzle and a horrifying smell, but barely any reaction from Arden. Slowly a smile came to his face.

"Magic? *Ha!* Pain? *Ha!* Magic is nothing. Pain I can ignore. Goodbye," he said, pushing the pole harder.

The world began to fade. She released the spell. The black metal of the halberd was beginning to burn her neck, and she needed what little of her mind was left to stay conscious. Her vision darkened. Struggling was becoming more difficult. Distantly, she heard a shuffle of feet. Desmeres had finally decided to take action. He rushed behind the hulking man, brandishing a rather meager-looking dagger. With a neat thrust he struck at Arden's back.

A lesser blade would have plinked uselessly off of the thick plate armor, but this was one of Desmeres's masterpieces. The narrow, sturdy point pierced the plate, the leather, the mail, and easily an inch of flesh before its momentum gave out. This surely crossed the threshold of pain to be ignored and injury to be acknowledged. Sure enough, Arden released the halberd with one hand and, with speed and power that even out of this behemoth seemed surprising, knocked Myranda's would-be rescuer hurtling across the room and into a wall. The brief decrease in pressure against her throat allowed Myranda a second gasp and a few more moments of life.

She renewed her struggles and searched her mind for something else that might ward off her attacker. Nothing was forthcoming, and it was not long before she sensed the world slipping away from her again. In a last, desperate effort, she tried to pry his fingers away from the weapon. As soon as her left hand touched his right, he pulled quickly back. Myranda drew in a long, pained breath. She scrambled away, or tried to, but the same absurd speed that he had displayed before reappeared. In the blink of an eye, his expression turned from shock to anger and she felt his hand latch onto her shoulder. His grip was like a vice. She fell to one knee and cried out. In the distance, almost immediately, she heard the shatter of glass and rising wind.

A flash of red and gold streaked across the room and collided with the monstrous man. He was staggered by the clash, and suddenly he could be heard grunting in anger. Myranda crawled to the table and clutched her staff. Jumping to her feet, she turned. Myn was there, her jaws clamped down on Arden's leg. The teeth couldn't pierce through the armor, the pressure was more than enough to cause pain that would cripple a normal man. This brute seemed unaffected, merely frustrated by the sprightly creature's heroic effort to both evade his attacks and throw off his balance. Finally, the bounty hunter caught the little dragon by the neck.

"You put her down!" Myranda ordered.

She held her staff at the ready, and her mind equally so. Arden threw the dragon with all of his unnatural might. The little creature might have been injured, had she not struck the recently recovered Desmeres first. The impact sent them both flying backward and into a cabinet filled with expensive plates. Myranda's anger flared. There was no point in keeping up the charade now. He would kill her regardless. She summoned to mind a spell, a quick burst of wind. It would bring this man quickly to the ground. Once he was down, she would have more options, provided she could keep him there.

Myranda knew that she was far from an experienced spell-caster, and this situation called for the one thing she had yet to manage--speed. If this spell was to do her any good at all, she would have to put all she had into it to ensure it would have the strength it needed in the time she had. There were two things she failed to factor in as she poured her mind like a waterfall into the task. The first was the fact that she was terrified, angry, and desperate. She had not yet learned the discipline to keep these emotions from fueling the spell. Second, the staff she held had been altered by Desmeres.

The result was, to say the least, sufficient. The wind tore through the room with the scream of a banshee, pulling in windows and tearing open doors. When it struck Arden, he was not merely knocked down, he was launched. His massive body soared across the room and shattered the chair propping the door closed, as well as the door itself. The exit was not a clean one, as the tumbling body struck and splintered the door frame. Arden spiraled through the night air and rolled to a stop fifty paces from the doorway.

Myranda was trembling from the exertion and the emotion of what had just transpired. She normally would be helplessly spent after the monumental spell she cast, but still she stood--winded and dizzied, but steady. Slowly, cautiously, she walked through the doorway. Myn limped quickly after her. Desmeres followed on his hands and knees. For a long moment, all was still. The night itself seemed to hold its breath.

Impossibly, Arden stirred. First, he rolled to his knees, then stumbled to his feet. He stooped to retrieve the halberd that landed nearby. Myranda held still, waiting for what was next. With the weapon in hand, he stood and turned to her. One arm hung horribly twisted. Calmly, almost serenely, he popped it back into place with a wet snap audible even from the doorway where Myranda stood. Once he was recovered, Arden's face shifted quickly into a grimace of fury and hatred.

"Kill them! Kill them all! I order you to kill these traitors!" he howled.

The Elites! She had forgotten that he'd had an escort. Myranda's eyes darted all about. No men charged her. None even stood. Here and there, amid a splash of crimson, lay a lifeless soldier. Myranda was both horrified and relieved by the sight. Lain had not been idle while Arden had been inside. He'd eliminated the entirety of the escort. When the bounty hunter realized that no help would come, the unnervingly serene expression came to his face once again. His eyes took on the clear, keen, intellectual look they had shown earlier.

"Yes, yes. Things are moving, aren't they? The coming months will be quite interesting indeed. I am afraid I must withdraw for the time being. One of you has got a nasty sting that I was ill prepared for. Not to worry-- the general will be by shortly to collect," he said, turning to walk away.

"Oh no she won't!" Desmeres called out, suddenly finding the strength to stand. He 'rushed' at the warrior, though his hobbling gait was anything but swift.

Lain's silent appearance was considerably more threatening, Desmeres's bravery intended only to conceal it. He swept across the courtyard toward Arden, seemingly from nowhere, and silently as the savage wind continued to tear across the plain. Arden did not see him, he couldn't have, but still he raised the halberd. The gem mounted in the blade darkened, almost seeming to invite the black of night inside. He swung the weapon in a wide arc. The gem left a dark scar across the air in front of him. Quickly, the streak of black rippled like a wave through the courtyard, growing wider and thicker as it moved. By the time it reached Lain, it was like a wall.

Lain stopped short and held his sword defensively. The runes scribed on the blade burned like embers and a narrow slice of the black wave dispersed away, though not quite enough for Lain to escape unscathed. Myn, knowing that her teeth and claws would have no effect on this, dove behind Myranda for protection. The young sorceress tried to throw up a hasty shield spell and brandished the staff as she had seen Lain do. The black splashed against the pale, half-cast shield, easily shattering it. Her staff deflected a bit more, leaving only a wisp of black that licked across her leg.

The sensation was entirely new to her--and agonizing. Everywhere the black touched felt cold and numb, unwilling to support her weight. Deeper, beyond her body and into her soul, came a searing pain, like the black was eating away at her very spirit. Unlike a normal wound that could be pushed aside, this pain seemed to seize her mind and would not let go. It was blinding.

Slowly the affliction released her, though the numbness did not. Myranda opened her eyes to find that she had fallen to the ground. Myn, who had escaped the black wave, was on top of her, lavishing the affection upon her that she had been unable to show since the young girl had had to become a Tesselor. When the tide of black subsided, Arden was gone. Lain, seemingly unaffected by the onslaught, moved quickly inside the mansion. Desmeres had ducked inside earlier and similarly was unharmed. He and Myn helped Myranda inside. They huddled into the sitting room, the first room that had a door to lock.

"Well, Arden has picked up some new tricks. I didn't think him capable of casting a spell. It must be the new weapon. Where in the world did he find a weapon that can do an active mystical attack? *I* haven't even found a way to do that!" Desmeres said, as lightly as though he were simply making conversation, turning to Myranda. "Good work with *your* spell, by the way. I wouldn't have thought you'd have it in you."

"Your weapons need work," said Lain.

Now that they were away from prying eyes, it was clear to see that while it had seemed he had escaped injury, such was not the case. One of his hands was curled like a dead spider and was shaking involuntarily. The fact that he was sitting betrayed something wrong with his legs as well. Desmeres launched into a defense of his weapon treatments, offering various excuses for the incomplete protection from the spell, though eventually admitting he would have to continue research in those areas. Myranda was about to offer Lain help when she realized that she had yet to deal with her own impairment, and was not sure how to do so. She set her mind to this. As she did, Lain closed his eyes. His breathing slowed, indeed, nearly stopped. Very slowly the shaking subsided and his fingers uncurled. By the time Myranda had managed to restore feeling to her own leg, Lain had recovered fully, and his breathing was beginning to return to normal.

"We haven't much time to lick our wounds, I am afraid," Desmeres said, looking nervously out the window. "Whatever managed to spirit Arden away so quickly could certainly--"

There was a knock at the sitting room door. Instantly, Lain slipped out the back door; Desmeres followed, whispering a quick recommendation that she answer it and call for help if it was trouble. Myn was coaxed from the room. Myranda picked up her staff and unsteadily approached the door. At this point, she didn't know what to expect on the other side. Holding the crystal at eye level and readying a spell in her mind, she pulled the door open. It was Udo.

"Mistress Tesselor, what happened here! There are dead soldiers all over, the entrance is a shambles," Udo said.

"Udo," she said with relief. "Are you alone?"

"Yes," he said.

"Come in. Please," she said.

He did so, and she closed the door behind him.

"Udo. I . . . I have to go," she said.

"That much I might have guessed, Mistress Tesselor," he replied.

"There was . . . I don't . . . it was the Red Shadow," she said, formulating a likely tale in her head.

"The Red Shadow, Mistress?" he said, stunned.

"Yes, he . . . he came to kill me. The Elites had followed and fought valiantly, eventually fending him off at the expense of their lives," she said, hoping that keeping it short and simple would keep it believable.

"I didn't think he would come someplace like this," he said.

"Where a Tesselor can be found, that monster is quite likely to follow. I must leave--now, before he returns. Do you suppose that you can handle this place by yourself?" she said.

"Well, I don't know, I--" he answered.

"I know you can. Take care of these people, and yourself. Now go," she said.

It was by far the worst she'd done thus far at maintaining an image of wealthy superiority, but in the state she was in, it was quite the best she could manage. When he had left with more questions than answers, Desmeres, Myn, and Lain returned.

"Clever use of Lain's alias, but points off for affection and concern. At any rate, we need to be as far from here as possible before sunrise," Desmeres said.

"But where will we go?" she asked.

"I might have a safe house near here that is still standing. It is our best hope," he said.

"But--it is Trigorah that is coming! Perhaps you could reason with her. She might be able to get you your money. Then I could join her and--" Myranda said.

"Out of the question. That woman is going to be seeing red when she arrives, most of which has been spilled from the veins of her Elites. She will be utterly unreasonable. No, I am afraid that you will have to come with us," he said, matter-of-factly, though in essence this was a threat of kidnapping.

If Myranda had any more energy, she might have argued, but after the clash all she wanted was to get as far from this place as possible. She grabbed the simple cloth bag she'd brought with her, changed back into the filthy but less conspicuous clothes within, found a few horses, and was off. Myn and Lain chose to run. They had made a brief attempt to locate the horses that the soldiers had ridden in on, but the battle had caused them to run off, so they reluctantly chose the only other ones available. Thanks to the fact that the horses were draft horses, bred for strength rather than speed, the pair on foot was quite able to keep pace.

They traveled east. Thoughts rushed through Myranda's mind as she trailed Desmeres's horse. A strong wind stirred the loose snow around them as they traveled, yet in the distance, both ahead and behind, all seemed still. Why did it seem to follow them? The Elites. Had Lain not killed them, they would assuredly have killed her. After all, they were with Arden, and were willing to allow him to do the same. She had convinced herself that the Elites, at the very least, knew of her role in the discovery of the other Chosen and would help her. Now it would seem that Trigorah alone knew.

Myranda wondered . . . did she really? Or was all of this a delusion and the Army wanted her for another reason entirely? Indeed, did she even matter? She had done nothing of value in discovering the others since she helped conjure the other Chosen One, and that had been Lain's doing, not hers. Was it a coincidence?

#

Little did Myranda know she was not the only one concerned with her place in the world. In a tiny darkened room, in the depths of a trance, Deacon struggled over the same dilemma. He was staring longingly into the motionless heart of a crystal in the palm of his hand. Many days ago, he had delved through his writings and refreshed his memory on every aspect of the spell called Distance Seeing. Much to his despair, this spell was as hindered by the confounding influence of the mountain as most others.

Regardless of the monumental effort he'd put into catching even a glimpse of Myranda, he found it impossible to locate her. He spoke at length with anyone and everyone who might know more than he, and the only piece of information that was even remotely helpful came from the mouth of the Elder herself. If he wished to see someone through the impenetrable veil of the mountain, the target would have to make itself visible, like a beacon in the night.

The problem with this solution was that there was no way for Myranda to know that he was trying to find her. The only way that he would be able to see her would be if she were to execute some powerful spell at the very moment that he was searching. From his point of view, this left only one option. He must look for her at all times, dedicating a small part of his mind to probing the outside world.

This slowed his work immensely. Days passed with no benefit, but he remained vigilant. Finally, he was rewarded. A twinge at the back of his mind alerted him that there was something to see. He plunged his mind entirely to the task of seeking it out. Slowly, a flickering image formed. At first he thought he had made a mistake. The woman he saw was dressed in a manner he had only heard of. Elegant--even extravagant--clothes. It was not until the image reached its peak of clarity that he was certain that it was Myranda he saw. She was pinned to a wall, her life in danger.

As she faded, so did the image. He watched anxiously as she recovered and struck back, and finally was struck by a strange magic he had never before witnessed. The image faded with Myranda on the ground, joined by Myn and a man he did not recognize. When it did not return, he released the spell.

He had hoped that seeing her again would ease his troubled mind, but the burning only increased to see her in peril and not know if she had escaped. The few apprentices who studied the prophecy were not convinced that Myranda's purpose was as she thought. Opinions were split down the middle as to whether she was more or less important than she supposed, and few agreed upon the degree.

Deacon sat in the darkness and thought. He could not live like this. There had to be a solution. As always, he turned to his books. There he would find something. There was always something. He scanned page after page of volume after volume, stopping only when the sun appeared to the east. An unrested mind did no good.

#

With the sky lightening, the group could not afford to travel any further. In order to improve their odds of escaping detection, they had let the horses free and continued on foot for the last few hours of night. They now found themselves at the center of a treeless plain. There was no point in the plain that could not be seen from one of the many nearby roads. The best cover that they could manage was a low point between two gentle hills. As long as no patrols passed on the western road, they had a chance to remain unseen. There would be no dinner that night. At least, not for Myranda. They couldn't risk a fire, and she couldn't eat meat raw as Myn and Lain did.

The day was spent lying on the cold, snowy ground, trying her best to sleep. She was left once again with the inadequate robe from Entwell, now without even the stolen blanket for warmth, which, combined with the wind that had yet to relent, made sleep all but impossible. Again, this seemed to be a problem only for her. Lain, as usual, did without sleep entirely, as did Desmeres. Myn took up her usual spot and dropped off to sleep instantly. Myranda gave up the fight for sleep and, much to Myn's dismay, joined Desmeres, who was crouched watching the horizon. He seemed to be smiling, an odd reaction given the circumstances.

"What could you possibly be happy about?" she asked.

"There is something on the way that may lend us a hand," he said.

"A friend? I didn't think you had any," she said.

"I said something, not someone," he said.

Myranda glanced about. She couldn't see anything helpful, but she did see something ominous. It was something in the color of the sky, and in the increasing sting of the wind.

"A blizzard is coming," she said nervously.

"Exactly. We will be safe in a blizzard," he said.

"Safe!" she said, stifling a cry of disbelief. "We are in the middle of a plain, no shelter in sight! How will we be safe?"

"Safe from detection. It would take a lunatic, a fanatic, or an idiot to try to hunt us down in a blizzard. We might even be able to move across a road without being seen," he said.

Myranda thought of lecturing him on the dangers that staying still would entail, let alone traveling, but she knew that her words would fall on deaf ears. She decided to focus on her own survival instead. She pulled to mind a handful of spells that might do something to warm her when the blizzard appeared.

It was not long before the storm began, suddenly and intensely. There was a whipping wind and a wall of snow. Against all logic, the group began to move on. The violent wind, as though it had a devilish mind of its own, blew directly in their faces, slowing their already snail-like pace. Lain's face, or what she could see of it through the snow, seemed to have a minor look of concern. It was barely noticeable, but no emotion left much of a mark on him since he had abandoned the Leo act for his stoic self.

"Keep an eye behind us!" Lain ordered through the piercing wail of the wind.

"Why? There is nothing there but snow. The same as in front of us and on all other sides!" Myranda replied irritably. She stabbed her staff half of its length into the snow and used it as leverage to take another step.

Despite the meager precautions she had taken against it, the cold had robbed her of most of the feeling in her face and limbs. As a lifelong resident of the north, she knew the difference between annoying cold and dangerous cold. The storm had crossed the line. A few minutes more and the cold would do damage. A few minutes after that and the damage would be permanent. Images flashed in her mind of the foolhardy hunters she had known, and the incomplete hands that served as a reminder of just how foolhardy they had been.

Periodically, she would cast a spell she had pieced together from Solomon's teachings to warm her enough to continue for a few more minutes of travel. Myn would puff a few breaths of flame for much the same effect. Desmeres made do with a sip from a flask he carried, and Lain . . . Lain simply made do.

The fresh blanket of snow was already getting thick. It was impossible to tell in just what direction they were heading. Every way they looked returned the same white maelstrom. Even the veritable sixth sense for direction that Myranda had picked up from her life of travel in the sunless north seemed to desert her. Their only hope to stay heading in the correct direction was to keep going straight into the wind. That meant trudging through drifts rather than walking around them. Before long, every step was an effort.

"How far to the safe house?" she cried out to Desmeres, trying to resist the urge to gulp the freezing air with her mouth. One pure breath of air this cold would ruin her lungs.

"I think that it is a small distance down the road at the end of this plain. If we were still on horseback, we might have reached it in half a day! Now . . ." He trailed off. Even *his* impenetrable confidence seemed to be wavering.

"Now we are going to die out here!" she yelled.

"Now, now, we are not going to die!" he called back. The tone of his voice made it seem as though he was trying to convince himself. He was rummaging for something in the pockets of his jacket.

"She will not die, because my orders are to take her alive," came a voice from behind them.

There behind them was General Teloran. She stood tall, with the ageless grace and unmarred beauty shared by all elves, dressed in her full Elite armor. Only the helmet was missing, torn away by Myn in a prior encounter and not replaced. The wind, coming from in front of them, had carried no trace of her scent. The snow and wind had concealed her approach.

A thousand questions flooded the minds of the group. Whether it was fanaticism, lunacy, or idiocy that motivated her, Trigorah had followed. The faintly glowing gems set in the blade of her sword flickered, signifying that some sorcery had provided the means. For a moment, only the whistling of the wind could be heard as all present stood anxiously waiting. The next sound was the hiss of Lain's sword as he drew it free. He knew not to wait for threats, for bargaining, for trickery. The pair simply clashed.

Swordplay between two greater masters was a sight seldom seen, and it moved at a speed difficult to imagine. Weapons were a blur as they pushed each other's skills to the limit. Slowly, obscured by the wind, snow, and sheer speed of the combat, the gems on the sword seemed to be gaining in radiance.

"Keep moving! She is here for you!" Desmeres ordered as he pulled his dagger from its sheath with one hand while he continued to rummage in his pocket with the other.

"But we can end this now!" Myranda cried. "There doesn't have to be any more fighting!"

Desmeres ignored her and cautiously approached the battle. He stayed a few steps away, as though he was waiting for something. Then there was a flash. The mystic energies that had been building in Trigorah's sword were released in a bolt. Lain expertly maneuvered his sword to block the attack, but the white-blue bolt seemed to shatter on contact with the enchanted blade. Shards of light scattered in all directions. A fair amount struck Lain, searing the white clothes he wore black. Only a slight tremor in his limbs and a cringe on his face betrayed the savage pain that was tearing though his body. He took a step back as Trigorah took a hand from the blade and put it behind her back. Desmeres quickly took Lain's place. His small dagger seemed no match for the sword, but Trigorah readied her weapon as though an entire army faced her.

"Desmeres. I thought you were more intelligent than this. To be seen with that beast. He is an enemy of the state. Even if there was not a standing order for your death, I should kill you for associating with him," she said.

"You can try," he said, pulling out a small vial from his pocket. At the sight of it, she backed away several steps.

"She is ours. It is treason to interfere with the actions of the Alliance Army. Do not think that you can bargain your way out of this," she warned, raising her weapon from a defensive position to an offensive one.

"Oh, the bargaining is already done. The price is set. I am simply awaiting payment. By now you should know our policy. If you send a messenger with a knife in its hand and no gold, we send it back with a knife in its back and no prisoner," he said, breaking the top off of the vial with the dagger. "And I don't see any gold."

The contents of the vial fizzed viciously. Whatever it was that he threatened her with, it had evil-smelling fumes that fought through even the powerful wind to fairly scald the noses of friend and foe alike. In one smooth motion, Trigorah's other hand came back into view. In the palm was one of the crystals that had nearly killed them last time.

"I've got more men nearby. All I care about is my mission, and my mission is the girl. I don't care if you, the dragon, or the malthrope die. I may even get killed in the blast. So long as the girl survives, my men will find her," Trigorah said.

"Fine then. Let us just see whose toys are more lethal, the Army's or mine," he said.

Slowly he raised the vial. Slowly she raised her crystal. Slowly Lain backed away. When Myranda saw the assassin replace his sword and begin to retreat, she knew that unless something drastic was done to stop them, these two fanatical elves would destroy each other. Without thinking, Myranda rushed between them. She turned to Desmeres to beg him to stop and instantly found an arm across her chest and a blade held offensively to her side.

"What are you doing!?" Desmeres said.

Lain drew his weapon again.

"I am sorry, but this is something I must do!" Myranda said as Trigorah began to pull her away.

Lain leapt forward, ready to strike Trigorah down and reclaim Myranda. In less than the space of a heartbeat, Myranda's head filled with a hundred conflicted thoughts. Finally, in a move based more on instinct than reason, Myranda cast the very same spell she had used to repel Arden the day before. The wind doubled in force and reversed on itself. Thankfully, it was nothing compared to the previous blast, but it was enough to knock Lain out of the air. Trigorah managed to make it a few more steps into the snow, enough to hide those who had moments before protected Myranda, dragging her new prize along. A reddish form fought its way through the swirling wall of white. Myranda prayed that Lain had not made a second leap, for while she may have had the strength to repel him once or twice more, she was not sure she had the heart. Instead, it was something far worse. Myn was following her. There was anger, fear, and confusion in the beast's eyes.

"Myn, no!" Myranda said, tears welling in her eyes and stinging her cheeks with the crackle of ice.

Myranda tried to gently cast the beast away, but the charm that hung at her neck left her unaffected.

"Please, Myn! Stay with Lain. I am sorry. I will come and find you again, I swear, but please, let me go now," Myranda pleaded with the creature. She could see Trigorah's hand tightening around her sword's grip. If the little dragon drew much closer, the weapon would not remain still.

The dragon stood, trembling from a mixture of cold and anguish. Everything inside the beast told it to follow, to save the one human she cared about, but that one human told her to stay. If it was what Myranda wanted, then it would be done. The noble creature stood and watched as her protector in her earliest days slipped away through the snow. When Myranda was gone from sight, and the faint sounds of crunching hooves through snow had disappeared, she turned longingly to Lain, who now stood by her. He did not follow either. Instead, he looked on with uncertainty in his eyes.

"Do not follow," said Desmeres as he made his way to them. "Trigorah knows me well. She'll know that if she doesn't pay, we will come to get her. If she does her job, she will know where to find us."

Looking to the vial, Desmeres tossed it into the snow. It landed out of sight, but brilliant flashes of red and blue managed to color the snow for nearly a minute as the contents of the container took effect.

"That was the antipode vial. I'd never tested it before. I intended it to invert the temperature of whatever it touches. Interesting. It apparently continues to do so until the mana is spent. Back and forth between freezing and burning. Can you imagine how effective that would have been on a living target?" he said, though Lain had continued in the direction of the safe house, the dragon in tow. Desmeres stood for a moment, considering the possibilities before following.

#

Myranda was thrown onto the back of a horse and was being whisked along in moments. She and her "captor" cast nervous glances behind them, even as four other Elites appeared out of the rushing snow to join them. In minutes, they reached the road where Myranda and the others had left their horses a day earlier. As they continued along the road, an ominous form she knew all too well emerged from the wall of white. A black carriage. Trigorah leapt from the horse's back and threw open the doors. Before Myranda could step in, the general turned to her.

"Staff!" she demanded.

Myranda gave it to her. It was quickly thrown into the dark interior. Myranda took a step to follow it.

"No!" Trigorah quickly reprimanded. "Up front with me."

She opened the door and shoved Myranda inside. A soldier who had been standing guard by the door had already climbed onto the horse she had ridden. Trigorah stepped up on the running board of the carriage and turned to her men.

"Listen! We do not stop moving until we are inside the fort! Speed will not be enough to protect us if that beast chooses to follow! If there is even the hint of his appearance, we face him together! The carriage will continue without us! Do not face him alone! He has taken too many of your brothers-in-arms! If that blade of his touches you, it will already be stained with my blood, that much I can assure you!" she dictated before ducking inside.

Once inside, she continued to issue orders.

"Turn around and put your arms behind your back!" she demanded.

Myranda obeyed. Her wrists were quickly and securely bound.

"Now face me!" she ordered.

Myranda turned and a collar of sorts was snapped into place around her neck. It bore a jewel much like the one that was fitted to the end of her staff. As soon as it touched her skin, she felt an odd sensation. It was faintly painful, as though someone was pressing on a half-healed bruise. She turned her mind to healing the pain, only to feel it increase to a sharp, piercing burn that did not subside until she broke concentration.

"What is this?" Myranda asked.

"A precaution. Unless you enjoy agony, I would advise against using any sort of magic," she said.

The carriage lurched to a speed far faster than the designers had intended. It rocked and bounced so violently, Myranda felt certain it would flip over. As she tried to remain in her seat in the passenger cabin, a space clearly intended for one, she could feel the gaze of her captor. Trigorah's eyes were locked on Myranda, almost burning with intensity. The sound of rushing wind, pounding hooves, and creaking wood filled the cabin, but still there seemed to be a painful silence that only a voice could break. After all, Myranda had dreaded this woman, running in fear from her and her subordinates. Now, only a short time after deciding that she could be an ally, she sat beside her. Myranda spoke.

"It was kind of you to allow me to ride here with you. I have spent time in the rear of a carriage like this before. It was--" Myranda began.

"Do not mistake caution for kindness. You have escaped from me too often to be left unsupervised," she said.

Immediately the silence seemed to push the tumult of wind and hoof back outside. Myranda spoke again.

"I know why you wanted to find me. I want to help you," Myranda assured.

"I wanted to find you because I was ordered to," she answered. "You can save your pleading and groveling for my superiors--if you make it that far."

"Surely they told you why they wanted me. Surely you asked," Myranda said.

Trigorah sat silently.

"You must have questions," said the girl.

"Many, but it is not my place to ask questions. I am not the interrogator. You will meet him again soon enough. After being assaulted by you, I am sure he will be pleased to meet you again," she said.

"Again . . . Arden? Arden is the interrogator?" Myranda asked.

The general was again silent. She reached out and snatched away the bag that Myranda had dropped when she entered. After pulling the dagger out and eying it briefly, she placed it back inside and scowled.

"You do not have the sword," she fumed.

"No, I haven't had it since Lain first captured me," Myranda explained.

"Lain . . ." she hissed. It was the first she'd heard of her target's name.

Trigorah's scowl somehow turned even more serious. Myranda could tell by her look that she was contemplating how best to attain the sword.

"The only way to get the sword and stop them from following is to--" Myranda began.

"Pay them. I know," Trigorah interrupted.

The general turned the idea over in her mind again and again. To pay was to fail, to admit that she could not do as she was ordered. And yet, the price had been so high already. The best of her men and the better part of a year had been spent in pursuit of this girl and the blasted sword she'd taken. Perhaps the time had come.

"It must be done," she said.

"Excellent. Once you pay Desmeres, we can attempt to convince Lain to--" Myranda planned enthusiastically.

"Quiet! Your future depends entirely upon what the other generals decide. I will deal with Lain when the time comes," she snapped.

There was a defensive tone to her last comment. Myranda had quickly learned how much General Teloran valued duty. After spending so much time attempting to apprehend Lain, it must have become an obsession.

"How long have you been after Lain?" Myranda asked.

Again, silence was the only answer--a silence that would not be broken for hours. The carriage stopped only once, only long enough to change horses. The cabin was hardly a luxurious one, built to keep those outside out, and those inside in. As a result, there was barely a slit for a window.

Myranda tried to turn her mind from the hunger that had been steadily gnawing away at her. Periodically, she would glance at the general.

The elf sat stoically, her eyes always locked on Myranda, as though at any moment the girl would mount an escape. Her armor, though no doubt exquisite when it was first made, showed the wear of decades of use. Here and there, Myranda recognized a shiny gash in a plate as one left by Myn. Trigorah adjusted a sagging plate on her arm, only to have it fall away again. The belt that held it had been torn through, as had whatever clothing she wore beneath it. Myranda wondered how long ago it had happened, and if she was responsible. Between the tattered edges of leather and cloth, bare skin could be seen, as well as something else. Something that caught Myranda's eye. There was a gold armband. It was not cloth, but a cuff of gold that was clamped onto her arm in much the same way that the collar was affixed to Myranda's neck.

The sight of it stirred something in her mind. There was something someone had said. Beware those who wear gold . . . The look of recollection must have shown on her face, for Trigorah broke the long silence.

"What is it?" she said--a demand, not a question.

"Nothing, just . . . something an old man said once," she said.

Myranda decided it was best to remain silent for now. A combination of exhaustion and weakness from hunger allowed her to drift off, despite the uncomfortable bonds and violent motion of the carriage. It wasn't quite sleep, but it was better than nothing. Consciousness wavered in and out until she was jarred out of the doze by the abrupt end to her journey.

"Close your eyes," Trigorah ordered.

"Why?" Myranda asked.

The door was flung open and the light stung viciously at Myranda's darkness-adjusted eyes. Trigorah stepped out and a pair of the attending Elites pulled Myranda into the painfully bright light outside. She wavered briefly, forgetting that her hands were bound when she tried to catch herself on the edge of the carriage. Trigorah caught her and steadied her.

"Take a deep breath. This may be the last time you feel fresh air in your lungs," she warned.

Myranda's eyes adjusted and she took in her surroundings. She was in a courtyard kept meticulously free from snow, surrounded by a low, sturdy wall. Filling the courtyard was row after row of soldiers. They bore general-issue armor that seemed crude in comparison to that worn by the Elites. Not a face could be seen, each hidden behind a visor or mask. At the center was a square stone building that seemed a bit small to warrant such defenses. She was being led inside. The doors were pulled open by the two guards stationed beside them.

Inside was pure darkness; not the merest flicker of light could be seen. Eyes that had only just adjusted to the light were faced with the task of penetrating the darkness again. A faint glow that Myranda soon found to originate in the gem of her collar was the first thing she was able to see. The pale blue light did little more than transform the darkness into a collection of ill-defined shapes.

"Close your eyes," Trigorah ordered.

Myranda swiftly obeyed. There came the familiar hiss and sizzle of a torch being lit. Carefully, the girl opened her eyes. The dancing yellow light revealed a scene she wished had remained hidden. The whole of the interior was a single large room with only the occasional pillar. The walls were lined with bars, divided into dozens of different cells, all empty. They approached an arched doorway that led to a set of stairs leading downward.

The stairs led down only one floor. The next staircase was at the far end of the floor. In this way, it was impossible to move quickly up or down. Each floor had to be traversed in its entirety to reach the next. As she was escorted downward in just this fashion, descending further and further into the ground, some of the cells began to show occupants. She glimpsed at the people locked away. With each new floor, she found herself feeling that she had seen these faces before. Some seemed to show a look of recognition themselves. A few showed something far stronger than recognition. In the short time that the torch illuminated their faces, these individuals shifted from shock to anger and hatred. She left at least one person on each floor screaming for her blood. With their cries echoing in her ears, she shut her eyes tight and allowed herself to be led onward. Finally, she came to a floor that brought no new cries. She opened her eyes.

It must have been the bottom floor, deep below the surface. While this place was as large as the other floors, there were no cells. In fact, it was practically empty. All that could be seen was a pair of chairs, a pile of chains, a table, and the interrogator. It was he, Arden. From the looks of it, he hadn't changed from the ravaged armor he had been wearing when they'd last met. His halberd was in the corner of the room, far outside the sphere of light cast by the torch, but betrayed by a glow identical to the one from her collar. The look of clarity and intellect that had appeared fleetingly during their last encounter was now a permanent fixture on his face. Myranda's arrival added a look of pleased amusement to the collection of out of place expressions.

"Finally managed to bring her in, have you? Splendid. And the sword?" he asked.

"They were not carrying it. In the interest of timely and secure retrieval, I believe the best course of action is to pay the ransom," Trigorah recommended.

"Well, of course it is. Had we gotten the payment to them before one of the other squads had shown up and spoiled things, we would have been saved a considerable amount of time," he said.

"And lives," she added.

"Lives are cheap, time is precious," Arden said without a hint of humor. "Now, when I have spent some of that precious commodity with our first prize, you and I shall look into the acquisition of our second. Go, and leave the bag, and if that staff is hers, leave that, too. The brute work is aside; this is a time for skill."

General Teloran slammed the door upon leaving. Only Arden and Myranda remained in the room. He flashed a rather incomplete smile at her.

"Have a seat," he said. "Relax."

Myranda sat.

"I am afraid that I may not be able to relax with you around. Not since you tried to kill me," she said.

"I do apologize for that. Couldn't quite place the face. It is a good thing your former captors wrestled me off of you. My colleagues would have been quite perturbed if I had killed you before I had determined your usefulness. Now, to that end," he said, snatching up her bag before sitting across from her and leaning forward. "Let us have a look at you."

Oddly, he closed his eyes as he said this. After a few moments, he nodded thoughtfully.

"Respectably skilled wizard. Mainly elemental with a fair dose of the healer's art and a smattering of the esoteric. Not anything special, but . . . respectable," he said. He began to remove objects from the bag and place them on the table.

"Who told you that?" she asked.

"No one. I can see it. I can smell it, I can even taste it. You've got a good, dense aura about you, and the spirits seem to like you. They pay particular attention to you. With some experience, you could be a force to be reckoned with, as your little display at the mines would indicate. I'll have to see about getting you a better collar," he said.

"Listen, never mind all of that! You can untie me, and there is no need for this collar. I know what you want, and I want to help you," Myranda said.

"Do you now?" he asked, raising an eyebrow and putting down the dagger from her bag. "This should be quite interesting. Tell me, what is it that we want?"

"You want to find the Chosen! This war is destroying the world and you know that the Chosen are beginning to appear to bring it to an end. You want to find them and assemble them so that all of the fighting can come to an end," she said.

"That is . . . one interpretation of our cause. Now, why do I want *you*, I wonder?" he asked.

"Because I have a part in this, in the prophecy!" she said.

"You are Chosen?" he asked, eyebrows raised once again.

"No, but I can find them," she said.

"The Chosen will find each other," he corrected.

"No, the prophecy is changing, I have heard the spirits speak of it with my own ears," she said.

"You don't hear spirits with your ears," he said.

"They were speaking through a prophet," she said.

"All of the prophets north of the battlefront are in the employ of the Alliance Army. You couldn't have been listening to a prophet--and even if you had, we would have heard it as well," he retorted, finally losing interest in her and returning to his rummaging through her bag.

"Well, he wasn't . . . Listen, why are we arguing? We want the same thing!" she urged.

He ignored her plea, placing bandages and vials on the table one after the other, shaking his head in amused wonder at the labels as he read each one.

"Such flawed little mechanisms you are," he mused quietly.

"Untie me and I will show you! I have the Mark, the Mark of the Chosen, on my left palm," she said.

"Oh, yes, I am keenly aware of that little fact. The hands stay tied," he said. He had come to the book she had taken from Lain's shelves.

"Doesn't that prove something? Doesn't that prove I have some higher purpose?" she asked urgently.

"Perhaps. That is yet to be determined," he answered distantly.

"Can you read any of that?" Myranda asked, suddenly hopeful that at least one answer might be discovered.

"Yes. All of it. It will be quite immediately useful to me, I think," he said.

"There is a page, just past the middle of the book, that has a single line crossed out. Find it! Tell me what it says!" she demanded.

"Though I am not in the habit of doing favors for my prisoners, I don't think I will need to flip to the page to tell you what it says," he said.

"What do you mean?" she asked.

"It will say, 'Pay us the full price and you may keep her. The sword will be given to the courier upon payment. You can deliver the gold to the following location.' Directions follow, would you care to hear them?" he asked.

"Why would it say that?" she asked, confused.

"That is what every other page says," he said, holding the book up to her nose.

Both pages that she could see, and apparently all of those that she couldn't, bore the message he had read on an otherwise blank page, written in plain Northern, in Desmeres's hand. He must have taken the book she had stolen and swapped it for this one.

"I am curious, but that will not last long, I assure you. All will be determined in a moment," he said, standing and stepping behind her.

"What are you doing?" she asked.

"I am about to begin interrogating," he stated.

"But why? I will tell you anything you want to know!" she said.

"I don't know everything I want to know from you yet," he replied.

"Then I will tell you everything I know!" she said.

"You don't *know* everything you know," he stated.

Myranda's confusion briefly surpassed her fear, and it showed on her face.

"There is a plethora of information you have that you would just push aside as something I don't need to know, not to mention the facts that you know both halves of but you've never been bright enough to piece together. I shall have all of them by the time we are through. Since you are so eager to cooperate, all I ask is that you do not resist," he said, sitting before her again.

Myranda closed her eyes. She repeated to herself in her mind the reasons that she trusted the Alliance Army, the reasons they needed her, and the reasons she needed them. The short list of assumptions that had led her into their hands had been quite compelling and convincing when she'd first composed it. In the past few hours she had come to find it severely lacking. This monster of a man, a man in the employ of the Alliance, had made a disturbingly effective attempt on her life when they'd last met, and now she was to willingly submit herself to an interrogation at his hands! All based on an optimistic assumption! She was resigned that certainly this had been a mistake, but there was no going back now. Desperately she scoured her mind for some thought to calm herself. As she felt the hulking man's fingers touch lightly to her temples, she finally settled upon something Desmeres had said. Things could be worse. That Epidime fiend he spoke of could be the one interrogating her.

As she thought, a peculiar, somewhat familiar, and terrible sensation was beginning to stir in her mind. It was a subtle pressure that she'd often felt when her mind was at its bleakest. She could not describe it, but somehow she knew that this was far stronger than she had ever felt before. The source seemed to be the fingers at her temples. They were not moving at all, and yet she could feel them digging deeper and deeper. It felt as though they were pressing in not on her skin, but her mind. She began to repeat her mantra more intently.

At least it isn't Epidime. At least it isn't Epidime.

The sensation grew.

At least it isn't Epidime.

Where had she felt this before?

At least it isn't Epidime.

Slowly she realized that there was not one voice chanting in her mind, but two . . . two of her own.

Like a flash of lighting, the burning fear of realization swept through her. The other voice, she'd been haunted by her own voice in her mind before. That was the sensation, the feeling she recognized. It was an intruder in her own mind. Why? How? Her racing mind was further muddled by the second voice. Before long, she couldn't tell her own thoughts from those of this intruder. Finally, she silenced them all. She did her best to do the mental equivalent of closing her eyes and covering her ears. Silence . . . Stillness . . .

At least it isn't Epidime.

The thought was not hers.

"You!" she cried, eyes opened. "You *are* Epidime! You were the one who hounded me every time I was stretched to the limit, whenever my spirit nearly gave out! You were the one who tried to push me to the edge."

She shook his hands away and tried to stand. He grasped her shoulder, wrenched it painfully, and forced her to the seat again. She made a desperate attempt to cast a spell, only to be instantly and painfully reminded of the restraint on her neck. With his free hand, her mysterious captor summoned the halberd to him. Once within his grip, the gem mounted in its blade shone brightly. Immediately, the sensation in her mind intensified. It was almost too much to bear. She shut her eyes tightly again and turned the full power of her mind to the task of keeping the intruder out.

The restraint about her neck flared again. She pulled back, gathering her strength deeper within her mind. The burning at her neck decreased, but still tore at her. She retreated farther and farther into her own mind, hiding from this foreign presence. Myranda found that if she pulled all of her strength deep, she could avoid the effect of the collar and still keep the dark, infiltrating force at bay. It was a monumental effort, every bit as taxing as any of the trials she'd faced in Entwell.

Time passed, though how much was impossible to say. Her mind screamed for relief. As she felt her efforts waver, she began to think to herself in an attempt to keep her mind sharp.

This was a mistake. I should have known better, she thought, feeling a sudden intense impulse to open her eyes. A brief attempt nearly led her to lose focus. *Keep your eyes shut, Myranda, keep your mind focused. What was I thinking? The Army has brought me nothing but trouble for my entire life. Why did I think I could trust them? Was my assumption that they would help me even my own? Did he somehow force me into this leap of faith? But he agreed when I said that he wanted the Chosen so that the war could be brought to an end. Maybe there is still hope.* Perhaps this is a test of my loyalty. Perhaps I should give in; I have nothing to hide . . . No!

Remember what Desmeres said. Epidime is not to be trusted under any circumstance. He might be one of them, those creatures, like the cloaks that attacked me. But, then, Desmeres has lied to me before . . . or has he? No! He was always honest. He wouldn't have warned me about Epidime unless he knew that meeting him could cost me my life.

I must resist.

Is he weakening? No, no, just keep him out.

Don't stop until he does, Myranda, don't take a chance . . . Why do I think he is bad? Desmeres said to watch out for him, but did he say he was bad? No. This man may be reasonable. After all, he could have killed us all if he is as strong as he seems. And he did let me go on his own. He could have easily strangled me to death, but he let go. I wish I could see what is going on. That feeling . . . he has tried this so many times from afar. Trying to warn me. Why didn't I listen? Now I resist.

I should just let him into my mind. That would bring this torture to an end. I want to see what is going on. He is an intelligence officer in the Alliance Army. He has been one since the start of the war. He knows what happened to my father.

I must see what is going on.

There is no reason to keep my eyes closed.

Her thoughts weaved more and more deceptively as her eyes ventured open. Instinctively, she braced for a dizzying rush of pressure that would shatter her concentration and end the struggle. None came. The room was dark. Blue light pulsed dimly from her collar and the halberd, illuminating the table beside them. There were the potions, the bandages, the book, the dagger, and a gold glove. The glove . . . had it been in the bag? She searched through her memory and received a very strong yes as a response. Furthermore, something inside of her urged that she put it on. She reached for it . . . when had her hands been freed?

The thought dropped away unanswered.

She stopped suddenly when she realized that Epidime was staring, albeit through half-lidded eyes, directly at her. Surely he would stop her. She questioned why she had even wanted the glove in the first place, and when Epidime had moved from behind her to in front. The answers that came were numerous. She ventured her hand out again but stopped. This wasn't right. She had to stop this fiend from trying to invade her mind. A notion forced its way to the front of her mind.

The halberd.

Yes! she thought. *He uses it like I use my staff. If I can get it away from him, he won't be nearly as powerful. I may even be able to use it against him!*

She reached out, slowly. As she did, his grip on the weapon visibly loosened. A feeling of alarm in the back of her mind was brushed forcefully aside. Her hand, trembling in a combination of exertion and fear, was nearly upon the weapon when her fingers snapped shut around it of their own will. Her arm quickly pulled the halberd away from Epidime's grip while the gem within it surged powerfully.

Myranda tried to drop the halberd, but her hand would not obey. The gold glove she had felt the inexplicable need to put on rose into the air. Now there was no doubt that Epidime had been the source of her confusion. He was much more in control than she was now. Out of desperation, she searched her mind for anything that might chase him from it. Her thoughts were swiftly and forcefully torn away as soon as they arose. She could feel the dark influence of Epidime's will slipping past her defenses into the deepest reaches of her thoughts.

Finally, she pulled together all of the will she had left and forced it to the surface.

There was a brief, unnerving surge inward as she removed her defenses, but immediately after came what she was hoping for. Agonizing pain. By forcing her magic back to the surface, she incurred the collar's effect. She cried out aloud and in her mind, and from deep within her, a second voice cried out as well. She felt the intruder's grip loosen just a bit, but it was enough. She forced him from her mind. Before her, she saw the eyes of Epidime brighten back to life. She threw his halberd away and redoubled her defenses. The pressure of his invasion was gone, though; in its place was a loud grumble halfway between pain and anger.

"Well, that was a new one. Teloran! Get in here!" he cried.

Myranda hesitantly opened her eyes. He was standing, pacing angrily with his halberd in hand. The door swung open and Trigorah entered.

"Take her to a cell, I have had enough of her for today!" he ordered.

"Have you managed to learn anything?" she asked, gripping the wavering girl by her upper arm and hoisting her to her feet.

"TAKE HER TO A CELL!" he repeated viciously as he rubbed his neck. "AND HAVE SOMEONE CHANGE THE CRYSTAL IN THAT COLLAR!"

Myranda was led up the stairs, where she was joined by a pair of torch-wielding Elites. She was suddenly acutely aware of just how much effort she had put into her defense when she found that getting her legs to cooperate was just a bit past her mind's ability.

The Elites fairly carried the ailing girl to the nearest cell, one floor up. After being dumped inside, the door slammed shut behind her and the jingle of keys followed by the click of a lock could be heard. After sufficient time to gather the strength to do so, Myranda raised her head to look around. The cell was sparse, to say the least. A pile of shredded cloth in the corner was likely intended to serve as a bed. The only piece of furniture was a chair, though by the looks of the ankle and wrist shackles attached, it was intended more for restraint than comfort.

She tried to stand, stumbling against the bars in the process. The motion was accompanied by a jingle around her neck. She felt at it to find that a chain ran down from either end of the collar she wore and connected to a crystal larger than her fist. Just as before, it hurt when it touched her, only now she could *feel* it leeching her strength away.

There was, at least, one benefit to the larger crystal. It provided more light. Without it, she would have been in almost complete darkness.

She collapsed backward onto the chair, finding that standing was not worth the effort at the moment. A moment later, her eyes came to rest on something that most definitely was worth the effort. A bowl. A *full* bowl. She leapt with a strength she didn't know she had at the food. When she reached it, she found that food was a rather generous word for the contents of the bowl. It was a substance that would have brought dishonor to the word gruel. More correctly, it seemed as though someone had mopped up a kitchen spill with a loaf of bread and wrung it out into a bowl. Of course, neither this, nor the possibility that the stuff was poisoned, was enough to keep Myranda from gulping it down without so much as a spoon.

The sound of boots clicking upon stone only just penetrated her hunger-crazed mind as she finished draining the bowl. When she was satisfied that she had swallowed every last drop of the horrid stuff, she looked up to see who had chosen to witness the spectacle. Standing before her was Trigorah.

The general looked down at the girl, forcing her to realize she was still huddled in the corner where she had found the bowl. With great effort Myranda stood, attempting to salvage what little dignity that she might have left.

"Come to gloat?" Myranda asked.

"I don't gloat. Particularly at a victory that is not mine. You have been asleep for ten hours. Epidime was beginning to fear you might die rather than wake," she said.

"He was worried I might die?" she said. "I would think he would have preferred it."

"Another perhaps, but not you. Seldom does he encounter a subject that offers a challenge," Trigorah said.

"I am a challenge, am I?" Myranda asked.

"You resisted him for more than six hours. You forced him out in a way that no one had before. For this you have earned his interest," Trigorah informed.

"Well, I am honored," Myranda said defiantly.

"Don't be. It only means that he will continue to try. Harder and harder. And when he does find his way in, I doubt he will take the time to leave your mind as he found it. He might not leave any of it at all. Frankly, you will be lucky if you've enough wits about you to remember to keep breathing when he is through with you," Trigorah said.

Myranda drew in a deep breath.

"Come here. Give me your hand," Trigorah said.

"No. Why?" Myranda resisted. Though she had been drumming it into her head that Trigorah, at least, could be trusted, the events of the day had shaken that belief.

The general held out a loaf of bread and a canteen. Myranda snatched them away. A bowl of glorified water was hardly enough to curb a days-old hunger.

"Why are you giving this to me?" she managed between swallows.

"I can't be sure he will feed you . . . you deserve a chance," she whispered, leaning closer. "Listen to me. No one has resisted him. He has been through my mind and a hundred others. Whatever he wants to know, he *will* know. Just . . . fight him. Do your best. Someone has to show him that . . . that we *can* resist."

"We . . . what do you mean? It is true? He isn't human or elven or . . . anything like that?" Myranda asked.

Trigorah cast a cautious look in either direction before slipping silently back into the darkness. Once again, Myranda was alone and in danger. It was hardly the first time that such was the case, but this time was different. This time it might be the last. She was in a cell, far below ground, waiting for a fiend to make his next attempt at forcing his way into her mind. She wracked her brain, desperately seeking some shallow hope to cling to.

There was one.

It was possible that those who held her would make the same mistake they had before, that they would not pay the price on her head. That would bring Lain to rescue her again. It was far from likely. The pair of generals seemed to agree on nothing but the fact that her previous captors must be paid. That didn't matter. It was hope, a shining light at the end of the tunnel to lock onto. Until then, she had to save her strength. Epidime would be back.

A week passed in the most wretched manner possible. She was restrained at all times. Each day she would be fed a thin bowl of food by one of the guards whose faces were hidden behind a mask, and submitted to a variety of Epidime's attempts. Most were marathon sessions that pushed each to their limits. Others were short, subversive attempts under the guise of all manner of other things, ranging from attempts to recruit her to offers to release her. In a way, the worst part was that each day she was moved to a different cell. A feeling of safety would have been impossible, but now she was denied even a feeling of familiarity.

She was reflecting on this fact and trying to ignore the horrible taste that was clinging to her tongue when Epidime approached for the day's torture. This day promised something new. Epidime had brought a second chair bearing similar restraints into the cell.

"Well, Myranda. I believe the time has come to meet some of your neighbors. You know this one very well. He hasn't stopped cursing your name since we found him," Epidime remarked smugly, as he forced a shaggy, blindfolded old man into the second chair.

The old man hung his head low. Drooping in the chair, he swayed slowly, almost deliriously. There was something familiar about him, but she couldn't place it. A scraggly, gray beard adorned his chin, and wiry gray hair ringed a bald head.

"Well? This is the quietest I've heard you, old man. She is here, in this room. Haven't you anything to say?" Epidime said.

"I am waiting for her to speak," croaked the old man. His voice was raw, as though it had been badly overused. It, too, had a familiarity to it.

"Why?" asked Epidime.

"I want to know where her throat is . . . so I can wrap my hands around it," he said.

The old man raised his head, revealing a worn and soiled priest's collar.

"You are the priest. The one I met just after I found the sword!" Myranda realized.

He lunged forward with all of the strength his feeble body could muster. Epidime easily pushed him back to the chair.

"I am. I knew that you would only bring sorrow. Look at me! Look what you have done to me. You witch! You wretch! Because of you, I will be spending the last years of my life in this stinking, festering hole in the ground. I pray nightly that you meet an end suited to your treachery! I take solace in the fact that you were finally brought here! I hope you never see the light of day again!" the old man spat with disdain. He leapt to attack Myranda again, but Epidime held him back.

"Why is he here!? Why do you have him?" Myranda demanded.

"For the same reason everyone else is here. They may have touched the sword. The prophecy, if properly read, holds that the sword will find its way into the hands of a Chosen One. We *will* have the Chosen, but to be certain of that, we must capture anyone who may have touched that sword," he said.

"You condemned us! ALL OF US! You carried that sword like a plague and MADE CRIMINALS OF US ALL! CURSE YOU! CURSE YOU, YOU WITCH!" he cried before his voice gave out and he was left wheezing and gasping.

"I will give in. I will give in right now if you will release them," Myranda said.

"Oh, no. These captives will never be released," Epidime said flatly.

"But why! Surely you read their minds! You must know that they are of no use to you!" she cried out.

"Indeed," he said.

"Then you could have let them go!" she cried.

"No. You see, we had to keep them here, if for no other reason than the fact that any one of them might have been very important to you, and thus a useful piece of bait, without knowing it. It was a long shot, but it wouldn't have been the first to pay off. As luck would have it, you are one of those poor souls who cares about everyone. I was thinking that we might empty out the nearest village to fill the remaining cells. What do you think? Imagine the pressure that would put on you," he said with a grin.

"Please, I beg of you. Release them and I will let you into my mind," she said.

"If you submit to me now, I will kill them all," he said.

"What! Why? You wanted me to give in!" she said.

"On the first day I did. Then you lashed out at me. You *injured* me. That is rare. Very rare. Unprecedented for your kind. Generally, I would kill someone for that--but not you. There was something special about you. You know, I had everything I needed from you after the fourth hour of our first session. Everything I had been asked to learn from you.

"You have nothing new to offer me that my fellow generals might need to know. I know Lain is Chosen. I know that another Chosen has been summoned. I even know what it looks like. The things you needed to protect were left out in the open, yet even when I had them, you continued to resist. You continued to defend something within your mind. You dared to believe that you could be stronger than me.

"For that reason, you will be broken. If all I wanted was your mind, I would have struck in your sleep. I want to show you that you are not strong enough. I want you to show me how strong you are. You will be tortured, twisted, torn, and shattered. You will try your best, and you will fail. You will be made an example of. And then, when you finally haven't the will to resist me, I will leave just enough of you to watch as I execute each and every one of these people before your eyes," Epidime stated. Chillingly, his voice was plain and calm, as though what he had said was to be expected.

"You are the death of us! You are the death of *us all!*" the priest managed.

Epidime hauled him out of the cell and handed him to a guard to be led away.

"You know, I have managed glimpses at what you've been keeping from me. A flash of your mother's face, a whisper of your father's voice . . . minutia. Trivialities. Pointlessness. Random, worthless events in your life. I have a feeling that when you are broken that is all I will find. Memories that you hold dear. Regardless, I will have them. I will see every cherished scene of your mind. Every moment in the garden with your mother, every precious visit from your father. Keep that in mind. And sleep well tonight," Epidime said.

The week before was nothing compared to the week that followed. Every day, another of the prisoners was brought before her. She had at least seen--though often only in passing--each one of them before. Simple town folk, shopkeepers, everyone who might have touched the sword. Some did not remember her. In those cases, Epidime forced her to explain to them that she was the reason that they were locked away. For most of the prisoners, their crime had not been explained to them until that moment. The anger, the sadness, the confusion, all rushed forth in a tearful burst of emotion.

At the precise moment that Myranda felt that the heart had been torn from her body, Epidime would make his attempt. It was agony in its purest form. And each day was worse. He would handpick more and more pitiful stories. Sobbing mothers torn from children. Soldiers yet to see their families after returning from the front. Worst of all, she knew that there could be no victory. If she gave in, they would be killed. If she was broken, they would be killed. All she could do was buy more time. All she could do was delay the inevitable.

After another week, Epidime approached alone, but Myranda was not so naïve as to assume that today would be any easier. He carried a black cloth bundle. On his face was a smile of pure delight. Myranda didn't waste the strength to imagine what sort of torture he'd come up with this time. She merely prepared herself.

"Well, Myranda. What do you suppose I received today? It will interest you greatly, I am quite sure," he said.

Myranda did not speak. She pulled together her mind, ready for anything he might try. Slowly, he dropped away just a hint of the cloth. He touched the thick, black covering carefully, as though it was an animal that might bite. Myranda's thoughts flashed to Myn, and a prayer passed through her mind that the creature was not inside the bundle. That prayer was answered, but the truth could hardly have been worse. The top of the cloth dropped free to reveal a splendid, bejeweled, engraved hilt. The hilt of a sword. *The* sword.

"Here it is. The source of your sorrow. I suppose you may still harbor some illusions that you have some sort of value. That you might be important, and that is why we wanted you. No. It was all for this. The trials of your life of late have all been due to your association with this piece of metal. You could have been anyone. Anyone at all. This weapon means more than you ever will. And now it is mine. You do know what this means, don't you?

"Don't think I haven't seen it. That slim thread of hope weaving through your mind. That Lain might come, that he might somehow vanquish me and rescue you and perhaps even all of these others. That will not happen. They have been paid. They have accepted. You are now as worthless to them as you are to everyone else," he said, venom fairly dripping from his words.

Myranda turned all of her strength to keeping the hopelessness from showing through. He would not have the pleasure of seeing her pain.

"Unfortunately, this little prize means that I shall have to leave you for a while. I am under orders to aid a colleague with a few projects he has been working on, and this may just come in handy. However, lest you forget me, let me leave you with this to torture you in my absence. There is a moment which, despite my recent additions, remains the most devastating of your life. The massacre. It has come to your mind often recently, hasn't it? You've wondered . . . how could it happen? The leaked intelligence that would have allowed the attack was never delivered. Even if it had been, how could the attack have been so successful, the destruction so complete?

"Kenvard was a capital, and close to the front. It was fortified. It could have held off a force a dozen times the size of the one that had swept through on that day. It had before. How could it happen?

"It was our men. There was no southern force. I handed down the orders from General Bagu personally. Leave no one alive. The leaked information was to cover it up, to provide loose ends that would tie up nicely in the minds of the people. Of course, I cannot say for sure precisely the names of every soldier involved, but I can tell you this: they were skilled, loyal, obedient, and trustworthy. They all came from the very top . . .

"Your father was at the top, wasn't he?" Epidime said, lowering his voice as he spoke so that his last words were a whisper.

With that, he stepped into the darkness, only the gem of his halberd visible, staring at her though the black like a mocking eye until he was out of sight. She waited until the distant grind of heavy doors signaled the monster's exit. When she was certain he was gone, her head dropped, her mind burned. Anger, fear, frustration, hate, desperation, and more battled for control over her mind.

Had he not truly slipped away, Epidime would have found no challenge at all in defeating her now. Her cries echoed through the halls. The pair of guards at her door had no reaction. She didn't take the care to bury her magic inside of her, and spurred on by the intense emotion, the crystal at her neck was burning at her viciously. She didn't care. Nothing could match the pain in her heart.

The torrent of emotions did not abate until she passed out from exhaustion. She slept a dreamless few hours and awoke in the same pale blue-tinged darkness she had lived in for the past two weeks. The rest had done little to restore her strength, or else she likely would have begun the entire process over again.

Instead, she sat weakly. Her temples had a dull, constant ache. As her head hung low, she realized something. The crystal that hung down from her neck had changed. Even from the little of it that she could see, it was clear that the surface had begun to fracture. She shook her head, hoping to clear the cobwebs a bit, and looked around her. There were other things that had changed. Here and there, she could see scorches on the walls. She faintly remembered turning her mind to flame spells in attempts to spill off some of the anger. The force she had put into them would have been enough to reduce the bars to little more than bubbling pools, but the crystal had done its job--for the most part.

Myranda's clouded mind slowly began to clear. As it did, the possibilities presented by this new knowledge began to develop. A pair of the masked guards approached the door of the cell. She sat still as one replaced the damaged crystal and the other administered the daily swill.

Myranda knew that these were merely nearmen, and couldn't possibly read her mind as Epidime had been attempting, but she had learned to err on the side of caution and thought only the most innocuous thoughts in their presence. When they had gone, she began to plot. Some of her spells had gotten through. When she poured out all that she had, some tiny effect could be brought about. It would be painful, but she may just have hope of escaping on her own. She would have to focus, despite the pain of the collar, on spells with a concentration she seldom managed without her staff. It wouldn't be easy, but it was hope. Hope would sustain her.

Comforted by the fact that her day long outburst had brought no reaction from the nearmen, she set about her task.

#

Far away, her struggles were viewed by pained eyes. Deacon had felt that if he could only see what Myranda was doing, it would put his mind in order again and he could get back to his work. First, he was plagued by the fact that images were few and far between. Now he had the opposite problem. Night after night he saw her, restrained and tortured. He poured through books for some solution, some way to know precisely what was happening. The images would persist for hours sometimes, but they would waver and twist, leaving Myranda herself as the only solidly recognizable thing--and they were always silent. Sometimes there were others, but recently she was alone.

He would focus on the images and try to get more information from them, but he simply lacked the strength. Worse, the other wizards had grown weary of his pleas for help in the matter interrupting their own studies and would no longer even speak with him. Finally, only two would listen to him, Solomon and Calypso. Of the two, Deacon found Calypso to be the most helpful, and took to confiding in her almost daily.

Disturbed by his latest visions, he took his usual place by the lake and waited for her to appear. A mermaid, long, flowing hair and emerald tail shimmering in the sun, surfaced from the lake. The very moment that she did, Deacon began. Calypso had become accustomed to his habit of skipping pleasantries and diving directly into his points.

"From what I was able to see last night, I can say for certain that the crystal around her neck has been changed. Are you certain you have never heard of this practice? A crystal used as some kind of torture?" he asked. "Perhaps I should look through the library for it again."

"If it wasn't there the third time, it won't be there the fourth," she said. "You know what you need to do."

"I need to know what is going on," he said.

"It won't help," she warned.

"What do you mean? Of course it will! I can't get her out of my mind because I am not certain of her place in the prophecy. When I know what has been happening to her, I will be able to study the prophecy in search of elements of these events. I will find them. Then I will know that all will be well and my mind will be at ease," he said, as convincingly as possible.

"You know, you really are very creative. If you won't think rationally, at least follow your own rules. Logic says you should follow the clues to the truth, not chose the truth that suits you and cater the evidence to fit," she said. "You are purposely overlooking the real root of your problem because you know it is a sickness for which there is no cure."

"Oh? And what is that?" he asked.

"I won't call it by name. You would only deny it and scurry away to your rationalizations. All I'll say is that I know, and deep down you do, too, that you will only find some kind of relief if you find a way to go face to face and--" Calypso began, only to be interrupted.

"Speak to Hollow!" Deacon blurted.

"What!?" Calypso asked, left blinking from the sudden and unjustifiable leap of reason.

"Hollow! I need to find her place solidly in the prophecy to put my mind at ease, and the only man who can do that with absolute certainty is Hollow!" he said, leaping up.

"Deacon, listen to yourself! Hollow only speaks when he has something to say, which is only once in a great while," she said.

"Then I will coax it out of him," he said, running off.

"The man isn't a man at all, he is an empty shell. You would have better luck coaxing an answer from your own echo. You are being foolish, unreasonable, and overly optimistic. Those are all symptoms, you know!" she called after him before shaking her head and whispering to herself, "That boy is going to lose his mind."

#

Elsewhere, Myranda had spent the majority of two days focusing her mind fully on the task of unlocking the collar from her neck. After having no success, she decided that the restraint likely was specially designed to prevent removal in this fashion. In all likelihood, all of the restraints were similarly designed, but she couldn't afford to assume that. As painful as any attempts to escape were, the pain was preferable to the hopelessness of imprisonment--or, worse, dwelling on what she had learned of the massacre.

She turned her attempts to the wrist restraints attached to the chair. Almost immediately, she could feel progress. At the end of an hour of intense trial, she heard a click that made her heart jump. The lock hesitantly released and she felt the metal shackle swing lazily open. Her left hand was free! The pair of guards, nearmen, patrolled silently, as they always did. It had become clear over the days she had spent under their guard that they could do little more than they were told. They were, however, acutely sensitive to sudden changes, and always offered a look in her direction when the grunts of effort and pain came to an end.

Myranda kept her hand in the shackles as it had been before. As the wrist shackles were behind her chair and she was facing the bars, the fact that one had opened would not be noticed. After a few moments, the guards turned back to their silent patrol. With a free hand, it would be possible to hold the crystal away from her chest by the chain and spare herself some of the pain, but she quickly dismissed the thought as far too risky. Instead, she attacked the second shackle just the same as she had the first. She was tired, but the freedom dangling tantalizingly before her was enough to keep her going. Eventually a second click signaled the release of her other hand. As she spent a few moments resting, she realized that there was a problem. She was facing the bars, and thus her ankle shackles were plainly visible. If she was to make good her escape, she would have to free both legs without the guards noticing.

The young woman's mind ached from overuse. Weeks of resisting Epidime had forced her to push herself to the limit frequently enough that she had discovered precisely how far she could go before breaking. If she attempted anything as taxing as the shackles had been, she would not have the strength to stand when she was through. Indeed, it had been so long since she had stood without the aid of a cruel hand clutching each shoulder, it was possible that she already lacked the strength.

Myranda shook her head. If ever there was a time for desperate acts, it was now. When the plodding footsteps of the guards seemed to be at their quietest, she grasped the chain at either side of the accursed crystal and lifted it away from her chest. The effect was astounding. The fog in her mind cleared noticeably, and she felt a fair amount of her strength return. Two swift spells slipped past the weakened effect of the restraint and popped her final two shackles open. Distantly, the footsteps began to quickly grow louder. They had heard!

Myranda stood on shaky legs. She could not get a good look at the stone around her neck, but she knew that they had changed it before, so there must be a way to release it. She searched with her fingers, but everywhere she touched it burned slightly, robbing her of feeling. The footsteps were nearly upon her now. There was no more time to waste; she would have to be ready. Crouching behind the chair, she smashed the crystal with all of the strength she had against the seat's hard back. It fractured. She smashed again. A piece fell away. With a final attempt, the crystal shattered, creating an eye-searing flash and cutting her hand badly. Then there was only darkness.

Instantly, she felt a strength she had not felt in weeks. A month ago, she would have counted herself as near death when she felt like this, but at this moment, it may as well have been the peak of health.

Without the crystal's glow, there was total darkness. That likely meant little to the nearmen, as they had been patrolling without light, but to Myranda it meant that she could not see them and they could see her. She crouched behind the chair and thought feverishly as she heard the steps come to a stop just beyond the bars. What would they do? They would have to secure her and apply a new crystal. That meant they would have to open the door. If that happened, she might be able to push past them and out of the cell, but then where would she go?

The pair of guards began an exchange in a language that was utterly foreign to Myranda. Finally, one set of footsteps retreated into the distance.

Myranda waited a moment, but there was only silence. One of the guards had likely gone for help or replacement restraints, and the remaining one was clearly not going to open the door. With more opposition on the way, the time to act was now. She lashed out with a sleep spell. She didn't have the strength for anything more powerful. The guard stumbled briefly, but did not fall. The spell simply wasn't strong enough. There were only two things she could think of that might do any good now.

She charged out from behind the chair into the darkness, quickly colliding with the bars. She reached through and grasped the unseen guard. At the same time, she chanted the words of the sleep spell aloud, quietly but intensely. The physical contact and incantation combined were just barely enough. The guard collapsed to the ground.

The girl quickly turned her mind to the lock on the cell. Almost immediately, she found that the larger lock was hopelessly more complex than the shackles had been. With nothing else to do, she fought furiously with it for a moment before collapsing against the bars, sobbing.

"I'm just not strong enough," she sobbed.

After a moment a voice came out of the darkness.

"You stupid girl," taunted the voice. It was the blind priest in a nearby cell. "You stupid, stupid girl. Open the door!"

"I can't. I don't have the strength! I cannot undo the lock!" she replied.

"You learn to run and forget how to walk! The keys! I heard them jingle as the guard fell!" he fairly commanded.

"Of course!" she replied, reaching through the bars and feeling about until her hands came to rest on the keys.

There were only three keys on the ring. The second opened the cell door.

"Where are you?" Myranda called into the darkness.

"Here. Why? Planning to put a knife in my back? It would be the most honest thing you've done in your wretched life," the priest hissed.

"I am going to let you out. It is pitch-black and--" she whispered.

"The door stays closed, witch," he whispered angrily.

"I am trying to free you," she whispered urgently, finding her way to the door. When she tried to fit the key into the hole, a quick hand swiped it away.

"I am a priest. It is my place to forgive. But I will *not* owe you. Now go, or I will keep the key and you will never escape this place with your life. Free the others if you choose, but as far as I am concerned these bars are here to protect *me* from *you,*" he warned.

"If that is what you wish," she said.

Another time she would have demanded that he come with her, but time was short. Other captives in other cells began to realize that Myranda had escaped and were calling for freedom. She remembered from her trip through with Trigorah that a torch was on either side of the stairway of each floor. Stumbling through the dark as best she could, she found her way to one and lit it. The mystic effort was enough to rob her of her balance. It was the last spell that she would cast without passing out.

In the flickering light, she saw dozens of sets of arms reaching pleadingly out to her. Taking the torch in the palm of her badly bleeding right hand, she made her way to each door, quickly unlocking them. The prisoners ran, only freedom on their minds. Only a few had been freed when three nearmen appeared in the stairway, blocking their way. Myranda worked furiously at unlocking more doors. She had stopped thinking of her own escape long ago. She simply *had* to release these people. It was her fault that they were here.

Suddenly, one of the nearmen was upon her. The other two, scarcely visible at the edge of the torch's light, waved swords to keep back the men and women already free. The fiend before Myranda chose its gauntleted hands, likely on orders from Epidime not to kill her. She waved the torch at the guard, causing it to step back. The silent, faceless brute raised a hand to strike her. Myranda stumbled away from the bars, barely dodging the blow. The attacker turned to face her and raised both fists for a hammer blow. A pair of powerful hands leapt from the darkness between the bars, seizing the guard by the face mask. A swift pull bashed the armored nearman's head into the bars, then again, and again. Finally, the hands released him and the guard crumbled to the ground.

The light of the torch revealed Myranda's rescuer. It had been months since she had seen him, but even without his decrepit armor she recognized the mountain of a man.

"Tus!" she cried, unlocking the cell as another of the guards rushed over.

Tus, a significant member of a rebellious group called the Undermine who had helped Myranda in the past, whipped the door open with all of his might. It smashed the charging nearman and dropped him to the ground. He snatched up the sword that the first nearman had refused to use and ran to the remaining guard. With a trio of clumsy, overly powerful strikes, the nearman fell. There was a dull surge of light and the nearman seemed to collapse into a wisp of dust, leaving only a pile of caved-in armor. A swift plunge of his sword into the chest of the other two nearmen brought about the same effect. Whatever these things were, they were not natural.

"This way. Caya is here. We will find her. You will free her," he said, more a statement of fact than a request or an order.

"I have to free everyone," Myranda said, opening another door. Tus grabbed the old man who ran from inside by the shirt.

"You will take the keys from the dead guard and unlock all of these cells or I will cut your arms off," remarked Tus.

The terrified old man nodded vigorously and turned quickly to the task. Tus turned to a woman who had witnessed the threat, fetched the keys from another downed guard and tossed them to her.

"You will follow us. You will open all of the cells we pass," he added.

Clearly fearing that what had happened to the guards would happen to her, the woman agreed. Myranda, though far from pleased with the method, accepted the result and agreed to follow Tus. Each floor brought another pair of guards. With a crowd of escaped prisoners to distract them, Tus seldom had much difficultly in dispatching them, leaving behind piles of ruined armor and motes of dust. Each defeated guard provided another set of keys and another terrified escapee was pressed into duty. Torches were lit, floors were emptied. Total chaos reigned. It was not until they reached the second to last floor, freeing all in their path, that the cell containing Caya was found.

The strong young woman within the cell had been the leader of the Undermine, and even after what must have been ages of imprisonment, the keen edge of defiance had not left her eyes.

"Myranda! I knew when I saw you that things would soon change! You are a godsend!" Caya declared, snatching a sword from Tus's latest conquest and looking dejectedly for a foe that would not come.

"You aren't angry? You are here because of me," Myranda said, confused that no apology had been demanded of her.

"I would have eventually found my own way to a place like this. But thanks to you, dozens of others did!" she said excitedly.

"I don't understand," Myranda said.

"No one believes what the army is capable of. What this war has turned us into! These people will be angry, hurt, disillusioned, and they will have nowhere to turn. That is the recipe for an Undermine soldier. Our ranks will be doubled! And I have you to thank," Caya said.

"But weren't you tortured?" Myranda asked.

"Not for more than a few minutes, if you call that interview in the chair torture. In fact, once you were brought in, that fellow with the halberd ordered these beastly guards to feed us better. He said he wanted us healthy and full of life," she said.

Myranda shuddered. Epidime had wanted them to be healthy when he killed them. He wanted their deaths to cause all the more pain to Myranda when he finally won.

"Let us go. If Tus left anyone for me to kill, I will see to it that you are not touched until we have made good our escape," Caya declared.

"No! I can't go with you," Myranda said.

"But you must!" Caya said.

"No. They may not want you as a captive anymore, but Epidime has a personal vendetta against me," Myranda said. "We are both better off if I am alone."

"Fine, then, but we will meet again," Caya said.

"You will be my wife," Tus stated.

For a moment the trio was silent.

"You already have a wife, Tus. Henna, remember?" Caya reminded him.

"You will be my new wife," Tus amended.

"Move, Tus. We've got recruiting to do," Caya said.

Tus agreed and the pair hurried back up the stairs. The fort had maintained a full complement of nearmen. They were vicious soldiers to be sure, but a frenzied mob that outnumbered them ten to one was more than they could handle. In minutes, the heavy doors were forced open and prisoners had run off in every direction. No more than ten guards survived the chaos.

These survivors took up arms and searched the fort thoroughly. The other prisoners were nothing, but Myranda would have to be found. When every cell and the whole of the courtyard had been scoured, the nearmen took to the surrounding fields. All that had been found was a trail of blood drops leading to a discarded torch near the doors. Hundreds of trails would have to be followed to their end. Myranda would be found. The soldiers marched into the setting sun on foot, the horses having been taken by the first of the prisoners.

For several minutes, there was no sound but the wind, and no motion at all. Finally, there was a stir in a dark corner. In the stable, little more than a simple shed beside the stronghold, Myranda struggled to push aside a feed tray filled with oats and crawled from her hiding place. She made her way to the water trough, broke the layer of ice on top and scooped greedily at the water. When her thirst was slaked, she turned reluctantly to the oats. She needed some sort of food. Raw oats would have to do. Reaching into the tray, suddenly she felt a cold, sharp, familiar sensation against her neck. A blade.

"Don't try to look. Where is the girl?" a harsh whisper demanded.

Myranda hadn't the energy to be afraid.

"You've found her," she answered, defeated and too tired to panic.

"Myranda!?" came a voice she recognized.

"Desmeres?" she said, turning weakly when the blade was removed.

"*You* caused all of this? What sort of a damsel in distress manages to escape on her own?" he said with a laugh of disbelief.

Desmeres was dressed in a white hooded robe with a white bag slung across his back. In one hand was a knife; the other held a much bulkier sack. The contents of the sack seemed to be churning violently.

"Desmeres, you can't turn me in again, I need to warn--" Myranda began, her voice wavering.

"I am not here to put you back in, I am here to get you out," he said, helping her to her feet and leading her to a window. "Did you lose weight? You feel lighter than . . . oh, my heavens . . . Myranda, if I didn't know it had only been a few weeks since you left us, I would swear it had been five hard years."

In the light, he could see the results of the captivity. She was visibly thinner, pale and ragged. Her clothes, hands, and face were smudged with dirt. Her right hand was clenched in a white-knuckled grip around a wad of her tunic, surrounded by a growing red stain. Every word was slurred, and she seemed on the verge of unconsciousness.

"Is Lain here?" she asked, worried.

"He ought to be. I--" he answered.

"And Myn?" she interrupted.

"Tied up in the sack. We were . . ." he attempted.

"Why?" she thwarted.

"She couldn't go with Lain, she won't listen to me, and I didn't want to leave her alone," he blurted before she could interrupt again.

"Why are you helping me to escape?" she asked.

"They didn't come through with the full price. Just a bit more than half," Desmeres said dismissively. "Myranda, what did they do to you in there?"

"Why would they . . . They know! Desmeres, tell me, where is Lain?" she demanded, suddenly, with an urgency that cut through her weariness.

"The plan was for me to create a distraction long enough for him to slip over the wall and inside. I was weighing possibilities when that mayhem started, which we both agreed was a bit more distraction than we had hoped for. He had to wait until the guards went off high alert, then slipped over the back wall. Presumably he is still inside. Why?" he asked.

"They've been trying to get into my head. They know he is Chosen. They will try to capture him--or kill him, I'm not sure. That *has* to be why they didn't pay the full price. They knew he would come back to get me! We need to find him!" she said.

"Relax, Myranda, relax. Lain and I have been at this for a very long time. I am not so naïve as to assume that this was a regrettable accounting error. We are prepared for every contingency. Now, I have some food here. I think you should eat something," Desmeres said, concern in his voice as he removed the bag from his back and began rummaging through it. Outside, the wind began to gust.

"Not now! I will not be responsible for another person being locked away in this place! We will find him and we will escape!" Myranda said.

A shadow darkened the doorway, drawing her attention. It was Lain, holding the bag Myranda had been carrying when she arrived.

"The sword isn't here," Lain said, similarly dressed. He tossed the bag to her feet.

"Lain! You have to leave this place! Run!" she said.

"That is the plan," Desmeres agreed. "But first, Myranda, open your hand."

"I am not hungry!" Myranda said, lying through her teeth for the sake of a quicker escape.

"But you *are* bleeding. Open up," he said, removing a thin glass vial from the bag.

She held the nasty-looking injury out. Desmeres snapped the vial. Instantly, Myranda felt as though he had poured boiling lead into her palm. She gasped and pulled it back.

"I am afraid that is supposed to happen. I am not particularly skilled at healing potions," Desmeres apologized.

When the pain subsided, Myranda opened her hand to see that the injury was closed, though the dried remnants of it still stained her palm. A moment later, the trio stepped tentatively into the fading light of the courtyard. All was still. They approached the doors, still open from the mob's escape. Lain held out an arm, signaling the others to stop. He took a long, slow, deliberate whiff of the air. A hint of concern came to his face.

"Not satisfied?" Desmeres asked.

"This wind. It is circling around us. It isn't bringing me anything useful," he said, scanning the horizon with his eyes.

"Perhaps there is nothing to smell," Desmeres offered.

In response, Lain locked his eyes on a spot in the distance, his hands moving to the hilt of his sword. Whatever it was, it was approaching from the air, and very quickly. Between the fort and the nearest cover was a field of snow and ice. Lain alone might have succeeded in reaching it before the form in the sky was upon them.

#

Deacon ran to the small hut at the edge of the village where they housed their prophet. A pair of apprentices, one an older man and the other a young woman, were sitting inside. They were both clearly desperate for a distraction from their painfully dull assignment. The winded young wizard who burst through the door was thus a welcome sight to them.

"Master Deacon, is there something wrong?" the woman asked.

"No, no. I have come to relieve you, Mera, and you, Karr," he said, slowly regaining his breath.

"Oh!" Mera, the woman proclaimed excitedly, but drooped as a thought occurred to her. "But I've six more hours in my shift. And Karr has three."

"I believe I have the seniority necessary to give you your freedom a few hours early," he said.

The pair was quite happy to have the afternoon returned. Neither was so foolish as to ask why one of the usually self-interested Masters would take such a fruitless job. Nor did they stop to mention the policy that at least two witnesses be present when monitoring the prophet.

Once they had left, Deacon positioned a chair before Hollow and sat. The old, frail figure showed no signs of life. His head hung limply down, his hands and arms clearly posed into some semblance of comfort. He gazed with the faded, cloudy eyes of a corpse. Despite all of this, Deacon could not help but offer a few moments of reverent silence. Finally, after a deep breath, he spoke.

"Hollow. Your connection to the spirits is unparalleled. I know that you only speak when the spirits direct it, but there is a matter of great concern at hand," he said.

The fragile figure sat motionless.

"I have been using my own limited skills to monitor a woman you spoke to directly during your last recitation. She appears to be in danger. I do not have the capacity to see for certain what is in store for her. I beseech you, oh great prophet, to speak on her behalf. Tell of her place on the path. Tell what the fates have planned for her," he said.

Silence.

"If I have read your predictions correctly, she could have a vital role in bringing the Chosen together. If she is in danger, the very prophecy may be in danger," he offered.

Silence.

"Listen to me . . . Tober." He spoke quietly, invoking the name that Hollow had once been called. "If there is anything left of you, you must believe me. I must know about her."

Silence.

"Damn it, old man! Listen!" Deacon cried, leaping up and hoisting Hollow from the chair by his tunic. It was like lifting a scarecrow. "I need to know! I need to know if she will be all right! I need to know that she will come back to us! That she will come back to *me!* This world cannot survive without her! *I* cannot survive without her! Speak! SPEAK!"

Withered fingers suddenly wrapped around his neck and he was wrenched into the air. Deacon grasped the old man's wrist and gasped for breath.

#

The forms in the sky grew nearer.

"Myranda, I think you and I had best slip inside until the threat passes," Desmeres suggested.

"I am not going back in there," Myranda said, pulling her staff and dagger from her bag.

The moment she touched the staff, a clarity she forgotten she could achieve seeped slowly into her mind. She was still weak, but she at least could think.

"Give me Myn," she demanded.

"Now is not the best time for a reunion. There is something on the way, and the only reason anything would be headed to this godforsaken place so quickly would be to kill one or more of us," Desmeres pointed out as he reluctantly lowered the bag to the ground.

"If there is fighting to be done, I don't want her to be helpless," Myranda said, cutting the bonds.

Myn instantly was on top of her, lavishing weeks of affection all at once. Myranda toppled to the ground.

"Yes. A helpless dragon would have been quite distracting," Desmeres jabbed sternly.

"Dragoyles. Two of them," Lain announced quietly, backing to the wall.

"No. Lain, I didn't bring my bow. The only time I have ever seen one of these killed was with a *very* well-placed arrow," Desmeres said, the beginnings of panic in his voice. It was the least composed she had seen him since they had met.

"What is a dragoyle?" Myranda asked, leaning heavily on her staff to climb to her feet.

Lain leveled a finger at the sky.

The creatures were quite near, and dropping down for a landing. Each was gray as charcoal, nearly black. The hide had a crude, rocky appearance. In form, they were like a malformed, bulky parody of a dragon, as though a sculptor who had never seen one had fashioned the dragoyles from vague descriptions. The limbs, tail, and neck all had a segmented look to them, like pieces that were joined together rather than grown. On their heads, a crown of cruel-looking jagged horns stuck out at random and unnatural angles. Hollow sockets were where their eyes should have been. In place of teeth was a serrated edge lining the jaws of the creatures, forming a lipless beak. Overall, the creature's head more closely resembled the skull of a dragon than the head of one. Only the bat-like wings seemed to be well-shaped, though as they grew closer Myranda could see that even *they* were more coarse and angular than they should have been.

These were undoubtedly the same type of creature she'd seen dead in the snow when she found the sword. Aside from a slight size difference and the placement of the occasional battle scar, they were identical. One was easily the size of an elephant, the other slightly smaller. On the larger creature's back was a rider, a woman Myranda didn't recognize, in a standard Northern cloak. In her hand was a halberd.

"Epidime had a halberd just like the one she is holding," Myranda warned.

Myn adopted a defensive stance. Desmeres pressed himself to the courtyard wall just beside the doors. Lain took a place on the opposite side of the door. Myranda and Myn joined him. The dragoyles landed with an earthshaking impact and the rider dismounted. Footsteps crunching in the snow could be heard advancing toward them for a few moments, then nothing but the whistling of the wind.

"You may as well show yourself, Lain. I know that you have come," the woman called out.

Lain cast a sharp look in Myranda's direction.

"I must say, releasing all of the prisoners didn't seem to me like the sort of thing you might do. And most of the soldiers are gone as well. You have been busy. No matter--I have reinforcements ready to deploy if I need them. Whether or not I do is entirely up to you, Lain. My orders are quite simple. Recruit you if I can, capture you if I can't, kill you if I must," she said. There was a quality to her tone of voice that chilled Myranda.

As she spoke, Lain was slowly sidestepping to the inwardly-opened door. Desmeres did the same, both ready to push them shut. Myranda put her eye to the crack between the door and the wall. The woman was tapping her halberd on the ground and looking thoughtful. The wind was steadily growing more intense. It was whistling in their ears now. The woman had to shout to be heard when she finally found the words she was searching for.

"Lain does not know a single spell, does he?" she said. "It is just as well that the soldiers are gone. The cloaks will make a far better match."

The woman turned and began to approach the creature she'd been riding. At the sound of the retreating footsteps, Lain streaked out from the doorway. He timed his bounding steps with hers. Myranda turned away at the ring of his blade. A horrifying slicing sound was followed by the sound of a body dropping to the ground. Myranda cringed, but even her weary mind realized that something was missing. There was no scream. Myranda turned and looked through the crack. The woman was fairly intact, save the horrid gash that ran from her right shoulder to her left hip. She was hunched against the halberd, which was driven into the ground. The dragoyles were, mysteriously, motionless. Lain kept a watchful eye on the beasts while he kicked the body to the ground and drove his blade through her heart. He then warily made his way back to the fort.

"Why aren't the monsters attacking?" Myranda asked.

"I have heard of this. They are either very well trained or mystically linked. Whichever it may be, they don't act without a rider giving orders. Lain once again proves why he is the field man of our duo," he says, a mixture of pride and relief peppering his voice.

"We need to move. Now," Lain ordered.

The others had no objection and moved as quickly as they could, which was frustratingly slow in Myranda's case. She felt like she had been awake for days--and quite likely had been. Her legs constantly threatened to give out on her. Myn slowed to keep pace. Lain was far ahead, with Desmeres midway between them. He turned when Myranda was too far back for her staggering footsteps to be heard. The captor-turned-rescuer called something out to her, but the wind had grown stronger still, and was screaming in her ears. He turned to repeat himself.

"If you do not hurry, I am going to have to carry you! And . . . Lain!" he cried. His eyes widened in disbelief.

Myranda and Lain turned in unison. The "dead" woman had reached up to the still-standing halberd and was hoisting herself to her feet. If there had been any doubt that the sword had missed its mark, a dark blood stain, visible even at this distance, confirmed the killing blow. Myranda knew that Lain was fast, but the speed he showed now was beyond belief. He closed the gap between himself and his foe in the time it took for the woman to get to her feet and pull the halberd from the ground. He raised his weapon, but the woman blocked his blow with hers. A heartbeat later, a flash in the blade's gem threw Lain backward, sliding him across the ground a fair distance and separating him from his sword.

"I wish you hadn't stabbed the heart. I shall have to make this fight a swift one," she said, her face white as death, but managing to convey a smug look of annoyance.

As Lain rushed to his sword, the woman twirled the halberd for speed and struck the larger dragoyle's back with the blade. It clanged as though it had struck stone, severing the rope securing a pair of bundles to the beast's back. The creature, despite the blow that would have cost a man his life, remained motionless. A gust of wind caught the contents of the bundles and cloaks, dozens of them, were scattered to the ground around the creature. A second flash of the gem caused the lifeless things to rise. The wind fluttered the garments--empty, yet clinging to outlines of unseen occupants. A second pair of bundles received the same treatment a moment later.

"You, beast. Kill the elf. Half of you cloaks help. The rest of you and this other beast can help me with this one. Kill the girl if you must, but aim to injure," the woman ordered, wheezing a bit and sputtering blood. "You caught my lung as well. How irritating."

#

"She with the white mark has had her place on the path threatened," Hollow spoke.

As before, Hollow spoke in a torrent of different tones, voices, and languages, though one seemed to speak far louder than the rest. He rose into the air until the chain securing his wrist to the floor grew taught. His head, legs, and free arm all hung limply, as though only the left arm had any life in it.

"Who? Who has threatened her? What should be done? What can I do?" Deacon managed to gasp.

He should have been thinking of his own safety. He should have been thinking about the fact that this was a momentous occasion. He should have been thinking about how many policies he had broken, and the consequences. He only thought about the answers to his questions.

"There are trespassers on the path. Shadows in the field." A shudder went through Hollow's body.

The fingers opened and Deacon dropped to the ground. Life was flowing into the other limbs now. They began to twitch. The frail form strained against the chains as it was jerked by unseen hands from one part of the room to another. Deacon scrambled back to a well-defined line on the ground, indicating the extent of the chain's reach. He rushed to take down the cryptic sentences that poured out as a hundred voices seemed to join the chorus of prediction.

"The light are darkened. Two fingers are not a fist. Selections. Decisions. White has become black. Gray may become white. Learners define learned. A long journey, necessary and deadly, is made safely in a single step. A worthy life can begin when an unworthy life ends," the voices whispered.

Deacon was hard-pressed to record all that he heard. Then, faintly, far below the other voices, the voice that had dominated the others in the first few sentences could be heard. It was quietly but insistently chanting a single phrase. Deacon strained to hear it. Something told him that of all of these voices, this is the one that had answered his pleas. This was Tober.

104

He tried his best to filter out the voices of the other spirits, each offering up precious hints at future times. His spare stylus was still. The voice was so soft, so quiet. What was he saying?

The door swung open and Karr entered. He had felt guilty abandoning his post, and was more than a little frightened that he would be punished for doing so.

"He is speaking! Deacon! Why didn't you call for the others? Why aren't you writing?" the apprentice cried, but the wizard remained still.

What was this voice saying?

#

The cloaks, at least fifty of them, drifted quickly to their assigned targets. The more massive dragoyle charged at Desmeres. He frenziedly rummaged through the bag as the beast pounded toward him, trampling a pair of the cloaks in the process. The hulking thing was steps away when he pulled out a large glass ampoule and hurled it at the creature. A clear liquid burst from the broken container and coated the monster's face. Instantly, the liquid crystallized and hardened.

Desmeres dove aside as an intended bite turned into a head butt that collided with the ground. In a mere moment, there was a swarm of cloaks drifting in ever-decreasing circles around them. Myn dug her claws into the ground, her gaze locked on the enormous creature that was thrashing about clawing at its face. Desmeres pulled a thin red flask from his bag and hurled it at the nearest cloak with lethal accuracy. It passed through where the body should have been and slid harmlessly to the ground without breaking.

"It's no good. There is nothing to hit!" he cried.

The cloaks were very nearly upon them. Desmeres turned to the dragoyle, which was raking the substance off of its face already. He pulled out a second red vial and hurled it at the beast. It struck, shattered, and splashed the creature with a wave of fire. After burning intensely for a few moments, the flames subsided, leaving the creature virtually unharmed.

Desmeres looked helplessly through the bag for something that might do some good. Meanwhile, Lain managed to snatch up his sword again, only to roll to avoid the crushing foot of the other dragoyle. The beast opened its maw and a cloud of black mist erupted forth. A swath of the dark stuff cut across the crowd of cloaks that Lain dove through. Everything that the mist touched hissed violently. The unlucky cloaks that received a coating released an unholy screech. Most of them quickly succumbed to widening holes being eaten through them. With a series of deft sidesteps and dives, Lain made his way to the woman. The creatures kept their distance, wary of injuring their master.

"Oh, to hell with it! Myranda, cover your eyes and brace yourself!" Desmeres ordered.

Myranda quickly did as she was told. Desmeres gave the bag a long, low swing and released it in its entirety at the beast. The bag struck with a shatter of glass, followed immediately by a sound that defied description. The roar of thunder, the crackle of fire, and all manner of whistling, rumbling, and howling explosions melded into one deafening sound. It was accompanied by the most dazzling of light shows. Shafts of red, blue, orange, and white danced momentarily through clouds of fire, smoke, and debris that trailed away in the mighty wind to form a long, billowing stream. The force of the blast shredded half a dozen of the nearby cloaks and singed a dozen others.

Desmeres was hurled backward by the blast. Myranda dropped to the ground, Myn crouching just in front of her. The rush of wind from the explosion momentarily outpaced the wind already whipping through the field. Through squinting eyes, Myranda hoped to see cloaks being torn away from her by the force of the lingering blast, but instead she saw a pair of legs, black as a silhouette and ending in a trio of vicious claws, cleaving the icy ground. The limbs seemed to fade into nothingness as they approached the flapping cloak, just as the clawed hands did when they attacked. Thus anchored, the horrid creatures managed to hold their positions.

Lain's sword clashed with the woman's halberd again and again. This person should have been dead, but somehow she matched his speed and strength. As the battle raged on, the woman seemed to smile, as though she appreciated the skill of her opponent. Unfortunately, the mismatched weapons were working in the woman's favor. Whenever Lain managed to step near enough to score a blow with his sword, the woman switched to the offensive, pushing him back to the length of the longer halberd's reach. With that much distance between their target and their master, the cloaks were emboldened to offer a few strikes. Pitch-black phantom limbs whispered into solidity, slashed at him, and vanished again in one lightning motion. Already, tears in his clothes were showing a mixture of orange fur and crimson blood. In front of him was the woman, behind was the dragoyle, and cloaks churned in a ring around them. There was little hope for escape.

Desmeres's explosion finally subsided, revealing a crater alternately frozen, charred, dissolved, petrified, and pulverized. There was nothing of the beast left but a handful of shattered, stony pieces of whatever it was that it had been made of and a sizzling puddle of the same thick, black substance that Myranda had discovered in the field where all of this madness began.

She struggled to her feet, awash in a sea of cloaks. They clutched and clawed at her, but did not attack. Myn snapped at them with her mouth and lashed at them with her tail, but regardless of what she did, the creatures were unaffected, and without orders regarding the dragon, the cloaks simply ignored her. The girl drew her mind into a failed attempt at a spell that robbed her of the strength to stand and she dropped to the ground.

Desmeres was on his feet again and sprinting to her, slashing with a pair of medium-sized daggers he had pulled from concealed sheaths. His style was a frenzied one, more focused on keeping the fluttering monsters away from him than killing them. The creatures had a way of sweeping in for quick slashes and retreating again with a speed and fluidity that no creature that had to rely on legs would be able to manage, and when met with the keen edge of his weapons, they tended to turn back before doing any real damage. With each step he took, they grew bolder, and by the time he reached Myranda, he'd received more than a few deep scratches without managing to destroy a single cloak. The elf snatched up the girl, hefting her onto his shoulders. Myn nipped and pulled at the creatures that attempted to pull her down.

"Clear a path to the fort!" Desmeres ordered, as a claw landed a painful blow across his back.

The dragon was reluctant until Myranda weakly repeated the order. Like a flash, the dragon leapt in front of Desmeres and, without a friend to worry about hitting, unleashed a shaft of her fiery breath. The cloaks scattered from the blazing attack. Fire quickly consumed all of the cloth demons that were touched, sending them streaking away, trailing streams of flame behind. As Desmeres trudged slowly toward the doors to the fort, periodic blasts of flame kept the cloaks at bay.

Lain had taken more slashes to the back and legs than he could stand. With a trio of swift jumps, he made his way to the other side of the woman. She turned quickly to face him, but he had turned his attention to the cloaks. With their master between himself and the massive dragoyle, he had at least a moment of safety from it as it ran a wide circle around her to reach him. He swiped his sword with all of his might and sliced through the three that were attacking him. The very instant his sword met the fabric of his enemy, something unimaginable happened.

The wind ripping across the field had been every bit as powerful as a blizzard before, but now it exploded into a gust that should have torn Lain from the ground. Instead, he stood, without a hair twitching on his head, while ice and snow around him was dragged and thrown by the force. The wind itself seemed to be avoiding him. Lain didn't take the time to consider the cause of the bizarre phenomenon, as even this mighty wind was not enough to faze the huge dragoyle that was now charging toward him. He sprinted with a speed that beat even his earlier showing toward the sheltering walls of the fort that the others were just now approaching.

Alas, they were not afforded the same mysterious protection and Desmeres had to fight for every step, while Myn dug her claws deep into the icy ground to find purchase.

The pounding charge of the attacking beast grew nearer.

Desmeres reached the doors of the outer wall of the fort and stopped. The unnatural wind was causing them to swing violently, like shutters in a storm. The creak of wood and the groan of hinges could be heard even over the wind. There was no way that they would be able to seek refuge inside safely. Behind them were ten cloaks, clawed hands and feet clutching the earth as Myn had, crawling like insects toward them. Suddenly, one of the doors became still before seeming to almost deliberately wrench itself from its hinges and cartwheel across the field toward Lain. He managed to dodge. The single-minded creature on his trail did not. In a monumental impact, the door shattered into splinters, knocking the creature reeling.

Desmeres stumbled into the courtyard of the fort and dumped Myranda to the ground as gently as circumstances would allow. The wind died down as Lain joined the others in the courtyard--or so it seemed until the trio made their way to the door to defend it. In reality--if such a word could be applied in light of the surreal events at hand--the wind was receding away from the fort, focusing on the remaining enemies. If there was any doubt that some mysterious force was trying to help them, this was the proof.

The cloaks clung tenaciously to the ground, no longer advancing, but refusing to be pushed back. The dragoyle had yet to recover from the impact of the door. Only the woman, who held her halberd high with its gem shining, was unaffected.

"What is going on?" Myranda cried, making an earnest effort to climb to her feet and failing.

"I . . . I don't know," Desmeres said, a look of wonder on his face as he watched the spectacle.

Wisps of flame began to appear, streaking longer and longer in the direction of the wind, as though the wind itself was turning to fire. It soon became apparent that this was precisely the case. Within moments, the whole of the field before them was awash in a sea of churning flames. The roar of fire blended with the screech of dozens of the cloaks that remained. The heat, even from the safety of the wall, was suffocating. Air rushing in to feed the flames moved with a force easily equal to the gales the flames had replaced. Trees in the distance bowed toward them, so strong was the pull. The maelstrom burned on for nearly a minute before the swirling flames drew into a tighter and tighter column, focusing into a single elongated form, positively brilliant in its radiance.

Myranda squinted at the form. Just barely visible in the center of the glow was the shape of woman. It was the second time Myranda had seen this being.

"The other Chosen," Myranda whispered in awe.

#

The apprentice took up a quill and scribbled furiously. The stylus slipped from Deacon's fingers. He understood the voice. Even now it was chanting, almost silent to Karr, but clear in Deacon's head. It was a command. It was directed at him alone. Such a thing was impossible, unimaginable. Hollow did not speak *to* anyone. If at all, he spoke *at* everyone. But there could be no question. He had asked what he could do, and this was his answer.

The chanting did not stop until Hollow fell silent a minute later, but even then his final words were those that Deacon had strained to hear.

The path is changing. Go where it leads.

#

The fiery form drifted in the sky, silently surveying the damage. Patches of ground hidden beneath snow for decades now smoked and steamed. Puddles of what had moments before been ice now boiled. The dragoyle, though much the worse for the experience, still lived. The woman, holding the halberd high, had also survived, as did three cloaks that were near enough to share the protection of the weapon.

Seeing that her job was not finished, the mysterious fiery savior shot through the air at the woman. With a few deft twirls of the powerful halberd, the enemy struck the charging form with the blade gem. The Chosen was deflected and sent hurtling backward. The brightness of the flames dimmed significantly and seemed to disperse briefly before pulling back together. She floated, her brightness wavering, before finally it faded to nothing and her form dropped to the ground. Where there had been fire, now the form was a continuous, crystal-clear mass of water. It was shaped perfectly into the same form as the fire had been. Where her feet touched the boiling pools, it joined them.

"Myranda is better bait than I anticipated. Another Chosen has shown itself. Quickly, capture her, too!" the woman ordered, her voice a barely audible wheeze. It was clear that the death that she had been cheating was preparing to claim her.

The cloaks obeyed, drifting hauntingly over the smoldering ground toward the fluid form. The watery woman dropped down into the pool below her, appearing to be nothing more than another puddle. They drifted near to it, remaining a cautious distance away. Not cautious enough.

Tendrils of water surged up and saturated the cloth creatures. The wind, in a short, severe burst, froze the cloaks solid. The watery form rose again, arms crossed and a faint look of satisfaction on her face. Her smug display was cut short as the foot of the now-recovered dragoyle smashed down over her from behind. The water splashed everywhere, and for a moment it seemed that with that simple maneuver, the bizarre being was defeated.

On closer inspection, the water soaked with exaggerated speed into the ground. A shudder nearby grew swiftly, culminating in a rift that opened. A sandy, stony version of the same being climbed out. The fingers were less human, narrowing down their length into cruel claws. A powerful blow from the deceivingly heavy limb was quite enough to get the creature's attention. A dozen or so more followed with a speed far swifter than a creature composed of stone ought to be capable. Old scars widened, cracks opened, and thick, black blood flowed. The relentless rain of blows finally reduced the weakened beast to a lifeless mound of battered rubble.

The stone form shifted its cool, penetrating gaze to the woman in the only snowy portion of the field that remained. Graceful steps sunk a few inches into the baked earth as the living statue moved toward the woman. She had dropped to her knees, one hand holding weakly to the halberd, likely the only thing keeping her from crumpling entirely to the ground. The glazed-over eyes of the woman turned to the ground. She spoke, weak whispers between constant wheezes.

"Stupid--" Wheeze. "--worthless--" Wheeze. "--creatures." Wheeze. "I must--" Wheeze. "--have a long--" Wheeze. "--conversation with--" Wheeze. "--Demont," she managed, before dropping to the ground and into a long overdue stillness.

The stone form reached for the halberd, embedded in the ground as it had been before. The face twisted into a scowl, and she smashed the weapon with a mighty backhand. It flew an impressive distance, crashing down beyond the edge of the charred region and disappearing beneath the thick layer of ice-crusted snow.

Behind the fort wall, Desmeres helped Myranda to her feet. With the aid of his shoulder and her staff, she was able to walk. Lain held his sword at the ready, not yet willing to trust whatever it was that had helped them.

"There may be something to this prophecy after all," Desmeres admitted quietly, as the trio approached the unearthly being.

The living statue turned to face them and, for a moment, there was silence. The surface of the creature's body was smooth as marble, and seamless. It, as before, bore the general appearance of a woman, the features dulled. The face lacked a mouth, and only a soft rise marked where the nose should have been. The mark that graced the sword, Lain's chest, and Myranda's scarred hand stood clearly embossed in the center of the forehead. In the place of eyes were pristine, lidded, white globes that had a faint glow. Its gaze was locked solidly on Lain, unblinking and unstraying. The shimmering eyes narrowed, the shine grew.

Lain suddenly stepped back and drew his weapon.

"What is wrong?" Myranda asked, concerned by the showing of hostility.

Lain did not answer. Instead, he stepped forward, making it clear that he was quite willing to use the weapon he held. The glow in the eyes of the being faded, and it slowly raised the stone talons that had made short work of the massive dragoyle just moments ago. Lain tensed, ready to defend or attack at any moment. In a smooth, deliberate motion, the being ran a talon along the blade. With a long, crisp ring of the blade, the stone creature collected a few drops of the fallen woman's blood. Almost immediately, a change seemed to happen. The blood vanished through previously absent cracks in the fingers. The cracks spread and connected, causing flakes of the stony surface to fall away. Beneath, pink and vibrant, was what appeared to be . . . flesh.

The change continued, flaking away up the arm revealing healthy skin behind. Soon the reaction quickened, cracking away large patches of the surface. Here and there, the flakes seemed to hang in the air before connecting with one another and taking on the texture of the cloth the woman was wearing. Before long, a full garment hung in the air. It draped itself around the shoulders of the now–nearly-human figure before them. The hood pulled into place, hiding the face just as the final plume of stone flakes drifted into nothingness. The hands of the being, now a perfect replica of the fallen foe, rose to the hood and pulled it back.

Everything, right down to the full head of long brown hair, was just as it had been on the woman. Had the body not still been on the ground in front of them, they would have believed the enemy had somehow torn herself back from the beyond yet again.

"You have done well, Chosen One," the being said. "I am impressed with your ability to blend with the lower creatures."

The being approached Lain. He held the sword tightly, tip leveled at the throat of the woman, keeping her at bay.

"What *are* you?" Desmeres managed through a rare look of wonder.

The being did not acknowledge him, her gaze locked on Lain.

"Answer!" Lain ordered, moving the sword to within a hair's width of her throat. The woman was unaffected.

"I am not in the habit of dignifying the questions of mortals with response. I will answer *you,* if you wish," she said.

"Do it!" Lain growled.

"I am like you. I am a guardian of this world. I am Chosen," she said.

"Why are you here?" Lain demanded.

"To join you in battle against the enemy," the woman said.

"I neither want nor need help," he said.

"Nor do I, but it is decreed by the powers that govern all of existence that it must be," she said.

Lain drew in a long breath of air. "The soldiers that survived your escape are coming back," Lain said, scanning the surroundings for the best route of escape.

"That show she put on likely has every soldier from here to the horizon on the way," Desmeres said.

Lain spoke to Desmeres in a bizarre language Myranda had heard spoken in Entwell. He responded with a nod.

"We need to leave--now," Lain said.

"Agreed," Desmeres said. Myranda offered a weak agreement.

"You aren't actually *afraid* of these animals, are you?" the woman asked, a hint of disdain in her voice.

"I do not want to deal with them. Not now," Lain said.

"Mmm. Yes. Then let us go," the woman said.

"You will not be joining us," Lain said, moving swiftly to the west.

Myn trotted to Myranda's side as Desmeres helped the weary girl to follow.

"I must. It is destiny," she said.

"Lain, you must allow her join us. She is Chosen," Myranda agreed.

"These creatures use this word . . . Lain . . ." the woman said.

"It is his name," Myranda said.

"Inform your mortals that they are not to speak to me," she said. "I cannot approve of their continued presence. The very fact that you have allowed them to label you as they label themselves speaks volumes of the fact that you have spent too much time among them. You are Chosen; you mustn't allow yourself to be lowered to their level."

Lain was silent. Myranda's reverence for this mighty being was quickly slipping away. It, like most elements of the prophecy she'd encountered, was not as she had imagined. Far from the noble, benevolent, caring being she had expected, the woman before her had managed, in the space of only a few sentences, to firmly define herself as a rigidly superior, tactless creature. Everything she said had a cold, sterile feel to it. In a way, her attitude was similar to the one Myranda had assumed as a Tesselor--but her tone made it far worse. At least Myranda's words had the sting of sarcasm. This woman spoke frankly, as though there was no doubt that anything she spoke was anything less than absolute fact.

"What is wrong with you? We are the people of this world! It is your duty to protect us, not lord over us," Myranda said, her irritation briefly pushing her weariness aside.

"Tell your human that--" the woman began.

"Tell her yourself and be gone," Lain growled.

He increased his westward pace to a speed difficult for the ailing Myranda to match, even with the help of Desmeres. The woman released an irritated sigh and turned, for the first time since that day in Entwell, to Myranda. She then proceeded, with infinite calm, to shatter any lingering hope Myranda might have had that she was the hero she'd hoped for.

"My duty is to the world, not the inhabitants. I am to protect you insomuch as you are a product of nature. Past that, I see little distinction between yourself and the charred ground you stand on, and were you to suddenly be changed from one to the other, I would hardly consider it a change at all. I have watched over this world since the dawn of time and have found the brief fraction of history that you and your ilk have inhabited it of no more consequence or interest than the eons that preceded it. Your society has proven itself to be shortsighted, dim, and quite likely to bring itself to a prompt end without any enduring influence in the grand scheme of things whatsoever. I consider it an enormous concession that I have even bothered to learn this sequence of squeaks and grunts that you call a language. I would not be speaking at all but for the fact that the one you call Lain seems unwilling to communicate by spirit. He is the only being besides myself worthy of any distinction at all," she stated before turning back to Lain.

With the infuriating being by his side, Lain wore a far more stern expression than usual. It became clear that she had no intention of heeding his order to leave.

"I haven't the time to deal with you at the moment. Keep out of sight. If we are pulled into another battle because of you, I will see to it that you do not survive it," Lain grumbled as they reached the trees at the edge of the clearing.

"I assure you, no weak-minded beasts that seek you and I shall discover us and survive to spread the knowledge," the creature said.

They trudged on. Lain had a determination in his stride that carried he and the seemingly indefatigable woman far ahead of the others. Now, among the trees, they didn't have to rely upon distance alone to hide them from prying eyes. This fact, coupled with the hundreds of different trails made by the other prisoners, made discovery of the growing group exceedingly unlikely. This was fortunate, because the chill air of the hardening night was beginning to take its toll. Myn had taken to puffing flame once a minute or so to keep warm, and before long Myranda was shivering uncontrollably. She was walking now simply out of reflex, shuffling in a daze, eyes closed. After her staff slipped out of her hand for the third time, Desmeres decreed that the time had come to stop until morning. He lowered Myranda to the ground and began to gather dry boughs from beneath the trees. He had already begun to spark flint against steel to start the fire before she realized what was going on.

"You can't start a fire . . . pine . . . too much smoke," she objected weakly.

"I am in no mood to spend the next few hours finding a more appropriate fuel, and we *need* this fire. It would be awfully anticlimactic if you froze to death tonight," he said, mustering a weak grin.

The cold, frost-crusted wood was not being cooperative. Myranda, moments before succumbing to exhaustion, whispered a barely audible request to Myn, and a burst of flame from her lips lit the stubborn wood quite nicely. Shortly after, Lain and the woman approached. He cast a stern look at Desmeres, but relented upon seeing the collapsed Myranda with Myn curled on top of her. The woman looked upon the sight with the same sterile stare she'd worn since her arrival. Lain sat cross-legged by the rather meager fire and closed his eyes.

"I was under the impression that our intention was to avoid detection," the woman remarked.

"I am afraid that the fire is a necessary risk. We mortals are quite fragile, after all," Desmeres said with excessive pleasantness.

"Infuriatingly so. Those two are sleeping, I suppose," she said.

"As *I* hope to be shortly," Desmeres said, adopting a similar posture to Lain. He then propped his elbows on his knees and his chin on his fists.

"Such a pitiful requirement, a mandatory period of helplessness at the end of each day," she remarked as she bent low to inspect the girl and the dragon. "And these eyes are woefully inadequate."

"What exactly are you accustomed to?" Desmeres asked.

The woman remained silent, inspecting the fire instead.

"Ah, I see. I must answer your questions but you needn't answer mine," he said.

This, too, was ignored. Suddenly, flames swept up around the woman and, in mere moments, she was consumed in flame. A moment later, it was clear that she was, as before, actually *composed* of the flame. At this distance, the wonder of the sight was breathtaking. The flame was like cascades of liquid gold flowing upward in graceful curves over her body. Behind the bright tips, the flame was a deep red, and behind that was a dark, almost black core that was just barely visible among the brilliant gold and red. The fiery being was more defined now than she had been before, looking more like the woman from whom she'd borrowed her form. The ground beneath her feet sizzled briefly before she stepped onto the campfire. Its flickering flames joined with hers and she took a seat.

"It isn't nearly as strong and pure enough a flame to suit my needs. I shall require a fair amount of time to restore myself to the strength I enjoyed this morning," she remarked in a voice similar to the one she'd had as a human, save for a peculiar crackling quality that underscored it.

"I shall endeavor to build a more appropriate one in the future. Have you any specific requests?" Desmeres offered with a yawn.

"Use the wood of several trees and fan the flames constantly with strong, focused winds. That should provide adequate intensity," she stated simply.

"I think that may be a fire more visible and taxing than I am willing or able to create," Desmeres said.

"I suspected as much," she replied.

After a few moments, the form of her body seemed to flicker away into the flames.

Lain sat in deep concentration as the others slept. It was often as near as he would come to sleep for weeks or even months at a time. His back was striped with slashes from the cloaks he'd battled. Many still leaked blood, contributing to long maroon stains along his own cloak. If he managed to sink deeply enough into this trance, the last of them should close. He had no use for magic, but the warrior's sleep had saved his life more than once.

It was no replacement for true sleep, though. The body was greatly rejuvenated, but at the expense of the mind. Dark thoughts from long ago had a way of finding their way to the surface. Few had even heard of the warrior's sleep, but those who *had* heard of it had learned of it first through the tales of those minds lost to it. Madness was often the price of the technique. For a few hours, Lain endured the twisted remembrances. Sometimes the faces of his victims would flash in his mind. Other times, some of his darker deeds would crawl out of the murky darkness and linger. One scene in particular came so frequently it seemed to become an old friend.

The setting was always the same. He was on the farm of his youth. The only man who had shown him anything but hatred, blind Ben, was being beaten before him. As he watched, he--lashed to a plow--was being beaten as well. He was too exhausted to continue. Ben, old and feeble, finally took his last lash with a whip and fell to the ground, dead. Shock, pain, rage. Emotions burned at his brain. The baser instincts inside of him screamed for revenge. Ignoring the increasingly intense lashes of the slave driver's whip, Lain tore at the leather straps that secured him. Tooth and claw reduced the last of them to shreds and he was free.

The acts he committed were unspeakable. Inexcusable. He tore through half a dozen slave drivers and guards before a team of them managed to force him into a shed. This would be the last mistake they made.

The shed they barricaded him into was filled with supplies for the harvest. Taking up a scythe, Lain slashed through both the door and the men who braced it. Before the thinking part of him returned, he had stained the blade with the blood of fifty men--or more. Only the other slaves and the youngest son of the owner were spared.

Those who found the aftermath of his rampage did not know what to think. It was as though a bear had mauled half of the men, while the other half were simply cut to pieces.

Finally, Lain forced the remembrances from his mind and pulled himself from the warrior's sleep. It was these soul-searing visions that served as a reminder to him that whatever horrid end he may come to, it was deserved. He knew that the life he had led could not be redeemed. He did not fear death. A part of him craved it, but the same instincts that led him to his atrocities that day continued to demand that he do whatever it took to give the lives back to those like him, through any means necessary. In doing so, perhaps he could prevent another from becoming the twisted demon that they had made him into.

As Lain hunted down a meal, the others slept. Once fed, he remained vigilant. With the wretched swirling wind--which, it seemed, had been the newcomer's doing--gone, the breezes again brought him smells from far away. Soldiers were numerous; the wind carried their scent regardless of direction. Most were in the company of horses. Some were joined by far more fearsome beasts. They all seemed to be growing nearer. With the others to slow him, an encounter was inevitable.

Each passing moment brought the first of what was sure to be a string of battles nearer, but Lain knew it was best to fight sooner with the group well-rested than to run now and face a battle later with his group useless. His group . . . Lain furrowed his brow. He had never been comfortable as part of a group. Now there were four who looked to him. He was not a leader. He was not a protector. This was not his place.

His solitude was broken when the rising sun roused Myn, who, in turn, roused Myranda.

The girl was far from recovered. Her strength was a fraction of what it should be, but that still made her several times stronger than the previous few weeks of captivity and torture had allowed. Thoughts and memories of what had occurred in that terrible place constantly leapt to the surface of her mind and had to be brushed away. She attempted to rub her sore neck. The collar that had severely limited her spell-casting was still locked in place, but without the crystal it was little more than a nuisance. Now that there was nothing to prevent it, her mind worked to heal her body as she slept--but even so, she was sore from head to toe. Slowly, she surveyed the status of her friends.

Myn was off faithfully hunting down breakfast. She must be healthy enough. Desmeres was sleeping propped against a tree. Here and there, a place where one of the cloaks had managed to reach his skin could be seen. One or two such wounds still had the look of fresh blood about them. They should be healed. Lain was crouched at the edge of the clearing. His clothes, formerly white to blend with the snow, now were streaked with the remnants of his injuries. He didn't seem to be bleeding any longer, but the wounds were still quite large, quite numerous, and quite deep. They must be terribly painful.

"Lain, you're still hurt. Let me heal you," she said, fetching her staff and using it to struggle to her feet.

He silently agreed. Within a few minutes, she had found all of the visible injuries and healed them. She knew better than to ask if he had any others. He would deny it. Instead, she turned her attentions to the sleeping Desmeres. His gashes were easily dispensed with, though the warm, tingling sensation of their removal was enough to wake him while she was still crouched by his side.

"Why thank you," he said with a yawn, admiring her work as the last wound shrank away. "I must say, you do a better job than those potions of mine. Mind you, you might wake me up next time you feel inclined to cast a spell. I may have an opinion about it. By the way, there is a nagging pain in my lower back that you missed. Yes . . . there . . . this is why I have made it a policy never to get my hands dirty."

Myn came trotting back with some manner of wild bird for Myranda. The girl cleaned it, fashioned a spit, and held it over the fire.

"What do you suppose you are doing?" came a voice from the flames.

Myranda, startled, fell backward. The form of the newcomer separated itself from the flames and shifted slowly back to her human form. Desmeres chuckled to himself.

"I am sorry, I didn't know!" Myranda apologized.

"No. Of course you didn't," the woman said. Her cold voice bore a hint of the tone of a weary teacher consoling a poor student. "A creature of your level could not be expected to understand the nature of my being."

Myranda felt a twinge of anger, but there was no use voicing it. She cooked her meal as best she could over the remnants of the fire. When she was through, Myranda offered the rest to Desmeres. Myn, apparently still holding a grudge for being tied up and bagged the day before, would not allow it. Instead, she quickly ate it herself.

"Well, if you could behave yourself, I wouldn't have had to bind you in the first place," Desmeres stated, correctly assuming the motivation for the act. "Ah, it is just as well. We need to move before someone spots the smoke."

"We shall stay here until I have fully recovered," the woman announced.

"We leave now. It is already too late to escape cleanly, but if we move quickly we may limit our encounters," Lain said.

"I cannot be expected to perform the acts of which I am capable if I am not allowed to recover fully," she said.

"How much longer will you need?" Myranda asked.

"With a fire this size? Several weeks more," she stated.

"Well, when the soldiers find you, lie to them about where we went," Desmeres said, quickly following Lain, who had already set off in the direction they had been headed in the day before.

"Wait! Lain, you mustn't leave her behind. You are both Chosen! You must remain united," Myranda called after him. He did not turn.

Myn trotted halfway to Lain and turned to urge Myranda on.

"Please, you must follow now. I am sure you are strong enough to reach wherever we are headed! If not, I will help you," Myranda pleaded.

"To suggest that I would *ever* require your aid is tantamount to blasphemy. Even in my weakened state, I am more powerful than you can imagine," the woman snapped, a rare hint of emotion flavoring her usually sterile voice.

"Then let us go! Quickly!" Myranda urged as Lain disappeared amongst the thickening trees in the distance.

The being tore a branch from a tree and dropped it on the smoldering fire. She quickly shifted back to flame and settled down.

"No! No, I . . . He isn't like you! He . . . has spent too much time among us. He doesn't even believe he is Chosen. He doesn't believe that the Chosen exist! He has become . . . tainted, disfigured by our way of thinking," she attempted, hoping that appearing to share her distasteful view might convince her.

"I am aware of what he has told you. I have been watching him since he left the cave. He is lying to you, no doubt in attempts to rid himself of you," she said.

Myranda looked desperately about. This could not be happening. These were the warriors who were intended to save this world. Now one refused to believe his place, and the other refused to help him.

"However . . ." came the voice from the fire. "The mere fact that he has been willing to suffer your presence for so long, let alone his consideration and even protection of you, betrays a fundamental . . . alteration of his character that will need to be reversed if he is to rise adequately to his true purpose."

Slowly she removed herself from the fire and shifted back to the human form. As she did, the last, lingering flames were drawn into her, leaving the fire fully extinguished. The woman walked with purpose in the direction of the others. Myranda remained behind long enough to disguise where the fire had been. Myn trotted quickly back to aid her and urge her along.

"Myn, this is going to be more difficult than I'd imagined," she said as she turned to follow.

When she reached the others, Desmeres was walking a few steps behind. The woman was beside Lain. All were silent. When he noticed Myranda, Desmeres took a few steps further back to join her.

"Well. Quite a pair, aren't they?" he said quietly. "So far, all she has done is order me to take a more fitting position. I appreciate people who make an accurate first impression quickly. It saves time."

"Where are we going?" Myranda asked.

"There is another safe house. Still a fair distance away. Of course, this one is much smaller. Barely built to house Lain and I. With you, the dragon, and our new ray of sunshine, things are going to be cozy," he remarked.

"What do we do next?" she asked.

"First we find the safe house. Once inside, we can start making plans," he said. "To that end, I've a few issues that you may be able to help me with."

"I imagined you might," she replied.

"You mentioned that Epidime used a halberd like the one the woman had. That was Arden who used the Halberd, not Epidime," Desmeres observed.

"Arden *is* Epidime," Myranda said.

"No . . . How could Arden be Epidime? Do you know this for certain?" Desmeres asked doubtfully.

"If that brute who tried to kill me at the mines was Arden, then I am convinced he is Epidime. I spent the last two weeks struggling to keep him out of my mind," she said.

"Keep him out of your mind . . . so he was attempting to read your mind?" Desmeres said, suddenly a good deal more interested.

"Read is too gentle a word. He was forcing his way in. He was trying to take it for his own," she shivered.

"Are you sure Arden was the one doing it? Is it possible that he was just an enforcer and the attempts were coming from elsewhere?" Desmeres asked.

"The attempts were doubly intense when he made contact. It was him," she said.

"Mind reading. It must have been Epidime. Arden is Epidime. He had us fooled. He had everyone fooled," Desmeres said quietly to himself. "I am not accustomed to being caught off-guard with information such as this. Information is the biggest part of my role in the partnership. This changes things."

"How so?" she asked.

"Well, for one, the contact I have in Arden's organization has just become infinitely more valuable. And . . . other things," he said.

"What?" she asked.

"Nothing that might interest you," he said.

"Why don't you want to tell me?" she asked, having heard too many such responses to take them at face value.

"Not to offend you, Myranda, but it seems fairly clear to me that we are not likely to receive the rest of the price on your head. Any attempts to secure it from this point forward would be folly. Not that I am disappointed. The half that they *have* given us more than triples the amount we've earned on our three best years combined. However, since you aren't terribly likely to join our cause, it does mean our bizarre little partnership is nearing its end. Soon we will part ways. With that in mind, you already know more about us than anyone alive today. If we tell you much more, you may as well go into business for yourself," he explained.

"I don't understand. When you were planning to hand me over, *alive,* to the very same people trying to hunt you down, you were willing to answer any question I had. Now that you have given up on turning me over, you begin keeping secrets?" she said. "Why? What was different then?"

"You don't want to know," he said, the earnestness in his voice a warning.

"You know me better than that. Tell me," she said.

Desmeres heaved a heavy sigh.

"It will strain our relationship. I would be lying if I said that I hadn't become fond of you in the time we've been working together. I would much prefer to leave on pleasant terms," he said.

"Desmeres, you and Lain have been trying to claim a ransom on my head for the better part of a year, and despite that fact, you remain my two closest allies in all of this," Myranda pointed out.

"Yes, twists of fate and quirks of incident have certainly cast us in the role of protectors more frequently than captors," he agreed.

"If I could come to trust you despite the fact that I *know* you had only the worst intentions in mind, what could you possibly say to 'strain our relationship'?" she asked.

"You would be surprised," he said.

"Only if you tell me," she said, growing impatient.

"Lain?" he said, raising his voice slightly.

"Tell her," came his response.

Desmeres sighed again.

"The plan was to accept full payment and exchange you and the sword at once. Lain would then follow the courier to where you were taken and poison you," he explained. His tone was not apologetic, merely anticipatory or the reaction he knew would follow.

Myranda stopped walking. She was silent for a time. Lain and the other Chosen continued on. Desmeres stopped a few steps later. He turned to her.

"I warned you," he said.

"That . . . how could you even . . . ?" She attempted.

"Is it really so much worse than merely handing you over? We were doing so with the full expectation that you would not last long once we turned you in. The poison would have been a quick death, far better than anything that they would have had in store," he offered.

"Are you still planning to kill me?" she asked.

"Against all good judgment, the decision has been made to let you live your life to its natural end," he said.

"Well, I am glad that--" she began.

The ring of a sword being pulled from its sheath cut her remark short. Lain held the sword to the neck of the other Chosen.

"If you try that again, I will do what it takes to kill you," Lain hissed.

"What the female said is true. You have been tainted. You are not one of these *things*. It is only proper that you and I join our minds rather than lower ourselves to their level with language. To threaten my life betrays so much of what they have done to you. It shows that these mindless, primal savages have managed to infect you with their temperament, and the suggestion that I could even *be* killed reveals the ignorance and weakness of mind you must have had to adopt to live among them. That ends here. If you do not leave these beasts behind and join me in our destiny, then I will cure your attachment to them in the simplest way possible," she said.

"That may well be the most subtle death threat I have yet received," Desmeres remarked.

Lain's ears twitched.

"We do not have time for this. We have been found," He said.

Before long, the sounds that his sensitive ears had picked up found their way to the ears of the others: hooves crunching on snow. There were at least a dozen men on horseback. They seemed to be coming from all directions at once. Myranda held her staff at the ready, preparing her mind for the task at hand. In this battle, at least, she would not be helpless. Desmeres unsheathed his pair of daggers. Myn unfurled her wings, drove her claws into the icy ground, and bared her teeth. Only the newest member of the group seemed unconcerned.

After a few moments, the first of the attackers became visible through the trees to the east. Even at this distance, he was clearly a nearman. The crude blank visor covered an inhuman face Myranda had yet to see.

With a few silent steps, Lain seemed to vanish among the trees. Myranda locked her eyes on the soldier. A blur of motion swept past him, a strike from Lain nearly too swift to be seen, knocking him from his horse. A pair of other mounted soldiers appeared from behind and drew Myranda's attention. After focusing briefly on the ground beneath her, Myranda thrust the tip of the staff earthward. A minor wave of motion shook the ground. It was enough to terrify the horses, who swiftly threw their riders. Thinking quickly, Myranda intensified the spell around the base of the trees nearest to the fallen nearmen. An avalanche of snow was shaken from the branches, burying the enemies.

Myranda turned to find that three more were rapidly approaching from the north, and four from the south.

Desmeres stepped to Myranda's back. Daggers were not well-suited to battling those on horseback. The other Chosen One merely stood, her arms crossed, with a look akin to boredom on her face. The riders began to circle around them. They all bore spears. Two bore nets as well. The nearest of them hurled his in an attempt to ensnare Myranda. She managed a brief burst of wind that blew the net over its caster, tangling horse and rider alike and sending them tumbling to the ground. Myn dove upon the helpless soldier and brought him swiftly to an end.

A faint flash of light and scatter of dust as the armor caved in confirmed that these were no humans they fought. A spear was hurled at Myranda. She dove to avoid it. One of the other soldiers raised his weapon to strike her before she could rise. Myn launched herself at the rider, clamping onto the spear-wielding hand and shaking it violently as she worked her wings to pull him backward. He struggled against the dragon, at one point pulling free a handful of scales in attempts at pulling her off.

A second soldier attempted to attack before Myranda could get to her feet. A gleam of steel later and one of Desmeres's expertly crafted daggers was protruding from the nearman's neck. The armor was empty by the time it reached the ground. Desmeres rushed to the unoccupied armor, retrieving his dagger and the discarded spear. Myn finally managed to pull her target from his horse and finished him with a blast of flame.

Four soldiers remained. Desmeres and Myranda turned to them.

The nearmen focused on the opponents in front of them, neglecting the one who was behind. Before their mistake was realized, Lain had taken two of them. The remaining soldiers turned to face the warrior, and a half-dozen more arrived before Myranda or Desmeres could take advantage of the distraction. Myn sprayed flame to keep the soldiers at bay, but they were quickly growing more bold. At the edge of the battlefield, completely ignored by the soldiers, was the other Chosen One. She stood, arms crossed, as though irritated by the distraction.

"Help us!" Myranda pleaded.

"I do not see why you fight at all. You should cease this at once," the being said.

Bizarrely, her words were heeded, but not by those she had intended. The circling soldiers halted and pulled back. Seemingly unimpressed by the event, the woman continued.

"We are Chosen. You are mortal. When *you* are faced with the trials that *we* must overcome, death is the only possible result. If you survive this battle or any other, it will be by our discretion, and every motion that we spend to preserve your lives distracts us from our true goal. The most useful thing that you could do would be to simply bring yourself to an end more swiftly and spare us further delay. Turn your weapons on yourselves," she declared.

The nearmen obeyed. Swords were drawn and plunged into the chests of their wielders. In moments, the entirety of the attacking party was reduced to dusty piles of armor. Myranda stood in open-mouthed wonder at the act. Desmeres scratched his head for a moment before shrugging, collecting the trio of liberated scales, handing them to Myranda, and gathering the reins of three of the now-riderless horses. Myn was content to simply stand down without an explanation, and Lain seemed more interested in concealing the armor beneath the snow than asking questions.

"What happened? What did you do to them?" Myranda asked, confusion swirling in her head as she absentmindedly stowed the scales in her bag.

As expected, the newest member of their group had no intention of answering her. Desmeres led a horse over to Myranda. Gritting her teeth and shaking her head, she mounted the steed with her question unanswered. He offered the reins of a second horse to the woman. She extended a hand and, rather than clutching the reins, took hold of a single hair from the mane and plucked it free.

A moment later the solid form of the woman wafted away, replaced instead by an intensely swirling mass of pure wind that held, briefly, its former shape. Quickly, the swirling form altered posture, assuming the four-legged stance of the animal. Limbs lengthened and narrowed. The overall form grew. Soon the general shape of a horse stood where the woman had. The wind suddenly intensified where the limbs met the ground. Steadily, this tighter swirl rose, leaving behind the solid approximation of a horse's hooves, then legs, then body. Before long, a replica of the offered horse stood before the original.

"Impressive. It wasn't strictly necessary, though, was it? You could simply have ridden the original, couldn't you?" Desmeres asked.

The animal gave no answer. There was the possibility that she lacked the capacity to speak in this form. It was doubtful. Somehow, the smugly superior look that had so marked the face of the woman managed to persist in the horse. The effect was absurd, an animal that showed weariness bordering on frustration with those around it.

When a passable job of concealing the battleground had been managed, Lain, Myn, and the shapeshifter moved onward on foot. Myranda and Desmeres continued on horseback. Lain's seemingly inexhaustible stamina allowed for a pace near gallop for the horses. As they rode, Desmeres conversed with Myranda as best he could.

"They follow orders," he said

Myranda's expression communicated her confusion.

"The nearmen. That is what she did. She was in the form of one of the higher-ranking leaders. The woman she killed. The nearmen were following orders. That is why they killed themselves," he said.

"Would they really do that?" she asked.

"In my experience with them, I would say they wouldn't have a choice. It was different once. There was a time when they were just as you or I. Now, I doubt that they've a mind of their own. They live--or, more accurately, *die*--to serve," he answered.

Myranda was still attempting to come to terms with such a horror of existence when they reached the empty section of forest that apparently contained the hidden entrance to yet another of the many storerooms and safe houses that Desmeres and Lain kept. Lain reached down to a patch of ground rendered featureless by a blanket of frost and ice that would never fully thaw. Gripping what appeared to be an icy stone sunken into the ground, he pulled open a hidden door.

Myranda moved toward the opening.

"Just a moment," Desmeres said, wrestling his boot from his foot. He dropped the article into the hole. A rush of air and quiet cluster of hisses emanated from the opening.

Slowly he lowered himself down. Lain sent the horses running off in the direction that they had been headed before entering. Vanishing into a swirl of wind again, the shapeshifter swept inside. Myn dove in after, and finally Myranda joined them.

A few weak flames flickered to life when the hatch was drawn closed. The vault they found themselves in was barely the size of a large room. Even before the five occupants had entered, it was well crowded with bundles, chests, and sacks. There was scarcely room to stand. The shapeshifter settled back into her human form, arms crossed and the smug expression bearing a shade more frustration than before.

"Make yourselves as comfortable as you are able. Before we search these bags for something that is not yet too rotten to eat, there are a number of pressing matters that must be discussed," Desmeres announced.

"There most certainly are," Myranda agreed.

"Foremost, this is not a halfway house for wayward wanderers, and Lain and I are not caretakers. It is long past time that each of us went our separate ways," Desmeres stated.

"Lain is Chosen and I will not leave until he has joined with the others of his kind and turned to the task at hand," Myranda declared once again.

"Yes, that has been established, but--" Desmeres began. The voice of the woman cut him off.

"There are no others of our kind," she remarked.

"What? No. There are five!" Myranda objected.

"There had been, but the enemy has been most thorough. We two are all that remain who may call ourselves Chosen. It is thus of the utmost importance that we be delayed no further. Each moment the forces against us grow more powerful. Where once victory was assured, now it shall be a costly endeavor, if it is even an achievable one. We alone shall not be able to quell the storm we are certain to bring upon this world through our actions. The death throes of the war may well make its final days bloodier than the decades that preceded it," she said.

Her cold tone was maddening. If what she said was so, then, if victory was possible, it may well cost more lives than it would save. The possibility had haunted Myranda. There was already evidence that as the fiends who controlled the Alliance Army grew more concerned, their actions grew more drastic. Their soldiers permeated the north. With the nearmen to consider, there was likely two warriors for every civilian. If they were to seek the death of the Chosen at all costs, the devastation would be complete, even if the soldiers of the south did not sweep in to take the land they had been fighting for.

Somehow, Myranda had managed to convince herself that when the five were united, they would be able to prevent this. Now a being better suited than anyone to know the truth announced that such a miracle would not come to pass. She wrestled with the implications.

"How? How can you know? How can you be sure?" Myranda demanded.

"I have spent centuries in a state of global awareness. I spread my mind to the far ends of the world with the sole aim of locating the other divinely gifted beings when they arose. Four beside myself surfaced. The murk and haze of time and space have since swallowed three again," she answered.

"Did you see them die?" Myranda asked.

"I grow weary of your questions. I spoke in hopes of dissuading you from your stated purpose. I have no interest in addressing the depths of your ignorance," she said.

"Perhaps you simply lost sight of them! Perhaps they still exist but have escaped your notice!" Myranda said.

"*Nothing* escapes my notice," the being fumed.

Behind her, Desmeres smirked at the remark.

"I will find them. There is still hope," Myranda said, resigned.

"Hope is a lie. Hope exists only for those who do not know the truth. For the truly intelligent, there exists only certainty. Who do you think you are, human, to even suppose that you might contradict a being such as I? I, who have existed since the first whispers of eternity. I, who am among the first masterpieces wrought by the gods," the being spoke. Strong emotion flavored her words as she progressed, but she endeavored to appear as cold as she had been.

"Fate led me to you. Fate led me to Lain. Fate led me to the fallen swordsman. Fate gave me this!" Myranda cried, throwing down her staff and opening her scarred palm. "Fate has a place for me. Fate has given me a purpose."

The being lashed out, grasping Myranda's wrist and twisting it painfully to gain a better view of the afflicted hand.

"Blasphemy. Sacrilege. It is far better that I relieve you of this limb than allow the symbol of divine purpose to be squandered on so lowly a creature," she said, the malice of her words seeping through her cold exterior. As she spoke, the grip grew tighter, the twist more cruel.

Myranda dropped to her knees. Myn leapt to her side, baring her teeth. The young woman turned her eyes to the emotionless stare of the shapeshifter. Slowly, the mark upon her forehead, the very one she now punished Myranda for bearing, began to reveal itself. It had only been present when she was in one of the elemental forms until now. An instant before the enraged dragon would have attacked her, the being relented. She rubbed her own mark, her face revealing a glimmer of confusion and pain ever so briefly before her expression and the mark each faded to nothing.

"You are not worth the effort," the being decided. "That mark speaks nothing of purpose. It merely labels you as a curiosity. If anything, you are a mistake, a failed attempt at greatness. The spirit of my fallen would-be partner--the swordsman, as you called him--must have branded you as a message of his defeat. With that message delivered your brief, pointless role is fulfilled. I was quite aware of his passing."

"Because nothing escapes your notice," Desmeres repeated.

"Precisely," the creature agreed.

Myranda held her aching wrist and stood.

"How can the powers that be have made such mistakes? How can the very beings created and selected to protect the people of this world care so little about them?" Myranda asked.

"Emotion is weakness. It sensitizes you to the trivial and blinds you to the important. Only in detachment can decisions be made clearly. Only in solitude can all efforts be directed to the appropriate ends," the shapeshifter recited like a mantra.

"Why do you even seek to save this world if you do not care about the people in it?" Myranda asked.

"It is not a matter of desire. It is a matter of purpose. Purpose is the rarest thing in the world. Few beings will ever be given a true purpose for existing. Fewer still will achieve it. I was placed here to perform a task of which I am uniquely capable, and so I shall do it," she answered.

"What of the others who share the purpose? Isn't it your duty to be sure of their fate? Isn't it your obligation to find them if you can?" Myranda countered.

"It is not your place to question my decisions or interpret my role," she said.

The debate continued for the better part of an hour. The shapeshifter, once unwilling to acknowledge Myranda's presence, was now determined to put the girl in her place. For Myranda, all of the confusion and disappointment caused by having her illusions of the heroes that would rescue the world dashed now had a target.

Desmeres sat in quiet amusement as they argued.

Myn was mindful of the shapeshifter. Unlike in Myranda and Lain's spats, here there was a clear enemy. Many times, the Chosen motioned as though she would strike the girl, but each time she held herself back. The creature mostly maintained her composure, but occasionally her anger would flare. Such bursts were brief, but notable. The ground would rumble in sympathy to her anger, and rushing winds could be heard even through the thick earth roof of the storeroom. The argument had not yet begun to subside when the sound of Myn clawing at one of the walls drew Myranda's attention. She approached the dragon and tried to find out what was the matter. The corner of the room she was in was pitch black.

"There, you see. You cannot ignore the plight of the lizard long enough to finish your pathetic point," the shifter remarked smugly.

"What is wrong?" Myranda said, ignoring the attack.

"It would appear something didn't escape her notice," Desmeres said, the constant grin widening.

"What . . . Lain. Where is Lain?" Myranda demanded.

The shifter glanced casually about to discover that the malthrope was indeed missing.

"I actually thought it was going to be difficult. I was confident that I could distract you, Myranda, but the newcomer was going to be tricky, and the dragon would have been next to impossible. Fortunately for me, you two turned on each other. He snuffed out the candle a moment before our latest ally first claimed that nothing escapes her notice. When she grabbed your wrist, Lain made his escape. I suppose what she says is true. Emotion does blind you," Desmeres said, pulling open a sack hanging beside him and retrieving a heavily-smoked piece of meat.

"The hatch never opened. I would have seen it," Myranda said.

"That may well be so--but, then, Myn isn't clawing at the hatch, is she," Desmeres pointed out.

Myranda lit the candle again with a swift spell and investigated the wall. Before long, she found where a secret handle was recessed. When she reached for it, Desmeres stopped her.

"I wouldn't. Not yet. You see, in case you haven't noticed, we make it a habit to trap all entrances and exits," he warned, chewing the leathery meal.

She turned impatiently to him.

"Here is what is going to happen," he began. "You and the shapeshifter are going to go off and attempt to find Lain. She may succeed, but you will not."

"I have found him many times before," Myranda said.

"You may find this difficult to believe, but until now, if you have found him, it is because he wanted you to. Because of the uniqueness of the situation, Lain was able to use himself as the bait to his own trap. Think about it. How have you found him before? The tooth? As you may have noticed--or, more disturbingly, as you may *not* have noticed--that little keepsake went missing from your bag at about the same time as the book you borrowed. Lain wanted you to keep it as a memento, but such an item is a shade too dangerous to us to remain in general circulation.

"All you have left is Myn. I'll admit, she would be a great help, but Lain above any other is savvy at disguising his scent. So you will leave and you will search, and when you realize the futility, you will try to find me. You will fail there as well. Finally, you may choose to search for the shapeshifter. I doubt you will be met with any more success there, either. And so your days will be spent in fruitless wandering, much as they had before, until you abandon this quest you have imagined for yourself.

"I don't say this to dishearten you or to dissuade you. I say it because you are a woman of great potential and the world deserves better than to have such a life squandered," he said.

"The world deserves a future, and if Lain cannot be turned to his task it will not have one," Myranda raged.

The shapeshifter allowed a hint of a grin show itself.

"Why aren't you furious?" Myranda demanded.

"Lain has illustrated that he is not so deeply altered by his time among you as I had first supposed. He has abandoned both of you. To locate him shall be a simple task, and without mortals to slow us, we shall strike down this threat at its roots soon enough," she said.

"You know I am half elf, and thus only semi-mortal," Desmeres reminded her, more in an attempt to irritate her than anything else.

The shapeshifter moved dutifully toward the small panel that acted as a door for the hidden exit and forced Myn aside. Desmeres quickly motioned for Myranda to restrain the dragon. She just managed to do so before the door was forced open, prompting the same burst of hisses that had accompanied the opening of the surface hatch. The arm that had pushed the panel was now perforated with more than a dozen tiny needles. The shapeshifter slowly withdrew and analyzed the arm.

"Pathetic," she declared as she shifted swiftly to wind, scattering the needles dangerously in all directions.

As Myranda dove for cover, the shapeshifter swirled through the hatch and after Lain. Myranda quickly climbed to her feet to follow.

"Wait," Desmeres requested.

"You have stalled me long enough," she said.

The dragon vanished into the narrow tunnel beyond the hidden hatch. Myranda started to sidle along after her.

"You are right. I *have* stalled you long enough. By now, even if you knew precisely where Lain went, which you don't, and even if he were standing still, which he isn't, you would either have to sprout wings or have a *very* fast horse to even hope to reach him inside of a few hours. A few minutes now will make no difference at all. However, if you will listen to what I have to say, a few minutes may well make all of the difference," he said.

"Go, Myn. Make a trail I can follow," Myranda said.

She scarcely had to finish her sentence before the little dragon was out of sight. Myranda squeezed back out of the opening.

"Say your piece," she said.

"First, I would like to give you one last chance to make the correct decision," he said.

"And what might that be?" she asked sternly.

"Join us," he said.

Myranda turned to leave again.

"It is the only sure way to see Lain again," he said.

"I notice you didn't court the Chosen One for such a position," Myranda said.

"I had thought of it, but she is even more single-minded than you--not to mention that, despite being uniquely suited to stealth, she can hardly list subtlety among her many virtues. No, you are a far better choice. You have already revealed yourself to be an able negotiator, and you are quite capable of playing a role when properly instructed. Our clientele would be far more willing to confide in a woman. There are countless reasons. For you, there is the possibility for security, contact with Lain--and, not that you care, enormous profit," he said.

"I will not help you kill people," she said.

"If you must simplify it so, then why not view your own cause from the same point of view? What do you suppose Lain will have to do if you finally convince him to end the war? A great many very important people will have to die to cripple either army. Unless you suppose that Lain will turn to diplomacy. And no level of care taken will prevent the chaos of the war's end from claiming at least a few innocent lives," he said.

"If we can find the others . . ." she began.

"Yes, yes. The other Chosen will find a way, despite the fact that at least one is certainly dead, and two more are affirmed to be likewise by the only being likely to know. I think you know better than to rely upon miracles to do what must be done. Regardless, I have your answer. Let me just offer you a bit of advice. You see, as the Alliance Army never paid for you, and likely never will, it suits our purposes that you never find your way into their clutches. As such, I urge you to seek the Undermine. Their resources should be enough to keep you from the light of day long enough for Epidimé to find a new pet target. The other generals stopped caring about you shortly after you were captured," he said. "Now go, follow. Take some supplies and good luck to you."

Myranda fetched her bag and supplemented its contents with some provisions. She also selected a heavy white cloak that hung on one wall. It was likely one of Lain's, as it dragged the ground when it hung about her shoulders. With the far warmer garment in place and staff in hand, she set off into the passage. It was a tight fit. The tunnel was clearly a natural one, irregular in shape and claustrophobic. The barely adequate light from the storeroom lapsed quickly into complete darkness. She conjured a light in her staff and pressed on.

Myn must have been far ahead. Not even the sound of her scratching claws could be heard. There was only one path, and it became mercifully wider, only to have the ceiling steadily lower until she had to crawl to continue. This was not like the cave. At least there the walls, floor, and ceiling had been solid. Here, great clumps of soil brushed loose with her every move, at times making her feel as though the whole of the tunnel would drop down upon her.

Two long hours of painfully slow travel finally brought the night sky over her head again. She doused the light to a mere ember and held it low, so as to avoid notice. The claw marks Myn left in the snow were easy enough to follow.

As she traveled, she thought.

She thought about how quickly Lain had run the day before. He had wanted the others to follow then, and still he kept a pace that could match a horse. She then thought of the speed he had shown when he faced that woman in the field after Myranda had escaped. How long could he manage speed like that? As she thought, a growing feeling of hopelessness hung numbly in the back of her mind. Tears welled in her eyes and the cold air stung where they ran down her cheeks.

Deep inside, she wanted to stop. She wanted to turn around, find Desmeres, and accept his offer. She would be safe. Comfortable. Happy. She shook the thoughts away. There was a job to do. She wasn't doing it for herself. This was for everyone else, all of those who had lost their homes, their brothers, their sons . . . their fathers.

Myranda doubled her speed. The cold air stung her lungs with each huffing breath. Forward, find him. Find the others. End this. Her mind and body were turned so mechanically to the task that she didn't even notice as the sky grew rosy with the rising sun. She marched heedlessly across roads and through fields. In the distance, a town grew near. Before long, it was quite near enough for the residents to see the bizarre sight of a young woman in an ill-fitting cloak encrusted with dirt marching, eyes earthward, through a snowy field. A memorable sight. A suspicious sight.

Perhaps by luck, perhaps by fate, she escaped the notice of the townsfolk. Carried by legs that burned with fatigue, she finally reached the creature that had led her.

Myn was sniffing and licking at the ground, confusion and desperation on her face. Myranda could tell that she had lost the scent. Through some trick, Lain had managed to wipe this last trace of his trail away. Myranda scanned the ground in the light of the morning sun as it filtered weakly through the heavy clouds. Downy white snow crusted with a layer of glassy ice, smooth and pristine, stretched out in all directions. Somehow there was not a single footprint to disturb it. Myranda's fists tightened. Her teeth clenched. Myn looked pleadingly to her.

"It is all right, Myn. You've done well. Now I must try," she said.

Slowly, she lowered herself to the ground. Her legs protested, but she paid them no mind. Myn eagerly nestled herself in the warmth of Myranda's cloak as the young wizard pulled her mind together for a spell. It was one of the first she had learned in Entwell. She shut her eyes tight, casting her mind out and searching the essence of her surroundings. She had detected him like this when she was in the Belly of the Beast. She knew what to look for. Slowly, her mind spread outward. The spirits of every person, every animal, every living thing around her gradually emerged from the darkness in her mind. She was first struck by how different those spirits seemed here than in Entwell. The flickering essences she felt here were to those of the hidden village as a candle is to the sun. The people of the world were weak, defeated. Their spirits were drained.

Next she became aware of something she had never felt before. Scattered among the mild essences of the people of her world were presences that seemed wholly opposite. Whereas the other spirits seemed to radiate, albeit weakly, these others seemed like voids, drawing in the light and strength around them. The more her mind cast outward, the more she became aware of these blemishes on the landscape. They could only be the D'karon.

She focused further. Somewhere far away, she saw a mass of bright, powerful souls. She looked to them. They clashed with similarly brilliant spirits, spirits that seemed no different. These were the men at the front line. The only spirited, truly alive members of her nation and they were one by one fading away, struck down. Elsewhere, a cluster of the black spirits clashed with the light, nearmen clashing with men. She wondered if the Tresson soldiers knew that the men they battled were not men at all. Did they, too, vanish when struck down? She looked elsewhere.

Suddenly she found something. There was an essence. It had the same intense quality to it as Lain's, but this was different than before. It was a measure stronger than the other spirits she had seen, stronger even than her own, and yet it seemed stunted, weakened greatly from what it could be. It was to the northeast, among the mountains on the coast. She focused more intently. She could almost feel its precise location.

Suddenly there was a wave of something, something unbelievably powerful. It came from the northwest. The intensity of it blotted out all else. It continued, growing more and more powerful until Myranda had to pull herself from her meditation or be overcome by it. There was no doubt in her mind what it was. Even her unfocused mind was vaguely aware of the pulsing, surging force. The shapeshifter. Only she was capable of a force of such intensity and purity. And where she could be found, so too would be Lain, surely.

She turned her eyes to the northwest. Even at this distance, violent winds could be seen shaking snow from trees. Then she turned to the northeast. Something was there. Something that may be very important.

"This way, Myn. We may not be able catch Lain by ourselves, but we may still prove Desmeres wrong," she said.

Myn cast a second glance, understanding and not pleased at the fact they would not be seeking Lain. Always faithful, though, the dragon stood, ready to move. Myranda looked at the sky. The clouds had the glow that seasoned northerners knew as midday. She hadn't slept or eaten yet. She should seek some kind of shelter and rest. With the aid of Myn and her staff, she struggled to her feet. Her mind lingered on the essence she felt. Rest could wait. She could eat as she walked. She would find whatever it was she had felt or die in the process.

As she plodded off, pushing aside weariness and hunger, she was unaware of the minds that followed her.

#

In a dark hut, surrounded by books, Deacon strained his eyes at the last flickering images of Myranda. The minutes that had just passed had brought with them something he had been hoping for since she had gone. Every day had been spent searching for her mind. The best of days offered a glimpse of her as she pushed herself to the limit to cast a spell.

Today was different. Today, she, too, had searched.

She was not aware of it, but in those minutes when she'd cast her mind far and wide, her thoughts and his had met. He'd seen her, clear as crystal. He'd heard her. What she said, what she thought, what she felt. He knew where she was going, what she was trying to do, and what had happened.

As the moment passed and the connection was broken, he turned back to his tomes. The words were burned into his head. *The path is changing. Go where it leads.* He searched feverishly for the pieces he would need. No spell existed that would meet his needs. Not yet. He worked now with a renewed intensity, for just as he knew what she knew, he had learned something that she did not.

#

Elsewhere, a darker mind was similarly intrigued by the girl's foolish decision to cast her mind so visibly about. Epidime took care to conceal himself as he felt her mind shift to and fro. He had been busied by other things, but the girl who had managed to resist him was never far from his mind.

He was a skilled observer of spirits and souls. When the time came, it would not take long for him to find her unless she learned to hide herself as he had, but her spiritual equivalent of an alarm bell chiming had quickly drawn his attention. Had the newly-arisen shapeshifter not suddenly presented herself as a far more enticing target, he may well have intercepted the girl and finished what he had started, but for now that could wait. Conquering the girl would be satisfying, but his purpose above all others was to learn, and the shapeshifter offered a peerless opportunity for that. He had already learned that the one called Lain had joined forces with it, or at least fought beside it more than once.

The pair was formidable. It was best, then, to make use of someone disposable and observe as he had before. When he had learned the latest target's allegiances, strengths, and weaknesses, he would return for Myranda. She would be simple to find. After all, he knew where she was going.

#

Far away, Lain sprinted due east. Desmeres had done his job admirably. The others had been delayed, and he had managed to put a considerable amount of distance behind him in that time. He knew better than to believe that he could easily put the shapeshifter off of his trail, but he had been pursued by mystics before. Though they used different senses, they followed the same rules. There were ways to obscure these senses just as any other. His task was complicated by the fact that she was undetectable to him, however.

When the being turned to wind or fire or any other elemental form, her scent was absent--or, at least, indistinct. Worse still, when she did have a scent, he could not be certain what it was. These concerns were now the last in his mind, though. The being had grown close. Very close. She might be by his side at this moment if not for the arena that lie between them. He knew the place well. It was stocked with all manner of vicious beasts, and of late had been used to punish those the Alliance Army wished to make an example of.

Long ago, the D'karon had turned their dark wizards to the task of creating ever more formidable beasts to fill the cages and face the condemned. Now the creatures that the combatants faced were twisted, crude, hideous parodies of nature, the results of those dark pursuits. The windy, swirling form of the shapeshifter had only just become visible to Lain on the edge of the horizon when the arena passed below her. Suddenly, she turned the totality of her considerable might to the task of eliminating these creatures, drawing the attention of the full complement of guards in the process.

The maelstrom she brought about had every bit the intensity of the one a few days earlier in the field outside the fort, and would no doubt result in the same rush of soldiers to investigate. He had to make it out of the area before that happened.

#

For a moment, the mighty being surveyed her work. The ground around her was littered with the broken remains of black-blooded abominations. They varied in shape and size greatly, but some things were common to all. There was a roughness to them, a tainted simplicity. They were creations, attempts at duplicating nature. While they failed on most levels, she did briefly admire the almost mechanical efficiency that some displayed.

She analyzed the primitive "blood" that stained her now-stone hands. Briefly she considered shifting to the form of one of the smaller beasts. She had squandered much of her remaining strength in striking these D'karon creations down. Spending some time in a simpler form would aid her recovery.

Her reflection on the subject was cut short by the arrival of a mass of armor-clad soldiers. She swept her gaze across the ranks. Humans. They were doing the work of the D'karon. She would be justified in bringing them to the same fate as the beasts. Indeed, destroying the whole of the structure was quite within her right--but she decided against it. For now, she would save her strength for travel. Her stone form gave way to wind, and she set quickly off in the direction Lain had been heading.

As she took to the sky, she marveled at her fellow warrior's uncanny ability to obscure his uniquely powerful spirit. There were beings half of a world away that she sensed more clearly than the divinely anointed creature she pursued. Even that infuriating human he seemed to show undue favor to was simpler to locate. It was, of course, a testament to his worth as a warrior.

Perhaps, just as she watched over him until she was certain he was worthy of his place, so too was he testing her. Yes, that was most definitely the case. Once she located him, he would be satisfied and together they would wipe the scourge of D'karon from her land.

#

The shapeshifter continued her search, but she had underestimated Lain's skill. In more than ten days of scouring the countryside, not once did she turn up the malthrope.

All the while, Myranda trudged toward her own goal. She had no horse, and no way to get one, but it didn't matter. Over low mountains, icy fields, and through thick forests, the human marched. She slept only when she had to and ate while on the move. Myn faithfully by her side, the girl pushed herself toward an indistinct point in the mountains to the east. She didn't know what she would find there, but she didn't care. With each step, she grew more determined and more convinced that ahead lie something, anything that could help her. That was all that mattered.

She now stood a short distance from the last town she would find before the mountains began in earnest. In truth, the path was already steep and rocky, but beyond here she would have to climb. Until this point, Myranda had avoided the towns. Indeed, Grossmer's mining village had been the last semblance of a town that she had set foot in.

She thought long and hard. Hunting had been difficult for Myn, and the bag she held had been stripped of provisions days ago. The mountains were nearly bare. Myn would be hard-pressed to turn up enough food for one, let alone two, among the rocky cliffs that stood intimidatingly between herself and the target she sought. She would need to enter the town.

The risk that she would be recognized was small. After all, only the Elites and Epidime knew what she looked like, and Epidime alone seemed to still be interested in her capture. Of course, there were still concerns.

Myranda looked down at Myn, who gazed pleasantly back. As well-behaved as the little dragon was, she would not be able to join Myranda in the town. It was a shame. The thought of a bed had appealed to her, but she would rather spend the night by Myn's side than in comfort. Not that it mattered. Regardless of what she needed, she hadn't a single coin to buy it with. She patted the little creature beside her on the neck.

"Well, another night out in the cold for the two of us . . ." Myranda began, before something she felt stopped her.

There was a dip in the scales of her neck, the place where the nearman had grabbed her. Her thoughts drifted back to Desmeres gathering up her discarded skin. He claimed it was valuable. She rummaged through her bag and found the trio of smooth red scales. As her stomach growled and she stared with concern at the rocky mountainside she would have to climb, she made her decision.

"Myn, meet me on the other side of the town. I will be there soon," Myranda said.

The little dragon quickly took to the air. Myranda had nearly forgotten the creature could fly. She shook her head as it flitted directly over the town. She should have told her not to be seen, but it was too late now.

Myranda headed into the town, unsure of how much success she would have there. A frosted-over sign proclaimed this place to be Verneste. When she entered, she realized that, for a town, it was rather small. The streets were utterly deserted, the people indoors, away from the harsh and constant winds. No one had seen Myn fly by, at least.

Squinting against the biting wind, Myranda attempted to determine what type of markets were lining the one and only street in town. Not until she scraped the icy snow from the fourth sign she encountered did she find something that might help her. In faded blue on ancient gray wood was painted a set of scales--an assayer or appraiser. They were common in places such as this. Miners were certainly the only regular visitors to this place, and the services of an assayer would be essential to determining the worth of their mine. At the very least, she could find the value of what she had to bargain with.

The heavy door swung closed behind her and, for the first time in too long, she enjoyed the heat of a fire and shelter from the wind. As she warmed herself by the low flames in the fireplace, she slowly took in her surroundings. There were scales of various sizes, ranging from a small one on a desk at the far side of the room to one large enough to weigh bags of grain. Cases with jars and pouches containing samples of various substances lined two walls, while a third case sloppily held an incomplete set of reference texts. There was no purveyor in sight, though beside the scale on the desk was a large chime with a small hammer tied to its base.

When Myranda had warmed enough that she had stopped shivering uncontrollably, she gave the chime a ring.

After a third ring, heavy footsteps could be heard above, and soon a door was pushed open by a weary-looking older gentleman. He wore furs that had yet to see a tailor, still in the shape they had been in when they left the skinner. His face was unshaven and weathered-looking, with wiry gray hairs scattered among the black. Plodding over to the desk with a pronounced limp, he slapped both hands down, cleared his throat loudly, and looked her in the eye.

"What have you got?" he asked.

Myranda dropped the three dragon scales on the counter. He glanced them over.

"Dragon scales. Haven't seen many of these in a while," he remarked, picking one up. "The dragon these came from was young, eh? Baby scales are hard to come by. Usually the hand that drops them on the table is missing a few fingers."

He smelled them.

"Fresh," he remarked.

He scraped at one with a fingernail. Satisfied at whatever it was he was trying to determine, he placed them on one end of the balance, placing small pieces of brass on the opposite side until he was satisfied there as well. After thumbing through the appropriate book, he scratched a few figures a scrap of paper with a quill.

"An alchemist would give you forty silver for the lot. Good luck finding one. I will take them for fifteen, if you can afford the loss," he said.

"That will be fine," Myranda said. Deep in her mind, her uncle's voice scolded her for failing to bargain, but she knew it was better to take what she could than risk lingering long enough for someone to become curious about how she'd managed to secure fresh dragon scales.

"I thought you might feel that way," he said with a grin that showed teeth at least as poorly-kept as the rest of him.

As she picked the coins off of the table, she noticed a rather official document among the scattered papers there. It bore the seal reserved for statements from the king himself, and judging from the state of wear the other papers showed, it was quite new.

"What is that?" she asked.

"Eh? Oh. I was supposed to hang that outside, but I thought the king would be better served by a message that would last longer than the next stiff breeze," he said, handing the paper to her.

It was indeed an official announcement. As she deciphered the excessively elaborate wording of the document, a slow realization dawned on her. The words proclaimed that, due to recent escalations on the battlefield, all large labor facilities would be hereby transferred in their entirety to emissaries of the throne to be owned and operated by the Alliance Army in order to assure strong and reliable supply lines. The owners, it claimed, would be rewarded handsomely with both gold and exemption from military service. Not only that, but recently dissolved mines, plantations, and similar places would be re-formed and re-staffed to bolster supplies. It went on to list the harsh and numerous consequences that would result from the attempted sale to those unaffiliated with the Alliance Army.

It was madness to suppose that such actions were called for, or even worth consideration. The one thing that the army had in spades was military supplies. Virtually all of the iron in the world was pulled from northern mountains like this one. The one thing that was in truly short supply was leadership, and the administration of dozens of enormous enterprises would take all that the Army could spare and more. At first glance, there seemed no justification, but Myranda quickly realized one.

Epidime had scoured her mind, and though he didn't manage to break her, he did claim that he had learned all that he needed. He must have learned what Lain's motivations were, that he spent every copper he earned to free those who were forced to work in the very places that were now forbidden to change hands. This was a blatant, heavy-handed, desperate attempt to smoke Lain out . . . and it bore the official seal of the king.

It was still not clear why the army was so interested in the Chosen. There was still the possibility that the military wanted their help, but from what she'd seen of those in command, the motives were likely far more sinister. The fact that a dispatch from the king himself was serving their interests chilled Myranda, as it meant that even he was not beyond their influence. Or, worse, that he endorsed their methods.

She pocketed the coins, replaced the page, and tried her best to force the maddening thoughts from her head. With the transaction complete and silver jingling in her pocket, Myranda reluctantly returned to the frigid street. There was a surprisingly well-stocked general market that replaced her ragged boots and provided her with a few days' rations of salted meat. The addition of a canteen, a pair of gloves, a blanket, and a more appropriate bag left her with five silver left. There was no reason to save any, so she fetched a few things that she didn't so much need as desire. A small knife with a sheath was a shade more useful than the dagger Deacon had given her--which, until now, had managed to do little more than perforate the bag. That, too, was fitted with a sheath that best fit it.

She dropped the last of the money into the keeper's hand in exchange for a small bag of potatoes. Myn would be pleased. It had been a peculiar discovery back in Entwell that the little creature positively adored potatoes, and was even willing to tolerate visits from Deacon in exchange for one or two.

The dragon was fairly prancing with delight as Myranda tossed her one of the treasured treats. The new boots made the difficult task of scaling the icy slopes a fair amount easier, and the pack that hung on her shoulder freed her hands for the task as well. With the aid of her staff, she and the dragon were covering twice the ground that they had before. Periodically, Myranda would stop to determine where the thing she sought could be found. It was drawing nearer.

When the wind stopped whipping long enough for the blown snow to settle, a pass between two peaks could be seen ahead. She felt certain that what she was looking for, whatever it was, was on the other side. If the weather calmed at all, she just might make it through within the day.

Alas, weather is seldom obliging. The winds grew steadily as the hours passed, and though it was difficult to differentiate fresh snow from blowing snow, by the time the light began to fail, Myranda knew that she was in the midst of a steadily growing snowstorm. The nearest thing to shelter was a claustrophobic alcove beneath an over-crop that would at least keep the snow from their heads. There was nothing to burn for a fire, so once again body heat would have to suffice.

They slept huddled together, Myranda's cloak and blanket wrapped around them both. Myn's snout was the only thing exposed, thanks to the oversized garment. She could have pulled it inside, but her reason for leaving it out became clear when she huffed out the first of several bursts of flame over the course of the night. The heat that surged through her body afterward lingered in the warm folds of the cloak, likely the only thing that made the night survivable.

#

Elsewhere, the shapeshifter dropped down to the ground and slowly shifted to her human form. Spending time in the form of wind was taxing, and she felt as though if she maintained the form for much longer she would be spent. Lain was near, she was certain of that. He had slipped into one of the human settlements, so it was just as well that she entered as one of them. She scanned around her.

In this form, her senses were as frustratingly limited as any other human's. Virtually no light was to be had, save the weak glow from windows, rendering the only moderately effective means of observing the world that humans had at their disposal, vision, even less adequate than usual. Wind whistled away her hearing, and all touch told her was how laughably fragile these things were. They were actually endangered by the cold. She shook her head, rid herself of the annoying sense, and began to alter one of the other senses into something that could reveal Lain to her. Unfortunately, without some sample of a creature to work off of, she was having limited success.

Her mind, though, remained sharp, so long as she maintained a form that wasn't much more complex than the one she now occupied. She quieted her thoughts and felt for the essence that had allowed her to follow Lain this far. She felt him tantalizingly nearby, but something still closer drew her attention.

It was a spirit--black, twisted, and parasitic. It was one of them, a D'karon, trying valiantly to escape notice. It failed. She turned her eyes to the source of the corrosive essence. Surrounded by four of the empty cloak creations was a scrawny, mild-looking human male with an out of place look of intelligence and confidence on his face. In his hand was a halberd identical to the one wielded by the remarkably powerful wizard she had faced when she first revealed herself. He smiled at her. As she surveyed her opponent, he surveyed her. She would have little trouble with this one. There was barely a trace of the energy that was present in the last halberd-bearer.

"Attention, people of the fair city of Fleer. I represent the great General Epidime. What is to transpire is of interest only to the Alliance Army. Enter your homes and remain there until morning. Any individual who disobeys will be guilty of treason!" the young man announced.

At the sound of the last word, the handful of residents who remained on the streets scurried quickly inside. When all doors were shut, the man spoke again.

"I do so hate prying eyes while I work, and this promises to be a delightfully informative experience. That body you are using is quite familiar. I do believe those fingers clutched this staff quite recently. I must be sure to inform our men that she is no longer to be obeyed," he said.

"You will not live to speak those words," she said, shifting to her stone form.

"I am confident the message will be delivered. I see you have chosen the stone form rather than fire. Surely this has something to do with the staggering decrease in your strength since the last time you clashed with this weapon. Tell me, are you tired?" he asked.

She flashed into motion. With improbable reflexes, the weapon was raised to block, and with equally unlikely strength, the blow was deflected.

"Oh, yes, you are *quite* tired," he said.

The cloaks floated backward into the shadows as the shapeshifter unleashed a barrage of increasingly powerful blows. Each was blocked, though the last brought what was certainly the crackle of bone from the man's right wrist. The man dropped the hand to his side and spun the halberd to speed with only the left. The shapeshifter raised her hand, meeting the blade with her palm. With an ear-splitting clang, the metal came to a stop. Her other hand gripped the shaft and tore it easily from the fingers of the man.

As soon as the metal left his skin, the look of confidence and intellect was replaced with one of horror and pain. He cried out and cradled the shattered right hand.

"What . . . a-a-ah! What is this? What are you? What is going on?" cried the man in a meek, almost whiny shell of his former voice.

"You allowed yourself to be subverted by a D'karon. You are tainted. You must be punished," the shapeshifter hissed, throwing down the weapon and delivering a bone-shattering backhand to the sniveling thing in front of her.

The man dropped lifelessly to the ground, his head turned sickeningly to the side. She turned to walk away, but stopped, her eyes drifting down to the halberd. The gem in the blade was still glowing faintly. She lifted her foot to grind it into the ground, but before she could bring her heel down, the weapon slid swiftly toward its former wielder. The right hand of the beaten man raised. The fingers crackled open and clutched the shaft of the weapon. The scrawny man lurched to his feet in a single motion, as though an outside force had drawn him up by the shoulders.

The shapeshifter turned to the risen warrior. He twisted his head back into place and smiled.

"Humans have the inexcusable habit of deserting their vessel far before it has lost its usefulness. I am wiser than that. You, too, show wisdom. You were not afraid to do what had to be done. That is an admirable trait. A lesser warrior would have pitied the usurped victim," he said.

"Weakness in the face of the enemy must not be tolerated," she said, approaching him again.

"I agree. You and I see eye to eye on a number of important issues. Have you considered switching allegiances?" he asked.

She began to swipe at him in vicious attacks with her stone claws. He deftly deflected each, backing away as he did. The strikes were clashing so powerfully that the stone of her hands was beginning to fracture and break away. Finally, the entirety of her left hand crumbled and she retreated to regroup. Her opponent did not relent. Swinging the long weapon and gaining momentum as he did, the man struck again and again with the blade of the halberd. Cracks began to widen on the shapeshifter's form.

Finally, the man thrust the spiked tip of the weapon into her chest. The force easily split the stone and buried the blade, complete with the crystal it bore, halfway into the Chosen One's body. A pulse from the crystal shattered the weakened creature, and she was reduced to a pile of rubble on the ground.

"I wonder . . . can it be so easy? Somehow I doubt it," the arrogant man considered aloud.

One by one, the pieces of the shifter darkened to black and ignited. Before long, hundreds of fist-sized flames had flickered to life. The fire rose into the air, swirling and reforming until the fiery form floated above her opponent, brilliant eyes blazing with fury. The crystal at the end of the staff took on a brilliant glow. As the Chosen swept in for attack after attack, the gem was swung with precision. Some manner of magic struck the insubstantial, flickering form as though it were solid.

Finally, the shifter hung momentarily still in the air before dividing into a half-dozen intense balls of flame and surrounding the enemy.

"Well, now, aren't we clever," the man admitted.

The fireballs closed in for attack, but an instant before the first made contact, he drove his halberd into the ground and summoned a mystic shield. The fire clashed again and again with the shield--to no avail. This was more power than he should have had. He, too, had been concealing his true strength. Finally they withdrew, merging again. For a moment, she floated, considering her options. Slowly, she noticed a draw on her already waning strength. She turned to see that, behind her, the four cloaks had manifested charcoal-black hands and were drawing off flame in long filaments, attracting it like iron filings to a magnet. Each of the four leeched away strength and gathered it into growing fireballs of their own.

The shapeshifter tore through the air after them. Just the slightest touch would ignite them. Had she more strength, she would be launching long tongues of flame after them, but she had barely enough to maintain her form. After dispatching only one of the cloth abominations, she knew that she couldn't afford to squander any more strength in her fire form. She dropped back to the ground and shifted to stone once more.

"Stone again? Show me something new!" her opponent mockingly demanded.

The three remaining cloaks now let their stolen fire fly. The first splashed across her stone form. Swiftly, she shifted to flame again, reclaiming the remaining two before returning to stone. The cloaks closed in, striking their phantom limbs against her rocky body. She dropped to one knee as lines were scored into her by the unnatural substance that composed the claws. In a burst of motion, she lashed out, managing to grasp two of them and tear them to ribbons amid unholy, disembodied screeches. The third pulled to a safe distance.

The shifter raised her steely gaze and locked eyes with her opponent, still protected by his shield.

"It is just as well you refuse to join our ranks. You would hardly be of any use to us," he taunted.

The stone eyes narrowed in anger. She thrust her hands into the icy, cobbled street. A rumble began to shake the town. Suddenly, the ground beneath the man erupted with a spire of stone. He was sent hurtling into the air. Quickly, she took to the air after him in the form of wind. With a mighty effort, she managed to separate him from his weapon and hurl it into the distance. She then forced him, with all of the speed she could muster, to the ground far below. She lingered for a few moments until she was satisfied that this time the broken man would not arise.

She then cast her eyes to the east. She had nothing left. She would be helpless in very short order. With no options left, she streaked through the sky. There was no time to find Lain. Until she could recover, she would have to make do with someone else.

#

Sleep had been fitful, made possible only due to sheer exhaustion. Now it was impossible. Something, something incredibly powerful, had shaken the mountain during the night. The sound, like a crack of thunder, pulled her from sleep. A series of low rumbles continued to reverberate throughout the mountainside and valley. Each grumbling roar grew nearer. This sound chilled Myranda more than the call of any beast. It was the sound of an avalanche, the mountain shrugging off its blanket of snow and ice. If the rumble reached her, she would be buried without hope of escape. She slid out into the open and strained her eyes as white snow gave way to black night without so much as a glimmer of anything else. The only thing that penetrated the whistling wall of white and black was the thunderous roar. It was close enough to make the ground tremble. Tiny cascades of powdery snow began to form. There was no sense running. All she could do was hope.

Gradually, the roar subsided, moving down the mountainside. Myranda took a deep, relieved breath of the icy air.

Her ears, so recently turned to the terrifying rumble, now turned to something else. The wind seemed different. For most of the night, it had been waxing and waning, but it had always surrounded her. Now the shriek of high wind seemed to be overwhelmingly from the west. She turned to the darkness, raising her staff and conjuring a light in the gem. It barely cut an arm's length further into the dense night.

Suddenly, a chaotic, swirling form burst from the darkness, knocking Myranda to the ground. It was the shapeshifter, but something was wrong. She seemed looser, less defined. The slivers of light that served as eyes had a look of desperation. Fear. The windy form dropped to the ground, the whirling wind tightening as it did when she changed form, but just as quickly it loosened again.

"I do not have enough . . . I need something simple. Something small!" she cried.

Her eyes shot to Myranda's hands. She grasped them, pulling free one of her gloves. There was another burst of wind as the bulk of her form whisked away. What remained dropped to the ground, tightening and intensifying. Snow swirled into the mix. After a few moments, the snow settled, revealing a curious sight. Beside the glove was a squirrel, presumably a duplicate of the one that gave its fur to line the gloves. The tiny creature looked up with as much dignity as such a small face could muster, and spoke.

"Congratulations, human. I have deemed you worthy to be assigned a purpose," she said. She spoke with the same clear, powerful voice that she always did. The sound could not have been more out of place.

"What are you doing here? What happened? MYN, NO!" she cried.

Her companion was moments from snapping up the little creature. She froze when Myranda spoke up. The newest form of the shapeshifter turned slowly to the dragon, mouth still agape. She looked fearlessly into the cavernous maw.

"I would prefer that you dispose of the beast, but in the current state of things, it may be of some use. Keep it in line and it may live," she said.

"What happened?" she asked the creature, stooping to pick it up.

"That is none of your concern. Suffice it to say that even *my* strength is not boundless. The greater portion of it has been stripped away by a number of confrontations and I shall require an amount of time to recover. Until that time, you shall escort me, giving your life, if you must, to keep me from harm," she said.

"I will do my best," she said, extending her hand.

Rather than allow herself to be picked up, the proud creature leapt to her arm and scurried to her shoulder.

"Your best is certain to be woefully inadequate. That is why you shall take me to Lain. He, and only he, is capable of providing protection, should it be truly required," she explained.

"You couldn't find Lain?" Myranda said.

"More pressing matters arose. Enough questions. You will find him. Forgo sleep, forgo meals. Until I am delivered to Lain, you shall not allow the pathetic weaknesses that plague your race to delay us. Is that understood?" the creature asked.

"I can't find Lain. I have something more important to find," she said.

"Human, you have been given your orders. Follow them," the creature said.

"I may have found another Chosen. Lain can take care of himself, and I can protect you. This needs to be done," she said.

"You will find nothing of use," the shifter said.

"You will never find anything if you don't look," she said. "And I intend to. If you do not wish to go with me, then you are welcome to continue your search for Lain alone."

The tiny creature on her shoulder gave a frustrated sigh.

"It was an act of the purest optimism to imagine that I might have coaxed a small-minded mortal into acting in a rational and intelligent manner. No matter. I will recover just as quickly on an ill-advised, dead-end trek as on an intelligent one," she proclaimed. "Pursue your foolishness. In a day or two, when I am myself again, I shall leave you to your pointless errands."

With that, the creature moved to the interior of Myranda's hood, curling about the back of her neck for maximum warmth, with her head facing casually forward.

"Proceed," she ordered.

Myranda had not intended to continue until morning, but now she couldn't bear to wait a moment longer. She was sure that she would find another Chosen, and now the infuriating shapeshifter would be present to see it. She marched forward in angry silence, Myn dutifully in tow. The wind and cold were especially biting at night, and with nothing but the light from her staff, the progress was slow. It became slower still when she reached the near edge of the stretch of mountain ravaged by avalanche. The ground was uneven and broken, great pieces of rock-hard snow jutting at odd angles, as though the surface of the mountain had been shattered.

After a few hours, the lack of sleep and general exhaustion began to take its toll, and Myranda was having trouble keeping her mind sharp. In the past, she would have begun talking aloud to herself or Myn. Now she had a companion, albeit a bothersome one, who might offer a reply. She should have known better. She should have known that any conversation with the shapeshifter would end just as the last had--with angry silence--but the desire to hear something other than the relentless wind clouded her judgment.

"Do you have a name?" she asked.

"I do not need a name. Names are reserved for the faceless masses, like yourself, who are not unique enough to be differentiated by merit alone," she answered.

For a moment, Myranda marveled at the creature's ability to concentrate so much condescension into so few words.

"If you haven't got a name, then how would you prefer that I refer to you?" Myranda asked through clenched teeth.

"I would prefer that you did not refer to me at all," came her predictable reply.

"Well, I must refer to you occasionally. Why don't I give you a name?" she asked.

"Because names are labels, and labels are intended to describe. I do not maintain a single form long enough for any name to remain appropriate for long. Perfection is the only term that can consistently be applied to me, and even that falls short, as perfection is static and I am ever-changing," she said.

"Call it a limitation if you must, but I have difficulty conversing with a being without a name. Will you at least allow me to choose a name that I shall call you?" she asked.

"It is clear that you will not rest until I have allowed you to demean me thusly. Since your thoughts and actions do not matter in the slightest, I suppose I will permit you to assign me a title. Anything to aid your addled brain," she relented.

"You are a woman, correct?" Myranda asked.

"I typically assume a female form," she corrected.

"Well, then, I shall call you Samantha," she said.

"Absolutely not," she said.

". . . I thought it didn't matter," Myranda grumbled.

"I will not be associated with so common a name. Choose something more fitting," the shifter replied.

"Then . . . Alexia," Myranda offered, feeling that the attitudes offered by her own alter-ego and the shapeshifter were quite in line.

"No," the shifter said.

". . . Gwendolyn," Myranda attempted.

"No," she replied.

"Well, what do you want?" Myranda asked.

"Something that reflects my nature. I am fluid, I am eternal, I am ethereal . . ." she began.

"Then why don't I call you Ether?" Myranda asked.

"Ether . . . Ether," the creature repeated, as if to test the sound. "Well, it is hardly unique, but it will suffice."

Myranda smiled at the minor victory.

"Tell me, Ether, why did you have to take a simple form to recover? Why didn't you just step into a fire as you did before?" she asked.

"I suppose this was to be expected. I allowed you a single concession, and now you expect me to answer your every question," Ether said.

"You do not have to answer if you do not want to," Myranda said with a sigh.

"No, no. I shall answer. Perhaps if I address your ignorance, you will become a more reasonable creature. It taxes my strength to exist in the form of wind, fire, or water, and though I can exist as stone effortlessly, it requires great effort to move and restores strength slowly. With the whisper of energy that I had left, were I to shift to flame, I would have passed my breaking point and lost my form completely before I could be exposed to a pure enough or strong enough flame to recover. Had I turned to stone, I would have had to remain motionless for many months in order to regain the strength to change back. By taking the form of a small, simple creature, I can regain strength at an acceptable rate while not becoming completely helpless," she said.

"It doesn't require effort to be in the form of a squirrel?" Myranda asked.

"It does, but it requires less than it restores. Anything smaller or less complex than, say, a large horse, will allow me to recover," she said "Anything larger is taxing."

"Do you have to eat or sleep?" she asked.

"Only if I remain as a completely faithful replica of a creature with such impairments for a period long enough to incur such a price. I typically alter a form to remove such weaknesses," she said.

"Do you know what the creature knows?" she asked.

"No. I am privy neither to memories nor instincts of my form," she answered. Her tone indicated that her patience was flagging.

"If you do not have the instincts, how is it that you know how to move and behave in a new form?" Myranda asked.

"In the same way that one who builds a device knows how to operate it. I am exerting my influence over untold millions of component parts, each infinitesimal in size, to allow myself to assume such a form. Determining how the end result should function is comparatively no task at all," she said.

"What would happen if you lost form?" Myranda asked.

"Now I simply will not respond to questions to which you most certainly know the answer. You were present at the very ceremony that revived me from such a state," she snapped. "Honestly. How is it that you have survived so long if you do not even recall what little you have learned?"

"I did not realize that--" Myranda said, attempting to defend herself.

"Enough, focus on walking, lest you forget how to do that as well," Ether ordered.

Any attempts to foster further conversation with the creature were fruitless. Myranda resorted to one-sided conversations with Myn and herself to keep her weariness at bay. The sun was just beginning to rise, shedding some level of natural light on the mountainside.

Myranda, though relieved of the task of providing her own light, immediately wished that the darkness had remained. In the light of morning, it was clear that there was still a long way to go before she reached her goal.

#

Desmeres sat at a poorly-lit table in yet another of the many safe houses and store houses that he and Lain had maintained over the years. He scratched the last stroke of a very official-looking document and rolled the expensive parchment into a scroll. Heating blue sealing wax until it dripped onto the document, he opened a well-locked box and pressed the seal hidden within into the soft wax. When he took it away, what remained was the official seal of the king of the Northern Alliance. For such a seal to be applied by any hand other than His Royal Majesty's was a treasonous act, punishable by public torture and execution.

He laid down the document beside a half-dozen just like it, each identically sealed. As he did, he noticed a similar document had appeared and, though weathered, it also bore the seal of the king. This one, unlike those beside it, was not a forgery. Knowing that it had not been there a moment ago, he knew that only one person could have placed it there.

"How long have you been here, Lain?" he asked.

He stood and turned to find himself face to face with the man he addressed. The assassin did not answer.

"Managed to escape that shapeshifter, I see. Unless, of course, you *are* the shapeshifter . . . no. Somehow I feel that she would not have been able to resist the fanfare of a noisy forced entry," Desmeres considered.

"They are preventing me from performing my task," Lain said, his voice fairly shaking with anger.

"Yes, Lain, that is a fact of which I am keenly aware. I have dispatched messages to a half-dozen prospective sellers. All six returned, accompanied by a message from the king recounting the terms of his new policy. More disturbing than their return was the fact that they were returned to the entrance of the storehouse we had taken Myranda to prior to her capture by Epidime. I paid a man to find a courier to send the messages. Neither I nor he had been anywhere near that place at the time. We did not take the care to keep that girl in the dark, and now *he* knows far too much about us.

"Right now, I am attempting to send messages claiming special exception from the king's ruling. If they meet a similar fate, then I am afraid that we shall have to either move to Tressor and try our luck there or pose as emissaries of the king. That is, unless you can find a new way to spend your gold," Desmeres said. "Which I suggest."

"He is taking back their lives. The people I freed are being taken back," Lain said, his fury dripping from every word.

"Yes. That is regrettable. Nothing can be done, short of bringing the war to an end," he said.

"Then that is what must be done," he said.

"Lain. You and I both know that if such a thing can be done, you are the one to do it. At any other time, I would support you fully. But they are clearly trying to elicit precisely this reaction. The most fundamental lesson learned on the warrior's side of Entwell is to *never* give your enemy what they want from you," Desmeres reprimanded.

Lain pulled open a chest and began equipping himself with the weapons within.

"Lain, think about what you are doing. I am in too deep already. Until you come back to your senses, I am afraid you and I will have to part ways," he said.

"Then our partnership is terminated," he said.

"So be it," he said, turning to dispose of the six acts of treason he had just completed. "I could certainly benefit from a few years free of assassinations and espionage. If you survive, do see me about weapons periodically. Regardless of the state of your mind, your hand remains one of the few worthy to hold my creations."

He turned to find, not to his surprise, that he was alone once more. He shook his head slightly. It is a risk all beings face if they live long enough. The thing that you allow to define you will eventually destroy you. The passion to free those cursed by the life he had been burdened with had kept him focused for all of these years. Now it would kill him.

Someday, Desmeres's own passions might do the same.

The thought made him smile. He wondered what his price would be. What would he be willing to give his life for? He pulled from his pocket the tooth he had taken from Myranda and held it up. The price would have to be very high . . . *Very* high.

#

The walls of the valley funneled the already vicious wind into a frenzy of blown ice and snow. Myranda trudged with eyes shut tight to keep the biting wind out. Ether was curled up in the hood, safe and warm. Myn puffed flame every few moments to ward off the cold. The only thing that kept Myranda's aching muscles in motion was the promise of what lay on the other side of this valley. Just a few more minutes and she would reach it. Just a few more steps and she would be there. Finally, the whistling in her ears died away and the ground sloped downward. Her eyes opened and her heart dropped.

Ahead lay a small, flat-bottomed ice field. In the center was a fort that would have resembled the one that she'd been tortured in had it been complete--but it was not. It was a husk. Walls were crumbled inward like a fallen cake. Huge bricks littered the field around it, some at the bottom of craters. Some disaster had happened here, some earthshaking explosion. This must have been what had caused the avalanches. The tiny head of Ether's current form peeked out into the cold. She didn't say anything. She didn't have to. Her smug sense of satisfaction at the sight seemed to radiate out from her.

As Myranda approached the wrecked structure, her hopes flickered. The lower levels were intact. She managed to find a secure set of stairs and began to weave a route through the rubble. As she did, Myn sniffed curiously, intrigued by some scent within.

Soon Myn was moving so quickly, dashing between cracks and shattered pillars, that Myranda could not keep up. She was making her way further down into the intact floors. With a light conjured in her staff to guide her, the grim consequences of the cataclysm that struck this place became clear. Great mounds of nearman armor lay scattered along the walls. The force that had brought the former owners to an end had been enough to twist and char the thick metal. Here and there, the remains of a human could be seen. There was barely enough left of them to be recognized.

A chill shook Myranda as the increasingly intact floors became all too familiar. The design of this place was precisely the same as the fort of her interrogation. Empty cells lined the walls. Here and there, a chair bore the same restraints that had held her.

Myranda finally reached the lowest level. A large section of the ceiling had been torn free and was lying propped against one wall. Iron bars were embedded in the floor, but they were peeled back like flower petals. Myn sniffed at the edge of the propped-up ceiling. Quietly, Myranda could hear something from the space underneath. Was it . . . weeping?

Ether had heard it, too. She leapt to the ground and began to approach the sound. After a few steps, whatever was making the sound moved suddenly. Myn leapt back. Ether stopped.

"You. See what it is," she ordered.

Myranda crept cautiously to one side of the propped up slab, holding out the staff. The light fell upon a sight she would never have expected. Shivering, hugging her knees, and sobbing was a creature not unlike Lain. She was a malthrope, an adult, but there was something peculiar. She was covered in stark white fur, from the tips of her fox-like ears and muzzle to her toes. Her clothes were ragged shreds, fluffy white tail drooping pitifully through a tear in her trousers. When she opened her teary eyes, pink irises stared briefly at Myranda until they closed tight again in terror.

"No . . . No . . . stay away," she managed between sobs.

"Calm down. We aren't here to hurt you," Myranda tried to reassure her.

"It was the monster. The monster came again. I . . . I . . ." the creature said before breaking down and sobbing incoherently again.

She had the tone of a frightened child. Myranda tried to reach out to comfort her, but the poor thing scrambled backward to avoid the touch. She crawled quickly out from under the slab, where Myn approached and inspected her. The little dragon was not defensive as she usually was, but nevertheless the sudden appearance of the dragon terrified the pale creature all the more.

"No. I'm sorry. I didn't want to get out. I know I'm not supposed to get out. Look, I will go back. I'm sorry, I'm sorry," the creature stammered.

She edged around the dragon and ran into the darkness.

"No! Wait!" Myranda called.

She strengthened the light, hoping to catch a glimpse of where the creature was running to. There was no need. She had stopped in the middle of the room, crouching in the center of the ring of ruined bars.

"I didn't break them. The monster did. I'm sorry. I'm sorry. I don't know where the chains are, or I would be wearing them. Please don't punish me," she pleaded.

"No. No. Stand up," Myranda said.

The creature quickly snapped up straight, holding her hands rigidly at her sides. Myn had grown curious again, approaching and sniffing at her. She began to tremble visibly at the dragon's approach, but concentrated on remaining standing perfectly straight.

"Calm down. This is Myn. She won't hurt you. Here, give me your hand," Myranda said.

The terrified creature swiftly obeyed, as though she were afraid that she would be chastised if she didn't. Myranda reached into her sack and retrieved a potato for Myn and placed it in her hand.

"Now offer it to her," Myranda said.

The creature held down the vegetable, shut her eyes tight, and tried her best to keep the rest of her body as far as she could from her fingers. Myn sniffed the treat, and swiftly snatched it up. She then licked at the fingers that had offered it. The malthrope couldn't help but smile and a giggle at the odd sensation.

"There, see? She likes you. Now calm down. What is your name?" Myranda asked.

"You . . . you didn't tell me yet," she said.

"What do you mean?" Myranda asked.

"I didn't have to learn that yet," she said, tears beginning to flow again. "I swear, if the others had told me, I would remember."

"What others?" Myranda asked.

"The people . . . the teachers who were here before the monster came," she said. "Aren't you the new teacher?"

"No," Myranda said.

"Then you have to leave! You have to leave now! Only the teachers can be here. And the people who they bring. Did they bring you?" she asked.

"No," she said.

"Then leave. Leave now! Before they come back! They are--" She stopped suddenly, looking cautiously about and lowering her voice to a whisper. "They are bad people. They make you learn things. Even if you don't want to, they . . . they *make* you. *They make you!*"

She began sobbing again. Ether climbed to Myranda's shoulder.

"Well, will you accept now that there was nothing here worth finding?" she asked.

The weeping creature gasped.

"Who said that? They are here!" she panicked.

"No, no, no, it is just Ether--here, see! She is a friend," Myranda rushed to explain.

She grabbed the creature from her shoulder and held it out to the terrified one in front of her.

"If you do not release me this instant, I will incinerate you," Ether said with stifled anger.

The frightened creature's eyes widened in terror at the bizarre sight. She quickly ran to the slab of ceiling and crawled underneath it, screaming all the way.

"That thing talks like one of them! And it shouldn't talk at all!" she cried from her hiding place.

Myranda apologized to both Ether and the terrified creature. She shook her head at how quickly she had come to dismiss the new form of the shapeshifter as perfectly normal.

"I should have warned you. She is a shapeshifter," Myranda explained.

"I don't know what that is. Go away! I don't have to listen to you, you aren't my teacher," she cried in reply.

"Please. I just want to talk to you," Myranda said.

Something had apparently caught Ether's attention, as she scurried to one of the blackened stains on the floor.

"You probably haven't eaten in days," Myranda said, pulling some of the meager and practically frozen provisions from her bag.

"Go away. Go . . . you have food?" she asked, venturing a peek from her hiding spot.

"It isn't much, but . . ." Myranda began. Before she could finish, the creature had sprinted out and snatched the piece of salted meat from her hands.

She turned it and sniffed it, tentatively sampling it with her tongue. Suddenly, she tore it to pieces with her sharp teeth, sloppily speaking as she wolfed it down.

"This isn't--" Gulp. "--food. This is much better. Food is nasty wet stuff. It comes in a bowl and it has no taste. Also, there is--" Gulp. "--never this much of it," she said, making short work of the meat.

When she was through, she stared longingly at the bag the food came from.

"Do you want more?" Myranda asked.

"N . . . Yes?" she attempted, nervous of reprisal.

"Here," Myranda said, offering another piece.

Without a word, she snatched it away and swallowed it down. Myranda offered her canteen, which was emptied in an equally desperate manner. When the creature was through she sighed and smiled, licking her lips and sitting down on the ground.

"I like you. You are much better than the teachers," she said.

"I like you, too. Now, can you tell me your name? What did the teachers call you?" Myranda asked, joining her on the ground.

"They called me very bad things. Things I don't want to say. There was a tag that they made me wear. What did it say? I . . . V . . . Ivy?" she said uncertainly.

"Well, Ivy, my name is Myranda," Myranda said.

"Myranda . . ." Ivy repeated thoughtfully. "I think they talked about you."

"The teachers?" Myranda asked.

"Yes. I don't remember, though. I hardly remember anything they teach me. That's why they're so mad all of the time," she said, shuddering.

"What is this place? How long have you been here?" Myranda asked.

"I don't know. I have been here forever, though. Longer than I can remember," she said.

"What did they do here?" Myranda asked.

"They kept me behind those bars and tried to teach me things. All sorts of things. They tried to teach me about places, and people, and things like that. And they tried to teach me how to fight. They did that a lot. I didn't want to. Then they brought in this man. He had a glowing stick like yours, only pointier, and he would put his hand on my head and *make* me know things," she said, shuddering again.

Dark memories of the soul-searing time she spent with Epidime flickered in Myranda's mind. In her simple way, Ivy may have been describing his torturous ability to manipulate the mind.

"This man, the one who forced thoughts into your head, what did he look like?" Myranda asked.

"He looked like a man. I don't know. He was big. I don't want to think about it," she said, shaking her head as if she could shake his image out of it.

"Ivy, what about the staff? What did it look like?" Myranda asked. "It is very important."

"It was . . . it was . . . a two-handed, casting type, hook-and-spike poleax, a style of halberd, best suited for battle mages and paladins," she said definitively, as though the words had been read from a text.

Myranda was surprised by the precise answer, and it showed on her face.

"Well, I didn't forget *everything* they taught me," Ivy explained.

"That man. Did you hear the name Epidime when he was about?" Myranda asked.

"Yes, but not just that. It was always *General* Epidime. There were other generals, I think . . . one was named Teht," she said.

Myranda remembered it as one of the names that Desmeres had mentioned.

"What did she look like?" Myranda asked.

"That," she said, pointing.

Myranda turned swiftly, staff held defensively. There was no need. The form she indicated was slumped in the far corner of the room. She, for all outward appearance, was human, but the thick black liquid that should have been blood betrayed her true nature.

Myranda had heard of nearmen who were different. This must have been an old one. Whatever had killed her had been massive. She had more injuries than could be counted, though from the looks of it, they all came from the collision with the wall and single blow that had hurled her into it.

"I should be sad that she's dead. I'm not. She was horrible. They all were. I'm glad I can't remember half of what they did to me. I'm glad the monster came," she said.

"The monster. Tell me about the monster. What did this?" Myranda asked.

"I don't know. I didn't see. They were teaching me something and yelling at me and then there was this shaking and this light. After that, all I remember is screaming. I was screaming, they were screaming. And there was the light. Terrible light," Ivy replied, trembling.

"I have heard enough of this. Human, kill the beast," Ether ordered.

"What? No!" Myranda said.

Ivy was startled by the out-of-place voice and ran behind Myranda for protection.

"Do not disobey me, human. Do as you are told," the tiny creature warned sternly.

"I will not kill her!" Myranda declared.

"Human, if I am to tolerate your presence by my side during this quest, then I expect nothing short of blind obedience. Now--do as I say!" the shapeshifter fumed.

"I will not kill her and neither will you!" Myranda said.

"I have no intention of killing her. I have ordered *you* to do so," Ether said.

"No. If this was truly important then you certainly wouldn't trust me to do it. What is this? A test of loyalty?" Myranda asked.

"Open your eyes. This place reeks of the D'karon. Their tainted influence permeates the air. That thing that you are shielding is no different. We are surrounded by death and destruction, yet that beast is unharmed. She speaks some absurd tale of a monster that rendered a fort and all those within to rubble, and yet spared her. It is a trick, a ploy, and you have been fooled by it. There is a stain on the floor there. It is Lain's blood. Months old.

"End that menace before it is too late. I will not touch that thing. You believe that you have a place in this prophecy? Well, this is it. Bring a moment of meaning into your useless and wasted life. Perform one valuable act before your frail, impermanent body succumbs to the ravages of time and the elements," the shapeshifter raged.

As the creature continued, her words were ever more hateful and venomous. Myranda weathered them as she had a dozen times before. Myn was not so patient. She had learned the language well, and was quite aware of the vicious tone. She would not hear such words aimed at her companion. Before Myranda could stop her, Myn puffed up her chest and blasted a column of flames at the tiny form.

"Myn, what have you done!?" Myranda cried. A fear that had been growing in the pit of her stomach as the argument had progressed suddenly surged. Behind her, the trembling malthrope whimpered, crouched into a ball and hugging her knees.

The flames lingered for a few moments before intensifying and taking a familiar form. The shapeshifter had recovered enough to make use of them, it would seem. A few moments later her human form stood before them.

"Even in anger, your beast proves more useful than you," she said. "Now, kill the whimpering animal behind you or I will kill you."

"Tell me why!" Myranda demanded, standing firm despite the fear that grew inexplicably stronger inside of her.

She cast a glance at Myn, who had stepped forward to defend her friend, only to droop her head and slink backward again. Myranda hadn't seen the creature show such fear since that day in the cave when the water caught up with them.

"If I were to do her harm, I would be chastised for it," she said.

"You certainly would!" Myranda agreed.

"Not by you. What possible repentance could something as frail as you force upon me? I would be chastised by the only beings capable of such a feat. The gods themselves," she stated.

"How?" Myranda asked.

"The mark! Why do you suppose we who are Chosen must bear it? The mark is a link to our divine origins. It is intended to ensure loyalty by punishing any act that shows allegiance to the enemy. The burning of the mark purifies the body and soul of misdeed. There are some misdeeds too great to survive. Murder of another Chosen is foremost among them," Ether said.

"That is the purpose of the mark?" Myranda said.

"Of course it is. I suppose you thought it little more than a label to indicate one's status. If a Chosen One's superiority is not immediately apparent, then he or she is hardly deserving of the distinction," she said.

"Well, then why would you be punished for hurting Ivy? Unless . . ." Myranda realized, turning swiftly to the slowly calming creature. "Ivy, have you a mark--anywhere on your body--that looks like this?"

Myranda showed her left palm. The creature looked at it through teary eyes and tugged the neck of her ragged shirt. There, just over her heart, was the mark. The fur was black instead of white. It had clearly been present since birth.

"She is a Chosen! She is a Chosen and you wanted me to kill her!" Myranda screamed. "Why!?"

"She is clearly a ploy of the enemy. If we allow her to join us, it will mean our end," Ether stated simply.

"How could she be a ploy? You said it yourself! If she were loyal to the enemy, the mark would have destroyed her," Myranda said.

"The penitence is meted out by the soul. A being as naïve or foolish as she may just be ignorant of its own treachery until the moment he or she takes specific action against a truly pure warrior," Ether said.

"Even if that were true, why would you kill her? She is still Chosen, and there are precious few left!" Myranda said.

"Foolish child. The Great Convergence has yet to occur," Ether said.

"And it never will if you destroy every Chosen you find," Myranda retorted.

"Do you know nothing of the quest you hope to assist in? Until the Great Convergence occurs, there may arise as many Chosen warriors as the gods deign fit. A fallen Chosen may be replaced until five of them unite and turn to the cause. It is thus our duty and obligation to rid this world of the Chosen who have strayed from the pure path, lest they gather and keep the truly virtuous from their place. Now strike that beast down!"

"No! There is no reason to. She is coming with us!" Myranda declared.

"I can come with you!?" Ivy cried, jumping up, a look of pleading hope on her face.

"She cannot!" Ether demanded.

"Of course you can!" Myranda contradicted at the same time.

Ether grasped Myranda by the neck of her cloak and shifted to stone, lifting the girl effortlessly into the air.

"I could easily kill you and leave that thing here to die," she stated.

Myranda coughed and struggled in the unbreakable grip.

"Hey! Put her down!" Ivy objected, a flash of anger in her eyes.

Myn, suddenly recovered from her bout of fear, leapt out and clamped down onto the stone arm casually raised as a defense.

"You are tolerated only so long as your benefits outweigh your liabilities. I will not allow you to endanger my purpose," Ether said. Her voice was as steady and emotionless as ever. She seemed not to be threatening or warning Myranda, but informing her.

Myn shook her head violently. Her teeth scraped, cracked, and finally crumbled the stone of Ether's arm. The shapeshifter's hand dropped to the ground and shattered. Slowly, she turned to see the damage, dropping Myranda suddenly to the ground. She and her fallen appendage shifted to wind, rejoined, and with visible effort returned to her human form.

"However, until I am able to secure a more sizable surplus of strength, I shall allow you to remain by my side, provided that you can ensure me that the animal you insist upon shepherding can control itself," Ether allowed.

"Myn will behave," Myranda said, climbing to her feet.

"I was referring to the newest beast in your menagerie," Ether corrected.

"Is she talking about me?" Ivy asked.

"I believe so," Myranda replied.

"She's mean," Ivy pouted.

"You will have no arguments from me," Myranda agreed. "Now, if you are to join us, you will need something warmer than the rags you are wearing. Did they keep any extra clothes for you here?"

Ivy shrugged.

Myranda thought for a moment, reluctantly pulling what she knew of Epidime's fort to mind. During her escape, she had come upon one or two storerooms that she had briefly considered as hiding places. Perhaps similar ones could be found here. Ivy must have been wearing something when she was brought to this place.

Myranda led the way up the stairs, with Myn and Ivy scampering with eager enthusiasm alongside her. Ether followed, conjuring an extra layer of clothing to ward off the cold that this form seemed so weak against. Doing so required a measure less effort than altering away the weakness. She briefly considered having Myranda tell the dragon to blast her with flame a few more times so that she could be off and done with the foolish girl, but the human would see it as a request for aid, and the thought of such an inferior creature feeling as though she had been able to help her was distasteful enough that she would rather await a more independent method to recover.

Ivy looked with interest at the other floors, inspecting bars and cells as though she had never seen them. Myranda found the first storeroom. There were weapons and armor for the nearmen. Ivy rushed in, excited by the new things inside. Shortly after, she came running out with a club that looked as though it should be a bit too heavy for her. She managed to carry it with little difficulty.

"Can I bring this?" Ivy asked.

Myranda could feel the stern gaze of Ether without looking. If this newcomer was a danger to them, it was best not to allow her to be armed. At the same time, if she was to be of any help, she would need to be able to fight, and thus she would need a weapon. Myranda looked over the club. Such a brutish weapon looked out of place in Ivy's hand. It was perhaps the size of her leg and striped with iron bands and blunt iron studs. It was a cruel weapon, and the newest Chosen held it as though it were a plaything. Myranda pushed the thought that this innocent creature might be something to fear out of her mind.

"If you are careful with it," Myranda decided, pausing for a moment as she realized how motherly she sounded.

"Thank you!" Ivy gushed in a sing-song tone as she hurried off to inspect more of her surroundings.

They were making their way slowly through the more battle-scarred floors now. In truth, though, it was only Myranda who was moving slowly. Ivy was navigating the debris with a dancer's grace, even with the heavy club in her hand, and Myn was right at home among the rubble. Ether squandered a bit of her freshly-regained strength in order to whisk immediately to the surface in the form of wind.

Near to the surface, Myranda found the caved-in remnant of a second storeroom. It had at least a few things that had some use, and was most certainly where the possessions of those imprisoned were kept. Most of what was found within was unusable, but Myranda was able to salvage a second canteen and bag, and a hodgepodge of clothing. An over-large, heavy wool shirt and a pair of leggings that were fairly close to her size, the former dingy white and the latter gray, supplemented her rags. One of the ubiquitous gray cloaks, also quite oversized, was the final touch. When all was said and done, the outfit seemed to suit Ivy. The saggy clothes and sleeves that hung past her hands were a complement to her childlike demeanor.

One floor above was the wind-whipped field. Myranda cast one look at the wind and snow and was suddenly reminded that she'd had too little sleep and too much exercise that day. The thought of spending the night on the frozen ground was hardly an inviting one. She decided that it was best to spend a few hours resting in what little shelter the ruined fort offered. Shards of broken support beams were gathered together to start a fire, which Ether immediately took advantage of. The sight of a dragon starting a fire and a woman turning to flame and stepping into it had managed to become commonplace for Myranda, but Ivy marveled at it.

"Does the dragon belong to you?" Ivy asked.

"In a way, we belong to each other. She is more of a friend than a possession," Myranda said, eating the last of her meal that was a bit smaller than it should have been, thanks to her generosity earlier.

"Oh. That's nice . . . Myranda? Why did you come here?" she asked.

"I came because something inside of me told me that I would find someone very important here--and I was right, because I found you," Myranda said.

She settled back against the wall, Myn climbed on top of her, and she wrapped the cloak around the both of them.

"Myranda?" Ivy said.

"Yes," she answered, eyes closed and already slipping into sleep.

"Thank you," she said.

The words went unheard as Myranda dropped off into an exhausted slumber.

#

In Entwell, other wizards had begun to take notice of the events raging beyond their city. There were forces, bursts of mystic power, which could be felt even there. All agreed that a momentous time was upon them, but few could agree upon the deeper meaning. Eyes began to pore over the prophecy once more. The elemental had been summoned, that much was known. Was this truly the time presaged so long ago? Or would the events be scattered across years or centuries--or longer? Most eagerly awaited the answers. One was denied them.

When Deacon had provoked the unprecedented answer from Hollow, volumes of dense prophecy had been spilled forth. Most were even more indecipherable than those that had preceded them. It had taken much deliberation, but it was the decision of the Elder that Deacon's failure to alert others--and, indeed, his dismissal of those already present--was inexcusable. The missing words spoken that day would never be reclaimed, and it was solely his fault. As a punishment, Deacon was forbidden from viewing another word of the prophecy, or any other book. For five years, he would not be permitted any apprentices or apprenticeships, and his casting gem was taken away.

The primary goal of Entwell was to gather knowledge. His actions had violated that principle to the highest degree. As he had denied the world of knowledge, so he would be denied.

For a lifelong student such as he, this was devastating. For one so consumed, as he had been since Myranda's departure, it was doubly so. He struggled to retain the pieces of a spell he had managed to assemble in the weeks before the decision had been made. Permitted only blank paper, he recorded what he remembered, and set about fabricating the procedures and affectations that might fill in the gaps. He had to be careful. The spell drew dangerously close to lines forbidden to be crossed.

Days at a time were spent without leaving his hut. Shelves stripped of their books began to fill with loose pages covered in hasty revisions. The few phrases that he could recall of Hollow's last speech were nailed to the wall.

A long journey, necessary and deadly, is made safely in a single step.

He had underlined "single step" repeatedly. On the increasingly rare occasion that he left his task to eat, he would make his way to the waterfall, oblivious of the whispers of his fellow villagers. Most were convinced he had slipped into madness. He would eat, and as he did, he would stare at the waterfall. It would not relent for weeks, months even. Impossible to leave . . .

#

Myranda was shaken awake by Ivy. There was terror in the creature's eyes, and before she even spoke, Myranda could feel the flutter of fear growing in the pit of her own stomach.

"They are coming! They are coming!" Ivy whispered insistently.

"Who?" Myranda asked, suddenly wide awake.

"The teachers! I can smell them!" she said.

"So soon?" Myranda said.

Ether stepped from the fire and took on her human form.

"It was to be expected. A fort staffed by a general was likely to be resupplied and restaffed frequently," Ether remarked.

With strength to spare after the hours of recuperation, she whisked into the form of wind and launched herself to the surface. Myranda tried to follow, but Ivy caught her by the sleeve.

"No. Don't go! Stay here with me! We can hide!" Ivy urged.

"Myn, keep Ivy safe. I need to find out what we are facing," Myranda said.

Myn did as she was told, though she clearly wished to stay by Myranda's side. Dutifully planting herself in front of the frightened creature, and fighting off an unfamiliar and unwelcome fear of her own, she faced the stairs to the surface. Ivy crept up and hugged the dragon's neck.

"Don't let them get me, Myn. Don't let them get me," she whispered.

The dragon shifted uncomfortably. She wasn't certain she liked this newcomer, but she had been given a job to do.

#

Myranda squinted her eyes against the wind. They had slept through most of the day. The failing light showed a few rows of soldiers and a pair of equipment sleds. Perhaps fifteen soldiers in all. They were nearmen. She could tell by the way they moved. Pulling the sleds were . . . wolves? At this distance, she couldn't quite tell, but they seemed too large. There was one more, behind the rest, but he seemed . . . different. Myranda pushed it out of her mind and considered her options. She was well-rested now, and Ether had some of her strength back. Victory was not out of the question if they were to clash, but it would be best if battle could be avoided. Perhaps she could conjure some manner of illusion to conceal them. She weighed this option with a few others. None seemed likely to succeed.

A moment later her decision was made for her: Ether drew herself back together into her flame form and streaked toward the soldiers. It would be battle.

Like a comet, the fiery form roared through the air. Swords and shields were raised, but she still managed to destroy two of the soldiers with her first strike. The others scattered.

Myranda approached the battle, but kept her distance, more out of fear of Ether than the soldiers. She was moving so swiftly, striking at soldiers one after the other with such intensity, that Myranda felt certain if she moved any closer, she herself would be burned. The final row of soldiers, those nearest to the man who must have been their leader, drew back arrows. Two were aimed at Myranda, three at Ether. The arrows flew. Myranda threw up a hasty shield spell that only just stopped them. Ether laughed as the first two flew uselessly through her burning form, but the third was different. The head glowed faintly, and when it passed through Ether she shrieked in pain as a long stream of her flame seemed to follow it.

The injured being retreated to a position well behind Myranda. Eight soldiers remained, as well as the pair of what were most certainly no normal wolves. They seemed to be made of stone, and they were nearly the size of horses.

Myranda conjured a wind as powerful as she could manage, hoping to force them back and away from the fort that held Ivy. The advancing soldiers began to slow, but the leader raised his hand and Myranda's spell instantly died away. She tried to restore it, but to no avail. Suddenly, the stone form of Ether charged past her. The leader signaled for the wolves to be cut free. Both met the charging shapeshifter. She knocked one aside and grappled with the second.

Myranda was forced to shift her gaze from the spectacle as a trio of the soldiers drew near enough to be a threat. She thrust her staff into the snowy ground at her feet and focused her mind. Icy vines erupted from the ground and entangled the first of the soldiers, but before the others could be trapped the leader again swept the spell away. The single immobilized soldier fought at the vines. The twang of bowstrings released a second barrage of arrows, all directed at Myranda. She held up her staff and focused her mind on the arrows. Their paths shifted and struck the soldiers she'd attempted to entangle. Myranda looked away as they vanished into dust. The creatures would have killed her, and they were barely living things, but still she felt horrid that she had to kill them.

Another volley of arrows was launched. Myranda attempted to divert them but the leader's influence quickly righted them. She continued to fight against his will. She could feel his strength against hers. After a final burst of will, she dove to the side. The head of an arrow hissed through her cloak and across her thigh. She cried out. Her staff sunk deep into the snow as she tried to regain her footing. The pain was terrible.

She struggled to keep her eyes on the remaining soldiers. They were approaching her. When she finally made it to her feet, she was surrounded. She tried to summon a spell to mind, but the leader of the soldiers forced it away. He stood before her. The man looked more like a nobleman than a soldier. His clothes were nothing short of regal, the kind more at home in a king's court than a battlefield. Nothing resembling armor adorned his body. He was either very stupid or very powerful. He had jet-black hair and a face that would not be out of place on a statue of a god. With a gaze that seemed to cut through her, he surveyed his foe.

"Myranda Celeste. You are every bit the warrior I had expected. It is gratifying to meet you face to face. I am General Bagu, perhaps--" he began.

Myranda pulled to mind the last of her skills she had learned in Entwell. With a thrust, she landed a powerful blow with her staff. The man reeled backward. The break in his concentration was enough to let through a blast of magic to scatter the other soldiers. She tried to get some distance between herself and the recovering men, but found herself eye to eye with one of the stone wolves. Claw marks scored the stony hide as it slowly moved toward her. It left behind a mound of shattered stone. Finally it stood still, awaiting a command. The real danger was behind her.

She suddenly felt a crushing force closing in around her. She couldn't move, she couldn't breathe. Her feet left the ground. Slowly she was turned. The five bowmen stood before her, arrows readied, their tips fairly pressing into her flesh. The leader approached her, fury in his eyes.

"You have found your way to the last of the original Chosen. Should more arise, you would have been valuable. But your threat outweighs your benefit," he seethed. A pulse of will snapped one of Myranda's ribs.

She turned all of her own strength of mind to countering his. Despite her best efforts, the force was barely lessened. The best she could manage was to hold him off enough to stay alive.

"Destroy her," the man ordered, clearly deciding now was not the time for a battle of wills when a simpler means of execution existed.

Arrows were drawn back, but before they could fly, a charging form tore through the line of bowman. Myranda struggled to turn to see the form, but the force around her tightened. The air was forced from her lungs. The leader raised a second hand. At the very edge of Myranda's vision, the thrashing form froze.

"Clever," he admitted, drawing the form nearer.

Now Myranda could see. It was the stone wolf. The fingers of the leader twisted cruelly. Waves of black swept over the body of the creature. It howled in pain, but behind the howl was a scream. Ether's voice. The stony form shifted slowly to the stone form of Ether as additional mass of the wolf crumbled away from the human shape at its core.

"You shall be an adequate prize," he smiled.

Suddenly he turned. Anger flashed in his eyes. The form of Myn hung, writhing in pain in the air. Flames spewed from her mouth until it was forced closed. Myranda focused her mind. The spell that held her was astoundingly powerful. Ether had shifted to flame and now struggled with all of her considerable strength, yet the grip barely wavered.

"Let her go!" came a voice from behind him.

Ivy's club came down, but it stopped inches from the head of the man who held the others at bay. He turned, and in a moment she too was suspended in the air. She began to scream in a combination of pain and terror. Myranda suddenly felt the hot sting of fear in her stomach. She had been frightened before. This was different. It was fundamental . . . primal. She felt it rise as Ivy's desperate struggling increased. Myn seemed to be similarly affected. It was as though Ivy's fear was spilling over to the others. Only Ether and their captor seemed unaffected. Soon the fear was almost more unbearable than the pain.

"Let me go! I can't go back! No! NO!" she cried.

The grip was loosening. Something about Ivy's struggles was having an effect. Suddenly, there was a torrent of magic. It felt akin to the force that had been gathered to restore Ether, but it came all at once. A flash of blinding blue light filled the valley and a deafening shriek echoed from all directions, then swiftly faded to nothing. The hold on them was released. Myranda fell to the ground. Ether did not. She blasted directly at the powerful man. He was quickly consumed in flame and lifted into the air. The fiery form hurdled through the air and into the ruined fort. A few moments and a series of earthshaking blows later what was left of the ruins began to cave in. A flickering form erupted from the flying dust and debris.

Ether landed before Myranda. The flames of her body were weakening. The bright eyes wavered.

"Quickly . . ." the voice pleaded.

"Myn, fire--NOW!" Myranda cried.

The dragon unleashed flame that seemed to wrap around Ether. After a second and third burst, the shapeshifter seemed restored. She immediately shifted to wind and launched skyward.

"The leader is not dead. I intend to withdraw until I am better prepared to finish him. If you value your life, you will leave this valley," Ether called out. Threads of fear were woven into her voice.

Before Myranda could object, the windy form had disappeared into the distance. The ruins were still collapsing. If that wizard truly had survived, Myranda hoped that the mountain of shattered stone would delay him long enough for her to escape. She closed the wound in her thigh, moved her ribs back into place and healed them, and climbed to her feet. Myn rushed to her side to help her.

She scanned the valley, but there was no sign of Ivy, save one. It was a single footprint, more than a dozen paces from where she should have landed. Where were the others? The last of the bricks of the fort crumbled into what was now little more than a pit filled with jagged stone. Deep beneath it, Myranda could already hear a deep rumble. She would have to move quickly.

Running in the direction the footprint faced, Myranda found another, more than one hundred paces on. Together they seemed to be indicating that Ivy had made her way down the mountainside along the steep but direct path that had been taken by the soldiers. Of course, with such massive strides, running hardly seemed the appropriate word. Somehow Myranda would have to find a way down with similar speed, or the leader who had nearly taken her life moments ago would be upon her to finish what he had started. Her eyes turned to the only other things in the valley, the supply sleds. They were small, the sort intended to deliver minor cargo. She turned one to face downhill.

"Myn, burn the other sled, then find Ivy. When you do, lead me to her," Myranda said.

Myn quickly obeyed, taking to the air once the sled was aflame. Myranda pushed the sled and climbed on. It gained speed quickly. Soon the landscape was whipping by at a terrifying rate. The path was a gently curving one, but at this speed, she had to lean all of her weight to one side of the sled to manage the turn. She could have used magic to steer, but a general throbbing in her body assured her that she had not yet tended to all of her own injuries, and she had the others to think about. It was best to save her strength.

Here and there, at the base of a treacherous crater, Myranda would spot another footprint. Myn was still overhead, far ahead of her, searching. The pass was growing more narrow, the curves more sharp. A sound from behind like a clap of thunder served as a reminder that she must not slow.

Finally, Myn glided down and kept pace ahead of the speeding sled. She'd found something. Myranda did her best to stay behind the dragon, and miraculously managed to guide the sled safely through a series of successively narrower forks in the pass. After passing though a point in the path only slightly wider than the sled itself, the pass opened again. In the distance, at the end of a long, deep furrow that looked to have been scooped out of the snow, was Ivy, motionless and face down. Myranda managed to bring the sled to a halt. She climbed down into the furrow.

Ivy's body was hot, almost scalding to the touch. A fair amount of the snow around her had turned to slush. The edges of her cloak were frayed and charred, yet her boots seemed little the worse for wear. One hand still clutched the club, the surface of which had been blackened and charred as well. Myranda rolled the creature over; her face had been in a hollow in the snow that looked as though it had been melted--or perhaps boiled away. The melting snow was slowly filling it with icy water. She was breathing, but only barely, deeply unconscious.

Fairly soaking herself to the bone in the process, Myranda dragged Ivy to the sled. She loosened the straps and removed packs and bags that had survived the ride thus far until there was enough room for Ivy to lie. Whatever mysterious heat had kept her warm thus far was fading fast, and soaked as they were, neither of them would last long in the snow. Myranda flexed her knowledge of water magic, wicking away all that clung to their bodies. She then pulled off the rough canvas that had been wrapped around the cargo and threw it over Ivy.

Carefully, Myranda probed with her mind, sweeping again and again for any kind of injury. Mysteriously, impossibly, Ivy was completely unharmed. Her only plight was that her spirit was utterly drained. It was only with the whisper of strength that remained that the once-powerful essence clung to the body. If this creature could recover, time alone would serve as the cure. With nothing more to do, Myranda sat on the edge of the sled and gave her racing heart a rest, Myn by her side. She tried to grasp what had just transpired.

In one day, she had found one Chosen and lost another. The one who had left her was anything but what she would consider a hero. Ether was self-absorbed and obsessed with her own superiority. The other was a study in contradictions. She seemed full grown, but behaved like a little girl. She seemed not to know a word of magic, yet she had a soul powerful enough to break that wizard's grip. Her will seemed weak, yet she was capable of forcing her emotions on others unintentionally. She could not land a single blow on the wizard, yet she was able to traverse half of a mountainside in a heartbeat.

Myranda's head throbbed. She willed away some minor injuries Myn had sustained while in the wizard's grip, then tended to what was left of her own. She could not sense Bagu drawing nearer. Perhaps he had yet to escape. Another attempt to find him revealed that she could not sense him at all. Briefly she wondered if he was concealing himself, but she pushed the thought aside. If he had followed her this far this quickly, there would be nothing she could do to stop him. He had no reason to hide.

Standing again, Myranda looked over the supplies she'd uncovered. There was a longbow and some arrows, including a quiver of the crystal-tipped ones. Those might be useful. Another bundle seemed to be entirely chains, ropes, and shackles. Ivy must have been difficult to restrain. She separated a rope from the bundle. There was not a scrap of food or a drop of water. The nearmen must not need it, and if her own stay was any indication, the tiniest amount of that horrid swill would last months at the torturous rate at which they rationed it out.

Myranda secured the useful items to the open space left on the sled and began to push it carefully along.

By the time the mountain turned to flat land again, it was well into the long cold night. The tundra was not nearly as cold as the mountain had been, but it was quite a bit colder than the field she had left on the other side. In her years of wandering, Myranda had never been so far north, nor so far east. She was nearly to the coast. Had she taken a few turns differently in her descent of the mountain, her trip may well have taken her to the shores of the North Crescent Sea. The sea was entirely separated from the mainland by the Eastern Mountains, and thus few ever saw it.

Of course, it had been her view every morning while she was in Entwell, but the thought had never occurred to her when she was there. Perhaps because it was such a paradise, the thought of an icy, forbidding sea would have been out of place. For a moment, she let her mind linger on more pleasant times. She thought of all she had learned, all of the people she had met. She thought of Deacon . . .

A gust of icy wind and a hint of light struggling through the clouds above the mountain shook her back to reality. If her sense of direction was not failing her, she was on the thin strip of flat land between the Eastern Mountains and the Elder Mountains to the north. Were she to follow the southern edge of these mountains west for a few days, the walls of the northern capital would come into view. It was the most heavily fortified and largest city in the kingdom. Nestled among the mountains and with a pair of legendary walls, the Tresson army could sweep across the whole of the Northern Alliance and be turned back by the forces defending the capital for years.

In the past, the place had been called Verril. When the three kingdoms united, it came to be called simply Northern Capital. It was a name as sterile and utilitarian as any that had been created since the war began, just another in a long line of changes that stripped the culture and history from the land and its people.

With the capital so near, this was a dangerous place to be. It was clear now that the D'karon were the real enemy, and that they made up the better part of the Alliance Army. The capital was the point of command for that force. The generals in command of the army, and potentially the throne, would be there. Until the full might of the Chosen could be brought together, she had to help them as best she could to evade the grip of these powerful men. That meant taking the ailing Ivy as far away from here as she could until the poor creature could recover.

Moving the sled proved to be a far more difficult task without the aid of a slope. Fortunately, as she had been forced to learn, the mountainside was riddled with caves. She came upon one large enough to conceal the three of them, but small enough to be certain it was not otherwise occupied. Before Myranda could even request it, Myn scampered off and returned with a pair of snow rabbits. Myranda was unwilling to risk lighting a fire, and the planks of the sled were the only wood to speak of, so she rendered the meat as edible as she could with magic alone. This being her first attempt, the results were less than ideal, but she managed. Again her mind turned to Deacon. He was a master of that particular trick. Somehow, he'd compressed the entire procedure to the snap of a finger. Had she known what lay in store, she might have asked to be taught that instead of some of the other things she had learned from him.

She fumbled through the bag for the stylus he had given her. It was still with her. She turned it about in her hands. Holding it reminded her that somewhere there was a place that was untroubled by the war. Somewhere there was a person like Deacon. Perhaps she could return there. Perhaps that was the place that would keep the Chosen safe until they were united.

Alas, there were far more reasons why she could not or should not return than why she should. The way could well be blocked now and for months to come. Even if it were open, the journey was perilous and she doubted that she remembered it well enough to navigate it safely. Aside from all of that, there were other Chosen to find . . . or were there?

A comment made by her recent foe echoed in her mind. She'd been too frightened and distracted to consider it before. He'd said that she had found her way to the last of the original Chosen. Lain and Ether were each original, and the swordsman was dead. Even if Ivy were an original, there should have been one more. The D'karon must have killed it. A dark feeling came to the pit of Myranda's stomach.

If this war was ever to end, it would mean that the D'karon would need to be defeated, but they had managed to kill two of the mightiest warriors ever to exist, and capture two others. Only Ether had evaded their grasp entirely, and that was largely due to the fact that for thousands of years she had barely existed.

Two things were now quite clear. First, the foes she faced were far more powerful than she had thought, and second, there were two Chosen that remained to be found. The second point was made more distressing by the fact that there was no prophecy to guide her in her search. What were the two that remained? An artistic prodigy and a strategist.

Myranda turned to the still body of Ivy. Neither could be considered a description of the creature she had found. She was one of the new Chosen; a replacement, somehow. But that contradicted what the man in the valley had said. Had he been trying to confuse her?

Myranda climbed from the cold ground to the edge of the sled. The cold would be distracting, and she could not afford that right now. She had found Ivy; she could find the others the same way. She clutched her staff, closed her eyes, and opened her mind. Ivy's essence flickered weakly beside her, and upon her lap was curled the small, pure spirit of Myn. She spread her consciousness.

As her mind swept outward, she could feel the mountainside scattering her concentration more and more as it crept further south. Finally, there came a mountain beyond which all else was obscured. This, no doubt, was the same mountain that the cave of the beast wound through, leading to Entwell. She shifted her focus. The faint, defeated souls of the people of her land glinted like stars reflected in a glassy lake--save one. One burned like a sun, drowning out those that surrounded. Ether.

She strained to see more, but ever outward there was the same until her mind swept across the vast darkness that was the sea beyond the western shore. Nothing offered even a whisper of the strength that she had felt in Ivy, or that she had seen in Ether. Not even Lain could be seen. Here and there, a presence seemed to flick in and out of sight, like an insect flitting past. Nothing more revealed itself.

The mountainside and its unique ability to blind the mind's eye concealed most of the south from her. There was the chance that what she sought could be found there. She focused harder. There had to be a way to look beyond. She strained, pulling and stretching her mind with all of her might. Slowly--agonizingly so--she could feel her vantage point changing, moving forward. The shift was accompanied by a peculiar feeling. It felt something like losing her balance, but in a far more profound and fundamental way. Whispers of the stronger souls to the south peeked tantalizingly at the edge of the hazy disruption the mountain caused.

Suddenly, the feeling of disorientation grew a thousand-fold. She felt as though she was falling. At the same time, all semblance of physical distraction dropped away. The cold, the sound of the wind at the cave's mouth--it all vanished. The faint flickers around her became infinitely more vivid. The spirits of the people of the villages, once barely detectable, now shone brilliantly. Between them--and, indeed, everywhere around her--was a general glow. It was fluid and alive, shifting like wind.

Tight clusters of black voids seemed to draw in this ambient glow. The nearmen. Three voids stood out among them. One was in the distance, where she reasoned the capital must be. Another was far to the west. The third was in a field, not far from her. Also in the field was something she could not immediately identify. It was muted, weaker than it seemed it should be, but undeniably there.

It was Lain. He was concealing his spirit somehow, but it was certainly him. A similar essence, muted and concealed, was further to the west. Another Chosen? She tried to focus more intently on this unknown form, but her mind had reached its limit. It didn't matter. She had a direction. She had hope. For now, that would be enough.

She tried to release her concentration. Instead of the world rushing in, she felt the tumbling, spinning disorientation increase. She felt as though she was slipping away. Quickly, she focused again, trying to get her bearings. A realization swiftly dawned upon her. She was viewing the world as though she were high above the field to the west of the mountainside. She was not in the cave. She was not in her body.

For the first time, she turned her attentions to herself. She tried to move, but the muscles she tried to manipulate did not exist. She moved only when she willed it so, manipulating her "body" solely through magic. She was unconstrained by the physical world, drifting to and fro according to her mind's desire. Though the motion was easy enough to master, it was not effortless. She could feel her focus weakening. She did not know what would happen to her if she weakened to the point that she lacked the will to move. She didn't want to find out. Desperately, she searched for her body, but in this state only magic and spirit were visible, and her body had none. Instead, she sought out Myn.

The dragon remained faithfully on her lap, and with the familiar essence to guide her, Myranda's spirit reached her body. The very instant she slipped her astral limbs into her physical ones, she jerked into full consciousness. She was cold. Very cold. Her body must have been near death during her absence, leaving her chilled to the core. She began to tremble violently, waking the dragon. Puffing a few breaths of flame to ward off the chill, Myn slipped quickly back into slumber. Myranda, spent from her ordeal, soon followed.

#

Far across the field, high in the sky, Ether soared. A few bursts of dragon fire were not nearly enough to restore the strength she had wasted in her battle. She cursed herself for her weakness.

The D'karon were far more formidable than she had anticipated. Of course, she'd had to compensate for the weakness of the human. That was surely the primary cause of her difficulty, but allowing herself to grow so weak was inexcusable. She trained her mind on the essence of her fellow Chosen. He was certainly below, but somehow he was still capable of concealing himself from even her keen senses. He was a testament to the superiority of those who could rightly call themselves Chosen. Not like the beast the human had found.

The blindness of that weak-minded and softhearted girl was astonishing. Any fool could see that the creature she had found had been corrupted by the enemy. How else could it have escaped her notice? The thought of the human having some ability that she lacked was laughable. Still, she had proven useful. And she did bear the mark . . .

#

Lain drew in a deep breath, analyzing the air for any hint of Myranda's scent. The wind was sweeping down off of the mountain, but the traces of her were weak. She was ahead, but she had come from the mountain, not through this field. He didn't care. The important thing was that she was near. Even he was not certain how he had known where to find her, but long ago he'd learned to trust his instincts on such matters.

The wind shifted and Lain swiftly sampled it. It carried a foreign scent, one far too near and far too fresh for comfort. He dropped low to the ground. The cloudy sky brought little in the way of light, but he'd been blessed with eyes that needed scarcely any. There was a form, far to the south, that stood motionless in the field. It seemed to be considering its surroundings. After a time, it turned south.

Lain held perfectly still for more than an hour. Not until the form had vanished completely from his view did he allow himself to continue. He immediately resumed his journey toward Myranda. He had not eaten in days and he was nearly frozen, but none of that mattered. Nothing mattered but the purpose to which he had devoted his life. No one must suffer as he had. If the war stood between him and his goal, then the war must end. There was no other option.

As he drew nearer, Myranda's scent grew stronger. The dragon, Myn, was with her. And . . . something else. He couldn't place the scent. It toyed with him, undeniably present, yet barely noticeable.

He slipped into the cave's dark interior. Myranda and Myn were asleep in a heap hunched against a sled. Something was asleep atop the sled. He drew in the scent, but still it eluded him. His eyes fought to make out the form strewn with makeshift blankets. He approached it. Only the head showed. It looked like . . . His heart began to beat harder. His legs seemed to weaken. His mind would not accept what was before him. Could it be? After all of these years? It was . . .

#

Myranda was shaken awake. Lain's face was inches from hers. Eyes she had rarely seen show a drop of emotion were saturated with angst, confusion, urgency.

"Who is she! Where did you find her! What happened to her!" He demanded, voice desperate.

"Lain! Where did you come from?" Myranda asked, sleep reluctant to release her from its grasp.

"Answer me!" He demanded.

"There was a ruined fort in the mountains. She was inside," Myranda said.

"Tell me that she isn't one of them," he said, almost pleadingly.

"She is not a D'karon. She is on our side," Myranda assured him.

Rather than a look of relief, a far more desperate look came to his face.

"TELL ME SHE DOESN'T HAVE THE MARK! TELL ME SHE IS NOT A PART OF THIS SUICIDE!" he demanded, shaking her violently again.

"S-she does. She is Chosen," Myranda shakily answered.

Lain released her and stepped away. The shaking and yelling had awoken Myn. She was overjoyed at the first sight of Lain, but something was wrong. He looked broken, devastated. He dropped to his knees, eyes distant and unfocused. His gaze shifted to the ground.

"In my life, I have been everywhere in this war-torn land. I have been past the southern most of Tresson cities. I have been inside the Northern Capital. I have seen both oceans. In all of my years, I have seen only three of my own kind. I only truly knew one. Since I last saw any of them, five long decades have passed. I had come to accept that I was the last, that my race would die with me. It didn't matter anymore. Now I find one of my own. Not just one of my kind, but one of my kin, and fate has chosen that she must . . ." he stated, trailing off.

His fists clenched.

"Kin? She . . . she is in your family? You know her?" Myranda asked.

"I've never seen her, but her scent is almost identical to mine. What happened to her?" he asked, voice distant and defeated.

"Some soldiers and a wizard approached. We fought off the soldiers, but the wizard nearly destroyed us. She managed to break his grip somehow and she was gone. I found her half of a mountain away, like this. She hasn't moved since," Myranda said.

"She is weak . . . Will she live?" Lain asked.

"Time will tell," Myranda said.

Lain was silent for a time. Myn nudged his tightly-clenched fist. The fingers opened and stroked the adoring creature. The pained look on his face faded into a look of contemplation. His eyes closed.

"The war must end," he declared.

"You saw the proclamation from the king," she said.

"What does it matter? It is what you wanted," he said.

"Why have you come to me?" she asked.

"I know you. I know that you are devoted to this cause. I know that you have talents that will be indispensable," he said.

"Won't Desmeres be of more help than I?" she asked.

"He is not foolish enough to involve himself," he said.

"You called this suicide. Do you believe that?" Myranda asked.

"We are too few and too weak to bring this war safely to an end. Powerful men wish for it to continue. The war is what gives them their power. They would sooner see their own children die than give up that power. Reaching them will be difficult, killing them more so. The consequences will be inescapable. This *will* lead to our deaths. There can be no doubt. But it must be done," he said.

"You are talking about the five generals. You plan to end the war by killing the leadership of the Alliance Army," Myranda said. His words did little to help her confidence, save one. He had said "we." From this point forward, they were in this together.

"It is the only way," he said.

"The army will crumble. The south will overrun the north," she said.

He was silent.

"Do you even care?" she asked.

"The south has no interest in the continuation of the war. They are a stronger, more able force. They have little to gain from this wasteland. They only wish to retain that which belongs to them. The day the soldiers on the north side of the border drop their weapons, those in the south will do the same," he said.

"So . . . the deaths of these five will bring this war to an end for certain," she said.

"It is by no means certain, but it is as likely a method as any," he said.

"Won't others arise to take their place?" Myranda asked.

"If more must be done, more shall be done," he stated.

Myn suddenly decided that she had been lax in her duties and streaked off to fetch a meal for her long-absent friend. Lain stood and turned to the sleeping form on the sled.

"Her name is Ivy," Myranda said.

He placed a hand on her head.

"I need to warn you. She isn't . . . she must have been in their clutches for a long time. Whatever they did . . . she isn't well," Myranda said, finding herself in the unique position of protecting Lain's feelings.

"What is wrong with her?" Lain asked.

"She can't remember anything. What happened to her, even who she is. She is like a child," Myranda said.

"It is just as well. What happens at the hands of the D'karon is best forgotten," he said.

"I don't think I will ever forget," Myranda said, shivering. "Epidime was the one who tortured me. He was among those who Ivy had to endure as well."

Lain shook his head.

"I faced Demont . . . playing against our strengths," he muttered.

"What?" Myranda asked.

"Epidime specializes in the mind, Demont the body. Had our captors been switched, we each might have been broken. They are testing our strongest qualities," he said.

"The general called Teht. Did she have a specialty?" Myranda asked.

"She deals with wizards," Lain said.

"We found her dead in the ruined fort," Myranda said.

"Then our task is made somewhat simpler," he said. After a moment more of contemplation, he came to a swift decision. "We must leave."

The suddenness of the comment and the conviction in his voice took Myranda by surprise.

"Leave? Now?" she questioned.

"There are a few more hours of darkness. We will need them. The longer that we delay, the more likely our discovery," he said.

"But where are we going to go?" Myranda asked, gathering together her things.

"Tressor. There are a number of people there who have yet to settle their debts. They shall be made to protect her," he said.

"But, the prophecy says--" Myranda objected.

"I do not care about the prophecy," he said.

"Surely even you cannot deny the truth now," she said.

"I deny nothing. I intend to keep this creature from the fate that I have chosen for myself," he said.

"But if you hope to succeed, you will need her help!" she cried.

"Myranda, it is a war. We face an army at best, a pair of them at worst. There are only two ways to face a force of such size. The first is to meet it with equal strength or greater. One hundred and fifty years of failure is all that can be shown for that. What remains is our only viable option: to strike with a small enough force to avoid notice, and to strike at the very highest level. Cut off the head.

"If the king were truly the seat of power, then the deed would already be done, but our targets are more numerous, and far too canny to allow themselves to be taken in a single blow. They will need to be taken one at a time, but in swift succession. I will require your aid to recover quickly enough from the injuries I am certain to endure. It is for this reason alone that doubling the size of the force should even be considered. Even allowing Myn to remain with us is a risk I hesitate to take. To imagine that a force of five--even five that match my skill--can slip through as easily as one is foolish. To suggest that a force which includes one such as the shapeshifter could do so is madness," he said.

Without another word, he wrapped the makeshift blankets more tightly about the unconscious creature and threw her across his shoulders. It was futile to argue any longer. His mind was clearly set. Myranda gathered the bow, arrows, and rope from the sled and quickly followed Lain. Even with Ivy to carry, he set a pace that was difficult to match. They had been back in the cold of night for several minutes when Myn came trotting up with her gift for Lain. When he showed no interest, she carried it faithfully behind him.

Lain seemed tireless as the sun struggled to turn the black clouds of night into the gray clouds of day. All the while, he seemed more cautious than usual, sniffing the air and casting nervous glances to the southwest. The short day passed without a single word from any of the travelers. Night was well and truly upon them again before the silence was broken.

Lain's previous departure had been a sudden one, and had left Myranda with a mind full of questions. The intervening time had done little to dull the edge of her uncertainties. The silence, and having Lain so tantalizingly near, had stirred the thoughts to mind with renewed intensity.

"Lain, earlier you spoke of Demont. You said you faced him. When?" she asked.

"When you were in Ravenwood with the white wizard," he answered.

"What happened?" she asked.

"The Elites were after you, and you were in Wolloff's tower. I knew it was only a matter of time before they found you. I too was a target. To keep them from you, I allowed myself to be taken," he answered.

"And they took you to Demont?" she asked.

"To be tested, though any other man but Demont would have called it torture. He wanted to break me, to know my limit, but in time he lost interest and moved on, taking only the blood he had collected from me. I was left chained to a bed of spikes, dangling over a pit of flames. I was alone. I managed to wrap a chain around one of the spikes and levered it free. By the time the guards had noticed, I'd managed to free myself and escape. The Elites were dispatched to find me. You found me after I'd finished them," he explained.

"That . . . that's horrible," she uttered.

For a time, she contemplated the ordeal he must have endured, but soon another question forced the thoughts aside.

"Lain. Desmeres . . . he told you about the book," Myranda assumed.

"The one you stole from me. He did," came the reply.

"I found the page . . . the entry with Sam Rinthorne. The one from the day of the massacre. There was one beneath it. I couldn't read it . . . but it was in Kenvard," she said.

Lain was silent.

"Lain . . . after the massacre, Kenvard was gone. How could . . ." she began.

Her voice was being choked off by a knot forming in her throat. Her vision was blurred by tears.

"It happened during the massacre," he said.

"What . . . who?" Myranda managed to ask.

"Rinthorne had hired me to find and seal the leak. Shortly after I recovered the intelligence, I was found. One of the Elites. They had been searching for me for years by that time. The man who found me. He was your father," Lain said.

The words shot like a bolt of lightning through Myranda's mind.

"He captured me. Before bringing me in, he found the intelligence. He read it. He seemed to think that something was wrong with it. A bargain was made. I was to be released, and he would destroy any information they had accumulated about me. In exchange, I was to go to Kenvard and save his family from the coming siege. When I reached the city walls, the gates had already been breached. The building he had told me to search was empty. In the chaos, I managed to locate two blood relatives by scent. You and your uncle. I cleared an exit; your uncle found it. Despite the fact I could not save the others, your father kept his word. Overnight, the hunt for me came to a halt, the trail rendered cold.

"I learned that shortly after that his treachery was discovered. He was put in the dungeon in Northern Capital," Lain said.

Myranda was silent. She felt numb, and not because of the cold. The cold, the night, the world, they were all a thousand miles away. Her mind was burning with his words. Lain, all those years ago, had spoken to her father. It was his doing that she had survived that horrible day, and if only her mother had stayed in her home, she too would be alive. And her father . . . the dungeon.

She had heard tales of it. Everyone had. It was legendary. Buried beneath the capital, it extended downward and outward like a system of mines. The worst of criminals were kept there. A man inside was as good as in his grave. He would never see the sun again. Prisoners there were forgotten, erased from the world. All of these years, Myranda had feared that her father had been killed in battle. Now she wished he had been. He couldn't have survived this long in such a place. Starvation, disease, torture . . . . He had likely come to a terrible end there. It was foolishness to think otherwise. He was dead now, perhaps after years alone in that wretched hole in the ground.

The girl's tortured mind was still struggling with this terrible revelation when Lain stopped and set down his load. There was no shelter to speak of, and the winds at the foot of the mountainside were constant. The icy fingers of night were the first things to break through the veil of agony her mind had erected. Surely he didn't mean to rest now. They would be in plain sight of anyone who might pass by.

"You don't intend for us to spend the night here, do you?" Myranda asked.

"I felt her stir. Ivy is waking," he said.

It was true. The creature was moving her head and groaning. She tried to sit up, and succeeded with the help of Lain. Her eyes slowly opened. She sniffed and threw her mouth wide in a long, deep yawn. She saw Myranda before her and smiled sleepily. Then she turned to see Lain. His hand was on her shoulder. She pulled back slightly, the hint of fear in her eyes. She sniffed and seemed to calm slightly, the fear turning to confusion or even recognition.

"Myranda . . . w-who is this?" Ivy asked.

"This is Lain. He is a friend," She said.

"Lain . . . I know that name, too," she said, looking nervously at Lain. "They said it a lot. He is a friend?" She mustered a meek smile again. Suddenly it dropped away. "A friend like Ether?" she asked suspiciously.

"No, better than Ether," Myranda said with a smile.

Lain cast a questioning look at Myranda.

"Ether is the name I've given to the shapeshifter," Myranda explained.

"Then the shapeshifter managed to find you," Lain said.

"I'm hungry," Ivy interrupted.

Lain looked to Myn. She was still holding a now partially-frozen prize from her earlier hunt. She proudly presented it to him. It was a rather meager offering, hardly enough for one. The two creatures exchanged glances and, without a word, rushed off into the night.

"Where are they going?" she asked.

"I imagine they are going to hunt down a fresher meal," Myranda said.

"You aren't going to go with them, are you?" Ivy asked, looking nervously into the blackness that surrounded them.

"I don't think I would be of much help. Ivy, tell me. What do you remember about our encounter outside the fort?" Myranda asked.

Ivy shuddered.

"I remember I was scared. Myn was scared, too. Then I heard you scream. I couldn't hold onto her, she ran out after you. I didn't want to, but,

I knew he would kill you. I tried to help, but he got me and . . . then light . . . then dark," she said.

She shut her eyes tight. It was as though it hurt her to remember.

"You were hurt then. I saw the blood . . . why aren't you hurt now?" she asked.

"I am something of a healer," Myranda said.

"Healer . . . but . . . how long have I been asleep?" she asked, looking up to Myranda.

"A bit under two days," Myranda said.

"How could you heal so quickly?" she asked.

"A spell," she said.

"You mean . . . magic. I thought magic only made things worse. All they ever tried to teach me was how to hurt things," she said.

"They tried to teach you magic?" Myranda asked.

"A little. Near the beginning. I was no good at it. I'm no good at anything, but I was so bad they stopped trying to teach me. They started using it on me," she said.

Her eyes shut tight again and the pained look returned.

"What other things did they try to teach you?" Myranda asked.

"Everything. Too much. I don't want to think about it," she said.

She tried to stand, but even with Myranda's hand to steady her, she dropped dizzily to the ground again.

"I wish Myn would come back. I like her," she said, yawning again.

"Myn . . . is she a year old yet? I can't remember," Myranda admitted. "How old are you, Ivy?"

Ivy smiled and held up a few fingers. Then the smile dropped away. She looked at the fingers, then her hands. A look of deepening confusion came to her face.

"I'm . . . I'm . . ." she stuttered. She was visibly upset.

"What sort of creature are you?" Myranda asked.

"I'm like y--no. I'm . . ." she said hesitantly. Tears were beginning to well in her eyes and they darted slightly, as though a long lost memory was fighting its way into her mind. "Something . . . something is wrong. I . . . I don't . . . I'm not . . ." she attempted.

Finally, the tears began to roll down her cheeks. Myranda knelt down and embraced her to comfort her. The creature hugged her tightly and began to sob. Feelings of pity and concern swept into Myranda's mind, along with the sadness of the creature forcing its way through. She had held up six fingers when asked her age. From the smile on her face when asked, she was initially sure of it. Six years old? How long had she been in their hands? She even seemed unsure of what she was. Had they changed her?

These questions swiftly drew others that continued to plague her. She knew better than to expect any answers.

#

Deacon closed his door and threw up an array of subtle but powerful locking spells. It was a useless gesture--there was no spell he could conjure that could not be broken by his peers--but in the light of his actions, he had to take some sort of precaution. Taking a seat at his desk, he reached inside his cloak and removed a small satchel. He unfastened the string and reached inside. Out came an impossibly large book he'd taken from the library, then another, then another. The satchel was the culmination of several months of work earlier in his training. It could contain anything that could fit through the opening. No one besides Gilliam ever knew that he had made it.

Quickly he began to transcribe the notes within. He had to be swift. The missing books would be noticed. Had this been any other time, he would have been ashamed--nay, disgusted--by his own behavior. Stealing the books had required the exploitation of every aspect of his art that the others distrusted, but it was necessary. The gaps in his spell were too wide. It might work, but only under the best conditions. That would not do. The severity of the circumstances was the very reason the spell had to be created.

Finally, when all of the new information was collected, he put the stylus down. It wasn't enough. The knowledge wasn't there, and without it the odds were against him. He closed the books and slid them back into the satchel. The odds . . . the spell could not be improved . . . perhaps . . .

#

Ivy had calmed down by the time Lain and Myn returned. They had tracked down a mountain goat. The look of pride on Myn's face was priceless as Lain dropped it down before Ivy. The grief-stricken creature instantly perked up at the sight of the meal. Myranda opened her mouth to offer to cook a piece of it for Ivy, but before she could get the words out, Ivy had torn off a piece with her teeth. Myn did likewise and Lain sliced off a piece for himself.

Myranda turned away. She'd had a hard enough time adjusting to Myn's eating habits. This was too much for her. When the meal had been finished, there was more than enough left for her. Her hunger overcame her revulsion. She cut away a piece and tried to apply a spell to cook it. Too little sleep and too much stress made it more of a task than usual. Ivy, licking blood from her lips with a look far more innocent and satisfied than such an act should ever allow, became intrigued.

"What are you doing?" she asked.

"Cooking the meat . . . or trying to," she said, pausing to let the frustration pass.

"Why?" she asked.

"I can't eat it raw like you. It would make me sick," she said.

"Are you sure? It tastes great. It the best thing I have ever eaten," she said.

"I'm sure," Myranda said.

"Why? I can eat it. Myn and Lain can, too," she said.

"Myn is an animal. You and Lain are . . . well, the three of you are better suited to a life like this than I am," Myranda said.

"So, Lain and I are . . . like animals then," she said.

"No, no, no, you're--" Myranda began to reassure her.

Suddenly Lain's fingers shot to the hilt of his sword and he turned swiftly. A stiff, steady wind began to blow in the wrong direction, against the mountains. This could be only one thing. Sure enough, the wind swirled tightly together and formed into the familiar human form of the shapeshifter, Ether.

"Once again you prove useful to me, human. You should be honored," she said. "Lain, your skill at evasion is a match for my skill of detection. You have proven yourself to me. It is time that you and I set about our task as Chosen in earnest."

"Oh, no. Not you!" Ivy whined.

"I am sorry that you have had to endure the presence of this abomination. As you have no doubt noticed, her essence has been sullied by the will of the D'karon. It is in the best interest of the world that the inevitable demise that her weak mind would have led her to be allowed to occur, such that another more worthy spawn of the gods may take her place," she said.

"See, she's mean!" Ivy said. "Why don't you go away!"

"I intend to," Ether said.

"Really?" Ivy said.

"Lain and I will have no use for the likes of you. We shall be on our way," Ether said.

"Wait, you are going to take Lain? But . . . Lain brought me food. He brought me a *goat*. It is my favorite food ever. That means he is nice. Why are you going to take him?" Ivy asked.

"I do not need to justify myself to you," she said.

"I have my own plans. You have no place in them," Lain said.

Ivy clapped joyously. Ether's eyes narrowed.

"I had anticipated such a reaction," she said. "What precisely is your plan?"

"None of your concern," he said.

"Ha ha," Ivy laughed mockingly.

"I naturally would have preferred that our partnership be a willing one, but it needn't be. Now that I have found you, you cannot be rid of me. I require no sleep, and I am not so foolish as to be distracted again. In time, you will either see that my help is invaluable or rid yourself of the mortals you have so burdened yourself with in hopes of evading me. In either case, the outcome is beneficial to me," she said.

"What? No!" Ivy objected.

Lain showed little reaction, but it was clear that he was not pleased. Ivy looked pleadingly to Myranda to produce some manner of solution. Myranda merely returned to the task of rendering the meal edible without a fire. Brief attempts to have Myn roast the meat directly on an improvised spit had resulted mostly in singed fingers and charred food, so magic was reluctantly put to work instead. Myn, satisfied that those who mattered to her were not upset, simply ignored those who did not, curling up in Myranda's lap. Defeated, Ivy crossed her arms and pouted.

Lain scanned the horizon and sniffed at the air. No one was near--at least, not to the east, out of which blew the stiff mountain winds. His real concern was in the south. The person he had seen had been heading in that direction. Myranda was not a difficult person to find for those sufficiently skilled, and Lain could think of no other reason one might brave this frozen waste save to find her. There were powerful people on her trail. Normally, he would face such a foe immediately, but now there was Ivy. She must be kept from harm. Nevertheless, the surest way to ensure her safety was to take her to the south as soon as possible. There could be no delay. He would have to take his chances.

The long journey had taken its toll on the others. A semblance of shelter was found. Shortly after, Lain crouched and slipped into his bizarre substitute for sleep and Myranda wrapped her cloak tightly about herself and Myn against the cold. Soon, the only members of the odd group who were awake were Ivy and Ether. Ivy shot Ether angry stares. Ether seemed to look through her with an air of unquestioned superiority. For a time, a there was a mutual feeling of dislike, but a few hours of boredom and curiosity weakened Ivy's resolve.

"So . . . Ether. You can change into anything?" she asked.

Ether stood silent.

"Ether?" Ivy asked, optimistically believing that she had not been heard the first time.

The shapeshifter turned away.

"Can all humans turn into different things?" Ivy asked.

Ether flinched. Ivy grinned.

"I am not a human. Humans are stupid, emotional, worthless creatures. I am beyond human," she stated sternly.

"Well, right now you're human. And you were one before, so you must be a human pretty often," Ivy reasoned.

"I assume this form to more gracefully interact with the weak-minded who could not comprehend my more fundamental forms," she said.

"But right now you're human, yes?" Ivy asked.

"Yes," Ether said.

"And later you will change shape, yes?" Ivy asked.

"As soon as the situation requires it," Ether said.

"So, humans can change shape then," Ivy said.

"Absolutely not!" Ether corrected.

"You are a human, you just said! And if humans can't change shape, then you can't change back!" Ivy said.

Ether turned to face her. Her eyes were narrowed and her fist clenched in frustrated anger.

"I will not waste time and energy forcing understanding into an unwilling mind," she fumed.

"Uh-huh. That just means I win," Ivy said.

"You did *not* win. There was nothing *to* win," Ether snapped.

"Well, you are talking to me now. You weren't before," Ivy said.

"Yes, a mistake I will rectify at once," she said.

She crossed her arms and turned away again. Ivy smiled.

"For someone who claims to be 'above' emotions, you certainly get mad easily," she said.

Ether whipped around, rage in her eyes. The sight before her was Ivy with a satisfied smile.

"Now *I* am going to stop talking to *you,*" she said.

Grinning triumphantly and crossing her arms, she sat on the ground and leaned against Myranda's back. She wasn't tired, not remotely, but she closed her eyes. She could downright *feel* the rage in Ether. The creature who acted so superior was no different from herself. It was a satisfying discovery.

For her part, Ether fairly shook with anger. She had never felt so manipulated, and she had never hated a being more. She had never *hated* before. The fact that this pretender had instilled such a feeling, such a weakness, only intensified it. Her rage was a fire that was fueled by its own existence. Finally, she released it in its most literal form, shifting to flame. The thought of directing her wrath at Ivy lingered in her mind, but instead she used it to reduce a sizable mound of snow to boiling water. The edge of her rage thus blunted, she shifted to water to spend the rest of the night restoring a fraction of her power.

When morning came, Lain was the first to rise, as he had never truly slept. The wind blew with frustrating steadiness from the mountains. It carried little of the information he sought.

Quietly, Ivy joined him. She looked him over with curiosity. He sniffed at the air, she imitated. She continued looking him over, comparing him to herself. He was like her. More like her by far than anything else she had seen or smelled. She had fur, he had fur. She had pointed ears, he had pointed ears. She had a tail . . .

"Where is your tail?" she asked.

He looked at her for a moment, then turned back to his task. Ivy frowned.

"When I was younger, it was cut off and sold," he said after a moment.

"That's terrible. Why?" she asked.

Again Lain hesitated before answering.

"It was more highly valued than I," he said.

"You and I . . . are we the same?" she asked.

"We are," he said.

"Then . . . is that going to happen to me?" she asked.

"No," he answered immediately. "That will not happen to you."

Ivy smiled. The sudden snap and crackle of ice drew their attention. Ether had chosen to rise. After climbing from the frozen pool, she shifted to her human form once more. Ivy gave her a sneer.

"Well, now that this exercise in weakness is over, I trust we can continue," she said.

"Not yet. Myranda isn't up yet," Ivy said.

"Myranda is meaningless. She and the lizard have fulfilled what little role they had," Ether said.

"Well, I'm not leaving without her," Ivy said.

Ether's eyes narrowed. Quickly she forced composure on herself. She would not give this creature the satisfaction of showing anger.

"Very well. If you wish to waste time and further damage our cause, by all means, do so," she said.

"No need," came Myranda's voice wearily.

She hoisted herself to her feet and stretched her stiff joints. She had barely slept, and was chilled to the core, but she refused to burden the others. Myn restored her own warmth with a few bursts of flame. Myranda opened and closed her hands a few times until the feeling began to return to her fingers with an agonizing vengeance.

Lain continued on his way, setting a pace that most easily matched. Myranda had to fairly run to keep up. As she did, she allowed tiny doses of magic to restore enough warmth to her ailing body to convince herself she was out of danger.

In the distance, there was a fair-sized stand of trees beside a small, icy lake. Myranda searched her memory for the name of either, but in all likelihood this unremarkable spot in this icy plain simply didn't warrant one.

"What are you thinking about?" Ivy asked, breaking the trance-like wandering of Myranda's mind.

"I was wondering if this place had a name," she said.

"Why?" she asked.

"Well, it helps me to keep from thinking about less pleasant things," Myranda answered.

"Well, you and I could talk. No one else seems to like to talk," Ivy said.

"Yes . . . I would like that very much," Myranda said.

Engaged in the rare luxury of mutual conversation, the journey seemed to pass more quickly. It was a little difficult at first. Ivy didn't know enough about herself to answer any questions Myranda asked, and Myranda had to take special care not to upset her again. Instead, Ivy asked scores of questions about Myranda and the others, and about the world in general. She seemed to be only vaguely aware of some of the most significant events of the past few decades. Hearing of the war bothered her, but she seemed very interested in anything Myranda had to say about Kenvard.

Ivy was mid-sentence when a gust of wind from the south caused her, as well as Lain and Myn, to lock their eyes on the horizon.

"What is it?" Myranda asked.

"I smell something," Ivy said.

"Nearby," Lain added quietly.

Myn planted herself in front of Myranda, claws dug deep into the frozen earth, teeth bared and wings spread. Whatever was near was a significant threat. Ether sampled the air with her human nose, and when it proved insufficient, plucked a hair from Ivy's head. After a few moments, she stood as a perfect duplicate of Ivy, complete with the sense of smell she desired. Myranda looked desperately about. There was nothing to see. Then . . . *he* appeared. Perhaps fifty paces ahead of them, near the bank of the lake, the spell he had used to conceal himself slipped away like a dropping curtain and there stood Arden--or, more accurately, Epidime.

"You disappoint me. I have been waiting. The party has grown, I see," he said.

He held his weapon, identical to that held by the wizards he had sent after them in recent days. Lain burst forward, sword drawn, ready to make short work of this foe once and for all. At the same instant there was a flicker in the gem of Epidime's halberd. Lain stopped suddenly and retreated slightly. Ivy gasped and hid behind Myranda. Myn dug her claws deeper, and Ether abandoned the malthrope form for her fiery one.

"What is wrong?" Myranda asked.

"So m-many . . . too many," Ivy stuttered, terror in her voice.

"Dragoyles. Dozens of them. I couldn't smell them until now," Lain said.

A second flicker and the landscape darkened with no less than fifty of the crude, horrid beasts. They stood as if posed, perfectly at attention and perfectly still.

"Attack now and I shall have them kill you. Try to run and I shall have them kill you. Behave and we shall have a calm, intelligent discourse. *Then* I shall have them kill you. I think that the choice is clear. Consider it for a moment. Consider for a moment the possibilities and opportunities that these precious few minutes will provide you. Perhaps you will work out some miraculous battle plan that will afford you a victory. Perhaps you will outwit me. It really doesn't concern me," he said with an alarming level of calm.

Lain stood, sword readied. Ivy cowered. Slowly her fear crept outward. Myranda could feel it tingling in her spine. Her hands shook as she held her staff defensively. Eyes turned nervously to Ether. She floated just over the ground. She alone might begin this battle prematurely. Fortunately, she lowered herself to the ground and shifted to stone. From her expression, her decision was motivated by the sheer size of the task ahead.

"Well done. Now, I must congratulate you. Bagu made a rather sudden and *very* angry appearance in the capital. I have never seen him so badly injured, nor have I ever seen him so furious. He immediately sent me out to find and destroy the lot of you, with special emphasis on the shapeshifter. That is rather out of character, and quite at odds with the standard course of action. Demont is the beast wrangler, he would be best left to leading these creatures, and the precision strikes are usually led by Trigorah. Worst of all, killing even one of you before all of the others have revealed themselves is a terrible waste of time. Frankly, I consider this an act of folly," he said.

"Use the bow. Aim for the mouth," Lain instructed.

Myranda nodded, slowly sliding the weapon from her shoulder. Epidime continued as though oblivious to the action.

"Now, I am quite satisfied with my knowledge of the shapeshifter. I do not object to her demise. I would like a look through Lain's head before he dies, and a second try at Myranda would be satisfying, but my real fascination at the moment is with that cowering bit of fluff behind her," he said.

Ivy shrieked and crouched down, hugging her knees and rocking back and forth. The spike in fear sent a visible shudder through her, and a similar one through Myranda and Myn. The event did not go unnoticed by Epidime.

"We put a great deal of work into that little project. I was beginning to wonder if any of it would bear fruit. Forced empathy is intriguing. What else do you have to offer, I wonder?" he asked.

The intimidating man took a step forward; Myranda drew an arrow and made ready to let it fly. Lain shifted his stance.

"Yes, I suppose the time for battle has--" Epidime began.

Before he could finish, Ether had shifted to her fiery form and burst toward him. He deflected the attack with his halberd and willed the dragoyles into action. The earth shook and the sky blackened as dozens of massive beasts leapt into the air and thundered across the ground.

Lain released a trio of dagger-like weapons he'd pulled from his cloak. Two met their mark, both beasts reeled back in pain. The less fortunate of the two let out a pained roar as orange light flashed brilliantly from its mouth. A moment later, the unearthly orange glow emanating from the hollows that served as the creature's eyes faded and the beast literally crumbled to the ground. The second recovered and tried to locate its target once more, but Lain swept in and drove his sword nearly to the hilt into the creature's mouth. With equal speed, he withdrew the blade and evaded the spray of the horrid black acid that came spewing forth from the beast as it flailed about before crumbling away.

Myranda took aim and launched arrows as best she could. It took all of her strength to fully draw back the bow, her hands shaking from fear and effort. She made up for her poor aim by guiding the arrows in flight. Despite the fact she did not hold her staff, and her focus was severely impaired, she still managed to knock a few from the sky.

Myn heaved great bursts of flame that did little more than draw the attentions of the beasts. As they approached, she took to the air, expertly avoiding their leaping attacks and puffing away clouds of black breath with the wind from her wings. She managed to distract a handful, but with so many, it was clear that Myranda could not afford to stand her ground for long.

"Ivy, I need you to try to make it to the trees," Myranda said.

"N-no! I c-c-can't!" she stammered. She had her eyes tightly shut and was fairly whimpering with every breath. Around her, somehow, there was a faint blue glow.

Ether was mercilessly assaulting the halberd-wielding wizard. He wore the same unconcerned, superior look he always did, not a bead of sweat betraying the unimaginable speed and precision of his reactions. Ether's fiery glow faded ever so slightly with every clash with the gem. Finally, she managed to land a single flaming swipe down the side of his face. Anger rather than pain finally found its way into Epidime's expression. He shifted and drove his halberd deep into her form. She cried out as the gem began to ravenously tear at the very core of her strength. She desperately tried to pull herself away, but the gem seemed to have a grip on her.

Myn was causing chaos. The dragoyles, mindlessly attempting to annihilate her, trampled, sprayed, and rammed each other. One or two had succumbed to accidental crashes and lay in broken heaps on the ground. Her nimble maneuvers kept her just beyond their reach, but as more and more of the beasts joined in the task of removing her from battle, the escapes became ever narrower.

Lain had his hands full evading the attacks of those beasts focused on him. The air was thick with the caustic breath, and even one as skillful as he could not avoid a whiff of the evil fumes occasionally, sizzling against his clothes and fur. Quickly slipping through an opening, he charged toward Epidime and the ailing Ether.

Epidime pulled his halberd free to block Lain's blow, allowing the shapeshifter to shift to air and launch skyward. As she rose up, she began to stir the air around her, drawing up the black mist, clearing the battlefield and concentrating the vile stuff. As dozens of the dragoyles spiraled after her, she rose higher and higher. Finally, she released the accumulated ball of acid at the trail of beasts. They had been immune until now, but even their tough and stony hide was not enough to withstand so concentrated a dose. A half-dozen of them dropped to the ground, writhing briefly before collapsing outright.

Lain hoped that the beasts would stay at bay for fear of injuring their master as they had in the past, but such was not the case, and he found himself dodging powerful blows from behind and lightning-fast strikes from in front.

Suddenly Ether swept down, clutching the shaft of the halberd and pulling steeply upward again. Rather than release it, Epidime was lifted into the air. Ether launched skyward, dragging the foe behind her. Despite the rapidly receding ground behind him, Epidime seemed unconcerned. He willed the unholy light into his gem and began to assault her with pulses of energy. She continued to climb. A string of the beasts followed. Finally, wave after wave of dark energy took its toll and Ether released the weapon. Epidime plummeted only a short distance before one of the creatures plucked him out of the air. He moved to the dragoyle's back and turned to the ground. Ether soared upward, far enough out of reach that their attentions were turned elsewhere. Her strength was already beginning to fail, and if she hoped to see this battle through to its end, she would need to choose her attacks wisely.

More than half of the arrows in Myranda's quiver were gone. Not nearly enough remained to fell the beasts that were focused on her. Despite Myn's best efforts, at least five had turned to her. Myranda searched her mind for something in her mystic arsenal that might be of use. Her eyes turned to the lake. She grabbed her staff, conjuring a blast of flame to melt away some ice, and drew out a long stream of water. Compared to her test in Entwell, this was effortless. She shaped a dozen or so spikes and froze them instantly. Maneuvering the ice was easier, and Myranda was able to direct most of the impromptu projectiles to their targets. Unfortunately, the ice was not as effective as the arrows, and only two of the beasts fell. The three that remained were joined by four more and the creatures were moving in fast. She and Ivy desperately needed cover.

"Ivy, quickly, we need to head for the trees!" she said, taking the shivering creature by the arm.

"I can't. I can't," she whimpered.

Myranda knelt to attempt to hoist the malthrope onto her back. Suddenly she felt a piercing, crushing pain in her shoulder. She was torn from the ground. One of the creatures had snatched her up in its jaws. Her shoulder was shattered. She drew together her tortured mind and made ready to unleash all that she had on the beast that carried her, but a voice stopped her.

"If you even attempt to escape, this creature will dissolve the flesh from your bones," said the voice.

On the back of the creature that held her was Epidime. The pain was unimaginable, and grew with each jarring thrust of the creature's wings. A long, fatal fall already stood between Myranda and the ground. Tears streamed down her face and she screamed out in pain. Suddenly there was a flash of heat. Myn was rushing at Epidime, spewing flame. He leveled his weapon at the dragon and released a powerful wave of darkness. Myn dodged with a nimbleness that the dragoyles still on her tail lacked. The first of the pursuers was destroyed by the blast. The next collided with Epidime's mount. The collision jarred Myranda loose.

Ether shifted to flame again and took full advantage of the confusion caused by the creature's collision, unleashing a flurry of attacks on Epidime. Warding her off and remaining atop the creature proved difficult. She scored slash after slash.

Myranda dropped like a stone. A moment later, small, deft claws gripped desperately under her arms. The little dragon had caught her and was putting forth a heroic effort to bring Myranda safely to the ground. Barely half of the woman's size, Myn could only hope to slow the decent.

Worse, doing so robbed her of the agility that had kept her safe. The ground was rapidly approaching and Myn was beginning to lose her grip.

Suddenly, the noble creature's grasp was torn free. One of the dragoyles had grabbed hold of her left wing and was whipping her like a rag doll. Myranda fell to a painful impact on the ground. The pain in her shoulder didn't matter, the fact that the air had been knocked from her didn't matter. As she struggled to pull her unwilling body to its feet, her eyes locked on the little creature.

Lain had managed to dispatch three more of the beasts when he, too, saw the dragon. He had no more daggers to throw, and the creature was well out of the reach of his sword. Myranda reached for an arrow, but they had fallen from the quiver. Scrambling for the one that had fallen nearest to her, she realized that the bow had been broken by the fall as well. Without an open mouth to target, the arrow would do no good anyway.

Hastily, she drew her limited knowledge of black magic to mind. She'd never truly believed that she would have any use for it. The thought that she would ever want to utterly destroy something was detestable, but in this moment, the only thing that mattered was freeing her friend, and punishing the beast that had her. Raising her staff, she cast a burst of raw, destructive magic.

Myranda was staggered by the effort of the unfamiliar technique. The crude, poorly-formed spell crackled viciously through the air, seemingly passing though the dragoyle. As it did, the monstrosity convulsed wildly, and one of the wings fell lifeless. Its jaws released a motionless Myn and both creatures fell to the surface of the frozen lake. Myn bounced horridly off of the surface before the dragoyle came crashing through. The whole of the lake surface broke into shifting sheets of ice, and Myn slipped through a crack into the frigid water.

"No!" Myranda screamed. She looked to the cowering, defenseless form of Ivy, then to Lain. With a glance, each knew what had to be done.

Myranda ran to the shore of the lake, shedding the bags and packs she had been carrying, and making her way onto the shifting ice. She had to make it to Myn. Lain took her place defending Ivy. He knew better than to try to carry her. It would rob him of the speed he would need to evade their attacks. For now, he would have to attack and distract those beasts that had remained focused on the ground. The rest were overhead, where Ether's clash with Epidime continued. In her insubstantial flame form, the beasts could do nothing to harm her, while she was quite capable of harming Epidime. Finally, she knocked the halberd from his hand. He suddenly gripped desperately to the back of the beast. A second creature snatched up the halberd and both turned sharply to the north.

Ether made ready to pursue, but as the swarm of beasts that had been interested in her turned their attentions to the ground, she became aware of what had been transpiring there. Lain was swiftly becoming surrounded. Ivy was curled up on the ground, paralyzed with fear. Myranda was sliding precariously across one of the pieces of ice on the lake. She turned again to the retreating Epidime. Her strength was waning. If he regained the weapon, she could not be sure of defeating him. Memories of the dire state she found herself in after their last encounter crept to her mind, sealing the decision. She returned to the battlefield.

Ether's arrival was not a moment too soon. Lain was having trouble keeping the creatures from Ivy. More than one deep gash betrayed the losing battle he was fighting. Ether shifted to stone, taking her place beside him. As the creatures approached, she delivered blow after earthshaking blow. Most of the dragoyles had already felt the bite of Lain's sword, bearing long scores across faces and along necks. The heavy stone hands opened these wounds, letting a weak orange light leak through before each creature fell.

Myranda reached the point on the ice where Myn had fallen through. Without a moment's hesitation, she plunged in. The cold of the water cut like a knife. She felt as though her chest had caved in. Her tightly closed eyes opened slightly. The pain seemed to surge through to the back of her head. In the pale blue light filtering though the ice, the motionless form of Myn drifted just ahead of her. She worked her frozen limbs, moving toward her friend. The shattered shoulder was nearly useless, her hand clutching loosely at her staff, but still she struggled. Slowly, agonizingly slowly, she drew nearer. Her lungs screamed for air, her shoulder screamed for relief, her body screamed for warmth, but she pressed on.

Finally, she reached out with her good arm, grasped the dragon, and fought to the surface. Her heart dropped. The ice had shifted. Three great sheets had butted together above her. Her air wouldn't hold out much longer. The pain and cold had left her mind in a shambles. With supreme effort, she conjured up a current that would carry her to the shore. She closed her eyes and gathered as much focus as she could.

A dragoyle heaved a great black breath at Ivy. Lain, left with no options, scooped her from the ground. The acid missed Ivy by a hair, but Lain was not so lucky. His leg was coated with the stuff. In moments, it had seeped and sizzled through the cloth and begun to eat away at the fur and flesh beneath. His teeth clenched in pain, but he remained silent and moved as quickly as the worsening leg would allow. With a very large, very slow target available, the dragoyles lost interest in Ether and focused entirely on Lain. He was swiftly surrounded. One hand tightened around the grip of his sword. The other slowly lowered Ivy to the ground.

"Ivy. You need to fight," he said.

She rose shakily to her feet. The club she carried had never left her hand. She raised it.

"I can't do this . . . I can't do this," she whispered, looking in terror at the beasts before her.

Suddenly, the creatures were distracted. There was a growing roar coming from the lake. As they turned to survey this new threat, they were met with the sight of the lake seemingly leaping from its shores and attacking them. Vast chunks of ice and torrents of water flooded over the battleground. Ivy closed her eyes and turned away, stifling a scream. Ether shifted to water and slipped into the ring of dragoyles. She merely raised her hand and the water parted around them. Some of the beasts were caught in the torrent, washed aside or smashed with ice. The rest had sprung into the air. As the water receded, the forms of Myranda and Myn were left behind.

Myranda drew in a long, painful breath and crawled to Myn. The dragon's wing was barely more than a few shreds of tattered skin, and she wasn't breathing. Myranda turned her mind to healing and searched the creature's body for injury besides the wing. As swiftly as she found them, she eliminated them. Soon, all that was left was the ruined wing. Myn had not taken a breath in minutes; there simply was not time to heal the wing completely. She stopped the bleeding, satisfied that it would be enough to take her out of danger. Heat was conjured to warm her, the water mystically drawn from her lungs, and still the dragon did not breathe.

Calling to mind her wind magic, Myranda forced air into her lungs and out again. Finally, Myranda had exhausted all of her knowledge and most of her strength, and the dragon remained still. She was faced with an undeniable fact. Myn was dead. The soul had left the body. No amount of healing could bring it back.

For a moment the world seemed to vanish. The life-threatening cold, the shattered shoulder that trickled blood down her blue-tinged skin, even the shadows and shrieks of the creatures closing in. All were gone as sorrow seized the very core of her being. Tears streamed down her face. She cried the dragon's name, shaking the lifeless body with her good arm until the pendant that Myn had worn about her neck came free in her hand.

Myranda closed her eyes. Slowly she shook her head. No. This was not how it would end. Not this way. Not now. She sat on the icy ground beside the dragon and pulled the staff from her useless left hand. Distantly, she heard Lain and Ivy call after her. She pushed the sound out of her mind.

Just as she had a few nights before, she twisted and turned the entirety of her spirit. She could feel the bonds that held her to her physical form begin to loosen their grip. The spiritual plane began to replace the physical one. Finally, her spirit tore itself free. Once again, she was afloat in a sea of lights. In the distance, there was the weak and fading glow that she knew was Myn. She willed herself toward it.

"Myranda, Myn! Get up! We need to run!" Ivy cried, her eyes darting wildly from dragoyle to dragoyle as they drew closer.

Ether looked over the scene.

"The fool," she hissed, turning to Lain. "I suppose that you will not leave this place without the human."

Lain's only response came as an angry glance before scooping water from the ground to wash away the black mist from his leg.

Ether raised her hand and the water swept up around them, freezing together into a shell.

"The ice will keep them from us, but not for long. The foolish human has left her body," Ether deduced.

"She what? But why?" Ivy asked, jumping as the first attacks began to rain down upon the protective shell.

"The poison of emotion, and because of you," Ether said. "The lizard has died, the human will likely follow, and all because you were too much of a coward to be of any use to anyone."

"No . . . I couldn't . . ." Ivy said, fear giving way to despair.

"What did you expect? Your emotion crippled you, and the same wretched weakness has caused all that followed. You are worthless!" Ether ranted.

"No, I'm not worthless! I'm not!" Ivy cried, dropping her club, covering her ears, and shutting her eyes.

Ether continued, amid increasingly angry refusals from Ivy. "You are a horrid, malformed, ignorant monstrosity. The best thing you could do is die swiftly to allow a more able being to replace you. As it is, it couldn't be more clear that you are an agent of the enemy. A plaything of the D'karon."

Ivy slowly removed her hands and locked Ether in an infuriated scowl.

"I am *not* one of them," she said. Gone was the childish tone. Her voice was serious, and carried the hint of threat.

#

The astral plain was no place for an unprepared mind. Myranda fought to comprehend it. Time and distance were different than in the physical realm. She chased after Myn's spirit, but it was drawn ever further from her, as if by a current. Here, Myranda's urgency was a boon to her focus, not a detriment. The faster she *wanted* to move, the faster she *did* move. Her will didn't just mean something here--it meant everything. It *was* everything.

She focused entirely upon the vague form that seemed to retreat as quickly as she could follow. A galaxy of flickering lights rushed by her.

The souls of untold millions of living things. None of them mattered right now. She reached out with her left hand. Here, at least, it was healthy. A few moments more . . . a few inches further . . . contact. Myranda could suddenly feel the life force of her friend. She grasped it, drew it near, and turned back. If her last journey into this other plane was any indication, her strength would not last long.

All that lay ahead was the same sea of glowing currents and points of light. There was no hint of where she had been. Nothing that distinguished anything from anything else. For the second time, she had taken a treacherous journey to rescue her friend, and once again her return seemed impossible. She searched desperately about. Already her "vision" was dimming. The more distant of the lights were fading from view.

#

Back on the battleground that Myranda so eagerly sought, the argument was continuing. Ether found the strongest objections came when she implied a connection to the D'karon, and had thus ceased to do anything else. Ivy's anger became sharper, more focused. Lain stood with his back to them. Before him was the weakest point in the icy shield, and his sword was ready to destroy the creature unlucky enough to be the first through.

"Do not imagine that you can hide it. I have taken your shape. I know that there is not an aspect of your physical being that has not been affected by their machinations," Ether taunted.

Suddenly, the sharp anger in Ivy's eyes became brittle, a whisper of fear showing through.

"No . . . can you feel that? It's coming. The monster . . ." she said. Her tone lacked the edge of her previous comments, as though the frightened child was trying to fight her way to the surface.

"I suppose I am to be intimidated. This imagined monster that destroyed the fort and left only you alive. Do you think me a fool? The only monster here is you," Ether said with a smug sneer.

For the whole of the argument, Ether had been pushing Ivy closer and closer to a line. That line had been crossed. Her eyes clouded over, eyelids fluttering slightly. A deep, reverberating growl shook like a tremor. The air began to grow warmer, until water was running down the icy shield despite Ether's best efforts to keep it frozen.

"Your parlor tricks do not frighten me," Ether said.

Ivy dropped to one knee. Her fingers wrapped around the handle of the club, clutching the wood so tightly it creaked. The growl grew into a roar. Finally, there was a burst of energy. It erupted with a force that shattered the shell of ice, sending pieces flying dozens of paces.

Lain--along with the bodies of Myranda and Myn--was sent hurtling though the air, sliding to a stop a fair distance away. Ether's watery form was scattered. She swiftly gathered herself together, shifting to flame in the process. When her senses returned to her, they beheld an awesome sight. Ivy was floating above the ground. A viciously red aura enveloped her, shifting continuously with the crackle of raw energy. An unnatural wind stirred her cloak and rippled her long hair. The club burned where her fingers touched it, the iron barbs glowing white-hot. Her eyes, now featureless orbs of light that trailed tangible streams of energy, locked onto Ether. The shapeshifter felt the power this creature was spilling off. It was at least equal to her own at her peak, and she most certainly was well short of that at the moment. Best to keep her distance.

Ivy suddenly burst forward. Her speed was astounding. Ether darted directly upward. Ivy followed. The gap closed quickly, and a monumental swipe of the raging Ivy's cudgel virtually scattered Ether again. The attack was devastating. She was forced to shift to air, lest she give out entirely. Ivy halted, bowing her head and clutching at her chest. A deafening roar of combined anger and pain left her lips as, through her fingers, the burning of the mark could be seen. It only lasted for a moment, and seemed to further fuel the creature's rage. She surged forward again with renewed force.

Like a sparrow pursued by an eagle, Ether made sudden turns and drops, but to no avail. As all of the remaining dragoyles took to the air in pursuit of this latest target, Ether flew toward them, weaving between. Ivy tore through them with little resistance. One by one, the great black beasts were reduced to fragments of broken rubble. It was not until no fewer than four such collisions had occurred that Ivy's momentum began to flag. When she slowed, the beasts swarmed.

Soon, all that could be seen was a writhing mass of black creatures clustered about a red glow. Ether hung in the air at a cautious distance, slowly weighing the risks of remaining until the end of the battle.

#

Something caught Myranda's attention. Far away, and far below, there was a bright red flash, and it burned like a brilliant crimson ember amid pale white glimmers. It was the only unique point she could determine, and thus the only target that made sense. Pulling the essence of her departed friend behind, she rushed to it. Everything around her was fading.

So focused was she on the red beacon ahead, she failed to notice a golden light following her. She rushed forward faster and faster, and the glow easily kept pace. Only when it began to overtake her did she realize it was there. It moved with the force of an avalanche, and before long it was pushing her along faster than even her desperation had managed to propel her. It did not do the same for Myn. As Myranda was accelerated, she could feel her grip failing.

Ahead, the spirits of Lain and Ether, almost drowned out by the powerful red glow, emerged. Just a few moments more and she would reach her own body and that of her dear friend. She could restore her. At the very instant she made contact with her physical body, she felt her grasp torn from Myn. Her eyes shot open, and the cold and pain she had been spared while her spirit was absent overwhelmed her. She cried out, attracting the attention of Lain, who had dispatched the handful of creatures that had turned back to the ground.

"Lain . . . please . . . Myn . . . is she alive?" Myranda managed.

Lain moved quickly to the dragon's side. It was cold to the touch. He put his sensitive ear to the noble beast's chest. Not a whisper of a heartbeat. He turned to Myranda. The look in his eyes told her all she needed to know. With the pain of loss surpassing by far every ounce of physical pain and more, she let herself slip into unconsciousness, the fingers of one hand clamped about the staff, and the other about the pendant. Lain trained his eyes on the spectacle above just in time for a second epic burst of energy to scatter the beasts. Ivy, her aura significantly dimmer, plummeted to the ground, landing with an earthshaking impact.

When the dust settled, she was still standing. There were thirteen of the creatures left. Ivy's eyes were still locked on Ether, and she thundered toward her. She was limited to the ground now, but clearly remained a force to be reckoned with. Her footfalls left deep, jagged craters. She remained the primary interest of the remaining beasts, and as each swept in it was met with a powerful backhand or swipe with the club. Lain snatched up Myranda's bag from where the surge of water had washed it and threw her over his shoulder. His leg was unsteady, but he had little choice. One of the creatures had turned to him. If he was to have a chance at protecting Myranda and himself, he would need the cover of the trees. He moved as quickly as he could manage, the beast snatching up the lifeless body of Myn and taking to the sky with it. He had only just made it past the first of the trees when Ether's windy form joined him.

"Leave the human behind. We have more pressing battles ahead. She will only slow us," she urged.

In a moment, the rhythmic thunder of Ivy's footsteps had grown near enough to shake the snow from the trees around them. Ether turned to the approaching threat. Her aura had nearly faded to nothing. The beasts were at her heels, but she seemed to care only about Ether. As she drew nearer, her strength finally gave out. She dropped to her knees, and finally collapsed forward. Lain laid Myranda at the base of a large oak that still had some of its leaves. He then rushed out to the motionless Ivy.

"Do *not* risk your life for that *wretch*. If she'd had her way, she would have killed me!" Ether ordered.

The command fell on deaf ears. Lain dodged the diving attack of one creature, and snatched up Ivy. The unconscious creature's fingers were locked about the grip of the club, the studs that lined it still sizzling in the snow. He delivered her to the base of the tree and faced the dragoyles.

"I lack the strength to damage these creatures," Ether warned.

"Then keep their breath from me," he replied.

The oak prevented the creatures from attacking from behind. The attacks came from all other sides. To simply block them would not be enough. He lacked the strength to absorb such a blow, and he could not afford to give an inch of ground. His blade moved with a speed and precision that could scarcely be followed by even the sharpest eye. Quick slashes found their way to every joint, every gash, every fracture the others had caused. Ether's talents swirled the caustic breath away. One fell, and another. Gashes deepened. Here and there, a swiping claw caught Lain, but he could not allow it to slow him.

The black creatures succumbed, one after the other, until only two remained. They attacked simultaneously. The first was ended with a slash to the throat. The second clamped its stony beak down on his upper arm.

The creature did not shake its prey as the one that had snared Myn did. There was only a twitch, then another, before finally it dropped to the ground. Lain had delivered the killing blow through the side of the creature's head with his free hand. Slowly, he pulled the blade from the creature's skull and surveyed his own wounds. Most were minor. The last was dire. Blood flowed freely from his arm. The creature's bite had reached the bone. With his good arm, he tore away the shreds of the ruined sleeve and began to bind the wound, pulling the knots tight with his teeth. As he did so, Ether shifted to her human form and looked coldly over the battleground.

The icy ground was littered with the stony remnants of dragoyles. There were sizzling black pools of their breath, and everything was smudged with their thick, black blood. Ether kicked open the ruined skull of the nearest beast, interested to see what it was within their mouths that was so vulnerable. Inside was a shattered gem, the very same type that Epidime had been using to draw away her strength. She stepped quickly away from the thing, the memory of its searing effect still fresh in her mind.

She then turned to Lain. His white cloak and tunic was soiled from head to toe. Dark smears of black blended with bright stains of red. In a dozen places, torn fabric revealed torn flesh. The leg that had been exposed to the acid was still faintly sizzling in places. The fur was blackened, and where it had been eaten away, the skin was blistered. Most dire was the injury to his arm. He had reached over with his left hand to apply extra pressure.

Despite his efforts, an appalling volume of blood rolled from the wound in thin streams.

"The wound on your arm . . . is it mortal?" Ether asked.

"I am losing too much blood," he said.

"I cannot heal you. I had never anticipated the need to," Ether said. "However, I can seal the wound,"

She shifted one of her hands to flame. He nodded and removed the bandage. She ran a fiery finger along the gash, instantly cauterizing it. The pain must have been agonizing, but Lain merely shut his eyes and weathered it as he did everything else--silently.

The ordeal had left the survivors completely sapped of strength. The sun was setting again, and soon after the darkness had become complete, Lain entered the warrior's sleep. Ether gathered together a moderate pile of wood and lit a fire, shifting to flame and stepping into it when it reached respectable size. Ivy was deep in a dreamless sleep. Not so for Myranda.

She lay, propped up against the tree, her mind anything but at rest. The events of her life rushed by again and again, accompanied by whispered thoughts and regrets. The flood of images and voices was disorienting and indistinct. All of the voices were distant, slurred, mumbled. All of the images were vague and fleeting. There was a feeling of tumbling, of falling, as though her mind's breaking point had been reached, the dam had given way, and all that she was had begun rushing out.

Suddenly, a single, sharp, clear voice cut through the rest.

"Open your eyes, Myranda," the voice said.

In an instant, the other voices were silent, the images gone, dispelled by the man's voice. She did as she was asked. The pain in her shoulder was gone, the cold was gone, the fatigue was gone. The grove of trees seemed subdued, bathed in a weak, pale blue light. Everything was still; not the slightest flutter of wind stirred the leaves of the one tree that still bore them. Around her, she saw her companions--Ivy beside her, Lain in front of her, and Ether's fiery form in front of him. All were unmoving, even the tendrils of flame were motionless, frozen. She stood. There was a man before her. She knew him. He had sparse white hair, plain black clothes, and his eyes were closed.

"You . . . you are the priest," she said.

"That is how you knew me, yes," he said.

"Am I . . . dead?" she asked.

"You aren't alive, but neither are you dead. In a sense, you have been pulled aside," he said.

"Why? How? Why are you here?" she asked.

"All valid questions. Part of why I am here is to answer them," he said. "There are important things happening, Myranda. A crossroads has been reached, and the next few steps are of the direst importance. I cannot tell you which steps to make, nor what is to come, but I can tell you what you need to know to make these next steps wisely."

"I don't understand. Why now? Why me? Why you?" she asked.

"Sit," he said, indicating a log to his left. She did, and he joined her.

"Let me begin by saying that I am not simply a holy man stirred to anger by your pacifistic tendencies. That was merely a role I deemed likely to lead you in the correct direction. My true name--or, at least, the one by which I am most frequently known--is Oriech," he said.

"If you aren't a priest, then what are you?" she asked.

"A difficult question to answer. I suppose the simplest description of my place in this world is the hand of fate. For the most part, the course of history is left to its own devices. On occasion, there is an imperative, something that must be done to ensure the course stays true. I am charged with assuring such events," he said.

"You mean the prophecy," she said.

He sighed.

"To a certain degree, it can be viewed that way, yes," he reluctantly agreed.

"But that doesn't make any sense. You didn't help me. You didn't lead me! You forced me back out into the cold when I first met you," she said.

"And I told you to go to Bydell, where you met Lain. It isn't much, I know, but it had to occur at that time, in that way, or other more important things could not have been possible. I have done the same for each of the Chosen. Lain knew me as an old man named Ben. Others knew me by other names. Had I done my job better, this meeting might not have been necessary, but as it stands, things are not precisely as they should have been. There are things you believe that are not so, and things you need to know which you do not. Now is the time to rectify that," he said.

"So you can answer all of my questions," she said.

"No, not all. I am here merely to inform you of that which you already know, and which you would have known had the path not shifted," he said.

"Why? Why now?" she asked.

"The point of no return has been reached. The names of the Chosen have been written in stone. The Great Convergence has occurred," he said.

"What? No! How can that be? We have only found three," she said.

"I count four," he said.

"Lain, Ether, and Ivy," she said.

"And you," he added.

The words made Myranda's heart leap into her throat.

"It can't be! I can't be Chosen!" she said frantically.

"You are pure of soul--" he began.

"But I am not divine of birth. My mother and father were human. They were mortal," she remarked.

"You needn't be born of a god to be divine of birth. Your existence in this world must simply be the work of the direct will of the divine," he clarified.

"Then how? How am I the work of the divine?" she asked.

"I am not certain you truly wish to know that answer. It is not as . . . inspiring as one might hope," he warned.

"Tell me," she demanded.

He sighed again.

"The gods are many things. They are mighty, they are wise, and, above all, they are anxious for change. As such, they take great interest in the lives of mortals. One day, your mother and father became of particular interest to two of them. You see, the two gods question were in disagreement over whether love was a thing of the body or a thing of the mind. A wager had been made about it, and when it became clear that despite the duties of a soldier keeping them apart, your parents remained in love, rather than lose the wager, the more unscrupulous of the divine ones . . . tipped the scales in his favor. I cannot be specific and remain discreet, but suffice to say the physical aspect of the emotion in question was made firmly obvious upon your father's next visit. Nine months later, you were born."

"I was born because one of the powers that be cheated on a wager?" she said in disbelief.

"In a manner of speaking," he said apologetically. "It was for that reason that the possibility of your taking the place of a fallen Chosen was never given any consideration until recently. The divine circumstances of your birth were concealed even from the other gods, lest the treachery be known."

Myranda shook the absurd thought from her mind.

"I was not born with the mark," she said, holding up her scarred left palm.

In place of the thin white curve and point that had been left by the sting of the sword all those months ago, there was a black, distinct mark. A birthmark.

"The mark is not an aspect of the body. It is an aspect of the soul. It becomes visible at the moment of the quickening, the moment that you are selected. For most of the Chosen, that moment is their birth. In your case, it was the moment you touched the hilt of the sword.

"You see, the swordsman you found that day was to be one of the Chosen. His name was Rasa. When he was struck down, his spirit lingered within the sword. When you touched it, your soul was bared to him. Your worth was made clear to him. He chose you to take his place. And so the quickening occurred. For others, it might have occurred differently. Perhaps silently, perhaps with a drastic change of mind and body," he explained.

"But . . . even if I am Chosen, that still only makes four. The five of us need to be together in the same place, don't we?" she asked.

"That is one of the many misapprehensions you have been laboring under. There is more to the Great Convergence than five specific beings being within an arbitrary radius of each other at the same moment in time. More than anything, it is a moment of decision. Yes, you have met the final Chosen One, but just because that being is not present does not mean the decision couldn't be made. What you *do* correctly comprehend is the consequence of the Great Convergence. From this point forward, there can be no substitutions. If there is a fatality or a betrayal, there shall arise no one to take their place. It is of crucial importance that the integrity of the team be maintained. Every day another path to victory is closed forever. All five of you have a role to fulfill," he said.

"Who is the final Chosen One?" she asked.

"I cannot tell you," he said.

"Why not?" Myranda objected.

"Listen. This is a test of the worth of your people and of your world. The Chosen did not have to exist. Another foolish belief you have is that the Chosen were put here to guarantee success. That is simply not so. You were created to make success a possibility. You represent the bare minimum that is needed to fend off this threat," he said.

"Why would the gods test us against each other? What can possibly be proved by letting us fight one another? By making it harder for us to end this war?" she demanded.

"Therein lies your most dangerous misguided belief. The war is not the reason the Chosen were created. The war is merely a symptom of the disease. I ask you again to think of the actions of Ether. Her concern rests solely upon the destruction of the D'karon. That is the true purpose of the Chosen. That is why you were brought together.

"You are being tested against the D'karon. They are products of other gods. They are not of this world. They are not of this plane of existence. The war is a weapon in their arsenal, a brilliant tactic. They have kept us fighting against ourselves, doing their work for them. The gods could not care less about a war between men, or any other of their creations. It is merely sibling rivalry. With the D'karon, it is another thing altogether.

"You and all of the people of our world become pieces on a game board. Existence is a privilege. I exist only to keep the playing field level. I am forbidden from holding your hand through this. If we cannot defend this world through our own merit, we have no right to it," he explained.

Myranda struggled to accept what she had been told. Ending the war had been the most important thing to her. It had seemed like the most important thing in the world. Now that she knew the truth, the meaning it had carried before seemed insignificant. It was impossible to comprehend it all at once.

"I am sorry this had to be placed on your shoulders. This burden was not meant for you, but I want you to know that you have risen to the challenge better than any of us could have hoped," he said.

She shook her head slowly.

"How can you say that? I have been near death so often. I have been captured again and again. I couldn't even save the life of Myn! How can I be one of the Chosen?" she cried.

"Know this. The spark of the divine is in you. Your every act is an extension of divine will. Remember that. It is nearly time for you to turn back to your task. If you have any more questions, I shall answer those that I can. Remember, I am not permitted to answer any question that may distract you from your task," he offered.

"What happened to the others? The other Chosen?" she asked.

"Lain and Ether are as they were created, and you know what happened to Rasa. The others wound up in the hands of the D'karon. Their fate is best left unspoken," he said.

"There are so many parts to the prophecy . . . I have even heard that five must enter the final battle . . . but only four will leave. Is that true? Is one of the Chosen doomed to die if we are to succeed?" she asked.

"The prophecy . . . let me tell you something about prophecy, Myranda. We do not have a plan for each and every person. You shape your own lives. I and those like me do not seek to preserve a path we have selected for you. You have selected your own path. All we do is ensure that the way forward is clear. When a prophet looks ahead or questions the spirits and speaks of a tragedy you must avert, or a mistake you must avoid, you must remember that it was your decisions that led you to that point. To trust him is to distrust yourself, to second guess yourself before you've even had a chance to guess. Live your life now. The future will come regardless," he said.

"You didn't answer my question," she said.

"The future is not for you to know," he said.

"Then what of the past. My father . . . how did he die, when did he die?" she asked.

"I can tell you of the past. I can tell you the present. I cannot tell you that. No decision you make from this day forward is without consequence. Today you made a choice that wove a new thread," he said.

The very moment the words left his mouth, the stillness around her seemed to waver, a breath of cold could be felt, and a twinge of the pain of her shoulder reappeared.

"I have overstepped my bounds. Return to your task, Myranda. Tend to your friends," he said.

His wording was awkward, seemingly purposely so. She turned his words over in her head. Was he trying to keep something from her, or trying to tell her something? She found herself, against her will, returning to her place beside the others. The cold came pouring back, the searing pain. The color streamed back to her world. Ether's fiery form began to wave and flicker again. The same faint gold color that had been painting the skies to the west when her eyes closed now adorned the east. She had slept the whole of the long night through.

She closed her eyes again and focused on her ruined shoulder. The bones began to move and shift, snapping back into place with an all-too-familiar jolt of pain. Before long, it was usable again. She placed her hand on the ground to help herself up, the fingers touching something hard among the crystals of snow. It was the pendant that she had pulled from Myn. She tied it around her own neck before climbing to her feet.

Her motion caused Ether to step from her place among the smoldering coals and shift back to her human form.

"You, human. Heal Lain," came her command.

Myranda nodded and turned to the warrior's entranced form. The fact that he was still in this state was a testament to the severity of his injuries. Before she set herself to the task, however, his eyes opened.

"See to Ivy first," he said.

Myranda did as she was told. She searched the sleeping form for injury. Muscles were strained. Sections of her clothes were scorched and brittle. She had been though something severe, but there was nothing serious that needed attention.

"What happened to her?" Myranda asked.

"She illustrated just precisely what a danger she is to our cause," Ether fumed.

"She isn't in any danger. She was the same after she faced the wizard outside of the fort. Was she afraid? Did she run?" Myranda asked.

"She let her anger rob her of what little control she had. She abused the power afforded to her by her status as one of the Chosen and tried to destroy me," Ether said.

"I have never seen a more destructive force," Lain said.

Myranda looked to Lain. His injuries were many, and serious, but not beyond the healer's skills. Before long, all of the wounds were sealed completely and free of scars. Even the long, black burn along his arm was eliminated. When she was through, she finished healing her own wounds. With her task aside, she had nothing left to keep her mind from what she had learned. She shifted her staff to her right hand and took a deep breath. Slowly, she turned her hand over. The black mark stood out against her chilled white skin as clear as day.

"Ether. I have something important to tell you," Myranda said.

"I sincerely doubt that," Ether said.

"This is serious, Ether . . . the Convergence has occurred," Myranda said.

"Such things are no place for humor, human," Ether remarked sternly.

"During the night I was visited by someone who called himself Oriech--" Myranda began.

"Silence. You have no right to speak that name. So significant a figure would not waste a moment of his precious time on one such as you," Ether reprimanded.

"You know of him?" Myranda asked.

"Of course. Oriech is he who speaks and acts for the divine. The keeper of the purpose," Ether said, almost reverently.

"He spoke to me. He told me that the Great Convergence had occurred," Myranda assured her.

"Why would he tell you, a common mortal, rather than Lain or I?" she asked.

"I have been Chosen. Look at my hand," she said, offering up her palm.

"I have seen your disfigurement. It is an affront to antiquity that it may remain on your flesh," she replied.

"No, look!" Myranda urged.

Ether shifted her gaze to the palm. Her eyes narrowed.

"Impossible. You are neither clever nor powerful enough to conjure such a mark falsely. Doing so would surely destroy you. It must be so. You . . . of all creatures on this face of this world, *you* have been Chosen. A simple human. We shall have to carry you as a weight about our necks. The fates must care little for the welfare of their world to place the burden of its protection upon your worthless shoulders," she muttered, adding after a moment. "You have been given a place by my side, that much is certain, but I am by no means convinced that the Convergence has yet occurred. Were it so, then that beast, Ivy, a monster who would sooner destroy me and herself in the process than hear the truth spoken, would be fated to fight by my side as well. For all of our sakes, I must believe that you are mistaken. Else, all is lost . . ."

Lain silently hoisted Ivy to his shoulders and began to head south once again.

"Lain, there is more. This war, it is more than you think," she said.

He continued silently.

"You can't just take Ivy south. She is Chosen, they will never stop looking for her," Myranda urged.

"Lain, while it is true that we must be rid of this burden before the final Chosen appears and she is cemented into the group by the Great Convergence, it would be best to be keenly aware of this beast's location. If for no other reason than to have her as a last resort," Ether reluctantly admitted.

"I do not care about the Convergence. I do not care about the Chosen. I will have the head of any who seek hers," he said.

"You must not turn from your purpose," Ether reminded him.

"I had only one purpose. To buy back the lives of those who had them stolen. Now I have another: to see that this creature dies the natural death that the rest of my people were denied, and perhaps . . . just perhaps . . . to see her find another and preserve our kind for one generation more. I care nothing for the rest of the world. I have lived for more years than any mortal has any right to, and in all of those years I have seen nothing worth dying for, and nothing worth living for. This place and all those in it can shrivel and die. It has nothing for me," he said.

"You believe that concoction on your shoulders to be one of your kind?" Ether scoffed.

Lain remained silent.

"What else could she be?" Myranda asked.

"I have assumed her form. She is indeed similar to Lain. More so than mere blood relation can explain. The few alterations that make her anything short of a twin are crude, obvious, even clumsily made. She is a product of the heavy-handed tinkering of a moderately skillful practitioner of the dark arts. I cannot say to what degree she has been changed. There is not enough of her original form left to serve as a basis of comparison," she stated, as a matter of fact.

Lain stopped.

"From the looks of her, she wasn't even complete," she said. "What disturbs me most is that she still bears the mark. It should have destroyed her the very instant they began to work on her."

"What else do you know about her?" Myranda asked.

"The oldest tissue in her body is only a few months old. Either that is the oldest change the manipulators made . . . or that is the age of the original form. Also, Lain is most certainly the template upon which this forgery was built. There was a stain of blood on the floor of the room she was being kept in. It was nearly degraded beyond recognition, but it was undeniably his," Ether remarked.

"You can tell that much?" Myranda said.

"Simple human. I can tell *everything* about a form from a single touch, provided it has not been so badly tampered with as she," Ether said.

Lain's face was unchanged. There was no indication what was going on in his mind. A brief, shining hope had been stolen away from him-- something that had been enough to convince him, in the space of a day, to uproot himself and postpone the cause that had driven him for decades. Now hope was replaced by doubt, mystery. He lowered Ivy to the ground, kneeling beside her and looking at her sleeping face. Slowly he drew his sword. Myranda drew a breath, unsure of what he had in mind. He bent low and nicked her finger. A lone red drop spilled out to stain the white fur. He then cut his own finger and watched the drop roll down. The sword was put in its place, and Ivy was raised to his shoulders once more. He continued southward.

"You mortals have truly poisoned his mind," Ether reprimanded.

Myranda ignored her.

"Lain. I understand how you feel. But think about it. You can't just hide her away. She doesn't know what you have planned for her. She won't be happy when she hears that you plan to leave her," Myranda said.

"I do not care if she is happy. My only concern is that she survives," Lain said.

"I know what happened when she became too frightened, and you have seen what happened when she became angry. It is only a matter of time before something like that happens again. Will these friends you hope to leave her with be able to handle that? They certainly won't be able to hide it, and before long agents of the D'karon will be after her," Myranda reasoned.

"Then I will take her where she cannot be found. I will take her to those who can handle her," Lain said.

"Entwell," Myranda said.

Her mind flashed upon her time there. It was a paradise, certainly the happiest time of her life, and it was the perfect place for Ivy. But it would not do. It would waste time and leave them with an incomplete force.

"How do you suppose you will get her there? The cave is a terrifying place. What guarantee do we have that the way is even open? Do you suppose that we can afford to remain within the cave for months waiting for it to clear?" Myranda said.

Lain stopped once more.

"Lain, the best way to make her safe is to see to it that the world she lives in is safe. I give you my word that I will protect her with my life. As long as I live, she will live," she swore to him.

"Some assurance. The feeble of body protecting the feeble of mind. Were I you, human, I would focus on preserving my own fragile form. After all, that lizard of yours was far better equipped to protect someone than you, and--" Ether said.

"Don't you dare finish that sentence," Myranda hissed.

"Listen, human, do not think that your recently bestowed status as my comrade in arms in any way makes you my equal. I will not abide anything short of reverence from you," Ether warned.

"Reverence? What have you done to earn my reverence? You condescend to all around you. You care nothing for anyone. You *run away* from any battle that manages to even threaten you!" Myranda fumed.

"I have yet to face anything that could hope to do anything more than delay me, and it is just such a delay that I am bound by my purpose to avoid at all costs. You, on the other hand, have no respect for the purpose for which you have been so recently tapped. Look at you. You are wasting away. Seldom do we have an encounter of any kind that fails to leave you at death's door. You didn't eat yesterday, and with that anchor about Lain's shoulders, I do not imagine he will be providing a meal any time soon. You are the victim of innumerable weaknesses. You would do well to address them before attempting to offer aid to those infinitely superior to you," she said.

"I can take care of myself. Unlike you, I know what pain and difficulty is. I face it every day," Myranda said.

"The insignificant things that constitute pain and hardship in your pitiful life are nothing to the trials that lie ahead. Do not presume that--" Ether began.

"Silence," Lain stated with authority.

Both Ether and Myranda instantly obeyed. Seldom did Lain address either of them. From one who spoke so seldom, words carried considerably more weight. No explanation of his order followed, but none was needed. The group simply continued south in silence. Before long, the reality of the situation came heavily upon Myranda. Her stomach growled, and she could feel the nagging weakness that assured her she was more than simply hungry--she was truly starving. She rummaged through the bag. All that remained was the stylus, a rock-hard frozen potato, two knives, and her canteen. All the rest had been washed away or used up. She transferred the potato to the inside of her cloak. It was an old trick; her body heat would eventually thaw it enough to be edible.

Ether watched Myranda with her emotionless gaze, silently judging her.

Time wore on. The sun began to fade, and the air became colder. Myranda wrapped her hand around the pendant that Myn had worn. She missed her. Even the absence of the sound of her footsteps made the world seem hollow. Tears trickled down her face. She quickly wiped them away, more to avoid a comment from Ether than to keep them from freezing. It was a pointless act. Before a second tear could fall, Ether had begun her assault.

"So. This is sadness. Clearly the most worthless emotion," she said quietly.

Myranda ignored her, but she went on.

"What possible purpose can be served by mourning the dead? Fear keeps you from danger, and anger motivates you to take action. Mourning does nothing. For mortals, death is a certainty from birth--a fact that each passing moment you are keenly aware of. To alter your behavior in any way when an anticipated inevitability occurs shows a disdain for what little knowledge you have of your future," Ether stated.

"Myn was my friend. I cared about her," Myranda said.

"Well, she is gone. Any time spent thinking of her is wasted. She doesn't matter anymore," Ether proclaimed.

Myranda opened her mouth to object, but before she could, Ivy stirred. She stretched and yawned before being lowered to the ground by Lain. She looked about sleepily, her mind slowly taking in her surroundings.

"What happened . . . what was going on?" she asked, more to herself than her companions.

Slowly, the memory of her last waking moments returned, and a desperate, terrified look came to her face.

"The monster! It came back, didn't it! What did it do?" she cried.

Her eyes darted around. The surroundings were different. There were no enemies about. No one seemed hurt . . . but someone was missing.

"Where is Myn?" she gasped.

Myranda didn't need to answer. The look in her eyes was answer enough.

"No . . . NO! She's gone! She's dead!" she cried, a torrent of tears and sobs following.

As before, it didn't take long for the intensity of Ivy's sorrow to infect Myranda. Somehow Lain and Ether seemed immune, but the weeping creature was inconsolable, and Myranda had to fight her own sadness compounded with Ivy's. She offered her shoulder to cry on, all the while choking back her own tears. In the back of her mind, she prayed that Ether would remain silent. Mercifully, it would seem that sorrow did not bring a violent reaction similar to those that anger and fear had, but it would only take a few of Ether's venom-soaked words to turn this into a far more volatile situation. For now, the shapeshifter simply stood with her cold, judging stare.

It was several minutes before Ivy was able to fit words between her sobs again.

"Did you see the monster? Did you see it happen?" she asked, sniffling.

"There wasn't . . . it wasn't . . ." Myranda began, hesitating.

"The monster *did* come. I know it, I felt coming it. What did the monster do? What did it look like?" she asked.

"It was . . ." Myranda began. She was not sure what to do. Could she tell the truth? Surely not, but neither could she feed Ivy's fears of this monster by lying. For better or for worse, her decision was made for her.

"*You* are the monster," Ether said.

Lain and Myranda shot her a savage look.

"What?" Ivy asked.

"Ivy, listen to me, she--" Myranda began, but Ivy cut her off.

"No! . . . Let *her* tell me," Ivy said. "You were talking to me, right before the monster came. You were saying terrible things about me. What happened after that?"

She looked resolutely at the shapeshifter. The tears still trickled down her cheeks, but she knew that Ether would tell her what Myranda didn't want her to hear.

"Your fragile mind couldn't handle the truth. You lost control of the divine gift you have been given, transformed into a raging berserker, and tried to kill me. You failed pitifully, and in doing so, you managed to destroy the bulk of the creatures that had attacked," she said.

"But . . . I couldn't . . . how could I?" Ivy said, struggling to comprehend what had been said.

"Isn't it obvious? What do you suppose they were doing to you in that place? They were turning you into a weapon. Clearly they have succeeded," she said.

Ivy shook her head and looked pleadingly to Myranda, hoping to hear a contradiction. An apologetic look was all that came in return.

"But I helped, right? I . . . killed the things that were trying to hurt us? You aren't going to make me go away, are you!? I can stay with you, can't I!?" Ivy pleaded.

"The decision has already been made. You shall be delivered to the south and we shall continue with our task unhindered by your idiocy," Ether informed her.

"No. Myranda wouldn't do that," she said.

"It was not the human's decision," Ether explained.

"Well, if it was you, then I don't have to listen. You're mean," she said, crossing her arms.

"Were I to have my way, you would be festering in the bottom of that ruined fort. Lain is the one who deems this journey necessary," Ether said.

Ivy looked to the culprit. Lain's cold gaze stared back.

"Why? Did I do something wrong?" she demanded, tears welling up again.

"Something wrong? You are a menace! You--" Ether began.

"Quiet! I know what you think! Now I want to know what he thinks," she demanded.

"Very well. Hear it from the mouth of Lain. The message is the same," Ether stated.

She locked eyes with Lain. After a long silence, he spoke.

"You are a danger to yourself. I will not allow you to die," Lain answered.

"But I . . . I," Ivy stuttered. "I'll be careful! I'll stay hidden! I'll do whatever you say. Don't make me go!"

"I will not humor you, I will not coddle you. I will not be kind. What must be done shall be done," Lain stated.

With that, he turned suddenly to the mountains. A breath of wind had carried the scent of a long overdue meal, and with a burst of his startling speed, he was off after it.

With teary eyes, Ivy watched him go. She then turned to Myranda, running to her like a scolded child. As Myranda comforted her, Ether cast a judgmental gaze over the scene. Her face bore a vague expression of contemplation, peppered with a dash of revulsion. Myranda prayed that she would have the wisdom and decency to hold her tongue until Ivy had recovered somewhat. It came as no surprise when those prayers went unanswered.

"Explain," she demanded.

"Ether, please, just give her some time," Myranda begged.

"No. You. Explain this. Why does this creature have such an effect on the two of you? She is undoubtedly a source of tremendous mystic might, able even to inflict her emotions on others, but you behave with the same foolishness even when the effect is absent," Ether said.

"I don't expect *you* to understand this, Ether, but people need each other. We need to care about others, and we need others to care about us. Lain has fought it for most of his life, but now that he has finally found one of his own, he can't deny it anymore. He needs her. We need her. And she needs us," Myranda said.

"Mmm. It is actually quite fascinating. You see, the true reason for such feelings, as well as why they are nearly exclusive to mortals, is really quite simple. Love between a male and a female is merely a means to ensure the propagation of bloodlines, and love for others is at best a means to ensure that the brood persists. Creatures slightly lower than humans and the like devote the whole of their existence to these tasks. For creatures that have just enough intelligence to become distracted, nature must fool them into maintaining their kind. To know that you cannot explain this need, but value it deeply, speaks volumes of its fundamental nature," Ether said.

Myranda and Ivy shot her the same stern look. Ivy then turned to Myranda.

"Do you really mean that? You need me?" Ivy asked.

"The world needs you, Ivy. You are a very important creature," Myranda said.

Ivy sniffled. "The whole world? No. How?"

"You are Chosen," Myranda said.

"I know. They said it a lot when I was there, and you and Ether argued about it when you found me. What does it mean?" Ivy asked.

"It means that you, Lain, Ether, myself, and one more person are the only ones who can stop the people who started the war," Myranda explained.

"The teachers?" she asked.

Myranda nodded.

"I can't stop them. I don't think you can either. There are a lot of them, and they can do things that no one should be able to do," Ivy said with a shudder.

"Well, we have to try, because if we don't, no one will," Myranda explained.

"But if that is true, then why does Lain want me to go away, and why doesn't Ether like me at all?" Ivy asked.

"Lain is worried that if you die, then he will be the last of his kind. Ether . . . Ether thinks that there are others better suited to the task than you," Myranda said.

The shapeshifter's face became visibly more stern at the gently worded explanation. For the moment, at least, she kept silent. For a time, Ivy too was silent. She looked defeated, confused, and frightened.

"Where will I go? Who will take care of me?" she asked.

"Well . . . if you go to the south, Lain claims to have friends there," she said.

"No! No friends. You said Ether was a friend and she hates me. He was supposed to be a friend and he wants me to go away," she said, shaking her head.

"The only other place is a place called Entwell. It is a wonderful place, and there are wonderful people there. You will certainly be safe, but it is difficult to get there. It is a long trip through a dangerous cave. And once you are there, it will not be easy to leave," Myranda said.

She knew that telling Ivy this would hardly help things, but she could not bear to lie to her. It was instantly clear that the concept of trudging through a cave did not appeal to her.

"You have to talk to him. You have to make him let me stay. I don't trust his friends, and I don't want to go in any cave," Ivy said, fairly begging.

"Listen to her. She must have been well-trained. She plays this part perfectly," Ether said.

"What are you talking about?" Ivy said angrily.

"Ether, don't," Myranda warned.

"You are an agent of the enemy. You can do no good to that end if you are not nearby. So you beg to stay. This softhearted and softer-minded girl feels for you, but I am not so blind," she said.

"I am *not* one of them! I *told* you I am *not one of them!*" Ivy raged, stamping toward Ether and pointing an angry finger in her face.

Her anger had surged suddenly. The stir of feelings swirling inside of her turned eagerly to it. Anything that she could lock onto was preferable to the terrible uncertainty.

"Ether, no! What is wrong with you!? Are you trying to make it happen again? Are you trying to get us killed?" Myranda scolded, her own anger doubled by Ivy's.

Ivy turned to Myranda, a shocked, hurt look on her face.

"You . . . you think I would kill you? I would never . . . I could never . . ." she said.

When Ivy's anger dropped away, so did Myranda's.

"You're afraid of me. Then . . . then maybe I do need to go. But . . . but . . ." she said, flopping to the ground.

She put her hands over her eyes, weeping softly again. Myranda put her hand on her shoulder, only to have it pushed away.

"No. Just leave me alone," she said.

Lain returned with a pair of snow rabbits, a pink tinge on his teeth betraying that he had already had his share. Ivy refused to eat, and though Lain did relent and allow a fire to both restore Ether and cook Myranda's food, even the tantalizing smell of roasting rabbit failed to tempt the distraught Ivy.

Myranda felt terrible. It was possible that this was merely Ivy's own sadness spilling over, but she knew that even if that were not the case, she would hardly feel any better. She was the only one in the world right now who the poor creature felt cared for her, and now the feeling of trust was gone. There was nothing she could say or do to make things better.

She made herself as comfortable as she could on the ground and prayed that she was tired enough to slip into sleep despite the burning in her mind.

Once again, this went unanswered. Periodically, she would open her eyes. Shortly after she saw Lain settle down to rest in his own way, she heard Ivy stir. For a moment, she could feel that the creature was looking at her, inspecting her to see that she was asleep. When she was satisfied, she turned away.

"Um . . . Ether," she said, sheepishly.

The shapeshifter was sitting among the crackling flames. Her eyes were closed, dutifully ignoring the creature.

"I know you don't like me, but . . . I get the feeling you wouldn't lie to me. You don't care about my feelings," Ivy said.

"I am enormously concerned about your feelings. I am certain that if they go unchecked they will be the end of us," Ether answered.

"That's why you don't like me. B-because of my . . . my feelings," Ivy said.

"They are chief among a sizable list of faults," Ether answered.

"So, if I . . . control my emotions. Then you won't hate me so much," Ivy said.

"Why are you speaking to me? You know that no good will come of it," Ether said.

"I don't want to go. I want to know what I can do to stay," Ivy said.

"You were created specifically to infiltrate and destroy the Chosen," Ether said.

"I wasn't!" Ivy snapped, quickly composing herself. "I wasn't, but I know that you don't believe me. What can I do to prove to you that you are wrong?"

"There is nothing you can do. You cannot disprove what I know to be true," Ether stated.

Myranda could feel the frustration and irritation fluttering just below the surface, but whenever it arose, she pushed it down again. Carefully, she opened her eyes slightly. Ivy was kneeling before the flames, her hands clasped. Begging.

"Then tell me how I can help *you,* how I can abandon *them,*" she asked.

"Attempting to prove loyalty through treachery. Only a truly inferior mind could have produced such a flawed concept," she jabbed.

Ivy took a deep breath as Myranda felt another surge of anger come and go.

"Then what about Lain? What can I do to convince him?" she asked.

"Again, absolutely nothing. His concerns, well-founded, are that you will get yourself killed if left to your own devices, and his judgment is muddled by the same impairment that renders you such a liability. He cares about you. Even if you were to present to him a solid, sound, and irrefutable reason to change his mind, I assure you, he would not do so. It was among the first of my observations of mortals. Emotion robs them of reason," Ether said.

"Well . . . well, you aren't emotional, right? What would you do, if you were me?" she said.

"End my own life," she answered without hesitation.

"Why can't you help me!?" Ivy said, her objection choked off by a knot in her throat.

"Ivy," Myranda said, sitting up.

She turned, then looked away quickly, trying to hide her tears.

"You weren't supposed to hear that," she said.

"Listen, Ivy. I want you to know that I am sorry for what I said before. I didn't mean it," she said.

"Yes, you did. You were just too nice to say that before. That's why I didn't want to talk to you. You would be nice. You wouldn't be honest," she said.

"All right. You want honesty? I am afraid. I am afraid when you lose control. But mostly I am afraid we might lose you. That is what Lain is afraid of, too. I said it before. We need you. And even if we didn't, I wouldn't want to see you get hurt," she said.

"What do I do?" she pleaded.

"You need to learn control. That will come with time," she said.

"What about Ether?" she asked.

"Don't mind Ether. She can't help the way she is, just as you can't help the way you are. Don't take too much of what she says to heart. She hasn't learned to deal with people yet," Myranda said.

"I've no interest in learning so distasteful a lesson," Ether remarked.

"Well, what about Lain?" she asked.

"Lain . . . Lain knows that what we are doing is very dangerous. He is willing to risk his own life. He isn't willing to risk yours. I believe in you. I know that if you do the best you can, and we work together, then we can do what needs to be done, and we can protect each other. We just need to make him see that," Myranda said.

"So, if I prove that I can take care of myself, I might be able to stay?" she said.

"I can't say for sure, but . . . perhaps," Myranda said.

"Then I'll do it!" she decided.

"Good, we need you," Myranda said.

With weight of her words off of her chest and a flicker of hope to keep the group together, she settled down for sleep again. This time it came swiftly. The sky was still black when Ivy shook Myranda awake again. She had a strange look on her face. It was a mix of fear with a dash of excitement.

"Six of them. Human soldiers, a few miles away," she said breathlessly.

"Standard patrol, due south. They are headed away now, but they will swing further this way with the next pass. A few hours," Lain explained.

"I smelled them first. I knew they were coming," she said.

"We can't move yet, but soon--and quickly," Lain said.

"If they are to the south, where will we go? The mountains?" Myranda asked.

"No. It will slow us. West. Then south through the fields," he said.

Lain trained his nose to the south, sampling the air. Ether took her place beside Lain. She shifted to wind and prompted a gentle breeze. Ivy quickly took a place between them, mimicking Lain as closely as possible. Ether moved to the other side, only to have Ivy wedge herself between again.

"Now," Lain stated.

Ivy nodded. She rushed to Myranda and took her hand, pulling her forward. The four whisked across the field at Lain's pace. There wasn't nearly enough light to see what was ahead. Only Lain seemed to know. Ivy was just eager, even desperate to stay by his side. Ether swept effortlessly as wind. Myranda could hardly breathe, but she did her best to keep up the pace. If not for Ivy's firm and insistent aid, Myranda would scarcely have had a chance of staying with them. The malthrope had a look of determination, of focus. Without a word, Lain shifted his path. Now they were headed south.

Suddenly, Ivy froze. Her head turned and locked onto the darkness to the west. Lain stopped and turned. His gaze was enough to urge forward, but Ivy wouldn't budge. She was trembling slightly. Ether came to a stop, floating above her, looking down with mild disgust. Then she too turned to face the darkness.

"D'karon," she said, darting toward the source of Ivy's fear.

"Never mind her. Keep moving," Lain urged.

"I . . . I . . . no. We have to stay together. We have to protect each other. She'll be killed!" Ivy decided.

Without time for another word, Ivy was off, Myranda still in her grasp. Behind them, the rapid strides of Lain could just barely be heard. Somehow, he managed to sprint almost silently. The same was not so for Ivy, as each step crunched loudly on the icy ground. She cast a glance back and saw him quickly closing the gap between them. Myranda was holding onto Ivy with one arm and her staff and bag with the other, her feet barely touching the ground.

"He is going to catch up," Ivy said nervously.

"You need to slow down. We need to be cautious. Wait for him, we can do this together," Myranda urged with what breath she had to spare.

"No. If he catches up, he will stop me, and I won't get to show him that I can do this. You will have to run on your own. Promise you'll follow me," Ivy said.

"I promise," Myranda agreed.

The malthrope released her and doubled her pace. With nothing but her ever-present club to carry, she was now at least a match for Lain's speed.

Myranda ran for all she was worth. Moments later, Lain tore past her as though she were standing still. The pounding footsteps of Ivy retreated into the distance, and Myranda found herself alone in the pitch-black night, her legs burning with fatigue, her lungs frozen from the night air. The ground began to slope gently upwards.

At the crest of the hill, Myranda found Lain. She tried to pass him, but he grabbed her. Without a word, he pointed to the ground that sloped away ahead of them. It looked strange. In most places in the north, the earth was a frozen mass, unbroken and undisturbed for a dozen winters. The ground beyond the hill was different. It was churned up, almost as though it had been tilled and plowed. Soil was visible among the snow and ice, which meant the earth had been disturbed since the last snowfall.

"What is it?" Myranda asked.

Lain silently pointed. Myranda strained her eyes. Patches of the gray ground seemed to be moving. Bulges were rippling their way across the ground. Tracing their course forward led her eyes to Ivy. She was standing perfectly still in the center of the field, and judging by the steadily intensifying blue aura about her, she was petrified by the churning earth. As her fear grew, the aura grew brighter, making more of the field visible to even Myranda's eyes. She quickly scanned the area. The low hill they were perched upon seemed to ring the field. At the center was a structure low to the ground, made of an ancient-looking gray wood. There was one enormous door hinged at the bottom like a drawbridge, and a slight wisp of thin smoke streamed from a stout rectangular chimney.

Slowly, one by one, the bulges stopped approaching and sunk back into the ground.

"What are they?" Myranda whispered.

"I don't know," Lain said.

Ivy hesitantly took another step toward the fort. The instant her foot touched the ground, a handful of the bulges rose up again and began to move toward her. Again she froze, and slowly they submerged.

"Ivy! Hold still!" Myranda called out.

Ivy couldn't stop shaking. When the last piece of ground sunk back into place, the things were only a few paces away. She looked to her friends. There was concern on Myranda's face. Lain was steady as always. Not a drop of the fear that was fairly coursing through her veins. She could feel it passing a threshold, taking hold of her like it had before. Her fingers tightened on the grip of the club. Not today. She turned to the doors and sprinted. Out of the corners of her eyes, she saw more ripples than she could count streak past her. She pushed them from her mind and pressed on. She would prove herself.

Myranda watched in horror. Each step coaxed a half-dozen more of the threatening ripples to the surface. It was the steps. The bulges only rose when Ivy's feet hit the ground. The vibrations must have been alerting them.

Suddenly, directly in Ivy's path, one of the creatures responsible burst from the ground. It was a horrid sight. She skidded to a stop a hair in front of the beast. A worm writhed before her, leathery gray skin arranged in thick overlapping plates like armor. It was thick as her waist and longer than she was tall. The front split like a flower, with four jagged jaws snapping. A dozen needle-sharp tongues flitted in and out. The fear leapt back into her throat and burned at her mind. Reflexively, she raised her club.

"Ivy, no!" Myranda shouted.

The weapon came down with shattering force. When she raised it again, what lay beneath resembled a smashed cigar. A dash of yellow mixed with her blue aura and the beginnings of a smile came to her face. She turned to see if her friends had seen her conquest. The sight she beheld wiped the smile from her face and brought renewed intensity to her fear. Like a wave spreading across a still lake, the creatures burst from the ground in an ever-increasing circle around her.

Lain could wait no longer. He rushed into the field. With the threat thus revealed, he could navigate the field without surprises. There were thousands of the worms. The whole of the field was an undulating mass--but with each footstep, the worms shifted like a tide to the place it landed, opening a tiny patch of land behind. Where there was no clearing, a swift swipe of his blade made one.

Ivy's eyes shot from the threat that surrounded her to the savior that approached her. As frightened as she was by the danger all around, she was more frightened of being left behind by these people who had plucked her from her prison. She couldn't risk it. She couldn't risk being rescued. It would rob her of perhaps her only chance to prove herself. The worms jabbed at her feet, but she was swift. Her movements became fluid, purposeful. Her grace was easily a match for Lain's precision. Finally, she sprang with all of her might to the door and caught hold of one of the cross-planks halfway up. She flipped the club into the air and scrambled up the door, catching the weapon like a baton as it fell. The entire maneuver was so practiced, so effortless, it seemed choreographed. She planted her heels onto the top of the door and her back against the stone wall and pushed.

The door was enormous. It should have taken a team of horses to open, but with her already unnatural strength fueled by fear and desperation, the thick slat began to creak. Not quickly enough, though. Lain was nearly there. She struck madly at the slat with heavy blows of the club, splintering the wood. Finally, it split in two, the piece she was perched upon crashed to the ground, crushing the worms that had gathered to attack the last place her foot had found purchase. She dropped, rather less gracefully than she had climbed, through the hole.

Myranda stood motionless at the edge of the field, unnoticed by the worms that had swarmed over the huge plank of wood, rendering it a scattered pile of shards in moments. Lain managed to spring over the undulating mass and climbed inside the fort. Now it was left for her to do the same. When there seemed no more targets to destroy, the worms slowly settled into the ground as easily as into a pool of water. In a matter of heartbeats, there was nothing left in the courtyard but a series of furrows where the horrid beasts had surfaced and submerged.

Myranda knew she couldn't outmaneuver the beasts as the others had, but it was clear that the monsters blindly attacked anything that shook the ground. The more the ground shook, the more madly they attacked. She called to mind the teachings of Cresh, her mentor in earth magic. She focused on a point far to the left of the fort and began to force her will into the ground. Before she could even sense she was having an effect, the beasts were visibly migrating to the point. When they reached it, they began to thrash about, searching for whatever might be causing the tremors.

Before long, the blind, deaf creatures turned to blame each other. She maintained the tremor long enough to reach the door and climbed as best she could with her staff in her hand.

#

The image flickered away. Deacon's eyes closed. He turned back to his task. He had managed to secure the large bag of gold coins the village kept. It was the accumulated wealth of the entire village, with the exception of the small horde kept by the dragon Solomon, and oddly it was one of the least protected of its valuables. The coins were scattered about the table. Some were heads up. Others tails up.

"Heads," he said, tossing a handful into the air.

They dropped to the table and rattled to a rest, all heads up. He shook his head. It wasn't enough. He knew a dozen spells that could cause the coins to land as he chose. He wasn't casting any of them. He did nothing to the coins. What he had changed was the odds. But it wasn't enough. It didn't prove if the spell was sufficient. Heads. Tails. It could only be one or the other. Or . . .

He turned all of his training, all of his years of education, to the task of honing the spell. He swept all of the coins from the table and cupped them in his hands. Closing his eyes, he threw them in the air. They clattered down again. Bouncing. Skipping. Spinning. Finally, they were still and silent. Slowly he opened his eyes. Some coins were on the floor. Others on the other chair. Most were on the table. Every last one was standing on its edge. That was enough.

He scribbled a few more lines onto the tattered pile of pages that lay on the edge of the table and rushed for the door. When he was able to squeeze a rational thought past the excitement, he stopped and picked up his satchel. There were some things he would need.

#

Myranda dropped into the dark interior of the fort. When she conjured light enough to see, she found that it looked as different from the other forts inside as it did outside. The others had a wide open hall in the middle, with cells lining the walls. The cells were missing here. The whole of the floor was one enormous room, interrupted by the occasional wooden support. Each corner of the room was hidden behind a slatted wooden wall that didn't quite reach the ceiling.

Though there were no cells, the floor was far from unoccupied. Beasts, ranging from the size of a small horse to some that reached the ceiling, filled the floor. They were arranged in ranks, and all stood perfectly still. For a moment, Myranda thought they were statues, but if they were, the attention to detail was supernatural. Hair moved with the wind from outside, eyes gleamed in the light. As for their forms, they had a twisted familiarity to them: a massive black tiger-like creature, with horns like a bull and barbs sticking through its fur; an eagle with a downward pointing tail that tapered into that of a scorpion. Most looked as though the most awful parts of a dozen animals were assembled into a single body. Largest was a beast that resembled ten enormous snakes joined at the tails to a central body with a squid-like beak on both top and bottom.

Once it became clear that they were no immediate threat, Lain ignored the terrible wonders and disappeared down the stairs at the far end of the room. This place, it seemed, had at least two things in common with the other forts. It had the same roundabout stair system--and, judging from the chorus of creaks and echoes, it was at least as deep.

Myranda tried to follow, but something wasn't right. There was a powerful magic at work. Very powerful, like a constant pressure on her mind. The sheer intensity of the enchantment was almost disorienting. It must have been what Ether had felt, what had led her here. Perhaps Ivy had felt it, too. Myranda leaned heavily on her staff to gather herself. Her eyes turned to the ground.

Embedded in the floor in front of each of the beasts was a plaque. Engraved in each was a cold, analytical label for the associated creature. *Augmented Plains Predator Revision II. Venomous Raptor Revision VI.* Beneath each engraved label was another one, rougher, as though it had been scratched in afterward. *Raid Stalker. Needlehawk.* There was the air of a museum, that these were objects of pride. She turned to the door, recovered somewhat from the influence of the place, and followed the others.

#

Deep inside, many floors below, Ivy was rushing past shelves, stands, and figures she dare not look at. The terror was already burning at her mind. She had to find Ether and take her away from this place. That would prove to Lain that she could protect herself and help the team. That would let her stay. She sprinted down flight after flight of stairs to ever larger floors.

Finally, she saw her: Ether was standing before a large, heavy door. She had changed back to human form, and seemed to be contemplating something. She turned to Ivy, a look of mild disappointment on her face.

"What are you doing here, fool?" she demanded.

"You have to leave. You'll be hurt. You'll be killed!" Ivy urged, tugging desperately at Ether's arm.

Ether pulled away.

"Calm yourself, beast. There is nothing here or anywhere in this world that can threaten me. Least of all this place. The D'karon have gone from here. Only their creations remain," she said.

"They have? Then . . . then we don't need to be here. We can go . . . before they come back," Ivy said, relief in her voice. The piercing blue aura about her began to fade.

"No. There is a dark magic at work here. A powerful one. I cannot allow it to continue its work," Ether said.

"Yes! Yes you can! We can go! Please! Before something goes wrong!" Ivy begged, the bright blue light surging back.

"You are pathetic," Ether sneered.

"What was that?" Ivy gasped, turning to the source of a noise.

"I heard nothing," Ether said.

"Well, turn into something with better ears! There is something scratching around in this room," Ivy demanded.

Ether ignored her, turning to the door before her. It was the first door she had encountered since entering the fort. Whatever lay beyond it was considered more valuable than all that preceded it. There were plenty of

219

cracks around the door, and even a barred view hole. She should have been able to flow through it with ease in her wind form, but she had been turned away. There was some locking spell, an impressively powerful one, preventing her from moving forward. Runes were inscribed on the door as well, no doubt the source of the enchantment. Undoing the spell would be no simple task.

She touched the door, recoiling almost immediately. The spell that protected the door and the far more powerful one that had drawn her here were . . . unnatural. They seemed to reverberate with a familiar tone, but horribly twisted, perverted.

Ivy shifted uneasily from foot to foot, sensitive ears trained to the silence, simultaneously seeking and dreading the scratching she'd heard before. As she did, she slowly began to notice the surroundings she had been so dutifully ignoring. This floor was filled with orderly rows of shelves. Upon the shelves, in labeled progressions, were sequences of body parts of advancing quality and detail.

Nearest to her was a row of skulls. The first was a human skull, the word *Man* etched in a plate beneath it. Next to it were a line of eight others collectively labeled *Altered Intellectual Dominant,* with each skull additionally labeled with a "Revision" number. Scratched beneath the embossed label was the word *Nearman.* The gruesome sight was repeated a dozen times over on the other shelves and even lining the wall, where a dragon skull hung beside no less than fifteen attempted duplicates, the last few resembling the horrid dragoyle.

Ivy struggled to keep her fear in check.

"Would you hurry! Break the door down! Do what you have to do so we can leave this place!" Ivy pleaded.

"I must first determine what we may find behind the door, so that I might take the form best suited to face it," Ether said.

"It is the workshop and laboratory," Ivy said.

"How would you know that?" Ether scoffed.

"It says it on the door!" Ivy said, pointing at the arcane writing word by word as she spoke the words again. "Workshop and laboratory! And then a recipe or something! Please, Ether, just do what you want to do, or tell me what to do and I'll do it. I can't take this place."

"How can you read that? Why would they teach you their language?" Ether asked accusingly.

"I don't know, maybe they didn't mean to! What does it matter? Just open the *door!*" she demanded, punctuating her demand with a mighty thrust kick to the door.

There was a burst of orange light and Ivy cried out in pain amid a crackle of energy. She was sent hurtling backward, skidding to a stop near the stairs at the other side of the room. The blue aura that had surrounded her and illuminated the room was dimmed to nothing. She groaned dizzily, flat on her back and dazed.

Ether looked to the door. It hung precariously from one hinge, the other broken. Whatever enchantment had protected it was spent. Ether cast a swift glance toward Ivy, shaking her head slightly. Quickly, she turned to stone and passed through the doorway, making her way through the pitch-blackness.

#

Many floors above, Myranda scrambled to catch up to Lain. Floor after floor of monstrous beasts streaked by her. The ancient wooden floor boards creaked and groaned. Each footfall kicked up a puff of dust and dry rotten wood. Myranda wondered briefly why such a massive place would have been built of wood when the others were stone. Suddenly, as she was about to emerge from yet another staircase, a hand yanked her back. The hand covered the glowing gem on her staff, obscuring the light. A voice whispered in her ear.

"Douse the light and be silent," he said.

It was Lain. She obeyed, and was soon shrouded in utter darkness. He whispered again, his words barely louder than her pounding heart.

"Stay here, and stay perfectly still," he warned.

Myranda did as she was told. She did not hear anything. She didn't hear Lain leave her side. She didn't hear him navigate the room in complete darkness. The next sound she heard was a peculiar squeal cut short. A few moments later, the voice was in her ear again.

"Restore the light--slowly," he instructed.

The crisp, bluish-white light of the staff slowly grew bright enough for Myranda to see Lain drop a small, bat-like creature to the ground. Myranda could not discern any more details before he mashed it into paste with his heel. He closed his eyes and listened intently before continuing forward.

"What was that?" Myranda asked.

"A watcher. I've only encountered them a handful of times before. Expect opposition momentarily," he said.

With that, Lain resumed his swift pursuit of Ivy. Myranda was puzzled by the statement, but followed as quickly as she could. There had been nothing but frozen field for as far as the eye could see in all directions, but if he was not taking the time to explain, Myranda hardly thought it wise to take the time to question. It was a warning, and these days a warning was a luxury.

Myranda had scarcely made it to the next floor when the mysterious threat presented itself. Out from the wooden slats at each corner of the room slipped a cloak. Then another, then another. Suddenly there was a

221

dozen of them. Swiftly, the disembodied garments began to circle about Myranda, slipping between and over the shelves that filled the floor. Myranda conjured a flame, the only truly effective weapon against these wraiths, but doused it immediately. If she was to use fire here, she would have to take great care. The wood was decrepit and bone-dry. It would catch fire even more readily than the cloaks.

She rushed to the doorway after Lain. As she did, she placed her staff behind her back and willed some of the fabric of her own cloak, shredded and loose from overuse, into a bow to hold it in place. While still maintaining the light it provided, she then reached into her bag and brandished a knife in each hand. Dodging the swipe of a phantom claw and delivering a retaliatory slash, she slipped into the stairway and continued on. The creatures, save for when they chose to screech their terrifying cry, moved almost silently. There was no way of knowing how near they were, and once they were a fair distance from Myranda's light, the black cloth blended seamlessly with the darkness.

Myranda focused on moving forward. She had to avoid being surrounded before reaching the others.

#

Behind her, Ether heard the occasional shriek of a cloak, but she quickly dismissed it. The room that surrounded her was far more deserving of her attention. Leading down from the door was a long flight of stairs to the floor below. A small fire in a stone fireplace cast a dim glow. Over it was a cauldron simmering a foul-smelling fluid. Opposite the fire, barely visible in the dim light, was a tablet inscribed with more of the same runes. It was undoubtedly the source of the truly remarkable amount of raw power that seemed to permeate this place.

Stands held books with immaculate and detailed sketches of dozens of beasts, each labeled and described in the same arcane runes that had labeled the door. Just past the foot of the stairs was a narrow channel in the floor that seemed to have no purpose. A large platform stood in the center of the room. Upon it a now-unrecognizable creature lay, separated with a surgeon's skill into neat piles. The faint brown stains of blood could be seen on the surface of the platform. Tall glass jars contained most of what had once flowed through the creature's veins. An array of instruments and tools were laid out with care on a tray. The curving blades and needle-sharp claws conjured to mind images of their use that would haunt the mind of a normal being.

Everything in the room had a meticulous, obsessive feel to it--and the feel that life was meaningless to the person who created such a place. Ether's eyes turned to the far wall. Instantly, a fury began to build inside of her. There, like forgotten playthings, were a handful of nameless abominations. They stood motionless, just as all that she had passed in her descent, but these were different. They bore no resemblance to anything of this world. The products of a madman's cruel mind or a twisted reality, the creatures were an affront to Ether's very existence--masses of tentacles, pincers, and spidery legs in configurations that defied logic.

Ether stalked toward them, preparing to destroy the creatures, when a bright light and astounding power appeared behind her. She turned to see a disc of what looked to be darkness itself swirling into existence. It grew until its edge dipped into the channel in the floor. Slowly, the center of the disc parted like smoke, and there could be seen the form of a man. He stepped forward and emerged from the portal. Quickly, with a loud, thundering clap, the portal closed.

Ether surveyed the man. He was thin, almost gaunt. His clothes were of fine cloth, with no armor to speak of, and stained with various unidentifiable fluids. Around his neck hung a large piece of fractured crystal, faintly glowing blue. His hair was dark, with a peppering of gray. His skin was pale. Long, thin fingers gripped loosely the head of a silvery weapon. It was the size of a staff, but tapered into a blade along its length. Four similar weapons hung from his back, each head adorned with four tiny crystals, each crystal dim with blue light. He was a head shorter than Ether's current form.

The man who stood before her, in appearance, was no threat. In presence, however, the same could not be said. He didn't so much look at Ether as analyze her. His eyes were intense, piercing. There was no hint of fear. He seemed to radiate a feeling of command, of superiority.

"The shapeshifter. The watcher announced only the malthrope. Properly training it to identify a shapeshifter in an elemental form may prove an intriguing challenge," he remarked.

"Are you the one responsible for creating these monstrosities?" Ether demanded, pointing a finger at the twisted creatures behind her.

"I am," he stated.

"Then it is my duty to destroy you. You have bastardized nature itself," Ether proclaimed.

"Yes, yes. So you say. If you wish to do battle, I must request that we do so outside of this place. It is quite near to my records room, and I am not quite certain I have created duplicates of all of my notes," he said.

"Ether, something is happening upstairs! I think the others need our help! We--" came Ivy's voice from the doorway, but it swiftly caught in her throat.

The man turned.

"Welcome home, wayward one," he said, almost pleasantly.

Ether took full advantage of his distraction. She swung her stone fist with all of her might at the stranger's head. In a flash, the four staffs on his back extended, splitting into segments. Insect-like legs extended from along the length. The edge of the silvery things reached the floor and planted themselves. Ether's fist clanked off of their bodies uselessly. Before she could attempt a second blow, three of the creature weapons weaved like metal centipedes to her. Two wrapped around her ankles, digging their legs into hers, and buried the tips of their tails deep into the floor. The third planted the rows of legs nearest to its head and curled its tail like that of a scorpion, striking again and again.

#

A few floors above, Myranda finally reached Lain. Several dozen cloaks had been left in shreds on the floor, but dozens more stood between him and the next flight of stairs. The creatures had been keeping their distance until now, picking at their targets as they had in the past. This was different. They were united in a frenzy to keep Lain from this next door, and they were succeeding.

In her fight to reach this far, Myranda had felt the rake of the black claws of these creatures more than once, and she knew well that if Lain's sword and skill were not enough to quell the tide, her own blades would do precious little good. She had to use fire, but first she had to protect the ancient tinderbox that surrounded them from it.

"Keep them from me for just a few moments," she said, shutting her eyes and trusting that he could do so.

Lain shifted his stance, swatting the creatures away instead of trying to strike them down. Quickly, Myranda's plan became clear. The temperature of the room was dropping dramatically. As she drew the heat from the walls, floor, and ceiling, frost began to form. She pushed the spell as far as it would go, until the wood was fairly white with ice.

"Now don't let them leave," she said.

She unleashed all of the stolen heat, combined with as much as her mind could conjure at once, at the swirling swarm of cloaks. They took eagerly to flame, rising in a chorus of unholy screeches. Like paper thrown on a fire, the creatures flitted madly about, knocking the shelves to the ground. They charged at the pair of heroes, but never attempted to flee through the door they defended. Myranda deflected a few with a hasty shield spell, and Lain dispatched the rest in huge swaths with mighty swings of his sword. The injured creatures needed barely a slice to finish the job the fire had started and rob them of their will. Once that damage had been done, they fluttered uselessly to the floor where they sizzled at the frost and smoldered.

Before long, all that remained of the army of cloth wraiths was a cloud of choking smoke and a mound of charred embers. Lain sped through the smoke toward the door and Myranda followed, the mystic exertion reminding her of the tremendous spell that had disoriented her earlier.

#

Below, Ivy remembered why she had come there, and rushed down the stairs in an attempt to free Ether from her predicament. The centipedes were taking their toll on her. The strikes of the steel tail were chipping easily away at her stone body, and the blasted things were far too fast for her to strike at. As Ether reached her, the man gestured to the remaining two weapon creatures. They responded to the wordless command and flowed up the stairs, raising the door back into place. They then each planted their legs into the door and the wall, barring it with their bodies.

Ivy, the glow about her a piercing blue again, walked in a wide, cautious circle around the man, who did not assume the slightest of defensive postures. Slowly, he walked to a shelf on one wall. He opened a box upon it and pocketed a number of objects from inside. As he did, he spoke casually to Ivy, who was fruitlessly swatting her weapon at the attacking centipede.

"I see you carry a club. You were given the strength for such a weapon, but I would have expected a more elegant one," he said. "We never trained you with a club."

"Shut up!" Ivy demanded. "You were there. You were one of the teachers!"

"Mmm. Teachers. My little experiment, I am so much more than your teacher," he said.

"What did you call me?" she asked. The word seemed to cut her deep.

"Experiment. Altered Chosen Revision IV. The fourth attempt, and the only one with any degree of true success, though the second and third are not without their usefulness--and, with you as a prototype, the fifth is looking very promising indeed," he said.

"What are you saying?" Ivy cried, storming up to him and shouting in his face. The aura around her shifted sharply to red.

"One moment please," he requested casually, utterly unconcerned. He pulled from his pocket a gem the size of a small stone and held it up.

Ether had grown weary of weathering the attacks and grip of the centipedes and shifted to wind. Her turbulent form streaked at the stranger, who thrust the crystal forward. The instant Ether came in contact with the gem, she cried out in pain, the stone quickly taking on a bright white glow. More of her windy form streamed off and into the heart of the gem as long as Ether remained near it, and the effect it was having on her was clear. The intensity of the wind that was her body decreased significantly.

Finally, she pulled away, greatly weakened by the encounter. The gem maintained its brightness as he pocketed it. He snapped his fingers and the three centipedes formerly attacking Ether clattered along the walls and to the ceiling, where Ether hung recovering. The four small gems that shone like eyes on the heads of the creatures, Ether soon found, were of the same type as the one used to weaken her. Ether flitted fruitlessly about the room in an attempt to escape them, but the fleet-footed creatures were everywhere, it seemed.

"I am Demont. I am responsible for designing and producing some of the finest living weapons in creation, and you are unique among them. I really should work with Epidime more often. The direct link between body and spirit was a stroke of genius. Permitting the most basic of functions of the brain access to the vast reservoir of energy the soul has to offer makes even the most feeble mind capable of devastation," he mused.

"I'm not an experiment! I'm Ivy! You didn't make me! You couldn't have!" Ivy raged.

"Ivy, eh? Well, the body is my work. Nature must take the credit for the soul," he said.

Ether could not avoid the constant assault by her attackers. Soon she felt that she could not hold together any longer and dropped to the ground. One of the creatures dropped down beside her and Ether's form wrapped in an intense cyclone about the beast. There were a few moments of chaos, then silence, and where there had been three creatures, there were now four. The remaining centipedes ceased their attack, unsure of which was their foe.

Ivy turned back to the man and smiled. In the brief silence, an odd ringing noise followed by the clattering of one of the centipedes tumbling down the stairs in pieces marked Lain's entry. Demont's face turned not fearful, but stern. Half of the door fell away, sliding down the steps. The four remaining creature weapons clamored quickly to Demont's side.

Lain leapt at Demont but was intercepted by a pair of the centipedes. Ether, in her stolen form, tangled with another, and the last occupied Myranda. Ivy bared her teeth and charged, fear entirely supplanted by anger. She was clearly on the verge of becoming the chaotic form that had ravaged the dragoyles before. The red aura was blinding.

"HALT!" Demont ordered.

Instantly, the aura vanished. Darkness swept in. Myranda conjured light. She could not afford to wait for her eyes to adjust. Lain dispatched the first of his opponents. Ether was still entangled with hers. Ivy stood with a confused, disoriented look on her face.

"Much as I would like to see the cascading reaction Epidime described, I must not permit it here. This fort houses the only physical manifestation of a great many of my creations, and I do not wish to destroy it unless it is absolutely necessary," he said. "Now, listen closely, all of you. I do not feel that this place is an appropriate one to capture you, and with the exception of the human, strict orders prohibiting me from killing you have been reinstated. Thus, I must insist that you leave this place. If you do so quickly and willingly, I shall do you no more harm."

Demont made his way to a long case in the corner of the room. A final swipe of Lain's sword finished his opponent. He charged at Demont, but the case clicked open and ten more of the centipedes charged out to his defense. Myranda, who had yet to find something in her mystic repertoire to effectively combat one of the nasty things, now had six to contend with. Lain destroyed two of his own quickly, but the remaining three maneuvered well within the radius that allowed an effective sword strike, and proved more troublesome. Ether, however, managed to tear the beast she tangled with to pieces, and weaved her way quickly toward Demont.

Of all of the skills these creations had, intelligence was sorely lacking. They could not tell friend from foe, and with Demont distracted pocketing the loose notes, books, and tools from around the room, there was no one to guide them.

Ether sprung to Demont's leg. The needle-sharp legs of her current form dug deep into his flesh and she summoned all of the strength the abomination could muster. Like a flash of lightning, the blade of a tail sunk just a whisper into Demont's skin. Before it could slice further, a trio of the creatures latched onto the shapeshifter and tore her free. Dark blood ran from Demont's back as Ether was stretched taut by the creatures.

With little more than a nod, creatures began to peel off from attacking the others and assaulted the immobilized shapeshifter. Ether shifted suddenly back to stone, bursting from beneath the beasts. She charged at him. In a swift motion, he revealed one of the tools he had selected and drove it into her chest. It was a rapier-thin serrated blade, striped with filaments of the crystal. The filaments led back to the grip, which bore a delicate metal claw. The claw held a large, finely-crafted jewel. On contact, the web of lines illuminated and the gem shone brightly.

Ether reared back and grasped the cruel weapon, trying madly and futilely to tear it from her chest.

"It is a soul extractor, a simple tool. Merely a clarified and refined thir crystal. A lesser soul would be drawn from the body. Trapped entirely within. I suspect you exceed the gem's capacity. We shall see," he explained.

Ether's motion slowed. Ivy watched, as though from a great distance. Demont's command had shaken her to her core. It felt as though her mind had been pushed aside. There was nothing stopping her from moving, but she lacked the will to do so. Somewhere far away, she heard Myranda cry out in pain. Her fingers tightened on the grip of the club. Slowly her head turned. The creatures were all over Myranda. A flex of her mind repelled them, but as quickly as they were gone, others replaced them. Her face was scraped and bloodied. She was losing the fight. Ivy's lips drew back. Her teeth clenched.

Demont waded through the carnage. It dutifully parted before him. He reached the door at the top of the stairs. This monstrous man, this fiend who would endanger her friends, was about to go free. The thought burned at Ivy's mind. Finally she regained control.

With a mighty blow of her club, she smashed at the centipedes attacking Lain. He broke free from the creatures and sprinted up the stairs to swing his weapon at the general. A trio of the creatures hurled themselves in the way of the sword. It sliced through them all and cut a cruel gash along Demont's arm. All of the remaining centipedes scrambled to haul Lain away from their master. He grasped the injury, his face finally showing pain. It shifted quickly to anger.

"Congratulations. You have motivated me to disobey direct orders," Demont hissed.

He motioned to the rune-inscribed tablet before sprinting out the door. One of the beasts launched toward it, shattering the brittle stone. It was as though the whole of the structure shattered with it. The floorboards creaked; the cries of a thousand horrid beasts rang out at once.

The spell that had paralyzed the countless monstrosities on display above was broken. They were awake.

Trampling feet shook the ceiling. The cauldron held above the fire gave way, spilling its foul-smelling contents and scattering the flames. Myranda, momentarily left alone by the centipedes, put her mind to work. She swept up the liquid and guided it to the cluster of creatures. When they were mired in it, she froze it solid. She then tried to use what was left of it to extinguish the spreading flames, but it merely sizzled and blackened. Instead, she turned her mind directly to the task. The flames, as though guided by an unseen hand, had spread directly to the supports in the room. Already they were buckling and splintering under the weight. She turned her mind to keeping them together.

"Myranda, come on! We need to go now!" Ivy said, fear quickly moving in to take the place of anger.

"I need to keep the fire under control. Help Ether," Myranda managed, sweat running from her temple at the rising heat and massive effort.

"Why? She likes fire! Now that the teacher is gone we can go!" Ivy urged.

"With that thing . . . in her chest . . . no telling what will happen. Can't afford . . . to lose her . . . for any amount . . . of time." Myranda had to struggle to get the words out. The flames were slowly creeping forward, and the supports were beginning to split. She redoubled her efforts.

Ivy rushed to the motionless Ether. She tugged and pulled at the extractor, but the hands that had tried so hard to pull it free were now locking it in place. Looking at the rapidly failing supports, panic made her decision for her. She bent low and pulled the stone form forward onto her shoulders. One arm was hooked behind its legs, the other over its neck and still clutching the ever-present club. The weight was enormous. Straining desperately, her fear-fueled muscles hefted the shapeshifter from the ground. She turned her head to Myranda. Their eyes met.

"I will follow . . . I swear to you," Myranda said.

With that, Ivy made her way up the stairs. With each step she gained speed. Fear, determination, and a cocktail of other emotions powered her every motion. She emerged into the next floor. Madness itself lay before her. Nameless nightmares, maws belching flame, wretched black mist, and substances that defied description filled the room to every corner. In the center, a swath of shredded beasts led to Lain on the stairs across from her. His sword dripped a dozen shades of blood as he fought to clear the way ahead.

She rushed as fast as she could, but the gap he had created was closing. In her ears, there was naught but the thunder of unnatural cries. Her legs worked of their own accord. There was no hope of warding off the fear now. She could only hope to lend the urgency and purpose she felt to whatever it was that would very shortly rob her of her wits.

#

Lain sunk his sword to the hilt in yet another beast and tore his weapon free. His senses were under assault from every conceivable direction. There was no telling what these creatures were capable of. No two were the same. There was no time to learn their motions, to plan, to think. His instinct slipped directly from his mind to the tip of his weapon, guiding it to whatever patch of scales, fur, skin, or shell might suffer worst from its bite. The darkness that had made his first encounters with these creatures all the more difficult was now banished by the pale blue light pouring from Ivy. Her thumping footsteps increasingly shook the weak floorboards. Myranda was not behind her.

Before his eyes in the moment he could spare to see her, she changed. Her eyes clouded over. She surged forward with an impossible speed. The blue tinge of her aura vanished, leaving a brilliant white. The last few creatures before her were swept aside by the sheer force of her motion. With a single stride, she leapt up the stairs and past Lain. Foregoing the landing entirely, she planted a second stride on the wall of the twisting stairway. From there, she thrust herself to the floor above without touching a single step.

Tiny scampering creatures were crushed underfoot. Huge hulking beasts were outmaneuvered. Lain now followed in *her* wake. Keeping as close as he could manage, he slashed at any beast that ventured near enough to threaten either of them, and as many others his weapon could reach. Utterly unique creatures, similar only in purpose. Creatures made to kill. Prototypes, failed attempts, discarded imaginings. The first and last of their kinds. They leapt at him from all sides. The air was thick with their stench, their breath, their blood. He struck down as many as he could. He had to. His mind, in fleeting whispers, turned to Myranda. Every level of monstrosities that they left behind was one that still lay before her.

A distant creak and snap rang through the structure and the very floor beneath their feet shifted. Far below, a torrent of shattered wood, burning embers, and ruined creatures tore through a widening hole in the ceiling.

#

Myranda was thrown back. The fire was all around her, long ago having slipped from her control. She struggled to her feet; gasping a lungful of choking smoke and pushing aside the searing pain of the fire that lapped at her ankles, Myranda assessed her situation. The staircase was blocked by the very remnants of the floor it led to. Injured but threatening creatures began to pull themselves from the rubble.

Above, the supports for the next floor were giving way. She forced every last drop of her will into maintaining the integrity of the floor. Her life was lost. It didn't matter. All she could hope to do was to give the others a chance. Flames climbed to her legs, smoke strangled her lungs, and half-broken beasts drew menacingly close. With a strength she did not know that she had, she managed to force the shaky floor back into place.

#

Above, Lain and Ivy entered the final floor. The massive creatures found here were far too big to be swept aside by Ivy, despite the momentum that had continued unbroken since she had begun her ascent. Lain managed to inch ahead of her just as the tangled mass of snakes that dominated the room attempted to strike with one of its many mouths. The bite of his weapon caused the beast to recoil out of Ivy's path. As she approached the door, she lowered her shoulder, leveling the stone body of Ether with the solid planks.

With a force that was difficult to comprehend, the speeding hero struck the door, using the petrified shapeshifter as a ram. The planks fairly disintegrated on impact, the door destroyed utterly. Ivy was staggered by the blow, losing her footing and tumbling violently across the frozen ground outside. The stone body of Ether, though riddled with cracks after the collision, skidded to a stop just outside the walls in one piece. Lain darted out the door, followed by a flood of beasts and a vast billowing column of black smoke.

#

Many of the creatures below had been designed to breathe flame, and thus had set the fort alight in a dozen different places. It was clear now that the horrid place had been designed for just this purpose, to consume itself and all within rather than fall into the hands of an enemy. Myranda, still in the very heart of the structure, sensed that her task was done, that the others had escaped. She began to release her agonized mind's grip. As she did, like a waterfall, the ruined wood, ash, and fauna began to pour down before her. The floorboards she stood on and those above her head began to buckle.

Finally they gave way.

#

Ivy's aura faded as Lain rushed to her side, turning to the creatures that had filed out of the fort. With a rush of smoke and superheated air, the whole of the structure gave way. It collapsed into the pit it had been built in, disappearing into the black smoke that belched out. Red and orange flames cut through the smoke here and there, casting swaths of light upon the night-darkened field as the column rose into the sky.

The rumbling collapse of the structure was a blessing in at least one way: the worms that had guarded it now flowed into the fiery hole, destroying themselves in attempts to attack the source of the rumbling. Silhouetted against the smoky orange glow of the ruined fort were the only survivors of the collapse: the snake monstrosity, the horned tiger, and the scorpion-tailed hawk. Lain held his sword ready.

Ivy held her head, dizzy but still managing to get to her feet after her ordeal. She looked to the spectacle before her, seeing it but not comprehending. Her wits had returned, but the intense few minutes gone by were lost to her, a blur of sound and light. She wasn't sure how much time had passed, or even where she was. The last she remembered was being inside the fort--now there was no fort in sight. A piercing cry came from above and she looked up in time to see a needle-sharp black tail whiz by her head. She jerked away from it, reeling and falling back to the ground.

Her blurry vision locked onto a hulking form she had made sure to ignore when she'd entered the fort. Lain was standing in front of her, facing down a dark shape that moved toward him with alarming speed. The assassin slowly side-stepped. Each time he did, the creature charging at him turned slightly, shifting its path toward him and away from Ivy. She turned her eyes to the sky. A barely visible shape wheeled about and began toward her again. She felt about for the club that had finally slipped from her hand when she had fallen.

As powerful as her eyes were, the black form of the hawk against the black sky remained virtually indistinguishable. Her ears twitched as she tuned out everything else. They were far more sensitive than her eyes. She was just barely able to hear the rustle of wind past the beast. At the last moment, she raised her club, bracing it with both hands, clenching her teeth, and shutting her eyes. Her motion was well-timed. The beast had aimed a strike with its lethal tail directly at her heart. The force was enough to drive the fist-sized head of the tail entirely through the weapon, stopping just a whisper from its target. The creature madly flapped its wings, attempting to escape.

Ivy gripped the weapon tightly, swinging it out and beating it on the ground. The experimental beast was swung helplessly through the air before being hammered against the ground.

The huge, cat-like creation roared toward Lain. He carefully judged its speed. The distance between them quickly closed. Finally, he dove to the side. The tremendous beast was more agile than the creature that it owed its size and horns to, but only just. By the time he regained a firm footing, the beast was already upon him. A hasty swipe of his sword cost the creature one of its horns, but a powerful blow with its claws slipped beneath the attack and raked his abdomen. He pulled away, but the claws still left their mark. A second slice of Lain's weapon found the predator's throat. He retreated after the strike. The stricken creature writhed briefly on the ground before becoming motionless.

Ivy stood once more, planting a foot on the ruined hawk and tearing her weapon free along with a fair amount of the beast's tail. She sniffed at the barb that had nearly reached her heart. The smell of the potent toxin was intense and burned her nose. She turned to Lain. The experience had been enough to knock the cobwebs from her head. She was keenly aware of her surroundings, and of the severity of their situation. Moreover, she remembered what she had come here to do. To prove to Lain and Ether that she was strong enough to stay. She fought aside the constant burn of fear in her stomach and faced the massive beast that remained.

Now that there was no roof to limit the monster, it rose to its full height, lifting itself on the dozen stout snakes as though they were legs. It moved with deceiving speed, as even when all legs remained on the ground, the slithering of the limbs allowed it to glide along. Its target was the petrified body of Ether.

With great, bounding steps Ivy rushed to the beast. Lain circled around attempting to find the proper method do attack, but with a dozen pairs of eyes, there was no sneaking up on it. Ivy was not similarly concerned, and paid for it almost immediately. When she was in striking range, three of the limbs shot toward her. Before she could react, two had constricted her, squeezing her enough to force the weapon from her hand. They brought her swiftly to the clacking beak that was hidden behind the many legs.

Lain swept in. Snakes he had dealt with. He could read their movements. He knew when, how, and where they would strike. All senses alive and alert, he moved in. The attacks were swift and numerous. Lain dodged each as narrowly as he could. It was best to stay close. In that way, the beast could not attack without threatening to strike itself. When he reached the base of the limbs that clutched Ivy, he sliced neatly through them. They dropped to the ground, followed by an unnaturally small amount of blood. The wound where they had been connected closed quickly. The snakes writhed in pain enough for Ivy to escape, but they did not die. The core of the massive creature dropped down in an attempt to snatch up the escaping morsel, but instead sliced into one of its own severed limbs.

Ivy scrambled to safety, the piercing blue aura betraying the fear that had managed to surge back to the forefront. She snatched up the club from the ground as one of the other liberated snakes pursued her. She forced herself to face it, and offered a weak attack. Her state of mind robbed the strike of any accuracy; it barely grazed the beast, but it was enough. The needle-sharp tip of the hawk's tail delivered just a drop of its lethal venom to the creature. It jerked and convulsed, twisting and hissing in pain as though jabbed with a hot poker. As Ivy realized what had happened, the blue aura began to fade, a devious smile coming to her face.

Lain fought his way away from the beast. A pair of attacks had done little more than release two more snakes. Ending them, he retreated to a safe distance to consider a new strategy. Ivy, it seemed, had learned nothing from her last attack, as she again was rushing headlong toward the creature. He followed, preparing to release her from the grip that would inevitably result from her foolhardy attack.

When the first of the snakes lunged at her, she fluidly stepped to the side and hammered the tip of the tail deep into the serpent. The effect of the full dose of the venom was horrifying. As Ivy pulled her weapon away, snapping off the lethal tip of the tail inside the snake, she averted her eyes. The very flesh of the beast seemed to blacken and shrivel. Web-like lines of black wound along the beast's body, following the veins that swiftly delivered the poison to the core of the creature. Within the space of a few heartbeats, the entirety of the creature was convulsing and crying out in a chorus of agonized hissing.

When the beast was finally still, Ivy surveyed the aftermath. The monstrosity looked ruined, as if centuries of decay had reduced it to a mass of sinew and bone. Her face made it clear that she was not certain how to feel about her achievement. She looked to Lain, who approached her.

"I . . . I did it, Lain! Ether is okay! And I killed that . . . that *thing!* You don't need to protect me! I don't need to go . . ." Ivy said, trailing off.

She looked about with rapidly increasing desperation. As she did, a barely audible noise from above drew Lain's attention. It was a minute rustle, like the swoop of an owl. Lain trained his eyes on the apparent source of the sound. A stir in the rising smoke confirmed that there was a threat. Ivy suddenly grabbed Lain's shoulder and turned him to face her.

"Where is Myranda? She escaped, didn't she? She followed us, didn't she!? TELL ME SHE DIDN'T DIE!" Ivy pleaded.

Lain was silent. Ivy dropped to her knees, facing the burning pit that served as the final resting place for her friend. As before, sadness did not have any of the effect that her other emotions had. There was no one near who was weak or compassionate enough to have the emotion forced upon them. The poor creature began to sob as Lain resumed his cautious monitoring of the sky above.

"She . . . can't be dead. SHE SWORE TO ME SHE WOULD FOLLOW. Myranda wouldn't lie. She wouldn't make a promise she couldn't keep. And it's all his fault," Ivy said, leaping to her feet.

She was obviously fatigued. Wisps of red flickered about her as her weary soul reacted to the anger that was steadily building. Her eyes locked onto the sky above the fiery pit with far more certainty than Lain's. With teeth bared, she reared back and hurled her club. The weapon disappeared into the darkness before audibly colliding with something and plummeting back to the pit below.

Slowly, a peculiar form descended into the orange glow above the pit. It was Demont, riding a dragoyle unlike any they had yet encountered. It was smaller and more lithe in appearance. The wings were feathered instead of leathery dragon wings. The neck was longer and thinner, leading to a head that seemed to be a cross between the skull of an eagle and the skull of a dragon. It was clear that he was suffering greatly from the wounds he had received. His breathing was labored.

"Your survival . . . concerns me. Your ability to locate me . . . is all the more troubling," he said. "At the risk of . . . angering my associates . . . I may have to take . . . a slightly more direct role . . . in your demise . . . KILL HIM!"

The words burned at her mind. She turned suddenly and awkwardly toward Lain. She felt herself moving toward him. He held his weapon loosely, but defensively. He didn't want to raise the blade to her. A hatred greater than she had ever felt burned inside of her. She came to a halt. With great effort, she turned her eyes to the figure in the sky. She fought back into control of her body. Demont looked on with a stern face.

"It seems . . . your soul is stronger . . . than the body. Very well . . . we shall control . . . the soul, then," he said.

His fingers wrapped about the gem that hung from his neck. Instantly, Ivy dropped to the ground, limp.

"Rise," Demont commanded.

Ivy obeyed on a fundamental level. Her body rose like a marionette on strings until it was level with Demont, high above the field.

"Face me," he ordered.

She obeyed.

"Show me anger," he demanded.

The red wisps of light began to flow weakly again as her face twisted into a look of profound fury.

"More. MORE! I don't care if you have nothing left . . . FIND IT," he ordered, tightening his fist around the gem.

Pain mixed with her expression and her eyes took on a powerful golden glow. Finally, the full might of her vicious transformation spilled over. The first true outburst of its kind to be witnessed by Demont, it threw his mount backward with its force. When the beast he rode steadied itself, the display of power his creation managed brought a smile to his face.

"The mortal soul may yet be a worthy plaything," he conceded.

His smile was quickly wiped away when a blade burst through the neck of the beast he rode. During the moment of distraction, Lain had hurled his sword. The dragoyle's wings flapped a few times involuntarily before it crashed to the ground at the edge of the fiery pit. Still alive, fingers still clutching the crystal, the battered general pulled himself from the pile of rubble that had been his mount. He dragged himself away. As Lain drew near, he screamed an order to the still enthralled Ivy.

"WHEN YOU LOOK AT THESE CREATURES, YOU DO NOT SEE CHOSEN, YOU SEE DEMONS! KILL THEM BOTH!" he cried.

As she streaked to her task, he removed a gem from his pocket and shattered it on the frozen earth. A portal similar to the one that had brought him there opened.

Ivy launched herself at Lain. He rolled to the side and she gouged a deep trench into the earth where he had stood. He sprinted to the slowly-crawling general, but he disappeared through the portal moments before Lain could reach him.

Ivy turned her attentions briefly to the stone form of Ether. She rose high into the air and rocketed at the motionless form, shattering it with enough force to cause the pair of them and a fair piece of the field to collapse into the burning pit. A moment later she emerged, crying in pain and clutching her chest, the mark meting out its punishment. When the pain had subsided, she turned toward Lain.

He pulled his weapon and made ready for the clash, knowing full well it was a fight he could not win.

In a blinding streak of red light, Ivy attacked Lain. With the skill and precision of a lifetime warrior, he blocked the attack, but the force was too much. The sword was broken in two, and Lain was hurled backward. Ivy recoiled in pain, the mark on her chest glowing brilliantly through her ragged clothing. Lain climbed painfully to his feet. Blood leaked from a dozen old wounds and a dozen new ones. His sword was out of reach. Ivy hung ominously above the ground, her gaze locked on Lain. Behind her, the raging flames seemed to darken. The fire was dying out.

"Ivy. You do not want to do this," Lain said.

Ivy lowered to the ground. It was unclear if she was tiring, or if there was some other reason. Her arms were at her sides, fists clenched tight. Lain stood firm as she approached. Her eyes looked upon a friend, but her soul beheld something else. Filtered through the suggestion of the general, the images reached her burning mind as twisted monstrosities. She felt nothing but the need to destroy them.

"Look at me. Listen to me. Smell me. I am not your enemy," he stated.

Soon she was nose to nose with him. The raw energy pouring off of her burned at Lain, but he didn't so much as raise a hand. It would do no good. The brilliant orbs of light that were her eyes peered deeply into his own, as if they were testing his resolve. Flickers of truth fought through to her mind. She tested the air with her nose. She knew the scent. Her aura was beginning to dim, and the slightest hint of recognition was dawning on her face. She slowly raised a hand to touch his face.

From the pit, there was suddenly a low cracking sound. All eyes shifted to the source. Floating above the pit, drawing in the last of the flames, was Ether. The brilliance and intensity of the flame that made up her body was reminiscent of her first appearance, and every bit a match for the fiery red aura that surrounded Ivy. She held above her head a massive, flaming, blackened piece of wood. It was formerly the door of the fort.

"Get away from him, you *beast!*" she cried.

"Ether, no!" Lain warned--far too late.

The huge projectile sailed through the air. Lain dove aside and was showered by burning embers and ash as it collided with Ivy. Before the debris finished falling, Ether continued her assault. The symbol on her forehead burned even more brightly than the flame, but whatever pain it caused did not show past the anger on her face. She hurled herself at Ivy, raining blows upon her.

Tumbling to the ground, Ivy absorbed a massive amount of punishment. Suddenly, she exploded skyward, directly through the form of Ether. The flames scattered and reformed. Ivy shrieked as she peaked in her flight, the mark taking its toll swiftly. Ether shifted to wind and summoned an intense gale straight upwards. Ivy was pushed further and further up.

"Ether, stop this!" Lain demanded.

"She has proven once and for all that she is a tool of the enemy, a knife eager for a place in our backs. I cannot kill her, or it will mean my end, but I intend to see to it that she can never threaten us again," Ether raged.

With that she shifted to flame. The whole of the mighty column of air she controlled changed with her. Ivy vanished inside the towering flame. Ether continued the assault. The churned-up, snowy earth began to sizzle and boil. A single point, Ether's mark, shone through the flame.

Suddenly, the pain it was causing her became too much. She relented, covering the mark with her hands and crying out in pain. Lain's eyes turned skyward. High above, Ivy was plummeting. Her aura had dimmed greatly. She angled herself in the air as she fell, positioning her feet for a strike. Ether recovered just in time to for the blow to be delivered. Her fiery form scattered into a galaxy of embers. Ivy struck the ground beneath with enough force to form a crater, splashing aside a torrent of scalding mud and thawed earth.

Now her own mark administered its punishment for her attack. Her fingers clawed at the shining point on her chest, an ear-piercing cry splitting the air. Ether's form pulled sloppily together, the exertion now clearly showing. Through the pain, Ivy's eyes locked on her. Quickly, the shapeshifter changed to water. Ivy charged at her, but Ether vanished into the melted ice. Ivy skidded to a stop on the muddy ground, looking furiously about for her target. The very water itself leapt up all around her, first coating her, then immersing her in a swell of murky melted snow.

Ether's form separated from the mass of water that surrounded Ivy and quickly solidified into ice. The water around the raging malthrope followed suit. She thrashed about in it, her body slowly becoming immobilized. Her muzzle only just reached the edge of the water, peeking out of it, when the ice froze completely.

Ether's mark smoldered on her head, a slight smile of satisfaction on her face. It vanished swiftly. She was not satisfied. She shifted to stone. Like a wave spreading out from her core, the water she held in place changed to stone. Soon nothing was visible of Ivy but her nose. Ether slouched, the strength she had drawn in from the flames already nearly exhausted.

The mark on her head continued to burn at her as she began to walk toward Lain. Suddenly she stopped. She turned to the encased Ivy. Hairline cracks, crimson light shining through them, were spreading across the surface of the impromptu prison. Ether held up a hand and exerted her will. The cracks began to close. Her hand began to waver. The cracks opened again. Ivy burst from her bonds and dove upon Ether's stone form. She hammered her with blow after blow, breaking the stone form down into smaller and smaller pieces. The mark on her chest crackled with power as it sought to punish her appropriately for her actions.

Lain dove on Ivy's back. His prolonged touch was enough to break the general's control and make it clear to her that it was no enemy she was facing. Confusion swept in, mixing with the anger. Her strength was gone, her soul taxed to its limit. She pulled away from the mound of pulverized rock that had once been an ally. The fury began to drop away. Any dulling effects it had on the mark's effect went with it. A pure, intense pain burned at her chest, cutting her to the core. Just as her mind knew naught but anger before, now it knew naught but pain. It consumed her mind and pushed it past its breaking point. With neither the strength nor the will to remain standing, Ivy collapsed in Lain's arms.

Lain lowered the unconscious creature to the ground. In the eastern sky, the first rays of dawn were coloring the clouds. He surveyed the surroundings. It looked as though hell had clawed its way out of the earth. Smoke still rose from a pit that buried a comrade far below. The smell of death rose from it as the carcasses of the countless failed experiments smoldered among the ruined timbers.

His eyes turned to Ivy. She was alive, but only just. Unlike after her other outbursts, Ivy was not spared the physical consequences of her battle. Scrapes, gouges, and burns littered her body. Her fists were smeared with blood. Swelling marked where attacks had landed. He bent to lift her to his shoulders, but the sharp pain in his abdomen surged as he did. Ribs were broken, and blood poured generously from gashes on his chest. It was difficult to get a full breath. The hand that had formerly held his sword felt like it was grinding when he moved it.

He stood and found the two pieces of his sword. Tearing a few shreds of his clothing free, he bound the tip of his sword to his broken hand, stiffening it so that it would heal properly and providing him with at least some measure of a defense. After stowing the rest of the blade, he turned once more to the pit. Slowly, he approached its edge. He pulled in a painful breath.

She was gone.

Myranda.

It was inevitable. She had grown immensely, learned much, but she hadn't been ready. This was not the life she had been meant to live. This was not the death she had been meant to die. But she had been heading for it the moment she took her first step out of her world and into his. Now she was dead. The fierce pain in his chest and hand reminded him of why he had found her again. If for nothing else, he'd needed her skills. Before they had been drawn here, they'd been on the run. On the verge of discovery. Even if the column of failing smoke rising into a brightening sky was not enough of a beacon, the towering column of flame Ether had chosen to summon would lend an urgency to the patrol's steps that would bring them here in no time.

He was the only one left standing. And just barely. Without a healer, he might survive a battle, but he wouldn't survive long after. That was why this must not be a battle. More familiar tactics were called for.

Already he could hear them coming. The pounding of hooves. He moved far to the edge of the field, leaving Ivy far behind. The men must not reach her. His eyes focused on the approaching forms. Six soldiers, all with horses. The whole of the patrol had come to investigate. That was good. It meant these men were inexperienced. Proper protocol would have been to leave at least one behind to summon aid if the threat was great enough to warrant it. That would have complicated matters. Instead, once these men were down, there would be none to replace them for some time, and no message would be delivered.

He readied himself.

#

The most senior member of the patrol rode tentatively. He had been ordered not to approach this section of the field. There was a wide radius around this place that was completely off limits, but news of whatever had happened here was surely enough for his commander to overlook the violation. He hadn't seen land so ravaged since he had last been to the front.

Pausing briefly to scan the surroundings for some trace of the army that it must have taken to do this, his eyes came to rest on a handful of unidentifiable forms. The nearest was a prone figure midway to the smoking pit that seemed to be the center of the cataclysm that happened here. As he drew nearer, the form looked to be a malthrope. He hadn't seen one in years. It was an ill omen to find one here.

Behind him, he heard one of his men separate from the others.

"Halt!" he barked.

All but one horse was reined in. The commander gritted his teeth and turned his horse. The rearmost of the men had fallen a fair distance back, and was slumped forward on his horse. The other men were rigidly at attention.

"Soldier!" he growled.

When the man did not react he rode up to the offender. Blood trickled down the front of his armor. His throat was cut.

"DEFENSIVE FORMATION!" he ordered.

The men struggled to pull their steeds into the appropriate configuration while the commander glanced desperately for what had struck this blow so swiftly. His men were nearly in place, forming a tight, outward facing ring with himself as the missing link. As he coaxed his horse into his place, something slipping beneath the horses caught his eye.

"SCATTER!" he ordered.

The form leapt up and yanked back the head of one of his men, pulling a blade that seemed to be an extension of its arm across the soldier's throat before dropping from sight. What manner of demon was this? The body of the murdered man was pulled from the saddle. He had been the marksman.

The commander's sword was drawn. Whatever this thing was, it was behind the horse.

"ATTACK!" he barked, charging past the horse.

The men turned to him, but he was staring at the body of his fallen comrade and nothing else. The arrows of his quiver were missing. A clattering of wood drew his attention to his left. The fletched ends of the arrows, separated at their centers by jagged breaks, were just settling to the ground. Before he could spot what his men had, he heard a sound like an arrow in flight, but without the twang of a bowstring. One of the pursuing men lurched and fell from his steed. Then another.

"RETREAT!" the commander ordered, far too late.

The last of his men fell back, the frayed end of a broken arrow protruding from a joint in his armor. Then, as suddenly as it had come for his men, a sharp pain brought the darkness upon him.

#

His work done, Lain drew in another pained breath. He was a monster. He knew that. Anyone who would hope to survive a life like this had to be one. That was why Ivy must be spared it. As his many wounds painfully reminded him of their presence, he set about raiding the supplies of the soldiers. The arrows had been easy to break. Too easy. He quickly discovered that all of the equipment and weapons were of similarly lacking quality. Briefly, he considered taking one of the swords to replace his own, but until his hand healed, he would need a very light weapon. Each of the men carried a dagger. He selected three of them, and transferred any other useful resources he could scavenge into the saddlebags of the most able-looking steed.

Taking a deep breath, Lain lifted Ivy to his shoulders and threw her across the horse. He made ready to mount the beast and be off, but a thought came to mind. His eyes turned to the pile of rubble that had been Ether. He wanted very much to be rid of her, but her power, however misused, was unmistakable. That power could be useful.

More importantly, if she was still alive and he left her, she would most certainly try to find him when she recovered. If that happened, there would be a string of soldiers following her. Better to keep her where she would be able to do the least damage. He scooped up some of the largest pieces of rubble, one of which still bore the faintly glowing mark of the Chosen. Most of the rest of the remnants were indistinguishable from the dirt and stones of the field.

He mounted the horse and headed to the east. With the patrol for that area dead, it was the destination least likely to offer any resistance in the immediate future. In less than a day he would reach the foot of the mountains. From there he would head to Verneste. There was a weaponsmith there. He might be able to reforge Desmeres's blade. Lain would rather have found one of the storehouses to reequip, but he could not afford to encounter anyone before shelter could be found for Ivy long enough for him to recover. He set off.

Deacon glanced behind him nervously as he approached the crystal arena. Already the sound of angry cries and hurried footsteps revealed that his actions had been discovered. It was now or never. He stepped inside. The rosy light of dawn vanished as a magnificently starry sky opened overhead inside the arena. The stars bore little resemblance to what he was accustomed to. Azriel had a habit of conjuring up the sky that had been her nightly view in her homeland, rather than in this place.

Azriel was the eldest wizard in Entwell. In truth, she was its founder. For hundreds of years, she had made her home in a section of the hidden city that was composed entirely of the very gems that wizards used to aid their casting. It made spells effortless, and spared her the ravages of time. The centuries had brought her unparalleled knowledge in mystic arts, and her role as the final test for any who wished to be called a master of the mystic arts made her not just a figure of respect, but of fear among the spellcasters of Entwell.

In the distance, she reclined, gazing at the sky lazily, a book of spells open and resting in her lap. She had striking white hair, a tall, slender frame, and a black robe decorated with white flames that moved and flickered as though they truly burned.

"Deacon," she said without looking. "Making trouble, are you?"

"I . . . yes. But--please. The others will be here shortly. I request just a few moments from them while I explain," he said.

She raised her head, intrigued. With an absentminded wave of her hand, all of the scenery slipped away, leaving only the two of them in a black void.

"They shall not find us until I will it so. Tell me. What has motivated you to abandon our ways?" she said.

"Myranda," he stated.

"You will forgive me if I am not surprised," she said with a grin.

"I have been watching her. Ever since she left this place," he said.

"No small task." Azriel nodded. "But hardly an explanation."

"She is Chosen! It is proven. I believe she has spoken with Oriech himself. And I have been studying the words of Hollow. The ones that I shamefully coaxed out of him in the absence of the others. I believe they speak of me. I believe I must help her," he said.

"And how do you plan to do so?" she asked.

He pulled a bundle of pages from his bag and shakily handed them to her. She spread her fingers and they arranged themselves before her as if on a desk. As she read, her expression became more serious.

"You tread on dangerous ground, Deacon," she said.

She continued reading.

"Creative. Insightful. But incomplete. You propose some truly novel methods. Artful solutions to age-old problems, but it will not be enough. There are numerous assumptions of conditions that may never exist. This is impractical. It will not work," she said.

He pulled out a final page. The words were hastily sketched, runes scratched out and rewritten. She looked it over, glancing again at the first pages. A look of contemplation came to her face.

"You realize that this is not definitive. Even given a flawless application of the methods described, you merely make success a relative likelihood, not a certainty. You should continue your work. This has merit. It is brilliant, even revolutionary, but irresponsible. Given time, a tremendous breakthrough could result," she said.

"I can't. I have violated the terms of my punishment to come this far. I will certainly not be given the right to continue for years," he said.

"Then wait. A contribution of this magnitude is quite worth the wait. When you reveal what you have done here, you will have your name spoken in the same breath of some of our most revered visionaries," she said.

"I don't have the time. The last images I saw of Myranda painted a very grim picture. I believe it may already be too late. But I must try. I can't do it alone. With the benefit of the arena, I may be able to find her regardless of her state of mind, and I may be able to cast the many parts of this spell, but I cannot do both. You are the only one, aside from me, with the knowledge of gray magic necessary to aid me," he pleaded.

For a moment, Azriel was silent. She thought. When she spoke, her voice had a solemn tone.

"If you do this, regardless of the outcome, it will be the last spell you cast in Entwell. Casting a spell in this form, untested, upon yourself, shows a disregard for our principles that cannot be forgiven. You will never again be permitted to practice the mystic arts. Remember your mentor," she warned. "Gilliam lost his life to an untested spell, and one far less dangerous than this."

"I am willing to accept those consequences," he said without hesitation.

"Very well, then. Let us waste no time," she said, the air tingling as she drew together the first of the procedures described.

#

Lain rode on. The column of smoke from the ruined fort was visible, even at this distance, and he was only just reaching the forest at the foot of the mountains. Much care had been sacrificed for the sake of speed. Fortunately, he had remained unseen. Though the weapons of the soldiers were of the poorest quality, the same could not be said of the horses provided to them. A horse was far more likely to survive a battle than its rider these days, and as such, generations of war had done little to weaken them. Wide hooves caught the snow well, and powerful lungs drew the frigid air with no ill effect. Even so, the steed was heavily burdened and badly fatigued. Lain slowed to a walk when the trees were dense enough to make their discovery unlikely.

There was not a single part of his body that didn't scream out for relief. He could not remember when he had last eaten. The gashes across his chest still seeped blood and burned increasingly. They would not heal well. Many bones were broken, many more nearly so. It was a condition he'd had to learn to endure before Myranda had come into his life. He would learn to endure it again now that she was dead. Her skills would be missed. *She* would be missed. His mind lingered on her briefly, but he shook the thoughts away. Distraction was something he could ill afford. Not now.

He could not smell it, hear it, or see it, but something was wrong. It was a feeling he had come to trust. He was being watched.

Time and distance did not diminish the sensation. A tingling in his spine. A dull flutter in the back of his mind. He was certain now. Slowly, he brought his horse to a halt. He needed silence. Eyes closed, he drew in the air. He could smell animals nearby, a spectrum of smells, but nothing threatening. Slowly, the feeling faded. The concern it caused only grew. Whoever it was who followed was near enough to know of the discovery, and skilled enough to remain hidden. There were precious few beings he knew to be capable of such a feat, and only one seemed likely.

Now was not the time to call him out. For now he must continue.

Shortly after he began riding, his ears twitched at a distant crack of thunder. In the south, that might have signaled a coming storm. Not here.

Not this far north. He put it out of his mind. Whatever strange forces were at work, they were far behind him or not yet of his concern. The terrain was rocky now. A light but steady snowfall was beginning, whipped into a painful blast now and again by the constant wind from the mountain. He heard sound from inside his saddlebag. A whisper.

"Lain?" came Ether's wavering voice.

There was a strange quality to the voice, as though it came not from a mouth, but from thin air. Lain grunted a reply.

"The beast. Did she survive our encounter?" she asked.

"She did," he replied.

"And I assume you are carting her worthless hide along with us," she said.

Lain offered no reply.

"I suspected as much," Ether said. "I have ruminated on the subject of your obsession with her. It is my observation that mortals, in their quest to perpetuate their species, are driven to find and protect each other. Love is the name of this affliction. Even those unburdened by mortality seem to fall prey to this phenomenon. It is necessary for their mental wellbeing. I am quite certain that you, to a mild degree, have allowed yourself to be infected with this disease of the mind. Its target is Ivy.

"In the world of mortals, this quality may be seen as admirable, but it is a danger to our cause. You wish to be rid of her, and that is good, but your insistence on delivering her safely to the south is a delay at best and a threat at worst. She is a liability every moment that she is allowed to live, and while we cannot kill her ourselves, it is in our best interests, and in the best interests of this world, that we leave her to die."

"If you suggest such a thing just once more, do not expect to see another sunrise," Lain warned.

"It is as I suspected. Very well. While I believe that in time you might be cured of this affliction, time is not among our assets. We must, then, indulge your illness in a more helpful manner. If you must love someone, I shall permit you to substitute myself. You may thus find outlet for your affections without endangering the purpose for which you were created," she said.

"You suggest that I love you rather than Ivy," he replied.

"Indeed. You have my permission. You may begin at once, if you wish," she said.

Before Lain could react, a soft, weak laughter began to sound. It was Ivy. She began to stir.

"You--" Giggle. "--you love him. You say all of this about emotions being bad, and you love him," Ivy slurred, trying to open her heavy eyelids.

Lain halted the horse just in time for her to slide from the animal's back to the ground, tumbling to her seat. She continued chuckling softly.

"Ouch. That's why you don't like me. He likes me better than you," she said, finally wrestling her eyes open.

She looked around briefly, a puzzled look on her face.

"Where is she? Is she the horse?" Ivy asked, struggling to her feet and immediately stumbling into the steed to catch her balance.

"As though I would take the form of a beast of burden and carry *you*," Ether objected.

"What the!" Ivy exclaimed, moving unsteadily to the saddlebag from whence the voice had come.

When she beheld the contents, she began laughing uncontrollably. As she did, a pale yellow glow surrounded her. Lain felt a warm sensation in his twisted hand and gashed chest. He pulled aside some of the tattered cloth to see the wounds slowly closing. When her laughter stopped, so did the healing.

"She's a pile of rocks!" she sighed, wiping a tear from her eye.

"You *did* this to me!" Ether objected.

"I did?" she said, snorting with contained laughter. "I'm . . . very . . . sorry. HAHAHA!"

Again, Lain could feel his wounds healing. He didn't know what the D'karon had done to her, but apparently it was not limited to fear and anger. On the rare instance that a more positive emotion was felt intensely enough, it had beneficial effects. By the time the latest outburst subsided, Lain's chest was little more than sore, and his hand could move again.

"Silence! Silence!" Ether commanded. "How dare you take joy in the betrayal of your fellow Chosen!"

"I'm sorry. It's just that you are always talking about how you don't have emotions, and how you are better than us, and now you are helpless and in love!" she snickered.

"Blast the human for letting herself die. At least she could get you under control!" Ether cried out.

Instantly, anger roared up in Lain. How foolish could she be? Did she *want* to coax a more dangerous state of mind from Ivy? The creature stopped snickering, but did not seem angry.

"Myranda's not dead," Ivy stated. She looked around, confused again. "Where is she?"

"I've already told you," Ether replied.

"No, she isn't dead. She was just here, I was just talking to her . . . where did she go?" Ivy asked again.

"Stupid animal, you were dreaming," Ether said.

"No! I barely ever dream, and when I do, it is always about music. Lain, where is she?" Ivy asked.

"She was left behind, at the fort," Lain said solemnly.

"You mean she went *back* to the fort, right? Because she was just here. Shouldn't we wait for her to catch up? How far is it?" Ivy asked.

"We have to move on," Lain said.

"Oh. All right. I'm sure she'll find us soon," Ivy said, climbing onto the horse's back behind Lain, wrapping her arms around his waist and resting her chin on his shoulder.

"So, how did I do that to her?" she asked as they continued on. "I don't remember it, so I must have been transformed. Was I angry or scared?"

"Angry," Lain said.

"You were bending to the will of--" Ether began.

"Ether, do not say another word," Lain quietly ordered. "Ivy, we need to be silent."

"Whatever you say," Ivy eagerly agreed. She turned to whisper mockingly to Ether, "You got yelled at."

As they traveled further into the mountains, the horse's footing faltered more and more frequently. Soon they would have to leave it behind. As they rode, Ivy rummaged through the saddlebag that contained the provisions Lain had secured. She ate and offered to feed Lain as he guided the horse, but he declined. She even offered some food to Ether, who remained furiously silent. It was the first wise thing she had done in some time.

Lain did not know how or why Ivy had come to believe that Myranda had survived, but he had to travel as far as he could while the delusion persisted. While she was happy, this journey was infinitely simpler.

In order to avoid being seen, they had been traveling up the slope of the mountain in as direct a route as possible, avoiding roads entirely. The horse had been navigating ably, but now they had reached the point that would be more climbing than walking. Lain stowed the tip of his sword that had served as a splint and flexed his painful but functional hand. After transferring as much of the useful equipment as possible to their backs, the issue of Ether needed to be addressed.

"Naturally I shall have to be carried until I have recovered sufficiently to assume a more mobile form," she stated.

"Well, why are you still rocks anyway? Is it that hard to turn into something else?" Ivy asked. "At least try something lighter."

"The merciless assault you unleashed upon me, coupled with the abundance of strength squandered to quell said assault and the consequences my mark levied upon me, has taken a considerable toll. I would prefer to remain as I am until my flame form can less riskily be assumed," Ether explained with exaggerated calmness.

"Well, when I first met you, you were a squirrel. Why not do that again? Then you would be easier to carry, and you would be cute!" Ivy suggested.

"I have no interest in doing anything that would bring you ease or enjoyment," Ether said.

"Fine," Ivy huffed. "But this makes us even."

"Hardly," Ether replied.

Lain cut the bag free, Ivy slung it as comfortably as she could over her shoulders, and the group began to climb. At first, the going was slow, but Ivy learned quickly and soon the grace she had shown in the past began to appear here as well. Before long, they were scaling the face as quickly as one might a ladder. Alas, the long night quickly fell upon them, bringing with it the painfully frigid temperatures and heavier snowfall that Lain had hoped to beat. Climbing had been treacherous before. It was far more so now. Regardless, Ivy and Lain continued.

Ivy's fingers were numb, but she continued without a word. This was all part of the test to her. Another way to prove to Lain that she didn't need to be hidden away from them. Another way to earn her right to stay with him--and with Myranda. Why did Ether think she was dead? She remembered her in the fort. Fire all around her. Lain said they had left her there, but that couldn't be. That was no dream. It was too real. She was there. She said not to worry, that she would follow. She wouldn't lie.

Lain kept a careful eye on her at all times, mindful of any falter. Prior to his involvement in this, he seldom traveled with others. When Myranda became his constant companion, willing or unwilling, he had been forced to slow himself to accommodate her. He had never traveled with one who was so near a match of his abilities. Even when the fatigue began to show in her eyes, she did not slow. Even as the snow caked on her white fur and stung at her eyes, she kept pace. She was a testament to a dying race.

Before long, the slope eased, and the smell of burning firewood signaled their arrival on the outskirts of the town. The darkness and blowing snow concealed it from their sight--and, more importantly, concealed them from the prying eyes of any of the residents. Thus concealed, the time had come to decide what was next. They each dropped their loads and crouched on the ground. Lain silently thought while Ivy sat, the tattered remains of her cloak pulled tightly about her.

"Why did we stop here?" she asked, shivering. "I smell a fire over there, and I don't smell any of the teachers. Maybe the people there would share their fire."

"The people will share nothing with us. Listen closely. Do not allow them to see you. Our kind is hated by the humans. They will do you harm as readily as any of the D'karon," Lain whispered.

"But why?" Ivy asked, quickly adopting a whisper as well.

"It is the way they have been taught. It is the way it has always been. It is the way they all are," he replied.

"Myranda doesn't hate us," she said.

"Myranda was different," he said. "Don't expect to find another like her for as long as you live."

"Myranda was blinded by duty, compassion, and naïveté. She was that rare human who had true potential, but she lacked the objectiveness to make the most of it. I am almost tempted to mourn her passing, if such an act were not utterly without purpose," Ether added.

Ivy shot an angry look at the source of the voice. Pulling open the bag from where she dropped it, she tipped it, spilling the contents.

"Oops," she said flatly.

The disembodied voice of Ether began to object, but Ivy interrupted as though she didn't notice.

"Then why did we come here?" Ivy whispered.

"There is a man here who may have the skill to repair my sword," Lain said.

"Is he human?" Ivy asked.

"He is," Lain replied.

"So he is going to hate you, then. How are you going to get him to help you?" she asked.

Lain was silent. He had yet to determine an answer. Amid the whistling of the constant wind, the pile of stones that had been rolled from the bag moved of their own accord, clattering and gathering together into a mass. Suddenly, they shifted from solid stone to water, splashing to the snow below and seeping in, melting a good deal of it. Eventually, the pool seemed to leap up, twisting itself into Ether's human shape before giving way to flesh and cloth. The whole of the event had a labored feel to it, as though she would have been better served by a few more hours of recuperation before attempting it.

Ether cast a vaguely threatening look at Ivy, prompting her to flinch and raise her hands in defense from a presumed act of retribution.

"Give the weapon to me. I shall see that it is repaired," Ether said.

Lain considered the offer. Ether was not in the habit of being helpful. This was clearly an attempt to curry favor away from Ivy. The offer would have been a reasonable option, were Ether as capable of blending as well socially as she did physically, but such was not the case. Reluctantly, he retrieved the two pieces of the weapon. This would not be without its usefulness.

"I sincerely doubt that you are capable of doing so. But until I can determine a more appropriate method, you shall have your attempt. Listen closely. The smith is named Flinn. You must speak directly to him. If the sword is allowed to be taken by a go-between, it will not be returned quickly, if at all. Inform him that payment will be rendered upon completion of the repair. Under no circumstances should you reveal that you are Chosen, use violence, or threaten violence. Most importantly, do not appear to be anything more than a human," he warned.

"An act of the utmost simplicity," Ether said.

She made her way toward the city. When she was far enough away that Ivy knew she would not be heard, she spoke.

"Do you really think she can do it?" Ivy asked.

"No. But the scene she is certain to make will serve as an adequate diversion. Stay here, and stay hidden," Lain said.

He vanished swiftly into the darkness. Ivy giggled lightly, eyes trained in the direction of the town, eagerly anticipating a furious Ether storming back defeated. Every so often, however, something distracted her. Her ear would twitch, and she would look over her shoulder. There was a sound occasionally, just loud enough to be heard over the sound of the wind. A horse. Ivy crouched a bit further behind the drift.

Lain crept lightly around the outskirts of the city. He had never come to this place himself, but it was clear which of the precious few buildings was the proper one. Already the raised voice of Ether could be heard berating the young woman who greeted patrons. Lain moved swiftly to the roof. There were no windows to speak of, but near the sharply sloped peak there were vents to let the smoke of the forges out. A screeching clash of wills was taking place. Right now, all that he had to do was listen. Observe. It would be a simple act to find Flinn and offer him his life in exchange for this service, but he had long ago learned that a task performed on pain of death tended to result in a poor outcome. Indeed, confronting Flinn himself would end badly. Men such as he conducted lives separate from the public. They had go-betweens, front men. It was these individuals that must be the first targets. Through them a proper meeting could be arranged. One that would leave the primary target at ease, prepared.

As he listened, memories of a hundred such nights flashed through his mind. Prior to his acceptance of the assignment that led him to Myranda, this was the norm. This was how he conducted business. The crunching footsteps of an approaching horse prompted him to make a cautionary shift away from the road. The wind blew toward the sound. He pulled in a long, slow sniff. No scent from the horse or rider, but amid the burning wood and sizzling metal, there was a familiar smell. One of the women inside.

The smell wasn't precisely familiar, but he had smelled one like it. The blood wasn't the same, but the bloodline was. It was difficult to determine which woman it was, but there were only two inside aside from Ether. A moment later, after a blistering assault by Ether on the human race as a whole and the greeter in particular, the shapeshifter stormed out, followed shortly by the young woman. Her scent thus separated from the rest, he could be sure. It was she. She, then, would be the target. The screaming continued in the snowy road for a minute more before the young woman finally slammed the door on Ether.

Clutching the blade of the sword in a furious grip tight enough to prompt a dribble of blood, she set off toward the edge of town where Ivy was waiting. As she did, a man on horseback rode by her. The man's eyes lingered on the sword for a moment. The glimmer of recognition was unmistakable. Lain's eyes narrowed. The man's eyes were the only things showing, so bundled was he against the cold. He wore a suit of armor, its surface unmarred by a single nick or gash, only caked with the blown snow. The helmet hung from his saddle, as the thick hood and scarf could not be worn beneath it.

Lain scanned the street once more. No one in sight, and all doors closed. The man guided his horse to a small stable behind one of the buildings. Lain leapt silently to its roof. When the man emerged Lain leapt down and pulled him behind the stable, dropping him on his back and placing a foot on his throat. He pulled the scarf from his face.

"Desmeres," he hissed.

"Been a while," Desmeres croaked.

Lain removed his foot from his neck and pulled his former partner to his feet.

"You have been following me," he said.

"You couldn't know that," he said, looking at Lain incredulously.

"Do you deny it?" Lain asked.

"No, but you couldn't know that. Steps were taken . . . unless. You felt it, didn't you? That bizarre sensitivity to being watched. I'd forgotten about that," Desmeres realized.

"Why are you here?" he demanded.

"Look at me, Lain. If it isn't obvious, I have been remiss in my duties," he said.

Lain drew to mind what he had seen earlier, but kept his eyes locked on those of Desmeres. The half-elf knew him better that any other creature in this world, and at the moment it was not clear if he could be trusted any longer. Aside from the immaculate armor, he recalled a familiar shield had been hanging from his side, and a more familiar hilt protruded from his sheath. A sword hung, in its sheath, from his belt. It was *the* sword. The one that had begun this crusade.

He was dressed precisely as the fallen swordsman in the field had been, the one he had found and watched Myranda approach. The one who had sealed her fate.

"Why would you pretend to be Chosen?" he asked.

"Misdirection. Adding a dash of truth to a cauldron of lies," he replied. "A highly effective tactic."

"To what end?" Lain asked, patience wearing thin.

"To aid my new partners, of course," he said.

Lain's hand went to the grip of one of the stolen daggers.

"Then you have become a tool of the D'karon," he said.

"Surely it doesn't come as a surprise to you. Wasn't it to be expected? It takes the D'karon--indeed, the entirety of the Alliance Army under their control--to equal the skill and opportunities afforded by yourself as an individual. I approached them and offered my services. Doing so without being killed proved an interesting task. They were quite open to the idea, once my allegiance was established. Another challenge, might I add, but one I rose to. They eventually embraced my presence. All save Trigorah. Still bears a bit of a grudge, I am afraid. They have her on a rather short leash, however. She's been removed from active duty and confined to the capital. Odd.

"Regardless. I shared with them a few choice pieces of information, and proposed the idea of posing as a Chosen. I would appear to be on the side of the Alliance, thus making the public less likely to believe that the true Chosen might be opposed. In addition, it was believed that by appearing to be a genuine Chosen One, my presence might flush out the rest of you," he explained.

"Why follow me?" Lain asked.

"Why would they accept me into their fold if not to find you?" he asked.

Lain drew his weapon and placed the blade against Desmeres's throat.

"And tell me. What is it that you intend to do, now that I am found?" he asked.

"Very little," he answered.

"Why should I believe you?" Lain asked.

"One would hope that years of partnership and familiarity would be enough," Desmeres offered with a weak smile.

The blade pressed harder.

"You aren't worth enough, Lain," he added.

Lain twisted the blade slightly.

"I am serious. They have no interest in only one or two of you. And they certainly don't want you killed. They were sparse on the details, but they want no less than four of you--five, if possible--and simultaneously. And under no circumstances must any of you be killed!" Desmeres said urgently.

Lain removed the blade.

"Why?" he asked.

"They wouldn't tell me. All that they did was give me the names and descriptions of who to watch for," he said, rubbing his throat. "You, of course. They know a great deal about you. They also targeted the shapeshifter, and something they called 'The Fourth,' another malthrope. She was with you. And I suspect the shapeshifter as well. Conspicuously absent is Myranda. If you were to ask me, I'd say their plan is to take on the full force of the Chosen as a whole. I can't imagine why."

"Tell me why I shouldn't kill you," Lain said.

"I could refer to the aforementioned years of partnership, but more convincing is the fact that I have the ability to feed disinformation to your many enemies within the Alliance Army. They gave me an object through which I am told to keep them updated on my actions. I recently informed them that I would be checking this town for you. It might be useful to you if I were to report that I had found nothing and was moving on. Less useful would be a missing follow-up that might indicate the need for closer inspection," he warned.

Lain considered the statement.

"I can't say I know what they have planned for you. Having been in their clutches before, I imagine you know what to expect. One would assume another capture would result in more of the same for both yourself and the others," he added.

"How have you been following me? How is it that I was unable to detect you?" Lain demanded.

"The D'karon mystics have a number of rather unique specialties. Most wizards concerned with stealth deal exclusively with attempted invisibility. The odd eccentric has tinkered with rendering one's motions silent. Once accepted into their cloister, I found volumes of runes and enchantments dedicated to rendering one undetectable to all senses. Vision, smell, even senses I have never heard of. Indeed, senses I cannot fathom. And the crystals, Lain. The possibilities they afford," Desmeres gushed enthusiastically. "They are truly inspiring. I have been able to infuse your weapons with passive defenses, but these crystals can fuel active, aggressive spells. And the techniques they have can produce weapons so quickly.

"This sword is a replica of the masterpiece the swordsman had carried. I managed it in days. Not weeks, days! I have got a few blades in the works . . . it pains me to be away from them. Revolutionary. One in particular belongs in no hands but your own, Lain. When it is complete, you shall have it. No one else could do it justice. It is the pinnacle of my art, Lain. I don't care if it finds its way to my throat a heartbeat after it reaches your grasp. This is a blade worthy to taste my blood."

"Enough! How did you follow me?" Lain asked.

"Intuition. Familiarity. A secret or two I choose not to reveal," he replied.

Lain's eyes fell to his neck. Then back to his eyes.

"Very well," Lain said, taking a step away.

"Wait," Desmeres said.

Lain lingered just at the edge of a shadow.

"How did you break my sword?" he asked.

"It failed me in battle," he replied.

"Was it broken by another sword?" Desmeres asked, almost desperate for the answer.

Lain stepped forward, placing a hand on his shoulder.

"It was broken by the hand of another Chosen," he said.

Lain slipped fully into the darkness.

"The Chosen . . . it took the spawn of the gods themselves to break it . . . I can accept that. Very well. But listen. Do not let that pretender, Flinn, charge you a copper for what he will do to that sword. The techniques he will steal from it will make him rich *enough* without charging a fee as well," he said.

His request fell upon an empty darkness, but he knew Lain had heard it. He walked slowly back into the stable. As he did, he felt for something around his neck, finally pulling forward his chest plate to glance at where it had been. The tooth he had taken from Myranda, Lain's tooth, should have been hanging around his neck. It and the spell she had brought back were largely responsible for allowing him to track Lain so quickly. Realizing what had happened, he chuckled and shook his head.

"He certainly hasn't lost a step," he said, readying his horse to move on.

#

Lain returned to the spot outside the town where the others were waiting. There were more questions that could have been asked, more warnings that could have been delivered, but time was short. It was unwise to leave Ether and Ivy alone together. When he discovered them, they were predictably exchanging harsh words, though mercifully in whispers.

"There you are. Tell her what you told me. That you just wanted her to be a distraction," Ivy insisted, her teeth chattering.

"Do not indulge her madness," Ether said.

"It is true," Lain stated flatly. "You served your purpose. The situation is in hand."

Ivy stuck out her tongue at Ether, who stood with a stern look on her face, speechless.

"You *relied* upon my failure?" she scoffed. "How could you leave something of such importance to so remote a chance?"

Lain ignored the statement, continuing. "Be silent until the weapon shop closes. One of the humans inside may be persuaded to help us."

"That is spectacularly unlikely. All in attendance seemed unified in their desire to prevent the expedient repair of that weapon," Ether warned.

Lain remained silent. He crouched and slowly lulled himself into the trance that had come to replace sleep for him. Ivy huddled near to him against the cold, finally placing her head on his shoulder and dropping off to sleep. After staring at the scene with growing disgust, Ether took a seat on the ground and shifted to water--and, soon after, ice.

A few hours passed. His body at rest, Lain's mind remained active. He closed his eyes, his ears vigilant even in rest. Thoughts lingered in his mind. He thought of the dangers that he still faced, the tasks that still lay before him. Slowly, doubt began to grow.

He should have killed Desmeres. He could not be trusted. He should not be waiting here; it was a waste of very precious time. He should have left Ether. She is unpredictable and uncontrollable. His judgment was failing him. His skills were failing him. The end was coming, and swiftly. For the first time in his life, he had something to live for, something besides his vengeance to keep him going, but it was clouding his mind. He was making mistakes. If he continued to make these mistakes, he would be killed. If he was killed, Ivy would die. The last real hope for his kind, possibly the last living member of his race, would be gone.

Lain tried to force the thoughts away. Doubts were a death sentence. If there was one thing he had learned in all of his life, it was that the past is past. The only thing that matters is the future. If one does not believe entirely in one's choices, then one has already failed. He had to stay focused on his tasks. The greatest danger in the warrior's sleep was the threat of being consumed by the darkest aspects of the mind, the thoughts that too often drifted to the surface. Those who slipped too far awoke to madness, or not at all.

Distantly, the sound of a door opening signaled an end to the trance. Quickly his body awoke, fatigue reduced greatly. He rose to his feet, ignoring the stiffness and soreness. Ivy was jarred awake by the suddenness and gazed drowsily at her friend.

"What is going on?" she asked.

"Stay hidden. I will return soon," he said.

Before she could object or reply, he was gone. Lain's movements were barely affected by his injuries anymore. A few more hours entranced would restore him completely. As he slipped silently from shadow to shadow, a feeling of familiarity, of comfort came over him. Stalking a target. This was what he knew. This was his life.

He moved to the rooftops. With snow on the ground, he would leave footprints. There was no telling how long the repair would take. Footprints where they didn't belong might spark the people's suspicions. That would make remaining hidden more difficult. On the roofs, his movements would leave no trace for the casual observer. Soon he had found what he was seeking. Her scent was strongest here. It was her home. She had stepped inside just moments before. He listened closely. She was not alone. Two children were inside, and another woman. For a few moments more he listened. They complained that they were hungry. Swiftly, he darted to the back of the house, dropping down. There was a low door, already half-hidden beneath the piling snow on the rear of the house. With a smooth motion, he slipped the end of his broken sword between the door and the jam and slipped it up.

Inside, a brace lifted out of place and the weight of the snow began to push the door open. He squeezed through the opening and pushed the door silently shut, sliding the brace back in place. The room was a shallow basement. It was stacked nearly to the low ceiling with the firewood it had been dug to hold. A rat scurried away as he navigated the pitch-blackness toward the door. On the other side, he heard the clang of a heavy pot. The door opened and his target reached in to fetch a few pieces of wood for the fire.

Lain pinned himself close to the wall, hidden from the light of the doorway. As she knelt to load her arms with wood, he slipped into the kitchen. The stone chimney that ran up through the center of the house had a warm fire burning. There were openings leading to the den on one side and the kitchen on this side. It provided most of the light, all of the heat, and cooked the food for the home. Here and there, an oil lamp burned. The kitchen was well-stocked with pans, pots, and knives. Cabinets were stacked with clay dinnerware. This was a well–provided-for home. A narrow door to one side of a counter led to a pantry, similarly filled with roots, vegetables, bread, and smoked meats.

He slipped inside and silently shut the door.

In the other room, the children were arguing loudly. She shouted at them as she opened the darkened pantry and stepped inside, holding a lamp. Lain maneuvered behind her, unseen, and slowly shut the door. The sound drew her attention, but Lain easily remained behind her, reaching across and snatching the lamp away with one hand and covering her mouth with the other.

"Silence," he hissed as he lowered the lamp and extinguished it.

She obeyed, the room plunging into darkness.

"When you were young, your parents told you a tale. They told you of the day that freedom was gained in exchange for a single favor. That favor was the duty of your family to perform. Generation to generation, it would be passed down until the day that it would be repaid. Today is that day. Do you understand?" he asked in a bare whisper.

She nodded.

"Good. On the floor beside you, you will find the pieces of a sword. A very special sword. You have seen the weapon before and refused it. You shall take this weapon to your employer, Flinn, and present it to him. It must be reforged. Convincing him to do so will not be difficult. It must be finished in no more than a week. Convincing him to part with it will be difficult, but that is not your task. You must simply ensure that he begins work on the piece, reveal where the work shall be done, and bring the finished piece back here. Do this, and the debt is lifted. If I am satisfied, you will know, and your children need not hear the same tale. Do you agree?" he asked.

Again she nodded.

"Good," he said.

#

As the door opened, she turned quickly to see the face of the intruder, but he was gone. She pushed the door open, light flooding in from the fire. On the floor was a sword. As the children, two boys, chased each other around the house, the older woman came into the kitchen. There was a distant, disturbed look on the young woman's face.

"The boys are hungry, I hope . . . is something wrong?" she asked.

"Mother. Watch them for just a bit longer. There is something I need to finish," she said, stooping to collect the blade.

After carefully stowing the weapon, she put her heavy clothes back on and ventured outside. She traced the path she took every morning to the personal workshop of Flinn. Only she and a few of the apprentices knew precisely where it was. It was near to the town, but tucked into a small alcove near the mouth of an ancient mine. He was enormously secretive about his work and valued his privacy. He even redirected the chimney of his workshop into the mine, lest someone see smoke rising and find him when he was working. Once a day, she and the apprentices would deliver any supplies he needed and provide the day's projects, as quite often days would pass before he left the place for his home. She fumbled for the key that only she and her employer held. Unlocking the door and pushing it open, she entered. It was broiling hot inside, as always, and the air was choked with smoke thanks to the less-than-effective performance of his subversive chimney.

"What is it, Jessica?" called Flinn.

He was a stout, bearded man, perpetually smudged with the black of coal and stained with some dye or another. He was sitting at a cluttered, poorly-lit table, etching intricate designs onto the wide blade of a heavy ax.

"I have a sword for you to work on," she said.

"I have quite enough to do, miss. Enough to fill months. I've told you that already. Take it away," he ordered.

"Please, sir. This is terribly important," she begged.

"Important?" he said, puzzled. "And just how important? I've been offered fifteen hundred gold pieces for the battle ax of the baron's eldest son. I dare say that is quite important."

"It is a sword. It needs mending," she said.

"Mending? Good heavens, girl, I do not mend swords! I have apprentices for that! You should know better than to suggest it!" he said.

"Please, just look at it, sir," she pleaded.

Flinn looked up with a frustrated gaze. The desperate look in his chief assistant's eyes was enough to convince him that this was not something that would be easily brushed aside.

"Give it here," he said with a sigh, putting out his hands.

She placed a coarse cloth in his hands and uncovered the weapon. The instant the light hit it, his attentions locked onto it. He lifted the tip and examined the runes. Turning it, he looked closely at the break, running his fingernail along the layers.

"This is . . . Desmeres's work. Where did you get this?" he quickly demanded.

"It was left by a messenger. The work must be finished in one week. He will collect it from me," she said.

"One week? Nonsense. A masterpiece like this is to be studied. I need months. No. Years. I must have it. Find the owner and make an offer. Any price he requires. No. Better, bring him here. I need to know where he found the weapon. Yes. I must see this person," he said.

"I am quite sure you will meet him. I am not certain you can avoid it," she replied.

"Good, yes. Excellent," he said, distracted.

Flinn cradled the weapon like a child and carried it to his work table, sweeping it clear with a motion of his arm. Priceless weapons and tools clattered to the ground as he placed the object of his sudden obsession down carefully. His assistant opened the door and stepped outside. The dim, flickering light from inside fell upon the path she had made through the still-falling snow. A few paces further was a solitary pair of footprints. There were no steps leading to them, and none leading away. They were facing the door.

Simultaneously, a chill of fear swept through her and a decades-old weight was lifted from her shoulders. He had been there. He had seen where the work would be done. Her family's debt was nearly repaid. She returned home.

#

Inside, Flinn looked over the sword with a maddened eye. Fumbling through a nearby drawer, he spread a small pile of parchment on the table. He retrieved a bottle of ink and a quill and began to transcribe the runes from the blade to the paper, then a sketch of the cross section and profile of the blade. A small puff of cold air escaped his notice. He held up the hilt end of the sword and judged its weight, testing the edge with his thumb. When he reached for the quill again, it was gone, as was the page of notes.

"No. Where is it?" he growled, placing the sword carefully on the table and stooping to search the floor.

After sifting through the tools he had thrown on the floor, he stood again. The sword was gone. In its place was a single piece of paper, scrawled with a message: *Repair the sword in seven days, keep what you learn as payment. Fail and lose both of your prizes.*

Reading the last line, he cast a panicked look to a display case above the door to the rest of the workshop. It was empty. It had held a small dagger. The first of Desmeres pieces he had found. The techniques he had gleaned from it had changed his life. The weapons he began to produce, pale imitations at best, were head and shoulders above any other weapons for sale, and he had still only scratched the surface. The subtler nuances were still revealing themselves as recently as that month. He turned back to his work table. The broken sword, the dagger, and the notes were waiting for him. A chill wind swept past him again. He sat at the table, hunched over his work as though guarding it from grasping hands, and returned to his task.

#

Lain hurried back to the others. When he reached where they had been waiting, he found only Ivy there. He had suspected as much. Her arms were crossed and her brow furrowed, an irritated frown on her face. It was clear to Lain why. Ether had followed him, he had felt it. In some form or another, she had watched as he performed his tasks. Had he the opportunity, he would have put it to an end, but by the time he became aware, the need for silence was too great.

"Show yourself," he demanded sharply.

The intense wind swirled together tightly into her form and shifted to flesh again.

"Your skill is great, though I question your actions," Ether stated.

"Why did you follow me?" he asked sternly.

"In light of my recent difficulties, I felt it necessary to illustrate to you the degree of my own prowess," she said.

"I told her not to, but she didn't listen to me," Ivy huffed.

"I don't have time for this," Lain growled. "The sun will come up soon. We need to find someplace more secure. This will take time."

"There is a house on the north side of this place. Charred and empty," Ether offered.

"You have seen it?" Lain questioned.

"I observed all that this town and the surrounding mountainside has to offer a few moments after I had shifted to the wind," she remarked.

"We shall see," Lain said. "Lead us there. On foot."

Ether began to trudge through the deep snow in her human form. The distance was short, but the wind and snow made the travel slow. A heavier cloak coalesced about Ether's shoulders. Her feet sunk into the snow in light boots and emerged from the snow in heavier ones. She often removed the sensitivities to cold and hunger that plagued the mortal form, but in truth the windy form had taken most of what little strength she had restored. She needed to settle into this familiar form for a few hours more before attempting something like that again. It was with no small measure of relief that she agreed to remain as she was.

The sparse buildings of the town became more so, and a fair distance from them, just past the sign post of the town, was indeed the remains of a sturdy house. Two walls still stood, and though piled with snow and what remained of the roof, the floor seemed fairly intact. Lain considered it. It was situated such that the walls hid the rest of the ruins reasonably well, and the distance from the road was considerable. It was not the ideal place to hide, but they were not likely to find a better one. He inspected further, revealing a hatch leading to a basement comparatively untouched by the flames. With a nod, Ivy scurried inside, followed by Ether.

The basement was shallow, as most were in the rocky, frozen ground of the mountains. Light and snow filtered through a corner of the floor above that had broken under the weight of the wreckage. It looked as though this place hadn't been touched since the fire.

Lain crouched on the ground near the center of the floor. Ivy imitated him. He slowly began to enter the trance again, a task greatly eased by the lack of a constant, blasting wind in his ears.

As he did, Ivy wearily looked about. She was still tired, but this new place interested her. There were chests here and there, shelves piled with jars, some broken, some intact. There was a mix of smells she didn't recognize. Slowly, she edged away from Lain and carefully opened a chest, mostly keeping her eyes on him, fearful of a scolding.

When none came she began to look through the contents. Old, moldy blankets. She frowned and put them away. Trying to get the smell out of her nose, she sniffed the air, something catching her attention. Carefully, she followed the smell. Her whole mind tingled as she drew in the scent. Ether watched.

"What is it now?" Ether asked.

"I smell . . . rosin," she said.

"Why do you care about that?" Ether asked.

"I don't know . . . I . . . here it is!" Ivy said.

Tucked far into the corner, under a shelf and among a pile of other boxes, was a small case. She undid the latch and opened it to reveal a violin. Her fingers fairly shook as she pulled it from the case. She was transfixed by the sight of it. There was a look on her face of clarity, of focus, of remembrance that she had never shown before. Ether opened her mouth to object as she plucked a string, but instead she kept her silence. Part of her was interested in this behavior. More so, she was eager for the reprimand that Ivy was certain to bring upon herself from Lain.

Lain slowly pulled himself from the shallow trance to the sounds of quietly bending notes as Ivy's fingers twisted at knobs and her ears flicked. The strings were quickly coaxed into their proper tension. There was a skill behind her motions. This was not new to her. The plucking was soft. Certainly not audible above the whipping wind outside. For the moment, Lain tolerated it. A few more deft twists and each string produced the proper tone. She reached into the case and pulled out the bow and rosin. Testing the string, she applied some of the rosin. The serenity on her face was incredible. Finally, she raised the bow to the strings.

"That is enough," Lain warned.

She paid him no heed. The bow touched to the strings and a long, soft, crisp note was drawn from them, then another. Her movements were deliberate and flawless. It began as a slow, mournful, weeping melody. The song was barely above a whisper. Steadily, it grew brighter, quicker. Her fingers danced on the strings. The yellow aura that had surrounded her when she was laughing returned. A look of pure joy came to her face.

Again, Lain felt warmth in what remained of his wounds. The intensity grew as the tune grew louder, and soon Lain feared that if it grew any further, they would be heard. He placed a hand on her shoulder. She jumped.

"Lain, when did you wake up? Did . . . did you hear me? I can do this! It feels right, it feels natural!" she said. "Ether, did you see? Ether?"

Ether had a far-away, almost horrified look on her face.

"She is the . . . the artist, the prodigy spoken of in the prophecy. One of the originals. Damn her. She is . . . she was one of us," she said.

"What? What do you mean?" Ivy asked.

"The five original Chosen were created by the gods. The swordsman, leader of men. The one with the blood of a fox, master of all weaponry. Myself, unparalleled mystic being. The strategist and tracker. The last was to be the artist and prodigy," she said, almost fearful of her words.

"And I'm the prodigy?" Ivy said.

"There is the possibility that this was among the knowledge that was forced into your mind, but the effect it has upon you . . . it is deeper by far than anything I've seen," she said.

"So you've been treating me badly, and I am just like you!" Ivy said.

"You are *nothing* like me. You could *never* be like me. All this means is that the foes we face have the ability to turn a pure and perfect being into . . . you, and when you die your replacement will be as useless as Myranda was," Ether said.

"Hey . . . HEY!" Ivy objected.

"Quiet! Both of you!" Lain growled. "We will be here until my sword is repaired. If the two of you will be at each other's throats all of that time, something will have to be done about it," Lain said.

Ivy shrunk away like a scolded child, sitting in the corner, pulling her hood down over her eyes and pouting until her weariness caused her to slowly drift off. Ether waited patiently until the slow, regular breathing of sleep overtook her. Lain was still awake.

"Rather cold. A fire might be useful. For the two of you, of course," Ether suggested.

"We cannot risk the light or the smoke," he said.

"If the light and smoke are a risk, I can eliminate them," she offered.

Lain was silent for a time.

"It would be useful," Lain agreed.

Ether rose and gathered a few pieces of the lumber. She took weakly to flame and took a seat on the pile. A moment later the wood began to darken and warmth began to spread, but the flames of her body sunk to wavering black and not a wisp of smoke rose. Before long the basement was livable, even comfortable.

Lain did not reenter the trance. With his wounds healed, all that remained was weariness, and he could cope with that well enough. Ivy was deeply asleep, affording Ether as near as she was going to get to a few moments alone with Lain.

"Why?" Ether asked.

Lain shifted his gaze to her but remained silent.

"Why does this creature earn your affection while I am denied it? I do not desire the feelings you squander on her to be spent on me for my own sake, but for yours. It makes no sense to cloud your mind with her. What about her could be desirable that I do not possess tenfold?" Ether asked.

"She is of my kind. The two of us may well be the last. I must protect her," he stated.

"She is not of your kind. I am. She has been twisted and warped to resemble your kind. Indeed, *you* are not of your kind. Not as you use the words, at least. You were not born of malthrope parents. Your father was a god," she scoffed.

"I am what my life has made me, as is she," he replied.

Ether considered his words, swiftly dismissing them as yet another symptom of the damage that his time among the mortals has done to his perception of himself.

"The one you call Desmeres was near. I saw him as I followed you. I cannot imagine that you were not aware," Ether remarked.

"I was," he replied.

"It surely was not a coincidence," she added.

"It was not. He is in league with the D'karon, posing as a Chosen and tasked with our capture," he explained.

"And he still lives? You can no longer deny that sentiment has robbed you of reason and good judgment," Ether accused.

"For the time being, he can be trusted to serve his own interests before those of the D'karon. That means leading them astray until the price they are willing to pay is high enough to suit him. In the meantime, I have robbed him of his means of locating me," Lain said, pulling the enchanted tooth that had hung about Desmeres's neck from his cloak.

"Very well," she relented.

"Listen to me. I tolerate you because in times of battle you fill a need that I cannot. You can deal out and defend against mystic attack. It is for this reason alone that you were not left behind. I do not require your advice. You need not audit my decisions, dissect my reasoning, or judge my motivations. Keep your critiques to yourself and I shall do the same," Lain warned.

Ether chuckled. "I have attained a state of perfection. I am intrigued what possible critiques you might have for me."

Lain was silent.

"Speak," Ether demanded.

Lain drew in a deep breath.

"You were given almost limitless potential and an eternity to hone it. That should have made you invincible. Instead, you wasted the time convincing yourself that you were *already* invincible. You continue to waste your power by using every last ounce of it at every opportunity. Not every battle needs to end in an ocean of flame. You can take the form of any man or beast you choose, but in virtually all cases you choose instead to spill off all of your strength funneling the wrath of the elements. Myranda had the merest fraction of your strength and she made it last. She achieved her task and still had enough left to escape until this last battle. You finish each battle scarcely better than Ivy. She, at least, has no control over it. You do it on purpose. Perhaps worst of all is your squandered stealth. You can appear to be a human until the instant you open your mouth, rendering the skill all but worthless. How can you have existed since the dawn of time and managed to stay ignorant of the behavior of the most influential creatures in creation?" Lain fairly ranted.

It was a rare showing of emotion, one that he regretted immediately. It was pointless. Nothing he said would be heeded. Ether remained silent. Lain pulled open the bag and ate his share of the rations. The sun was rising. When the short day was over, he would find something to replace it. For now, there was only waiting.

Time passed slowly. Each of the trio had learned to deal with waiting. In Lain's work, patience was quite often the difference between success and failure. He spent his time carefully analyzing all that his senses told him. Once, a small group of D'karon passed through town, but they did not linger. Desmeres had been true to his word.

Ether was well accustomed to waiting. She had found herself capable of nothing else for an entire era. As for Ivy, her memories were filled with anxious waiting for another torturous session. All she had to do was to think about the fact that she was free from that fear forever and this waiting seemed like bliss.

As each waited, each thought. Lain traced the path he would take to the south over in his head a thousand times. The quickest: down the mountainside and due south along the foot of the mountains. The safest: directly through the mountains to the border. No. A compromise: down the mountainside, across the narrow strip of the lowlands toward Ravenwood, then south through Ravenwood. The forest ran nearly to the border, it provided excellent cover, and it would scarcely slow them at all.

Ivy mostly spent her time quietly fingering the bridge of the violin until the wind picked up enough for Lain to permit her to play. Then she lost herself in song until the wind died down or she grew tired. Ether made the occasional trip in the blackness of night to find more wood, as Lain warned that if enough of the debris disappeared, it might draw attention. Mostly, though, she thought. She watched Lain listen to Ivy's songs and she thought. She watched Ivy sleeping and she thought.

Once a night, when Lain was hunting, he would check on Flinn's progress. Each day, greater measures had been taken to protect his workplace. Armed guards. Additional locks. This mattered little to Lain. Slipping past such things had become second nature to him. Each day, he found himself inside, unobserved, and watching Flinn work. On the sixth night, it was clear that he would finish in time. The sword was already in one piece again. The edge slowly taking shape, the runes roughly etched. The remaining work was superficial. Lain returned to their shelter.

"Tomorrow we leave," he stated.

"Are you sure? Can't we wait a bit longer? Myranda can't be too far away now," Ivy requested.

She had spoken of Myranda increasingly as the days progressed. She was certain that the human was still alive, that she was growing nearer all the time.

"We will be heading west, back toward where we last saw her," Lain said.

She seemed satisfied. Lain never contradicted her belief. He would need every ounce of hope it provided to keep her moving quickly.

The day came. Lain had already delivered his final request to the woman he now knew was named Jessica, informing her to fetch the sword and leave it in her wood cellar. Suddenly, as he was concealing the last of the evidence that they had ever been there, he recognized a scent. He silenced Ivy and made his way to the broken corner of the floor. Peering outside, he saw, almost completely obscured by the swirling snow, a familiar form standing beside a horse. Trigorah.

There was something wrong. She was alone. Not a single one of her Elite was present. She was not even in her Elite armor, dressed instead as plainly as any Northerner. The only semblance of her rank was her weapon, clutched tightly in hand. She suspected something. Lain remembered Desmeres's words. She hadn't trusted him. She wanted to investigate the town he had dismissed. Her lack of her status symbols meant that she was here on personal business. Lain wasted no more time considering her motivations. She was a formidable investigator. She would find him if he lingered here.

The light of day had not yet faded. It would be tremendously risky to venture out. The fact that Trigorah was now so near made the retrieval of his certainly finished weapon imperative. She was difficult to defeat when equally armed. Were he to face her with only the poorly-made daggers he carried, defeat was distinctly possible. He looked to the others. His concern had not gone unnoticed.

"What's wrong?" Ivy asked, wisely whispering.

"Trigorah is here. We need to move," he said, drawing a dagger. "Leave everything."

Ether shifted to wind and swept into the icy gale above, returning and reforming.

"You need a distraction. I believe I can provide one to your liking," Ether offered.

Lain turned to her, silent.

#

Outside, Trigorah surveyed her surroundings. The townspeople all claimed to have seen nothing. The man called Flinn could not be reached, and his assistant seemed nervous about being questioned. That was more than enough to spark her interest. Desmeres had been through here. He'd reported that Lain was nowhere near. His previous report had stated with certainty that the malthrope was heading up the mountainside. He had to be heading this place. With a horse, Desmeres surely should have closed the gap between them, even if he had to use the road. Either he had gotten ahead of Lain and was too foolish to wait for his target to arrive, or he was covering for something. Either way, this was proof of his treachery.

It had taken her three days to reach this place, as well as four days and all of her favors to elude the sizable staff tasked with keeping her occupied at the capital. That blasted General Bagu had confined her to the military command hall in the capital since his trip to the project facility. He wanted her on hand--or in hand. It was clear her skills were wasted there, but he didn't care. By now, her disobedience had certainly been noticed. The consequences might be dire if she did not return with the prize she sought.

She had spent many years in on-again/off-again search for the assassin she now knew as Lain. She knew that he was clever, skilled. But things were different now. He was not alone. If Demont was correct--and she had never known him to be otherwise--then Lain would have at least two others with him. One was the project. That limited his options for shelter, if he was still near. By her estimation, it limited them to one. She mounted her horse and set off for the edge of town, where she had been told the ruins of a house could be found.

#

Lain whisked as swiftly and as silently as he could manage. In the distance, trudging back from Flinn's workshop was Jessica, bundled against the constant wind. She was carrying the sword. He managed to slip behind her.

"Your debt is paid," he whispered, pulling the weapon from her.

She gasped and flinched. By the time she opened her eyes, he was gone.

#

Trigorah came upon the shelter. There were three sets of footprints. Two led to the west, toward the steep slope. One led back toward the town. Distantly she could hear footsteps crunching their way unsteadily down the slope. In the wind, it was difficult to tell how many. She chose the closer prey, moving swiftly down the mountainside. Some distance down the mountain, the footprints split. Impossibly, two sets of footprints led in each direction, as though both of her targets had gone in both directions. To her left, the footsteps could still be heard. As she followed this trail, the two sets of footprints subtly spread to three. Illusions? No, this trail was real. She would have her answer when she reached its end. She doubled her speed. Soon forms emerged from the windblown snow. One was certainly Lain. Another was a woman. The last must have been the project.

The project was a variable. She was told that it was capable of all of the physical feats Lain was. Indeed, she'd been called into the facility of its design to act as an adviser on just what such traits should be emphasized. In addition, she had been briefed on its more unique aspects, but she had never been permitted to see it before. She would have to be on her guard. More so than usual.

"Halt!" she cried when she was near enough to be heard.

The three stopped and turned in unison. Lain stepped forward, fury in his eyes. The others seemed oddly calm.

"Lower your weapon, Lain. I am already acting against orders. Do not doubt that I will kill you and the others," Trigorah warned.

A savage growl erupted from him and he charged at the general. It was all wrong. His sword was held high, his body undefended. Even his motions seemed stiffer and slower than she knew them to be. With ample time to react, she blocked the attack and countered with a superficial slash across his chest. Blood flowed, but as it trickled down, it turned clear, then froze in the icy air.

His subsequent attacks were similarly fruitless, and those of Trigorah produced much the same result. Finally, she grew weary of the pointless battle. She thrust her weapon deep into the chest of what she knew could not be the true Lain. As soon as the first of the gems embedded in the blade touched his flesh, the afflicted area turned to water, crackling as it fell in the intense cold. As it did, the others recoiled as if they too had been struck. Soon the whole of the body had rushed to the ground, splashing all over Trigorah's ankles.

A moment later the other malthrope, the project, melted away. The woman smiled briefly before doing the same.

#

Elsewhere, Lain, Ether, and Ivy hurried down the mountainside. Lain was a few steps ahead of the others. Owing to some manipulation of her form, Ether had been easily keeping pace with him, but Lain turned when he heard the footsteps falter. A dozen paces back, Ether had stopped. Ivy was beside her, taking the opportunity to rest.

"She has found the first of the decoys," Ether managed.

Lain looked back; there was nearly half of a mountain behind them. The frost-covered tops of the evergreen forest below were now and again visible through the whipping snow. This diversion was working. If Trigorah could be delayed just a few minutes more, the wind would wipe their footprints away. The trail would be cold. His eyes shifted back to Ether. She seemed greatly fatigued, as did Ivy. Her eyes drifted to a tuft of fur caught on a nearby bush. Clutching it, she swiftly assumed the form of a doe, a shape simpler and faster on this terrain. Moments later the trio set off again with renewed speed.

#

Far behind them, Trigorah followed another set of prints to its end. There were the same three figures that she had watched dissolve away. The sole difference was a wooden box tucked under the arm of the project. This time, the woman she hadn't recognized before stepped forward to attack, while the project hid behind Lain, who held his weapon at a lazy ready. The attack was a weak one, or so it seemed. She raised her weapon in defense, but the blow shook her, as though the slow, backhanded strike had been made with a club. A resounding clang rang out as the next blow landed on her sword. Trigorah swiftly countered, the edge of her weapon barely chipping the arm that was each moment more visibly turning to stone. Before long, it was a living statue she faced. The blade struck again and again, but failed to sink into the rocky form.

Trigorah called to mind what she had learned of the opponent, the shapeshifter. She twisted the blade and struck with the flat. The shapeshifter's stone arm blocked the blow without budging. Quickly, Trigorah drew the blade along the raised arm. Gems were embedded in the blade of her weapon, designed to allow her to cast spells when the need arrived. Each time one of them came into contact with her opponent, the shifter shrieked in pain. Finally she pulled away, no longer able to withstand the horrid hunger of the crystals. The afflicted arm crumbled away. Soon after the rest of the shapeshifter followed. Before a blow could be struck against him, the decoy Lain wafted away as well.

#

Elsewhere, the trio of Chosen was well into the forest at the base of the mountains. Again Ether faltered. She did not have to explain why. Without words, they redoubled their speed. Due west. Already Trigorah was far too far behind to catch up, but she was not to be underestimated. She had the whole of the military at her disposal. They continued at a sprint for as long as they all could manage. Ivy was the first to slow. Ether matched her pace soon after. Finally, Lain relented. Every muscle in his body screamed for rest. Hunger had never bothered him, but he knew that if he did not eat soon, he would weaken. He could not afford it. He turned to the others. Ether slowly resumed her human form. Ivy was sitting in the snow, trying desperately to catch her breath.

"Wait here. I'll find something to eat," he said.

He swept into the forest. It didn't take long for him to find a boar. He brought it back to the others. Ivy sat cross-legged, wavering, as though she would soon collapse. Ether stood, an unfamiliar look of deep weariness on her face. She was clearly attempting to hide it, and failing pitifully. Lain threw the kill on the ground. Ivy looked at it wearily.

"Not hungry," she said flatly.

"Eat. You need strength," Lain ordered.

"I'm just . . . tired. I need sleep," she said.

"Eat. And you. I'll gather wood," he said.

"Unnecessary," Ether remarked.

Lain cast a stern look in their direction. As was often the case, his eyes communicated far more effectively than his words. Each of his companions slowly complied. Ivy's fatigue was more than apparent. She ate with none of the enthusiasm she typically displayed. Her attentions pulled fully away from her food briefly as Ether shifted to flame amid more flicker and flare than usual. When he was certain that the others had done what they needed to, he did the same, partaking of his share of the kill and settling into the warrior's sleep.

#

Far away, inside the hardened capital of the frozen land, a familiar figure sat, impatiently waiting. Before him was a great desk, covered with maps detailing troop movements, mounds of dispatches from various messengers, and a large sand timer, grains slowly slipping through to a barely half-filled bottom. The heavy door opened and in walked Epidime, battle-scarred halberd in hand.

"You beckoned, Bagu," he asked.

"Sit," Bagu ordered.

With an impatient sigh, he complied, easing into the chair opposite the desk with exaggerated care.

"Did you think I wouldn't find out?" Bagu hissed.

"That depends on which of my myriad secrets you've discovered," he quipped.

"Where is she!?" Bagu demanded.

"Again, you must be more specific. I have a considerable amount of knowledge regarding the whereabouts of the female population," he replied.

"You know that General Teloran is limited to the confines of the capital! She is no longer here," Bagu fumed.

"Yes . . . was that not generally known? She had a word with Demont, then headed off to the southwest several days ago," he said, realizing now the reason for which he was summoned.

The room seemed to grow uncomfortably warm as Bagu bristled with anger.

"Damn it, Epidime, you *will* take this seriously. Trigorah remains a vital element in our plans. She must be kept under control," Bagu fumed.

"If you'd left the leash slack, the dog wouldn't have pulled," Epidime remarked tauntingly.

"Save your wisdom for when I request it, General, and find Teloran," Bagu ordered.

"As you wish," Epidime agreed. He rose and headed for the door.

Leaving the room, Epidime walked briskly through a grand hall toward the massive doors of the palace.

"What brings you here, General?" asked the commanding voice of a slight old man seated at the end of the great hall.

"None of your concern, Your Majesty. Do not worry yourself," Epidime said dismissively.

"It seems that nothing is my concern of late. Nothing for quite some time," the king mused bitterly as a servant approached with a tray of food.

Epidime stopped suddenly and turned to the king.

"Were I you, my king, I would adopt a more . . . civil tone when addressing your generals. Common is the monarch who has fallen due to a lack of trust in those who defend him," Epidime warned.

"It is not my own fate that concerns me, but that of my people. My predecessors relinquished the reins of the army in our time of greatest need, in the hope that your aid would allow it to pass quickly. No man that lived then lives now. Perhaps the time has come to reclaim them," the King replied.

"General Epidime, go to your task. Erdrick, A word," Bagu ordered from the door of his chamber.

A grin came to Epidime's face as he made his exit. Bagu marched out of his lair and locked the king in a steely stare.

"The military that was left to us was a beaten force. Its back was broken. Defeat was in sight. Our men are what have given you these years, given you the chance for victory," Bagu reminded him.

"Peace is preferable to war. If defeat is the price, I am now willing to pay it," the king stated solemnly.

"You claim to care for your people, yet you would sacrifice their freedom with victory so nearly at hand," Bagu scolded.

"Their freedom was not mine to sacrifice, nor was it theirs. Their forefathers and mine gave it to the war long ago, and the war has been given to you," said the king.

"Very well, but when you speak of ending this war, do so with this thought in mind: our forces are strong, they are relentless, and they are many. They live only to do battle and to do my bidding. Should you take from them their present targets, in what direction do you suppose their blades will turn?" Bagu asked ominously.

The king remained silent.

"Remember this, Your Majesty. Your continued power is an illusion for the benefit of your people. The only true power lies in the hand that wields the sword," warned the general.

With that he returned to his lair. The defeated king sat in silence.

#

Back in the cold field, a few hours of sleep had done little to restore the trio, but time was precious. Or, at least, it should be. Lain was the first to rouse himself. He sniffed the air cautiously. The news it held concerned him. It was not that he smelled his pursuer, but that he *didn't*. The wind of the mountains should bring even the slightest scent directly to him. If she was on their trail, he would smell her. But Trigorah's scent was nowhere to be found.

Soon, the quietly crackling fire stepped away from its place and resumed the human form Ether had taken as her own. She stood beside him.

"I imagine that we should be on our way," Ether said.

Lain was silent, testing the air again. Nothing at all. He remembered what Desmeres had said. They had ways of concealing themselves. It was not her way. Trigorah was Lain's oldest adversary. Far older than his oldest ally. Long ago, Lain had learned that knowing one's enemy was infinitely more valuable that knowing one's friend. In his line of work, it was a lesson learned early or not at all.

He knew her well. She despised stealth. It was one of the things she hated most about him. To her, it was nothing more than veiled cowardice. She was a hunter. If he couldn't smell her, she was not downwind.

"She isn't following us," Lain stated.

"The D'karon general? I'd assumed as much," she replied.

Lain stared back at her sternly.

"One of my decoys has not been destroyed. I suspect she believes that she has captured one of us," Ether replied.

"You knew this all along," Lain hissed.

"The urgency of the pursuit was spurring Ivy on at a considerable pace. The faster we are able to relieve ourselves of this burden, the better," Ether explained.

Slowly, thoughts began to stir in Lain's head. He turned to the sleeping Ivy. With a tap on the leg, he awakened her. The young creature's eyes shot open. Almost instantly, she was fully awake. She looked about, fearfully, and clambered gracelessly to her feet.

"I slept too long, didn't I? She's here, isn't she! We should hurry, let's go!" she urged.

"For now, there is time. Ivy. I want you to sing something for me," he requested in an uncharacteristically gentle voice.

"You want me to . . . sing? I've never sung. Why would you want that?" Ivy said, almost nervously.

"Indulge me," he said.

"I . . . I don't know what to sing. It isn't reasonable for you to ask me to do that if I haven't done it before. Why would you think that I would even know how to? I . . . I play the violin," she offered.

As she spoke, a more familiar look came to Lain's face, the tiny, nuanced changed in his expression that only a few in this world had learned to read properly. Anger. Ether watched with eyes untrained to detect such subtleties of emotion. Suddenly, in a smooth motion that was over before Ether had even noticed it had begun, Lain pulled free a dagger and plunged it deep into Ivy's heart. A twinge of pain swept over Lain. Ether and Ivy released simultaneous cries, identical in all ways save the voice. Ivy fell limply to the ground, gasping for breath.

Ether was staggered, wavering on her feet. When she regained her balance, her eyes met with Lain's. The fury in his eyes was clear now even to her.

"Explain yourself," he demanded, his tone dripping with hatred.

Slowly, Ivy rose from the ground. Fear, pain, all emotion was gone from her face. Her features took on an even, practiced look of disinterest that matched Ether's perfectly. In unison, their mouths opened, and they spoke as one.

"It had to be done, Lain. She was destroying you," they spoke in eerie harmony.

Suddenly, the form of Ivy vanished in a burst of wind, the dagger in her chest clattering to the ground.

"Where is she!" Lain demanded, his sword drawn.

"Put her out of your mind. She was poison to you. She was making you sloppy; you were making mistakes," Ether said.

Lain swiped his weapon at her with incredible speed. She managed to shift to wind and whisk aside, shifting back to human again behind him.

"She may be one of the last of my kind. It is my duty to protect her!" he raged.

"Duty!? Your duty is to this world! And you are forsaking it! You are wasting precious moments to preserve what is nothing more than an attempt by the enemy to subvert you! Anyone could see that this has gone past duty for you. It is obsession! Devotion! It is--" she cried, stopping herself.

"Love!" Lain replied.

"Yes, love! And she doesn't deserve it! She is a thing! Weak! Ignorant! Impermanent! You and I both know that there is only one being worthy of you! I am powerful! I am eternal! We share everything! Purpose! Origin! And I am spurned for a failed experiment with the mind of a child!" Ether ranted. She shifted to Ivy's form. "I can be anything you require of me! Do you want a malthrope? So be it! Do you desire a human?" Her form shifted to Myranda's. "You shall have it! I can make myself into anyone that has earned from you what I am denied!" Ether raved, shifting back to her own human form and grasping desperately at Lain's cloak. "All I ask is for your trust! For your respect! For your affection! All I ask is that I be the one for you! That I have the place in your thoughts that is rightfully mine!"

Lain's grip tightened on his weapon. Hatred and anger swept over him in pulses and waves.

"You would speak to me of obsession! You don't even know what love is and you demand it of me? It cannot be demanded. You don't understand it. Ivy is like a daughter to me. You . . . I will not attempt to reason with you. You are dead to me. Tell me where she is," he said.

"I will not allow you to squander yourself on that abomination!" Ether cried.

Lain bared his teeth, clenched so tight they creaked.

"Think!" he hissed between them. "She is Chosen and you have betrayed her. Anything that happens to her now is on your shoulders. What price will fate demand of you if she comes to harm? How will your precious mark punish you if she comes to her end?"

Ether stood silent. Lain's words had pierced the thick veil of emotion. Slowly, the truth of her actions became clear to her--and the consequences painfully so. She'd felt the burning several times already, a sharp, sudden pain in her head where the mark could be found. She had ignored it, dismissed it. Even now there was a constant dull sensation.

"Gods . . . they've found a way to destroy me. I should have been destroyed the moment I led her away. If they kill her . . . we must find her. I led her away with some of the other decoys. Trigorah must have her! We must find her before it is too late! Until I can undo my mistake, her life is my own!" Ether cried, genuine fear in her voice.

She shifted to flame and burst high into the still-dark sky.

#

Far away, Ivy cowered fear and tried to catch her breath. She was still struggling to work out what had happened, but there had been little time to think. That woman, the one who Lain had run from, was near. In the initial sprint down the mountain, a great deal of ground had been put between them, but now Trigorah was on horseback. It was all Ivy could do to stay a few steps ahead. The fear that had gripped her from the moment she saw what had happened to her friends still burned her mind. The whole of the pursuit had been a constant effort to keep it from consuming her, from turning her into the monster. Doing so would allow her to escape, there was no question of that. What worried her was that when she awoke, if she awoke, there was no telling where she might be. So she had run.

Now she found herself in dank ally in a large town. The moon was behind the thick, perpetual clouds overhead. Despite the size of this place, there were very few people. After years of war, one would be hard pressed to find a town that didn't seem deserted. This, at least, was in Ivy's favor. It had allowed her to make it to this shadowy, litter-strewn alley unseen. Now she sat, her back against a cold, damp, stone wall, clutching a battered wooden box like a security blanket. A corridor leading behind one of the buildings was to her left. To her right, a few dozen paces away, the icy city street.

Quickly, she realized how foolish she was to have come this way. Lain had made it clear that the places of man should be avoided, but she couldn't help it. She felt drawn to them, like she belonged among these people. Now she regretted coming here. Every footfall that reached her sensitive ears turned in her mind to Trigorah coming for her. Breathing deeply, she tried desperately to clear her mind. She couldn't bring herself to believe what she had seen happen to her friends. They had just vanished. She tried to ignore the footsteps, replaying the scene over in her head. The way Lain swept away seemed so familiar, and the way Trigorah didn't seem to expect it, much less to have caused it. But if not she, then who? Did Lain do it? Did he know magic?

Ivy felt a strange tingling in her spine. She turned to the opening of the alleyway. Time seemed to slow. The tip of a polished sword caught what little light there was as it slipped into view. In that tiny reflection, Ivy's keen eyes locked with those of another. Trigorah. Praying that she had not been seen, Ivy clambered backward as quietly as she could, turning the corner in the alley. Crouching low, she trained her eyes on the ground where she'd been sitting. Footsteps echoed closer. The ground took on the white blue glow of the jewels in the general's blade.

Ivy turned away, her eyes now shifting down the length of the corridor, her legs primed for a sprint. An instant later, her heart leapt into her throat. There was nothing ahead but a few more paces of filthy, snow-covered cobblestone and a wall reaching up to the roofs of the tall buildings on either side. A dead end.

She turned again, but time had run out. The light of the sword was painfully bright after the blackness of the alley. Trigorah held it at the ready, her eyes coldly reading the malthrope, judging what this beast before her was capable of. Ivy closed her eyes and shielded her face with the box, backing to the wall behind her.

"What did you--how did--no! Please, no I--" she stammered hysterically, the blue aura of fear rising despite her best efforts.

"Silence," Trigorah ordered, her voice low but forceful.

"No, not here. Just not here. Please. There are people. If I change they might get hurt," she pleaded tearfully, as much with herself as with Trigorah.

"Silence! Listen to me. Creature!" Trigorah demanded with hushed insistence. She sifted through what she'd learned of the creature. Demont had spoken of a name she called herself. "IVY!"

At the sound of her name, Ivy stopped and looked slowly at her pursuer.

"Did . . . did you call me Ivy? The teachers never called me that . . ." she said.

Ivy drew in a long sample of Trigorah's scent.

"You were there. When they had me. But you aren't one of them, are you?" Ivy asked.

"I am a general of the Northern Alliance and I am sworn to defend it. Now tell me where the others are. I promise you that it is not our intention to bring any of you to harm," Trigorah said.

"Where are they? You KILLED THEM! And now you are going to lie to my face and tell me you don't want to hurt us!" Ivy snapped, a surge of red light painting the alleyway as the scene replayed itself in her mind again.

"That was not my doing," Trigorah said.

"Don't lie. DON'T LIE TO ME!" Ivy seethed. Deep inside, she knew that Trigorah could not have been responsible. Nevertheless, her emotions, denied fear as an outlet, sought anger in its place. She turned away, scolding herself. "Not here."

Her teeth clenched; the wooden box she held creaked in her grip. Ivy struggled to master her emotions. The last thing she wanted was to change here, in a city.

Very slowly, the red aura began to fade. Trigorah watched cautiously. At first, she had doubted the descriptions of the power that Ivy wielded. Their nature and intensity seemed unlikely, impossible. Now, though, she began to reconsider. She was no wizard, but it didn't take a mystic to know that the raw energy she had felt, and the speed at which it was summoned forth, was not the sort of thing to be taken lightly. Against her best instincts, she returned her sword to its sheath. Now was not a time to appear to be a threat.

"Ivy, look at me. I am not here to hurt you, and I did not hurt your friends," Trigorah said, holding up her empty hands.

Ivy's narrowed eyes seemed to stare straight through Trigorah.

"If you didn't, then who did? And why was Lain running from you?" she asked, the anger fading but still strong, and mixed with a healthy dose of suspicion.

"Those questions are not mine to answer," Trigorah replied.

"Don't tell me that! You *are* one of them! You can't just leave me be! You--" Ivy began to rant.

"Listen!" Trigorah's ordered.

Again Ivy froze. Trigorah's voice had the quality of a scolding parent. The forcefulness and authority broke through the emotions. Seizing the opportunity, Trigorah continued.

"I am not the only one seeking you. In fact, I believe that in pursuing you, I have made myself a target. We cannot squander our time here, screaming at one another. Let me take you someplace away from prying eyes and curious ears. Once we have the benefit of doors and locks, this battle of wills can continue. Until then, I want you to stay quiet, stay calm, and stay out of sight! Understood?" the general commanded.

Ivy nodded slowly. Any trace of anger was swept away. She felt compelled to comply--not in the unnatural way that Demont had willed upon her, but out of a sort of sudden respect, almost gratitude. It was as though the role of guiding hand that had been left vacant by Lain had, for now, been replaced. And there was something else. There was an air of . . . belonging. As though Trigorah was a piece to a puzzle that had long been incomplete. Something felt right about her leadership.

Ivy crouched down into the darkness.

Trigorah pulled her hood up and made her way quickly toward the street. She'd taken an enormous chance speaking to the unstable creature as she did. Good fortune seldom smiled upon her for long. Carefully, she took up a position on the city street, the opening to the alleyway that hid her prize within sight. If memory served, there was a rather large and quite well-staffed inn that would be able to accommodate her. An elderly man was passing by. Trigorah flagged him down. There was no need to ask the man if he was a veteran. He bore the scars and limp of a man who had fought until the military had no more use for him.

"You there, soldier," she called.

He turned and approached her.

"No one has called me that for some time, m'lady," he replied.

"Once in the service of this great land, always. I have a task for you," she said.

His eyes widened as he saw her face.

"You are the general. General Teloran. I am honored beyond words that you would speak to me," he gushed. "In my younger days, I was considered for service in your great Elite! That was before the Tresson swine ruined my leg. I want you to know that not a night goes by that I do not curse the name of that Undermine captain who took so many of them from you."

Trigorah raised a finger to halt the torrent of adoration.

"Noted and appreciated, soldier, but there is a matter of grave military importance that requires speed, tact--and, above all, discretion. Do you know the inn a few streets away?" she asked.

"Palin's House of Ale?" he asked.

"Precisely the one," she replied. "In a moment, I will be transporting a prisoner there for questioning. Go now and see to it that a suitable room is ready for me when I arrive. A stout door, locks on the inside, and no windows. We shall arrive by the back door. The way to the room should be free of prying eyes."

"It is an honor to serve the crown once more, General," he replied, turning and heading off as quickly as his infirm legs would allow.

Trigorah made her way swiftly back to the alley. The creature was standing in the shadows. The lack of the unnatural aura about her proved that she was, mercifully, still calm.

"When I say so, we are going to cross the road into the opposite ally quickly and quietly. Then I will lead you to a door and into a room inside. You will be silent until I say you can speak," Trigorah instructed.

Ivy nodded. As Trigorah waited tensely for the old man to make the preparations, she watched Ivy closely. The creature was shifting uneasily from foot to foot, her eyes locked on the alley across the way. The box she held was hugged close to her chest. A few more moments passed.

"Why are we waiting?" Ivy whispered.

"Just wait. If we move too soon, the way won't be clear," Trigorah said.

Ivy nodded. Trigorah judged that the time was right.

"Now," she ordered.

"Not yet. Wait," Ivy said, her voice hushed.

"I said--" Trigorah began scold.

Ivy ignored her, stepping further into the shadows. A moment later, Trigorah finally heard the crunching footsteps Ivy's sensitive ears had. She too ducked back further. A large, shabbily-dressed man lumbered by, dragging a crystal-tipped halberd. He paused briefly in front of the alleyway.

"I know him," Ivy breathed almost silently. There was a shiver in her voice and a wisp of blue light.

"Steady," Trigorah warned.

The lumbering figure continued. Trigorah watched as he vanished from sight. Epidime. Fortune had run out sooner that she would have liked. Suddenly, there was a motion beside her. Ivy bolted. Rather than call after her with an order that would certainly be ignored and likely draw Epidime's attention, she held her breath and prayed that she had learned some of Lain's accursed stealth. As she watched, she saw movements that could scarcely have been learned. Long, graceful steps, planting surely despite the icy stone. Soon she was deep in the far alley, gone from sight. Hiding.

Trigorah edged closer to the opening of the alley. Epidime was a fair distance away, and moving further. Stepping lightly, she too made her way across. It turned her stomach not to face him and proclaim her victorious capture of Ivy, but the creature was anything but securely in her grasp at the moment. If she could milk just a drop of information out of her, not only Ivy but the other Chosen too could be her prize. The other generals would have no recourse but to allow her to take her rightful place at the front lines then. Even Bagu would have to relent after having the renegade warriors delivered directly to him.

"Did I do good?" Ivy asked eagerly.

Trigorah shrugged off the odd reaction of the creature and silently led on. The tavern was just a short way ahead, if she remembered correctly. As she walked, she began to gather her questions to mind, readying her techniques. Her instinct screamed warnings about the sudden compliance, even *devotion* her prisoner was showing. It warned about Epidime and what treachery he may have in store. Nothing could be done for now to deal with such concerns. They were noted and brushed aside. The sound of boisterous laughter and loud conversation heralded the approach of the only building in this part of town that didn't seem deserted or rundown. She stepped up to a sturdy wooden door and gave it a push. Sure enough, it was not latched.

The pair stepped in quietly, closing and latching the door behind them. Inside, the heady aroma of spilled ale and roasting meat momentarily distracted Ivy. Her eyes lingered on the door at the far end of the long, dim hallway. She longed to be on the other side. Badly, she wanted to taste and smell and hear and see what was behind that door. A firm hand on her shoulder snapped her back to attention. There was one door open. It led to a large but virtually empty room. The place was nearly the size of a small banquet hall, but there was but a table and a pair of chairs to be found inside. They slipped in.

Trigorah drew the bolt on the door and tested its strength before turning to Ivy. The malthrope was already seated, placing her box carefully on the ground before folding her hands and smiling like an overachieving student. The general tried to work out what possible reason the creature might have for the complete reversal of trust. Before her escape, they were in the process of re-educating her. Demont had claimed that the process was not complete, but that a few safeguards had been put in place. Perhaps this was one of them reaching the surface. Regardless, best to take advantage while it lasted.

"Now, where are the others?" Trigorah asked.

"I . . . I was afraid they died, but you saw it happen, and you still want to know where they are, so I guess they are still alive. I don't know where. Do you know what happened to them?" Ivy asked. As she spoke, her nervousness melted away completely, as though she felt she was speaking to a friend.

"It is my belief that they and several others I fought were decoys," Trigorah said.

"Yes. Yes! Ether made a bunch of decoys. She said that she was the real one and that I should follow her . . . she was lying," Ivy said, her voice intensifying.

"Never mind that. Where were you heading before you split off? Why were you in Verneste?" Trigorah asked quickly, hoping to sidestep the angry realization that she had been betrayed.

"Um . . . Well, his sword broke . . . I broke it, I think. We were heading south. Lain wanted me to be safe, so he was taking me there, but he needed to get his sword fixed before we went to Tressor," Ivy said.

"So Lain is in league with the Tressons," Trigorah said. It was a suspicion she had long held, and one that fueled much of her disdain for him.

"Well, he has friends down there. They owe him favors, I think," she said.

"Would he continue south without you? Does he seek something else there?" Trigorah pressed.

"I don't think so. He was only going there so that he wouldn't have to worry about me when he tried to end the war," Ivy explained.

"How does he intend to do this?" Trigorah asked.

". . . I don't know. But he is going to do it. He's amazing," Ivy nearly gushed.

Trigorah suppressed a wave of anger at the hero worship.

"Do you suppose that he will realize you are gone?" she asked.

"Of course!" Ivy said.

"And he will come for you?" Trigorah said.

Ivy nodded vigorously.

"And the shapeshifter?" continued the general.

"Um . . . yes," came the answer, dejectedly. "She won't leave Lain alone." Ivy looked to and fro before adding in a conspiratorial whisper, "She likes him."

"And Myranda. Is it true that she--" Trigorah began to ask.

"SHE'S NOT DEAD!" Ivy retorted before the accusation was even made. "Everyone says she's dead, but I talked to her. I know she's still alive, and Lain knows it, too."

This was new. And if it was true, it would change things considerably, but something about her defensiveness made Trigorah believe that this was the wishful thinking of a naïve mind. Still, it was worth noting.

"Very well. Tell me about Ether. What types of things can she do?" Trigorah interrogated. The others had only the vaguest of details about the mystical creature, and the ability to produce duplicates had never even been considered.

"I don't know. Lots of things. I don't want to talk about her," Ivy objected. "Don't you want to know about me? I can do plenty of things, too!"

"The shapeshifter," Trigorah ordered.

Ivy grumbled and crossed her arms.

"No!" she pouted.

"This is not a game, Ivy. Do as I say," Trigorah warned forcefully.

"But . . . fine. She can turn into fire and water and all of that. Also, anything she touches she can turn into, and sometimes it takes a while. She gets tired quick because she overdoes everything, and . . . um, she hates crystals. One of the . . . ." She paused. ". . . teachers, shoved a crystal into her chest and she would have died if I didn't save her. What I did was--"

"We will discuss you later. First finish about Ether. Do crystals always work? Does she have a defense against them?" Trigorah said, refocusing the purposefully wandering mind of Ivy.

She grumbled again.

"No. I don't think so . . . wait. Yes. She turned into one of the silver crawling things that had a crystal right on its head and it didn't bother her at all. So, uh . . ." Ivy began.

"If she takes the form of a creature immune to that attack, she inherits the immunity as well," Trigorah deduced.

"Yes . . . I guess. Are we done with her?" the creature nearly pleaded.

"Very well. What would you have me know?" Trigorah relented. This was the most surreal interrogation she'd ever performed. In the alley, it had been like trying to juggle a tinderbox and a torch, and now it was like humoring a child that was starved for attention. She was beginning to wonder how much of the information she pulled from this damaged mind could be trusted.

"Well, I can play music, and I can dance, and I can sing, too. Do you want to hear?" Ivy babbled.

"Now is not the time for that. Where did you learn such things?" Trigorah asked. Certainly it hadn't been a part of the education they had given her during her development.

"I don't know how I know, I just know. And I am very good. Watch!" Ivy said, pulling the box from the floor suddenly and beginning to open it.

Before the latches could be undone, Trigorah's sword was at the ready.

"Stay your hands," she warned.

Ivy flinched, startled.

"Hey! I was just going to play the violin for you!" she scolded.

"Creature, as long as you are cooperative I will permit you to behave as you wish, but do not forget that you are my prisoner. Trust is acceptable, but obedience is mandatory. I am not your friend. I am your captor," Trigorah growled, her blade's point held a whisper away from Ivy's throat.

"You wouldn't hurt me," Ivy said dismissively.

"I will do what I must to achieve my ends. Consider this your last warning," Trigorah said with finality.

The general was accustomed to loyalty, obedience, and fear. She would *not* be dismissed.

"But we are supposed to be friends. Don't you feel it, too? You and I are supposed to help each other," Ivy said, confused by the threatening action.

"No. You only believe that because of something that was done to you while you were being created," Trigorah seethed. Her logic screamed for her to stop, to weather this behavior. She could not bring herself to head the warnings.

"Oh, what do you know? I mean, look at that ugly thing on your arm. Who would wear that?" Ivy said, in the same infuriating tone, pointing to the outstretched arm that held the sword.

Trigorah looked to the bulge under her sleeve that Ivy had indicated.

"You will not mock my band," Trigorah said, pulling back the sleeve to reveal a gold band engraved with runes clasped tightly about her upper arm. "This band was presented to me before I swore allegiance to the four generals. It represents my honored position at the head of the great army of this great land. The day I remove it is the day I forsake my superiors and forsake my kingdom. It has not left my skin since the day it was given."

Ivy twisted her head to try to get a better look at the runes.

"To quench the flames and dim the light? What does that mean?" Ivy asked, perplexed.

"What foolishness are you saying?" Trigorah hissed.

"That's what it says. There are other runes after it but that is what the little ones say. You mean you didn't . . ." Ivy began to explain, but suddenly she seemed distracted.

The creature sniffed at the air, concern quickly turning to fear.

"He's here," she said, terror beginning to spill off of her again.

Trigorah turned to the door. A sudden thunderous blow buckled the hinges. A second splintered them free. As the ruined tatters of door collapsed into the room, the hulking form of Epidime stepped inside. Ivy cowered behind Trigorah, who slowly sheathed her weapon.

"What are you doing!? He will kill us!" she shrieked.

"You have made a number of very influential individuals very upset, Teloran," Epidime scolded with his characteristic coolness.

"I have also captured one of the Chosen, something those same individuals could not do. I think that deserves some consideration," she countered.

"Ah yes. Ivy, as they call her. Demont's pet project. Tell me, how is it you managed to keep from lighting her short fuse for so long?" Epidime asked.

"Never mind that. It is quite likely that the others are coming, and I do not think it wise to face them here," Trigorah said.

"Why are you talking to him!? He is evil! We have to go!" Ivy said.

"Why . . . does this little beast trust you? That is a remarkable feat, General," Epidime admitted.

"Are you listening to me? We need to get to a more defensible position," Trigorah said.

Epidime still gazed at the trembling figure of Ivy.

"You didn't strike me as though you were in any hurry to leave before my arrival. Besides, I doubt we will find a position more defensible than the city," Epidime said.

"Up until your arrival, I had handled the situation with at least some semblance of tact. We might have escaped notice. And this isn't a fort, Epidime, there are civilians here," Trigorah protested.

"Collateral damage is a part of war," he replied.

Trigorah held firm. "You've seen what they can do. The entire city may be destroyed."

"Acceptable losses," came the logical reply.

"Acceptable? Hundreds of people would lose their lives for two? We are supposed to protect these people!" the general urged.

"An end best served by removing this threat to their freedom. Interesting that you are so eager to seek higher ground the moment I arrive. One might almost suppose you have other motives. A less understanding superior might even suspect insubordination. However, that cowering little prototype behind you has earned you the benefit of a doubt or two. Permit me to subdue our present prize. Afterward, I will even allow you to tell me what you have learned, rather than simply taking it from you," Epidime said.

"What? No! NO!" Ivy cried.

She tried to run, but with her mind still set on suppressing her emotions lest she ruin this place, she wasn't fast enough. The gem in the blade of Epidime's weapon was brought to bear on her head. A bright, intense flash of light and crack of energy surged forth.

A moment later, Ivy dropped to the ground, forced into a deep and unwilling sleep.

#

Not far to the south, Ether released an ear-splitting cry of pain. She dropped swiftly to the ground, crying out and clawing at the mark on her head. Far behind, Lain watched the spectacle. For the last few hours, Ether had been leading him like a signal beacon, tracking Ivy through some arcane means, but a gust of wind had brought a trace of her scent to him, and Ether would no longer be necessary. The smell was mingled with others. Hundreds of people. She was in a town. If his sense of direction had not failed him, this was a place called Fallbrook.

Two scents asserted themselves above the others. The first was the one that had been missing further south. Trigorah. The other was that of a man he had known as Arden, one he now knew to be General Epidime. Two generals. The situation smacked of ambush, but there was nothing to be done. For a few moments more, he watched the sky ahead. The dawn was throwing a pale gold against the clouds. If indeed the generals were prepared for him, darkness and the shapeshifter would be welcome, if not indispensable, allies. For the moment, it seemed he had neither. The one piece of luck had been the proximity of this place. Ivy must have been trying to find them to have come this far.

Any hint of cover had been left behind long ago. Lain was sprinting across open field. His trained mind cataloged dozens of mistakes he was making. From the deep, distinct footprints he was leaving to the proximity of a well-traveled road, he was keenly aware of his carelessness, but time afforded nothing more. His eyes focused on the town ahead, mapping out entrances and exits. Bringing to mind what he remembered of the rooftops and back alleys. Formulating what little of a plan he could. Working out where troops might be hidden, where they might gather and how to evade them. Determining where she would be. No time could be wasted searching. If this was indeed an ambush, he would have to know precisely where she was even before he reached the fringes of the city.

After a short distance, he found the smoldering form of Ether. She was standing, trying to regain her composure. The state she was in was almost beyond description. It seemed as though she was caught halfway between her stone and flame forms. Veins of fire swept slowly across a black stone body, glowing white-hot and flaring every few moments.

As she heard his approach, she turned to him. Her eyes, glowing like two embers, showed a mixture of fear, desperation, and anger. The sight of him was enough to spur her back into the air, the flame finally regaining its full force.

#

Ether's cry had not escaped the notice of the generals. Indeed, every eye in the city was turned to its source. The once–nearly-empty streets of the place were now peppered with the residents that the war had spared. Whispers passed quickly through the crowd. Tales had been told of a monster or demon that had spawned chaos in another town not long ago. It had assaulted one of the king's men. Was this that beast?

Trigorah and Epidime reached the street a step behind the last patron of the tavern.

"And you are certain that there are only two coming for her?" Epidime said thoughtfully, unfazed by the growing unrest around him.

"The shapeshifter and the assassin," Trigorah said. "A force that I hesitate to face without any reinforcements."

"There will be reinforcements. For the time being, we shall offer up some fodder," Epidime said.

The imposing warrior forced his way through the roiling crowd to the center of the street.

"Attention! The creatures that approach are enemies of the Northern Alliance. You are hereby drafted into the great Alliance Army. Defend this building with your lives!" he barked.

Fear and doubt turned instantly to pure chaos. Some searched madly for something to arm themselves with. Most ran in panicked mobs, seeking some form of shelter to hide from the carnage that was sure to rain down.

"Are you mad? These people won't last more than a moment against them!" Trigorah protested.

"A moment is all that is required," Epidime stated.

With that, the general disappeared inside the tavern. Trigorah's eyes were drawn skyward. The air was scorching with the heat thrown off by the form that hung in the air just over the street. The burning white slits that served as eyes for the shapeshifter came to rest firmly on Trigorah. Pitchforks, random debris, and anything else that the maddened crowd could find were hurled fruitlessly at the powerful being. They merely passed through her form, momentarily disturbing it and taking to flame.

"You. Elf. Bring the malthrope here or perish," came Ether's command.

Trigorah held her tongue, instead raising her sword.

"So be it," Ether thundered.

In the blink of an eye, the fiery form launched itself earthward. The impact threw back the throng that had gathered beneath her. The light from the flames faded and the shapeshifter was hidden from sight by the mob. Trigorah issued swift orders to stand aside, but these were no soldiers. No heed was paid as half of the crowd climbed over themselves to get a taste of combat and the other half scrambled to escape. Hammering footsteps rang out even over the roar of the crowd. The now-stone form of Ether charged effortlessly through them, those who would stop her tossed aside like dried leaves.

Trigorah's weapon was expertly placed to block the attack, but the force was like that of a charging bull. Ether heaved a backhand, knocking the blade aside. She gripped the warrior by each arm, pinning them to her body and hoisting her in the air. Helpless, Trigorah was slammed against the wall of the tavern, the wind knocked from her lungs.

"REVEAL HER!" Ether demanded.

The wake Ether had left behind her slowly filled in again as the townsfolk flooded toward her. A hundred hands grasped at her, trying to pry her grip on their beloved general free.

Their combined strength barely gave the elemental pause. With another powerful thrust against the wall Ether repeated her demand.

"REVEAL HER!" she cried.

"You shall never have her," Trigorah replied weakly, gasping for breath.

With a cry of frustration, Ether turned, hurling Trigorah into the crowd. The swiftness of the motion scattered the other attackers.

"Careful, shapeshifter, I have use for her yet," came the voice of Epidime from above.

Ether's eyes shot to the roof of the tavern, where Epidime stood smugly.

"And I suspect you still have use for this little creature," he said, holding forth a sinewy arm and dangling the limp form of Ivy off the edge by her wrist.

As his fist tightened around the unconscious creature's wrist, the mark on Ether's head flared. She dropped to her knees. The crowd swarmed over her. Epidime smiled, heaving Ivy's form back onto the roof. He turned, holding his halberd high. A narrow ribbon of white-blue light tore upward. Below, Trigorah was helped to her feet and rushed quickly to the writhing mass of crowd. Whatever had stopped Ether in her tracks would not last long. She had to take full advantage.

"Stand aside! Quickly!" she ordered, pulling people away.

Reluctantly, the frenzied crowd began to spread out. Suddenly there was a brief, sharp burst of wind from inside the center of the tangle of humanity. When the crowd had finally parted completely, Ether was gone. The general gripped her weapon tightly. She'd escaped, taken the form of wind. There was no telling where she was, or even if she was still near.

"Spread out! If she is here I want her found!" Trigorah ordered. "But do *not* face her. Leave her to me!"

The townspeople swiftly obeyed. Trigorah turned to the roof to see if Epidime had seen where the shapeshifter had gone, but his eyes were fixed firmly on the northern horizon. Knowing it was pointless to ask him, she simply turned to the task herself.

On the rooftop, Epidime's smile broadened. Several dark forms had appeared on the horizon. He turned to the crowd below. The chaos had died down a bit. That was unfortunate. Chaos always made things more interesting. No matter--more was on its way. For the time being, more fruitful thoughts could be turned to the shapeshifter's reaction to the dangling of Demont's little project. The injury of one Chosen had shown a direct correlation to the pain of another. That was a theorized effect of a betrayal between Chosen, and if there was to be a betrayal, this was the most likely pair.

The immediate question was obvious. Did this transfer of punishment extend to the ultimate extreme? If he were to kill the creature at his feet, would the shapeshifter die as well?

The question was an intriguing one. Logic indicated that it would. Briefly, he considered testing the hypothesis. The thought was quickly abandoned. The only truly sound plan that had been developed for dealing with the Chosen hinged upon all of them being kept alive. For now, he would have to sate his curiosity with a second demonstration of the effect. He looked down on the creature. She was stirring weakly. Impressive that the beast could recover so swiftly. Impressive, but inconsequential, as subduing her once more was simple enough. He inverted his halberd, bringing the blade close to Ivy's head.

Suddenly there was a clash, and the weapon was nearly knocked from his hand. He regained his grip, but before he could identify the source of the attack, a second came. The bite of a blade stung his arm with force enough to rob a lesser man of the limb entirely. He merely jerked his arm free and turned to see who had wielded the offending weapon. It came as little surprise that it was Lain who stood before him. Now prepared, the assassin's next two attacks were blocked.

"The shapeshifter, this monstrosity here, and now you. That makes three Chosen in one place. I must take care to stay on my toes, lest I bring about something prematurely," Epidime quipped cryptically.

Lain paid no heed, instead hurling attack after attack at the general. Epidime proved more than able to deflect them despite the gaping wound in his arm.

On the ground below, Trigorah was drawn from the alley she was searching by the sound of combat on the tavern roof. She was about to rush to her current partner's aid when one of the townspeople hurried up to her.

"What? What is it?" Trigorah demanded.

"We found her!" cried the villager.

"Where? Show me!" Trigorah ordered.

He pointed excitedly down the street. The general rushed off in that direction. She didn't make it two steps. Something caught her foot and she tumbled forward. Before she could turn, the sword was pulled from her hand. When she rolled to face her attacker, it appeared that it was the same random villager, but the truth was all too clear. The now-pointless disguise dropped away quickly, the stone form of the shapeshifter replacing it. With a powerful heave, she hurled the crystal-studded weapon far down the street. A heavy backhand robbed Trigorah of her consciousness.

Ether felt a strong need to finish what she had started, but she had a more important task at hand. Ivy was still in their clutches, and so long as she was, her own death was a very real possibility. Her instincts told her to take to the air and surge up to the rooftop, but the wielders of the halberds had proven capable opponents in the past. Better to avoid the risk.

On the roof, weapon clashed with weapon. Slowly, the damage to the arm was beginning to slow Epidime's movements. Lain carefully angled himself, shuffling inch by inch until he had managed to position himself squarely between the general and his prize. With Ivy safely behind him, the ferocity of Lain's attacks intensified. Epidime shifted his focus to defense. Before long the only attacks thrown were Lain's, and more than a few tasted blood. Despite this, Epidime seemed unafraid, even amused.

"Such dedication. Such focus. And all for that little thing behind you? What is it that motivates you so? Is it preservation of the species? Or is it something stronger," Epidime mused out loud, as though the battle was the least of his worries.

Lain ignored his words. The motion near the northern horizon had grown. He knew what was coming. There was no time to waste. He pushed forward, inching Epidime closer to the edge of the roof, limiting his options.

"Your composure is remarkable. Single-mindedness can be a virtue. I wonder, though. With such thought devoted to both your next move and mine, do you have any mind left to ask questions? Why does he insist on fighting on my terms when a simple spell would end the battle instantly?" Epidime taunted. "Is he toying with me? Is he stalling me? Is it a test? Part of some larger plan? Tell me, Lain, do these thoughts occur to you at all, or are you just a machine? Just a collection of parts working toward a single goal?"

Now Epidime could go no further. Snow fell at his heels as he reached the edge of the roof. Lain pushed harder, but the defense of his opponent did not falter.

"Well. I've got an answer for you. This is all just a pleasant distraction . . . until the real fun begins," Epidime said with a smile.

Almost as if on cue, a mixture of cries rose from the streets below. Some were cries of fear, others of excitement. The beating of leathery wings came next. Epidime leapt backward off of the roof, a blur of motion snatching him into the air. Shadows cast by the weak light of morning crisscrossed the ground.

Above, dragoyles circled, perhaps a dozen. One by one they landed in the streets and on roof tops, figures dropped from their backs. Some were nearmen, most armed as foot soldiers, but a handful carrying bows. Worse, more than a few carried bundles that seemed to split and multiply when they reached the ground. Cloaks. Dozens of them. Now high above, Epidime climbed to the beast's back.

"Fetch Demont's other toy. As long as we have her, we have them all!" He ordered.

The beasts and men alike obeyed immediately, though it was clear that it was not his voice that they obeyed. The gem of his weapon surged brightly before they took to action. A single nearman remained on the back of each dragoyle. The rest rushed the tavern. Ivy was struggling to rise as Lain reached her side. He pulled her to her feet.

"Can you run?" he asked, eyes trained on the beast that circled nearest.

"I . . . don't think so," Ivy slurred.

Three dragoyles now flew in a tight ring overhead. Lain silently weighed his options. He had his sword, two daggers, and nothing else. He couldn't fight them all off and protect her. Ivy was wavering. He could not carry her and hope to escape. There were no other options.

The creatures made their move. Two converged on Lain, the third lunged for Ivy. Lain dove toward her, grabbing her and forcing her out of the path of the attack. They rolled to a stop at the sloping edge of the roof. The two creatures collided, the first losing its rider, the second crashing to the roof. The beast that would have had Ivy instead struck the roof full force. Half-rotten shingles shattered. Ancient support beams groaned.

In an instant, Lain was on his feet. He took a dagger in his hand. These creatures had a weakness. Desmeres had learned it. The riderless creature dove to the street. Another thrashed wildly on the rapidly failing roof. One was on the verge of recovery. Its inhuman rider croaked a command in an unnatural language. The creature opened its mouth, ready to heave a breath of wretched black miasma at the heroes. A flash of steel later and the dagger was deep in the beast's throat. It released an earsplitting shriek, hacking and sputtering the corrosive breath on roof and rider.

Before any of the other beasts could mount an assault, Lain threw Ivy across his shoulders and leapt to the neighboring roof. As the stricken creature behind him seemed to come apart at the seams, oozing gouts of the horrid black poison, the ailing roof finally gave way, taking its occupants with it.

Lain's leap fell just short of its target and he collided painfully with the lower roof's edge. He held his grip, though barely, and dangled over the alleyway, which was now little more than a sea of nearmen and cloaks. The latter creatures swept high into the air, pitch-black talons manifesting from the empty cloth and clawing at Lain's legs.

In the streets, the last of the villagers abandoned the fight, running for the outskirts of the city and any shelter that could be found. The reinforcements called in by Epidime gave little consideration to the fleeing villagers, intent only on reaching their target. Only the unconscious body of Trigorah received any thought, a dragoyle swooping down and depositing her on the back of the creature ridden by Epidime. The general was watching with interest as Lain struggled to pull himself to the ledge when the stricken form of his partner was delivered.

"What is this? Interesting. That shapeshifter must still be about," Epidime said. His detached coolness persisted, as though through all of this he remained a casual observer. "I suppose I should flush her out. Now would be an unpleasant time for a surprise."

Ivy dizzily opened her eyes again, the leap having disoriented her. The sight before them shocked her to full consciousness. Just a few dozen feet below was a veritable ocean of nearmen and cloaks. She scrambled to get a grip on the ledge, pulling herself up as the blue aura quickly enveloped her. Had she not been so recently subdued, she would have been pushed over the edge already. For now, though, the terrified creature fell to a seat on the roof, her eyes darting up at the dawn sky speckled with more dragoyles than she'd ever hoped to see.

Lain pulled himself up behind her, screaming orders as he did.

"Stay down!" he commanded.

The words were far away, lost to Ivy in the cries of nearmen and shrieks of dragoyles. Lain ran to her, his eyes locked on one beast in particular that dove toward her. Time seemed to slow as the beast and the hero raced to their prize. Lain reached for his last dagger. There was no time to aim, no time to wait for an opening. He let it fly. The weapon soared heart-stoppingly close to Ivy, nearly grazing her ear. It met its target, plunging deep into the creature's hollow right eye socket, driving itself hilt-deep into the beast's skull. It screeched and veered away, the groping talons missing their mark. Instead of snatching her up into the air, the flailing claws raked down her arm. She cried out as she was thrown to the shingles. As she did, a second cry joined in agonized harmony.

The windy form of Ether launched up from the alley below. She had been among the creatures, silently striking them down as the others blindly fell over each other to reach the heroes above, but the time for that had passed. The force of her surge from below dragged cloaks and nearmen alike up behind her. Two more beasts dove at her allies.

Lain drew his sword and carved a long gash down the side of one, but the second was beyond his reach. Its claws clamped down on Ivy's shoulder. She was jerked into the air, screaming in pain and fear. The blue light about her was almost blinding, but it began to falter.

"We shall have none of that today, little prototype," Epidime remarked from his perch atop a nearby dragoyle, the gem of his weapon shining bright as he closed his will about her, flexing his potent spell again.

It snuffed away the aura, but only just. Ivy still struggled and screamed. In an instant, Ether was streaking to her, crying out as the pain inflicted on her ally was meted out as punishment upon her.

"Archers!" Epidime ordered.

Instantly, there was the twang of a dozen bow strings, but Ether paid no mind. She knew that arrows would have no effect on her. A sudden, searing pain tore through her, quickly surpassing that which her mark had dispensed and more. Her eyes turned to the radiant tip of an arrow as it tore through her windy form. Those blasted crystals. They'd tipped the arrows with them, just as some of Bagu's soldiers had! Ether was forced to waste precious time dodging the onslaught, but it was not long before she was back to her task, the skill of the bowmen woefully inadequate to properly strike her. A moment later she had reached her target. Epidime was not blind to this. He had planned for such a case. Ether shifted to stone the moment she was above the dragoyle, smashing down on the creature's back and knocking the rider to the ground far below. She then set about clawing and hammering at the black beast, its dark blood staining her hands.

"Release her!" Epidime ordered.

The dragoyle clutching Ivy obeyed. The hapless creature streaked earthward, her fear quickly taxing even the considerable efforts of Epidime's spell. Ether leapt from the dragoyle's back, plummeting like the stone she was before shifting again to wind. She swept around Ivy, slowing and guiding her descent. The young hero was scarcely comforted by this, the dizzying height and rushing wind doing little to settle her nerves.

"Quiet, you fool! You will be on solid ground again in a moment. I've saved you . . . I . . . I *have* saved you!" Ether began, suddenly realizing that for the first time since her betrayal she felt not the slightest pain of retribution. Her sin was absolved.

The respite from the pain was short-lived. Carrying her fellow Chosen slowed her and brought her back within the range of the archers, and they wasted little time in taking full advantage. The shapeshifter rushed to a rooftop with her precious cargo, but the closer she came, the closer the arrows came. More than one arrow whisked through her, missing the creature she carried by a hair.

Below, Lain leapt from roof to roof, staying ahead of the constant barrage of Dragoyles. His sword easily sliced through any nearmen who had made their way to the roof, and the cloaks that flitted about on all sides were too slow to catch him, though only just. Ether spotted him and hurried to the same roof he was headed to, the bell tower of a church toward the edge of the city. It was by far the highest part of the skyline, well out of reach of the nearmen. He climbed up the side of the tower as quickly as if it had been a ladder, and slipped in one of the windows. Ether swept in soon after, spilling Ivy to the floor.

"What is going on! Where were you? Why . . . *ah!*" Ivy began before the shock wore off enough to allow her mind to process the terrible pain in her shoulder.

"Clear a path. We need to get her to safety," Lain ordered.

"I've more important tasks at hand," Ether said, turning her eyes to the black form gliding toward them.

Lain didn't linger to attempt to convince her otherwise. Grabbing Ivy, he leapt down into the stairs of the bell tower and pulled the hatch closed above him, securing it with the brace that hung beside it. A heartbeat later, the walls shook as beasts battered it from all sides.

Ivy stumbled and lurched as she was hurried down the stairs. The pain was blinding, but behind it was a vague feeling of violation, like there was an unwelcome presence in her mind. It made things seem far away, like they didn't matter.

Finally, they reached the bottom of the tower, spilling into the shadowy main hall of the church. The doorway was directly ahead of them, but Lain pulled back and hugged the wall, pulling back Ivy as he did. This was the sturdiest building in the city, one of the few built entirely of stone and thus one of the few that offered any protection. Below, even over the din of the battle raging outside, Lain could hear the hushed gasps of anxious adults and the terrified wails of sobbing children. He needed to get Ivy to safety. Were he to be seen by the huddled mob below, there would be chaos. He could not afford it.

#

Outside, Ether streaked to her target. Epidime soared toward her. Crystal-tipped arrows hissed through the air from all angles, but Ether now had no fragile mortal to protect. With the benefit of her full attentions devoted to this single task, the archers failed to graze her with even a single attack. Epidime raised his weapon, the gem in its head burning bright. Ether watched it, carefully measuring its strength, the speed of the movements. The timing had to be right. A moment more and she was near enough. Epidime's weapon came down with tremendous force. The shapeshifter darted upward, the blade slicing through the air before her, just a hair's width from her windy form. Though the physical threat fell short, the mystic influence of the gem reached further, tearing away at her very essence in her most vulnerable form.

In a flash, the swirling form of her body tightened, drawing in with gale force, solidifying into stone. She dropped down onto the neck of the beast Epidime rode. The creature buckled under the sudden weight, nearly falling from the sky.

Epidime attempted a second blow, but Ether caught the shaft of his weapon in her stony grip. For the first time since the fight had begun, concern came to Epidime's eyes. With strength unnatural for even his massive frame, he attempted to wrench the halberd from her grip, but it held fast, her strength more than a match for his. Without a word of command, the creature they rode dove earthward, landing in the streets. Ether could feel the grip of her foe slipping with each tug, the core of his power wavering with each mighty pull.

There was no doubt now. Without the halberd, Epidime was nothing.

"Such a pathetic thing!" Ether spat as she felt victory near. "There is nothing to you at all. You rely on an artifact, a *tool* for your power? How could you have even imagined defeating a product of the *gods* with such a weakness?"

"A great thinker once said," Epidime began to quote, in a feeble attempt to maintain the cool demeanor that had until moments ago defined him, "wise is the man who focuses on an enemy's weakness, but dead is a man who ignores its strength."

A flash of the gem stunned Ether only briefly, but it was enough for the hoard of nearmen and cloaks who had gathered unnoticed around the battleground to capitalize. Ether's formidable stone form was nothing against the hundreds of grasping claws and clanking swords that rained down upon her. She fought valiantly to finish the task at hand, but the sheer numbers that pulled at her were too great. She was dragged into the writhing mob, her claw-like fingers carving long gashes along the back of the dragoyle before they too vanished among the crowd.

#

Lain led Ivy around the edge of the walkway that circled the top of the main hall. The injured creature was fighting back tears valiantly. The presence in her head had suddenly dropped away, and the full weight of the events of the last few minutes was once again resting entirely on her harried mind, but she managed to keep her silence and quell the fear that gripped her.

There were small windows lining the top of the wall, just below the ceiling around the perimeter of the hall, two large stained glass windows at either side of the walkway, and one great stained glass masterpiece between them. The duo edged toward the large window at the end of the walkway. It had broken long ago, the bottom of it replaced with planks of wood. If they could pull one aside, they could slip out and down the front of the building. Of course, there were more trying obstacles than a mere plank of wood blocking their path.

The creatures that had seen them enter still threw themselves at the tower. With each rhythmic assault, the walls shuddered. Before long, the bell tower would collapse. Worse, a large portion of the ground troops had been drawn by the dragoyle's attacks. They hammered on doors and shattered low windows. The people inside screamed for mercy. They had yet to see Lain or Ivy inside, and knew not why these beasts and men now threatened to tear their sanctuary down. All they knew was that an army of monsters had descended on their homes. There was a mix of abominations and soldiers tearing through the city, bringing all of the destruction of the war to their very doors.

Lain motioned for Ivy to stay where she was. She obeyed while her defender crept up to the window, evading the light it cast. Behind, Ivy huddled in the corner, cradling her wound. She was every bit as terrified as the people below her, but she couldn't allow it to show. She buried it deep within her. Even a wisp of fear reaching the surface would stir up her aura and they would be seen. Lain didn't want that, so it must not happen.

#

Epidime grinned, keeping a watchful eye on the chaos as he abandoned the back of the injured creature and summoned down a fresh one. His caution proved justified. No sooner had he taken to the air than the whole of the mass of attackers seemed to rise up. A black form could just barely be seen beneath them. An instant later and it surged up, sending the attackers hurdling helplessly through the air, raining down all around. In the center of the eruption was a dragoyle, but it was not like the others. A silvery tone was mixed with the black hide, and a brilliant white light shown from the hollows that should have held eyes.

Ether wasted little time. With the massive strength inherent to her new form, she trounced the foes foolish enough to venture near her, then took to the sky. Epidime would not escape this time. A silent command pierced the minds of the army of creations as her foe attempted to put distance between himself and her raging new form. Every nearman, every cloak, and every dragoyle moved as one, turning instantly to the new target.

The shapeshifter drew in a deep breath of air and heaved out a great cloud of miasma, blanketing the scattered forces below her in the caustic mist. As dragoyles swept in, she spat a second cloud of it in their direction. The beasts were unaffected, though the riders cried out in their unnatural language before falling to the ground below. Whereas before the creatures would have fetched a new rider, it seemed now that Epidime had taken a more direct role in controlling them, as they remained focused on Ether even in the absence of the guiding hands of their riders.

No matter. The shapeshifter had spent an eternity learning how best to use every aspect of a form, and even in the mere moments that she had occupied this shape, she was every bit as capable as the beasts she faced. What's more, she had the benefit of a more than rudimentary intelligence, something that her foes lacked.

The first of the creatures clashed with her, but its attack was smoothly evaded. Ether then countered, choosing her attack carefully. A single blow separated the creature's head from its body and both tumbled earthward. The entirety of the remaining dragoyles swarmed around her. Ether's skill with this form was more than formidable, but the volume of attacks was greater than she could withstand.

Rather than be overcome as she had before, she darted away. The others followed. The shapeshifter wove through the air as gracefully as this form would allow.

#

The constant rain of blows that pummeled the church from all sides died away suddenly and completely as the creatures were commanded to protect their master. Lain silently forced aside a board from the window and peered outside. The creatures, all of them, were distracted chasing one of their own, and it didn't take long to understand why. For once, the shapeshifter had used her powers wisely. He turned to help Ivy to the window.

Lain grabbed her good arm and guided her to her feet. The blood loss was beginning to affect her, and she had to fight to keep her balance. Her eyes were heavy. If something was not done about her wounds soon, she would lose consciousness. Death would soon follow.

She stumbled, nearly falling. Lain stopped her, but in the silence left by the departure of the attackers outside, it did not go unheard. In a flash, the hushed and huddled townsfolk below began to clamber anew in fear and anger. In the darkness below, the bolder villagers took up lanterns and headed for the stairs to the walkway.

Quickly, Lain widened the opening. Time was against them, and there was no use being quiet anymore. When it was large enough to crawl through, he tried to lead Ivy onto the narrow ledge beyond. Her head no sooner peeked out of the ruined window than a whiff of icy air and a glimpse of a dizzying height brought back her senses and the memory of dangling high above the city just minutes ago. She pulled back, refusing to face the drop again. The bang of a door being thrown open startled her. As Ivy turned toward the sound of approaching footsteps, Lain took matters into his own hands. Throwing Ivy over his shoulder, he hurled himself out of the opening, catching the ledge and dropping down as gently as he could manage.

It was not gentle enough, unfortunately. Ivy cried out in pain as they struck the ground. Heads peered out of the broken window above. Lain could fairly feel their gaze. They had been seen. Both of them. He turned and fixed his eyes on the horizon to the west. He had to escape, find shelter, and attempt to bind Ivy's wounds. It might already be too late.

The injured creature was muttering incoherent scoldings about being careful and warning her when he did such things. The assassin thrust aside all he'd taught himself to do, all that had become second nature to him. There was no time for stealth. There was no time for caution. The last real hope for his kind was fading away. That could not be allowed to happen. Not while he still drew breath.

#

High above, Epidime watched as Ether weaved between buildings, over roofs, through arches. The other dragoyles, clumsy by comparison, crashed into walls and collided with one another. A thought came to mind, causing him to turn his eyes to the ground. Beside the now-collapsed form of his former mount was the weakly stirring form of Trigorah. When a glance upward confirmed that the shapeshifter was distracted at the other side of the town, he guided his beast earthward. Casually dismounting, he fairly sauntered up to his ailing ally and watched her struggle to her feet.

"The shapeshifter . . ." Trigorah warned.

"She has her hands full at the moment. I am surprised at you. You aren't one to be so easily fooled. And I should know," he said.

"Save your mockery . . . what about the others?" she asked.

"Last I left them, they were holed up in the church," he said. "Demont's little project is wounded. They won't be hard to follow."

"If you think Lain will be easy to follow, then you learned nothing from me. He has skill enough to overcome any handicap. You need to find him before he leaves the city," Trigorah warned.

"The cogs are already moving in that regard. I will see to it personally just as soon as the more immediate threat can be dealt with. Ether's power concerns me and . . . do you feel that?" he said, suddenly distracted.

Trigorah held her aching head. "I felt nothing. Where is my sword? If you won't find him I will do it myself."

"I may have dallied too long. It is time for you to retreat. I cannot risk having you here right now. Not under these conditions," he decided suddenly.

"Not while Lain is so near. And not while you face three Chosen," Trigorah countered.

"I would reason with you, but I really haven't got the time, and this is a precaution I am afraid I simply must take," Epidime said.

In one smooth motion, he raised his halberd and struck the still-weak Trigorah. The blow was accompanied by a flash of the halberd's gem, betraying a spell that was no doubt intended to ensure that the strike had its desired effect.

His fellow general dropped back to the ground. A silent order went out to the fastest remaining dragoyle. As he mounted his own beast, the second pulled away from its pursuit, snatched up Trigorah, and turned north, disappearing into the distance. Epidime soared high into the air. It didn't take long before he spotted Lain. The fool was carrying the injured creature across his shoulders, running in plain sight. He swept down after the pair, but the leathery beating of wings drew his attention. Behind him, the dragoyle form of Ether was closing in on him. He managed to evade her, but the five dragoyles that pursued her were another matter. They were far more focused on catching their prey than avoiding this obstacle or any other.

Just as Myn had in her final battle, Ether used the trail of single-minded beasts as a battering ram. No fewer than three of them collided with him, the whole tangle of creatures falling to the ground like a stone. Now that only two remained, Ether could easily dispatch them, and she did so in mere moments. Circling to the ground, she eyed the mound of shattered dragoyle suspiciously as she resumed her human form.

"I cannot abide by that form. It is not without its usefulness, but I feel soiled by it," she hissed, confident that her job was done.

Her confidence, so often her downfall in the past, was again misplaced. As she approached the pile, a small portion of it stirred. Epidime pulled himself from among the broken bodies. Impossibly, the fall that had shattered the almost supernaturally hearty monstrosities had spared him. He was much the worse for wear, to be sure, as one arm hung limply at his side and an ankle was turned hideously inward. As he struggled free, however, his arm twitched, moved, and apparently recovered. He didn't even seem to notice the ankle until he tried to step on it. A moment later and he corrected the twisted limb.

"What *are* you?" Ether growled.

"For now? Human," Epidime croaked, his voice faltering.

He hacked and coughed, a pink mist of blood splattering his chin as he did so.

"In a moment, you will be nothing," Ether threatened, taking on her stone form and charging at him.

#

Lain had heard the collision and watched out of the corner of his eye as the broken mass had fallen. Perhaps Ether had defeated the general once and for all. Unlikely. All that mattered was that she had occupied him. There was a chance that he could escape. The edge of the town, and the field that lay beyond, was only a few hundred paces away. It was far from safe, offering little cover, but that was a blessing as well as a curse. Once he was outside of the city, he could at least be sure that no foe was lurking out of sight. If he could just reach it.

In the shadows, a whisper of motion caught Lain's eye. Then another, and another. He redoubled his efforts, pushing himself as hard as his weary, battered body would allow.

With a chorus of screeches, the shadows themselves seemed to leap out at him. Claws swiped at him from all sides as cloaks, still sizzling from the dose of miasma Ether had doused them with, flooded the street. One of the creatures caught his leg and he tumbled forward. By the time he regained his footing, he was completely surrounded by what was left of Epidime's ground forces. They floated and flitted around him, sweeping in to slash with their phantom claws. He stood over Ivy and drew his sword, knowing that these moments of delay might be the mortally wounded creature's last.

The way in which the creatures attacked, holding back and jutting in briefly to swipe at him one at a time, had been a blessing in the past. It had allowed him to pick them off slowly and to bide his time for an escape. Now, though, he needed to hold his ground, to destroy every last one of them--or, at least, disable them . . . and fast. The intermittent swipes now came frustratingly slowly. It was almost as though they were purposely wasting time.

Ivy groaned weakly. Lain sliced through another cloak. He breathed in long, greedy breaths, the frigid air burning at his lungs. The motions of his body and the sword were an afterthought, something akin to a reflex. As he fought, his mind worked feverishly to plan out his escape--where to run, how to treat Ivy's wound. There would be no room for error. Another slash, another foe fell. The fact that Ether had ravaged the beasts so badly was more than a blessing--it was a rare stroke of luck that made victory possible.

#

Just a few streets away, the shapeshifter's clash with Epidime was growing ever more intense. Ether knew that she'd spent most of the strength she had left. If she didn't end this quickly, she was not certain she would last. Epidime, however, seemed inexhaustible. His body seemed to be failing, but the mystical creature knew that the real threat came not from his body, but from his spirit, and it raged just as intensely as it had at the beginning of the battle. Despite this, he was limiting himself. His blows seemed as carefully measured as they were well-placed. Ether avoided most and blocked the rest, but she knew that he would not behave in this way unless he had good reason. His motivation, however, remained a mystery to her, and that concerned her.

His halberd swung in a slow, wide arc, forcing her backward. He then quickly circled around her, deftly avoiding a diving attack from his opponent. Ether's fatigue was beginning to show. Her attacks were becoming more frequent, and had the air of desperation that he had been waiting for. He shuffled a few more steps, watching with a grin as she adjusted her stance to compensate. Perfect. In a lightning motion, he thrust his weapon forward, unleashing a blinding lance of energy that struck her squarely in the chest. The force of it launched her like a comet, trailing energy and shattering through the wall behind her.

#

Hearing a distinctive crackle, Lain crouched and gathered up his precious cargo, rolling aside a mere fraction of a moment before the wall that had served as the backdrop for his battle thus far burst toward him. He rolled to a stop with cloaks on all sides. One grabbed each arm. Another grasped him about the throat. He struggled briefly, but their grip was too strong. In the rubble beneath the gaping hole in wall, the form of Ether rose. She was riddled with cracks, barely holding together. As the last pieces of debris from the explosion of force fell to the earth, Epidime stepped through the hole he had made. He looked about at his handiwork, smiling at the mound of rubble and the flicker of shattered lanterns from a nearby storefront.

"You should thank me. It is an important lesson in the art of war I have taught you today. Victory in a single stroke takes as much planning as power," Epidime mocked.

A sudden and swift move from Lain quickly wiped the smile from his face. The assassin caught the edge of one of the cloaks restraining him with his foot and pulled his arm free. He then managed to force the second one backward into the pool of burning lamp oil from one of the shattered lanterns. It took quickly to flame and screeched through the air for a few moments before fluttering to the ground, motionless. In the distraction, Lain managed to regain his sword.

The other cloaks, and a handful of surviving nearmen who had finally managed to navigate the city to their prey, began to descend on Lain, but Epidime stopped them with a thought.

"Listen, Lain. I know full well that you would sooner die than be taken captive, just as you would sooner give your life than lose that of the delicate creature at your feet. Alas, my orders are quite clear. Until certain criteria are met, you must be captured alive. All of you. Perhaps I could subdue you. Perhaps you could defeat me. Neither could happen before your precious Ivy fades away. That is her very life pooling about your feet. Every drop of blood is one she can't spare. Use your logic, assassin. Let me have her. I will heal her, you will escape. We will both fulfill the more important of our goals. If not, then we both fail," Epidime reasoned.

"Don't listen to him, Lain. Kill him," Ether ordered. She struggled to remain standing, straining under the weight of her own stony form.

"She wants Ivy dead. You know that," Epidime countered.

Lain's weapon lowered slightly. Ivy's eyes were locked on him, glazed and wavering. He drew in a slow, deliberate breath of air, eyes closed. He then exhaled, opening his eyes and tightening his grip on his weapon.

"So be it," Epidime sighed, raising his weapon for the coming battle.

He made ready to attack the stubborn hero, but something made him pause. Weapon still at the ready, he swept his eyes across the cityscape around him. A bitter wind was blowing, harder than it had been a moment ago--and then harder still. There was something else. A sensation. A presence. He shifted the halberd and gave the ground a sharp thrust.

A wave of black force rippled out from where it met the earth. It flowed across the street in all directions. Just before it reached Ivy, something disturbed it. It parted, like the water in a stream about a stone. As it did, the merest glimpse of something else could be seen, as though a veil had been briefly blown aside by a gentle breeze.

What followed happened with a speed few could comprehend. The fluttering black mist was drawn up by some unseen force only to be dispelled entirely, vanishing. A flash of light forced all to avert their gaze, and the icy wind surged, seeming to blow in from all directions at once. As Epidime struggled to regain his sight after the blinding flash, he beheld before him a pair of forms. Each was clad in a pristine white cloak, face hidden by the hood.

One held the crystal-tipped end of a shattered staff, a bow over one shoulder and a quiver of arrows over the other. The second clutched a crystal in one hand and an odd, twin-bladed weapon in the other. A sadistic grin came to Epidime's face, in his eyes a hint of the darkness that lurked in his soul.

"And then there were five," he said, his tone that of a monster unleashed. "KILL THEM ALL! NO ONE SURVIVES!"

The foot soldiers rushed in, Epidime turning to the opening he'd blasted through the wall moments ago and dashing through it. As he did, he raised his weapon. A ribbon of intense light erupted skyward, splitting above the city and encircling the walls. Instantly, a shimmering barrier coalesced just outside the outskirts of the city. A trio of nearmen followed their master as he sprinted from sight.

The staff-wielding stranger rushed to the side of the ailing Ivy. The other turned to the cloaks. A swift thrust of the crystal sent a bolt of light that struck the nearest attacker. In an instant, the cloak turned to glass, shattering as it struck the ground. A second cloak drew near, only to be struck by a second bolt that seemed to unravel the monster, leaving only a pile of frayed threads. A nearman was next, turned to stone by another attack. Behind the defender, the first figure crouched beside Ivy. The half dead creature struggled to focus her eyes on the white-clad form.

"I told them. I told them . . ." she wheezed.

The staff was lowered; a hushed voice whispered a few arcane words. Slowly, wounds began to close. Ether, still barely able to stand, dragged herself over to the pair.

"Finally. Finally more of my own arise," she chanted.

By the time she reached the others, the street was completely cleared of foes and Ivy was breathing the slow, deep breaths of a healing sleep. The defender turned--first with weapons raised at the approach of the shapeshifter, but lowered them quickly. The unused blade was slipped into the cloak, and the hood was drawn back to reveal a disheveled yet enthusiastic young man.

"Ether, I presume. I cannot begin to--" he spoke eagerly.

"Later, Deacon. The wall. We need to escape," the other cloaked figure advised. This voice was indeed familiar.

As the young wizard nodded and rushed off, Ether's eyes widened.

"You! How?" the shapeshifter gasped in an unprecedented showing of awe.

The healer stood, pulling back the hood. There, before Ether, stood Myranda. Lain rushed to her and for a moment their eyes locked. Then each gave a knowing nod. The assassin scooped up the slumbering Ivy and followed in Deacon's path. The shapeshifter, perhaps realizing the look of shock on her face, regained her composure.

"How can you be here? How did you survive?" she demanded.

"I'll explain when there is time. Have you much strength left?" Myranda asked with concern.

"I've more than enough," Ether lied. She attempted to straighten her posture but only succeeded in underscoring her fatigue.

Myranda was not fooled.

"I'll help you," she said.

Ether tried to push the human away, but lacked the strength even to do that. Instead, she slipped back to her human form and leaned heavily on Myranda as they made their way after the others. They didn't get far. Her partner dashed up to her, panting.

"It is no good. The power behind the wall is . . . incalculable. I've never faced anything like it. If we want to leave this place, we have to cut off the spell at its focus. We have to stop that wizard from maintaining it," he said.

A sudden surge of mystic power drew the attentions of the trio. Each had become finely attuned to such things. Without another word, both Myranda and Deacon rushed off toward Epidime. Ether began to follow, but didn't manage more than a few steps before she nearly collapsed. Her limit had been reached. For now, all that she could do was wait. Slowly, she turned and trudged toward the side street just ahead. Lain was waiting there. His sword was held low but ready, Ivy resting on the ground at his feet. Every muscle in his body was tensed, ready to sprint the very moment that the glassy, shining wall ahead was destroyed.

Myranda rushed into the courtyard ahead. Three nearmen blocked her path as Epidime stood before a mangled pile of defeated dragoyles. He raised his halberd and summoned forth the unholy glow that always accompanied his spells. The mass of ruined creatures before him began to shift and turn, waves of black twisting and crawling over its surface. The pieces rose from the ground, piling upon themselves.

Deacon raised his crystal and set his mind to halting whatever it was that Epidime had planned. Myranda waved her staff and a swath of white energy cut across the nearmen. They shuddered and stumbled before collapsing in a flash of light and burst of dust, leaving only a mound of empty armor.

As Myranda turned herself to Epidime, it was clear that precious little had been done to impede the work of their foe. The last pieces of a fiendish puzzle were slipping together. The pieces of the destroyed dragoyles were cobbled loosely into a towering, mismatched titan. The heads had been joined side by side, strung together like beads on a necklace, jaws separated and hanging in a similar strand beneath them, affixed at either end. The limbs were attached end to end, fore and hind legs shuffled with little concern for their proper place, claws affixed one on top of the other until each leg ended in a tapered spike. The shattered pieces of torso were assembled into a mosaic just barely cohesive enough to accommodate the limbs, and the remainder of spare parts curled into a massive, lashing tail.

"I've never felt a will so strong. The magic, the texture of it . . . It is different. Fundamentally so. There is only one way to end this," Deacon warned.

He did not need to say any more, Myranda knew what had to be done. As Epidime climbed to his perch atop the hideous beast, the pair that faced him burst into action. So too did their foe. The spindly creature skittered across the ground like an insect, the jagged spikes that served as legs slicing into the hard stone and earth like it was clay. It moved ponderously, in long, slow strides, but the span of the legs and the lashing tail made it seem as though it was everywhere at once. Deacon and Myranda split up, hoping to divide the attention of the creature.

Deacon stuck close to the buildings. He constantly tried to assault Epidime with spells of every type, but the diabolical wizard shrugged them off or worse, caused them to fade to nothing before they reached him. The beast he rode, if such a thing could rightly be called a beast, turned away from him, aiming its head at Myranda and its tail at Deacon. The disproportionately long appendage struck as though it had a mind of its own, one moment swinging in long slashes, the next gouging like a scorpion. It was faster than he was. Faster by far. Each strike was just barely turned away by a hastily erected shield spell, but the blows cracked it and warped it, as though something about the physical blow affected his magic as well. And the attacks were growing stronger.

Deacon knew that if he hoped to gain an edge, he would have to slow it down. Immobilize it. But how?

Myranda had far greater concerns. The heads, belching out their combined breath, sent great gales of the vile black stuff at her. Deft bursts of wind kept her safe, but the courtyard was quickly filling with the black mist. It pooled in sizzling puddles in the cracks in the street, and every moment there was less and less fresh air to whisk the danger away. The air around her became saturated. She could feel the sting on her skin. The ground was too dangerous. She had to get above it.

With all of her strength she leapt into the air, mixing in as much levitation as she could manage. The leap turned into a slow drift toward the rooftops. The cracked and broken heads lunged, trying to snap her out of the air, but she tumbled backward. The creature tried to lunge again, but it stopped and pulled back suddenly.

Epidime turned to see what held him. One of the creature's legs was embedded in the ground. The ground beneath the other hind leg seemed to slosh aside, losing its substance and parting like a liquid. The dark wizard realized what was next and commanded his creation to draw its leg free, but Deacon acted more swiftly, seizing the altered ground back again into not a mixture of stone and soil as it had been, but solid rock. The legs were held fast. As Epidime leveled his halberd to deal with this newcomer directly, an arrow hissing though the air and gashing his already badly injured arm reminded him of his primary target.

The battle was going on too long. He needed to eliminate one of these heroes *now*. Epidime ordered his beast forward. The head strained and snapped at Myranda, who was readying another arrow. Great plumes of miasma erupted forth, only to be blown in curling clouds back at Epidime. The horrid stuff burned relentlessly at him, but he paid it no mind. Myranda was far too important a target for him to fail now. With a horrifying snap, the monstrosity's hind legs gave way, tearing free and allowing beast and rider to crash forward into the building Myranda stood atop. The weak walls buckled, the ancient roof splintered.

Myranda rushed to the edge and dove to the next roof, losing her arrow. She landed on the sloped shingles, falling and struggling to grip the icy roof. Finally, she found a foothold and climbed to her feet, turning to the house that was crumbling beneath the unbalanced creature as it fought to gain footing on now incomplete legs. A flash of motion distracted Myranda. Through the broken roof, she saw a terrified woman scrambling to escape her failing house. Myranda's eyes swept over the town. The black acid was eroding walls, streets, and roofs. The poor people of this town were having their homes destroyed. Their lives were in danger.

With bow in one hand and staff in the other, she closed her eyes and opened her mind, drawing hard at the clouds above as she had in her exam in Entwell. With knowledge and purpose guiding the action, not to mention a considerable increase in power, the clouds above darkened and multiplied in seconds. A moment later, there was a crack of lighting and a roar of thunder as a torrent came pouring down from above. Her eyes opened to reveal a terrible storm summoned up in a matter of moments. Water diluted and washed away the wretched black acid.

"You've come far, Myranda. Quite far," Epidime allowed, taking note of this new display of skill.

Myranda ignored the words of her foe and leapt from the roof, rolling to the ground. She could not let him destroy any more of this city. The battle would have to be fought in the open--and finished soon.

Deacon wrapped his mind around the lashing tail, crushing his will around it like a vice and, with all of the effort he could muster, manipulating it. He had honed his manipulation skill to a fine edge. He could raise great stones, trees, anvils, but this was by far his greatest challenge. He managed to hold the lashing limb fast, but a will fought against his. He held his crystal out, straining to keep it still but slowly losing the tug of war. With a last, desperate twist, he managed to snare the tail around one of the grotesquely struggling legs still held fast to the ground and anchor it there.

Epidime swung his halberd without looking, a blast of black energy slicing through the air toward Deacon. He managed to dodge, and apparently blind to the danger of it, scrambled between the beast's remaining legs, under its head, and back to Myranda's side.

Lightning danced in the sky above him. Deacon called to Myranda.

"We won't hit him with a single strike he can see," he affirmed.

"Fine then. Let us strike at him with a *thousand* that he can see," she decided.

The words were cryptic, but they rang clear in Deacon's mind. Myranda drew back an arrow and fired it skyward. It arced upward, nearly disappearing from sight. Deacon then thrust his crystal high, a filament of brilliant light tracing upward until it met the arrow at the peak of its flight. Instantly, a section of the sky turned darker than even the storm clouds. The patch of black spread like a swarm of insects, separating into hundreds, thousands of tiny specks. Arrows.

The two heroes scrambled for the far end of the courtyard as the first of the rain of arrows struck. They moved in a wave, prickling the earth in an ever-advancing line toward Epidime. He raised his halberd defensively for a moment, but then let it drop. He turned a scornful eye to his foes, who now stood just ahead of where the first arrows had fallen. A handful of the plummeting shafts struck the head of the beast . . . with no effect. A constant stream fell upon him, vanishing just as they struck.

"Illusions. You would think to deceive me with illusions?" Epidime scoffed, genuinely angered by the simplicity of the ruse.

A moment later the grimace of anger vanished as an arrow, quite real, drove itself into his shoulder. It was true that the rain of arrows was false, but the one she had fired was not, and it had found its mark. Epidime gazed upon them with a look of calm, almost serenity as he pulled the arrow free. It should have killed him just as countless other attacks should have, but he stubbornly clung to life, a smile returning to his blood-tinged mouth.

"When will you learn that it will take so much more than you have to defeat me?" he asked.

Suddenly he began to cough and hack, his whole body heaving with the increasing outbursts. He closed his eyes and steadied himself on the creature's back as he struggled to regain control of his failing body. The sound of something hissing toward him through the air, alas, did not go unnoticed. His mind reached out and slowed the projectile. His free hand rose up and snatched it from the air. He spat and opened his eyes. What he held was the broken head of a casting staff.

"You threw your staff? Have you so quickly reached the bottom of your bag of tricks that you resort to this act of--" he began. He would never finish his sentence.

With the target held firmly in the hand of her foe, Myranda turned her mind skyward and drew down the true attack. A blinding bolt of lightning tore from the clouds above and struck the weapon, continuing through the man who held it and the beast he rode. Myranda maintained the state of concentration as long as she could, prolonging the bolt for seconds. All was white around them, in their ears a continuous, deafening roar, like a clap of thunder that would not end.

Finally she could manage no more. The lightning flickered away. She opened her eyes. The world was a haze. Even with her eyes firmly shut, the intensity of the lightning had robbed her of her vision almost entirely. There was little left of the beast that stood before them seconds earlier. Less still was left of the man--only a charred husk inseparable from the rest of the ruined rubble and the blackened halberd.

Myranda recalled her staff. The crystal glowed white-hot, and the augmented wood smoldered, but her spell had done its work. It had delivered its payload to Epidime and been spared most of the damage.

"That was . . . savage . . . and brilliant," Deacon admired, though his comment was unheard, the ringing in their ears easily drowning it out.

Myranda wished her staff was whole, as the cost of the spell was high enough to leave her nearly for want of the strength to stand. And, yet, she didn't feel as though it was over. Around them, the sudden and complete silence following the thunderous uproar had inspired the bravest of the townsfolk to peek their heads from their shelters. Deacon tugged at

Myranda's arm, drawing her attention and pulling up his hood. The wall was down. Now was the time for escape.

The hero turned to run, but the sight she caught out of the corner of her eye nearly stopped her heart. The halberd's glow returned weakly to the damaged crystal. She turned and saw the weapon rock free of the crumbling fingers of its former wielder and rise high into the air. Myranda's eyes turned to the ground as lighting cast three shadows. One was of the halberd. The second was that of a twisted, unnatural mockery of a human gripping the weapon. The third was that of a young child that had foolishly ventured into the courtyard from his hiding place. Myranda called out to the boy.

"No! Stay away!" she urged, but she could not hear even her own voice. Surely the boy could not either.

She looked to the sky, searching for the twisted form Myranda had seen silhouetted below, but there was none. The halberd hung alone, yet a second flash of lightning revealed the three shadows again as the halberd swept to the child's side. She summoned a bright light, prolonging the shadows as she tried to rush to the child. The twisted figure existed only in shadow, but it suddenly grasped the shadow of the boy. The child shook as if struck.

Myranda watched helplessly as the boy's shadow was somehow torn free. The boy dropped to the ground, then slowly rose as the twisted shadow replaced the stolen one. The boy reached out and clutched the halberd. Instantly, the look of innocence and fear was replaced by the look of cool, disconnected intellect that Epidime had worn. Indeed, he still wore it.

In a smooth, practiced motion with the halberd, Epidime summoned the swirling black form she'd seen Demont step out of. He guided his stolen body through just as Myranda reached it. Before she could do anything, the void in the air snapped shut, releasing a wave of black energy that knocked her to the ground.

Deacon was beside her in a flash, helping her to her feet. The air was still ringing in her ears, her vision returning slowly, but what she saw told her that she could delay no longer. People were now flooding out. They did not know what had caused this, why their town had been ravaged. Fear, anger and confusion filled their heads. It was a potent mix, and it needed an outlet. If she and her friends lingered, the townspeople could not be blamed for what they did.

Deacon and Myranda rushed to the edge of the town. There, Lain had discovered the horses that they had ridden in on and loaded Ivy onto the back of one. Ether was atop the other, and clearly out of her element.

"The sheer idiocy of using one body to control another . . ." she muttered as she struggled to determine how to guide the horse.

"I'll guide the horse, you ride behind me," Myranda said, climbing to the saddle as Ether grudgingly agreed.

Deacon climbed to the saddle of the mount that Ivy had been entrusted to. In truth, he displayed nearly as much difficulty handling the steed as Ether, but he managed, and a moment later the group as a whole was off, Lain trailing slightly behind on foot. The clearing clouds were shedding the light of the rising sun upon them, and they could ill afford to be seen. Worse, the rain that had spared the town and offered the means of striking down Epidime had soaked the heroes to the bone. In the bitter cold of the north, that was a swift road to death. Shelter would have to be found--and fast.

After nearly an hour, shelter was indeed found--in the form of a dense stand of trees tucked in a slight valley. Wood was gathered, a fire was started that Ether quickly took advantage of, and in short order Lain had managed to track down enough prey to provide a meal. As warmth slowly returned to frost-nipped limbs and it became clear that, for now at least, they had not been followed, Ether could hold her tongue no longer.

"Explain yourself," she ordered.

Myranda stared pensively at the ground.

"I think perhaps Myranda needs a few moments. I would be happy to--" Deacon offered helpfully.

"Are you a Chosen One?" Ether asked.

"I am not, but--" Deacon attempted to explain.

"Then do not speak in our presence. Myranda, answer," Ether again demanded.

"It was for nothing . . ." Myranda said, shaking her head.

"What are you mumbling about?" Ether snapped, unaccustomed to being so blatantly ignored.

"He was just a man!" Myranda replied angrily through clenched teeth, tears in her eyes. "Arden and Epidime were not one and the same! I killed the man, but Epidime still lives. I killed him for nothing! *Nothing!*"

"The weapon--the halberd. It would appear it houses some manner of entity. It was this entity that was your foe. This Arden fellow was merely the host," Deacon explained.

Lain watched from the other side of the fire, a knowing look in his eye.

"I've never taken the life of a human before. Never. And now I do so and it achieves nothing. That poor man had to die because I was too foolish to see the truth," she continued, her voice quivering.

"Yes, yes. I am sure it appears to you to be a terrible tragedy, but save your emotions for another time," Ether dismissed. "I require an answer."

"At the risk of angering you further, my esteemed Chosen, I feel that perhaps I could indulge your curiosity while Myranda--" Deacon attempted.

"I've warned you once," Ether stated sternly.

"It's all right. I owe them an explanation," Myranda said numbly.

#

And so she began to recount the tale, a tale that it is my great hope shall find its way to you as well. It begins where the others believed that Myranda's life had ended, in the lowest level of Demont's personal menagerie. Had I the strength, I would not rest until every last word was recorded. But, alas, the years weigh heavily upon me. You have my word. When next my stylus is put to work, all that remains will be revealed. The truth is too important to be lost to the ages.